FULL CIRCLE

FULL CIRCLE

All Closed Eyes Ain't Sleep, All Goodbyes Ain't Gone

Katrina Covington Whitmore
and
Betty Lipscomb Walker

Strategic Book Publishing and Rights Co.

Strategic Book Publishing & Rights Co., LLC
USA | Singapore
www.sbpra.net

For information about special discounts for bulk purchases, please contact Strategic Book Publishing and Rights Co. Special Sales, at bookorder@sbpra.net.

ISBN:978-1-68235-529-9

DEDICATION

This book is dedicated to all beloved Ma'dears in our lives, particularly Velma Jean Covington and Maggie Lipscomb Hinton. Your faith, love, and unquestioning support lifted and sustained us making us the proud women we are today. We just know you are looking down from heaven, prouder than ever, bragging to the angels about your accomplished daughters.

ACKNOWLEDGEMENTS

The authors Katrina and Betty would like to thank the people who made this book possible. Our in-progress readers, listeners and critics, Kim, Pam, and RoLayne; the generous family member who showed her faith in us by keeping us supplied with countless pens, reams of paper, and gallons of toner – thank you, Elizabeth. Thanks also to Martin for his help in this formidable endeavor. Many thanks also to Jean who patiently and willingly chauffeured the authors wherever they needed to go.

Finally, a heart-felt, special shout-out to our editor, who patiently and meticulously, with painstaking attention to detail, edited the entire manuscript more than once. Your outstanding efforts are appreciated more than we can say.

Chapter One

"Jenna Thompson...Jenna Thompson, how come you got a white girl's name?" Charlesetta removed the peppermint stick she was enthusiastically licking from her mouth, looking over at her friend. They were headed home from the general store having spent their pennies on stick candy, both carrying bags of other assorted sweets.

Removing the minty sweet she had been busily consuming, Jenna replied, "Because Ma'dear says she wants me to be able to do things without folk knowing right away that I am colored."

"Well, as soon as they look at you, they gone know."

"Maybe so, but Ma'dear says that maybe by the time they see me, it will not make any difference."

"Is that why you talk proper, too?"

"Ma'dear says it cannot do any harm to learn to speak using the same words that white people use without a heavy colored accent."

"What good is all that going to do you livin' here in Crawfish Holler, South Carolina?"

"It is *Crawford Hollow*, not Crawfish Holler, and I don't plan to spend my life in this Podunk town."

"Well, *excuse* me, Miss Jenna! No wonder er'body calls you Queenie."

"My oldest brother began calling me 'Queenie', the rest of my brothers and sisters copied him, so the name stuck. Then everyone else started calling me that, too, trying to make fun of the way I speak. But I do not care," Jenna said, tossing her head. "I like using proper English and pronouncing my words correctly, so forget them."

"Well, I cain't talk all hoity-toity like you, and I ain't got big ideas like you. I guess you gone live in Hollywood or California or something. You'll be too good to talk to someone like me."

"Charlesetta, don't be silly! We will always be friends." Reaching over, Jenna linked her arm through that of her friend. "We will both be strutting our stuff among the rich folk."

Lifting the corner of their skirts with their free hands, they began chanting, "Oh, strut Sister Sally…Sally, Sally…strut Sister Sally all night long," swiveling their hips and high stepping as they walked along, singing at the top of their lungs.

"*Queenie? Quee-nie…uh, Queenie…*" The strong voice, unusually deep for a woman interrupted them mid-song.

"Ma'dear," Jenna sighed. "I do not know how she knows when I am close to home. She is always coming to the door, calling me to do my chores, no matter what time I get home."

"That's 'cuz she's a witch…I mean a healer," Charlesetta amended hastily, when Jenna glared at her choice of words.

By this time, the two girls had reached the point where the road forked: one dirt-packed lane leading to the cluster of houses where most of the blacks in town lived, the other rock-paved road leading to the house owned by Jenna's stepfather where she and the rest of her family resided. Set well back from the road, it was surrounded by a huge garden where her mother grew vegetables for the table, and an extensive variety of herbs, tree bark, flowers and other medicines used in her healing. Hanging from the branches of the trees were strands of colored glass, bags containing clay, the bones of animals, effigies of spirits, river rocks, and quartz encrusted stones. Two women were walking up the road, both carrying small burlap sacks filled with the herbs and other ingredients needed for whatever potion they had asked Sister Albertina to prepare for them.

"Hi, Miss Lucille…Miss Millie," Jenna greeted the women as she drew close, bobbing her head respectfully.

"Hey, Queenie, your mama calling you 'cuz it's time for you to study up on your conjuring and spell-making?" Lucille asked curiously.

"That's right, you got the gift too, don' cha? You gonna be the next healer?" Millie asked half-fearfully, eyeing the slight girl with the head of thick, curly hair and the uncanny eyes.

"No, ma'am. I am going to help her get dinner on the table and the little ones cleaned up for supper." She refrained from telling them that she planned to use her healing skills as a nurse in a big city hospital, knowing that they either would not understand why she wanted to go through so much expense and effort to do something she was already learning to do for free, or they would not believe she could do it, that her destiny lay in the tiny town she was growing up in.

"Well, you have a good evening," Lucille said. "Thank your mama for helping us," lifting the small bag she held.

"Yes ma'am, I will, and you all have a good evening, too," Jenna said, turning up the long lane leading to her house.

Her mother, rubbing her lower back, was standing on the wrap-around porch in front of the open door leading into the kitchen. Heavily pregnant, Albertina was finding it harder to get around and almost impossible to navigate the four wide stairs leading to her back yard. This pregnancy was much harder than the previous ones, leaving her in constant discomfort, especially at night. Unable to sleep, she appeared weaker and more careworn every day, and the baby was still weeks away from being born. Jenna hurried up the stairs, clasping her mother gently by one arm, helping her to sit in the rocking chair by the door, and picking up a paper fan filched from the church, she began vigorously fanning the heavily perspiring woman.

"Ma'dear, you should not be walking around so much," she scolded as she wielded the fan, trying to get some air moving in the hot, humid atmosphere. "Rolanda," she called, "bring Ma'dear some water. Hurry, now! She is sweating something awful."

Moments later, her younger sister came scurrying through the door holding a battered tin cup filled with water and handed it to Jenna. "Here, Ma'dear, sip slowly. Sit here to get your strength back." Jenna held the cup to her mother's lips, retaining hold of it as she drank.

"I got to finish getting dinner on the table. Mr. Pettigrew will be home any minute," her mother said.

"Tell me what is left to do, and I will do it," Jenna said. "You sit there and rest. I can get Rolanda to help me. Where is Sugar?" Sugar was her older sister, her only full sister, the others being her half-brothers and Rolanda, the only other girl her half-sister. Their father was Rodney Pettigrew, her stepfather, her mother's second husband, a man she detested.

"She over in the apple orchard, talking to Walter Simmons," Rolanda said. "That's where she was last time I saw her."

"Probably doin' a lot more than talkin'. That gal likes boys a little too much for her own good," Ma'dear muttered. "She gone fool around and find herself in a mess o' trouble."

"I will send one of the boys for her," Jenna said. Turning to her sister she said, "Rolanda, find Henry Lloyd. Tell him to find Sugar and bring her home. Tell him to tell her Ma'dear said come home." Rolanda hurried away on her latest errand.

"Thank you, child," her mother said gratefully. "I don't know what I'd do without you. This baby is wearing me down, and Sugar gets more ornery and hard-headed every day."

"You need to take a switch to Sugar and stop having babies," Jenna said forcefully. "Don't you have enough children to suit that man? You know Doc Edmonds said when you had the twins it was dangerous for you to have any more."

"You know there'll never be enough chillen' for Mr. Pettigrew," her mother said wearily. "He won't even think about doin' nothin' to stop these babies from comin'."

"Two sets of twins and three single births is not enough? Seven of his plus me and Sugar and this one on the way is not enough? Is he crazy?"

"Don't talk that way about your daddy," her mother said.

"He is not *my* daddy," Jenna said fiercely, "and he does not pretend to be either. He is not even much of a daddy to his birth children except for Rolanda. All he ever does with the boys is beat them."

"That's enough," her mother said firmly. "Mr. Pettigrew is my husband, and you will respect him. He has put a roof over your head and food on the table most of your life. He has his shortcomings, but I will not allow you to bad-mouth him, understand?"

"Yes, ma'am," Jenna said stiffly, lowering eyes to the floor which still flashed with rebellion.

"Now, get that cornbread out of the oven, put the chicken and dumplings in front of Mr. Pettigrew's plate, take the greens off the stove, get those sweet potatoes out of the fireplace, put the butter and buttermilk on the table, and call everyone in to eat. I see Mr. Pettigrew at the gate. I'm not hungry, so I think I'll just sit here and rest a while. You be sure and say grace."

"I will," Jenna said, entering the kitchen, walking over to the stove and lifting the large pot of chicken and dumplings setting it on the place mat in front of the head of the table where her stepfather always sat. He came through the door as she was placing the butter and buttermilk on the table. "Good evening, Mr. Pettigrew," she said. "Supper is on the table, Rolanda is ringing the supper bell, and we can eat momentarily."

"Gal, how many times I got to tell you to call me 'Daddy Rodney'?" he growled.

You could tell me a million times and it wouldn't make any difference," Jenna thought, leaning over to fish the sweet potatoes out of the ashes of the fireplace where they had been baking, trying to ignore the lecherous eyes she could almost feel boring a hole in her back, traveling down and lingering on her legs and backside, *Because you are not my daddy and you do not act like my daddy, you big, fat, nasty, dirty old man.* Aloud she said, "Have a seat. I hear everybody else coming, so we can eat."

Her sister Sugar was the first one through the kitchen door. Short and voluptuous, with dark brown skin, big brown eyes, full lips, and a head of thick, blue-black hair that fell almost to her waist, she a man magnet, able to entice man or boy, black or white without even trying. More than one vicious fight had been fought over her and she always had a wide assortment of males wrapped around her dainty fingers. It was rumored the county's white Judge was one of her suitors, as was the white owner of the town's general store. Sugar always did seem to have the latest fashions, plenty of scented water and candy and makeup, a lot more than the money she earned selling eggs could account for; and Jenna had once seen an exchange between Sugar and her stepfather which raised unsettling suspicions.

"What's for supper?" Sugar asked, her lips glistening red from the lipstick applied to their lush fullness. *She's probably hoping no one notices they're even fuller than usual from the kisses she and Walter shared in the apple orchard,* Jenna thought. *They probably shared a lot more than that.* That Sugar was generous with her affections was a well-known fact. That she did not care whether the man was married, engaged, or courting someone else, another. She also did not care one whit that she had no female friends or that she was heartily despised by the town's entire female population, black and white alike.

"Oooo, chicken and dumplings," she purred, "and it's not even Sunday! One of the old hens must have either dropped dead or stopped laying eggs. Daddy Rodney," she said huskily, walking over to where her stepfather was seated and stroking his cheek with her painted fingernails, "you ain't going to eat all the best pieces and jus' leave the neck and back and gizzards for the rest of us, are you?"

"Baby, you know I got something special fo' you," her stepfather smiled breathing heavily, reaching into the pot extracting a breast and placing it on one of the empty plates stacked beside him, adding a generous helping of dumplings, handing the heaping plate to Sugar who smiled, nodding her head in satisfaction, moving to her place, and sitting down.

"Queenie, you next," he said, picking up a second plate and placing the neck and a gizzard on it along with a tiny portion of dumplings and handing it to her. The rest of the children fared better – sharing the legs, one thigh, back, and wing and generous portions of dumplings. "Call me 'Daddy Rodney', and I'll let you have this," he said, holding up the remaining thigh.

"What I have is fine, Mr. Pettigrew," Jenna said, deliberately emphasizing his name.

"Put that meat on her plate and add some more dumplings," Albertina said as she came through the door. "Growin' gals need to eat, plus she gone be up early in the morning huntin' and gathering wild herbs an' such for me."

A slight hesitation before he leaned over and carelessly dropped the thigh onto Jenna's plate, adding a messy spoonful of dumplings. "Good," Albertina said, reaching over and cutting the breast on Sugar's plate into thirds, placing two pieces on the plates of the smaller boys who had gotten no meat, ignoring her pronounced pout. "Now let us bow our heads," reciting a short prayer of thanks, "Amen."

"Amen," repeated everyone else at the table, raising their forks and spoons and digging in.

"Boy, did you git that fence fixed like I tole you?" Rodney looked over at his eldest son, his mouth full of food. "You didn' spend the day pluckin' that damn guitar, did you?"

"Yassir, I got it done," Henry Lloyd responded, "I had to cut down one of the trees when I ran out of already cut wood, but me and Dexter and Alfonso and Lorenzo did it."

"Yeah, well, I'm goin' over to look at it, and it better be right, that's all I got to say," his father growled, "else I'm gonna take a limb to all of y'all."

Henry Lloyd flashed his father a look of burning, intense hatred before looking down and resuming eating.

"What I dun' tole you about lookin' at me like that, boy?" Rodney said, half-rising, bunching his right hand into a fist.

"Mr. Pettigrew, let that boy alone so he can finish his meal in peace," Albertina said quietly. "If he said he did what you tole him, he did, and I ain't gone have you disrupting the dinner table over a look. Now, sit down and finish your supper."

A moment of charged silence passed before he sat down and continued eating. He never argued with his wife and almost always did as she said. If he did not, he knew that she would not hesitate to go for one of her many guns. She would shoot him, too, if angry enough. The missing tip of his right ear was proof of that. The healed-over hole in his weakened left hand attested to the fact that she wasn't above stabbing him either. Yet, she kept his clothes immaculate, and him well-fed. The many pounds he had gained since their marriage were proof of that. She treated him with respect, made the children do so as well, and never once had she denied him his marital rights even though the repeated pregnancies and miscarriages took an increasing toll on her abused body.

"Henry Lloyd, after dinner I want you to take a poultice I made for Mama Joyce over to her so she can start using it right away. That ulcer on her leg is causing her grief." Mama Joyce was Rodney's mother who lived on the other side of town on a huge plot of land her husband, Rodney's father, owned.

"Yes ma'am," Henry Lloyd said, giving his mother a grateful look, knowing the errand would take some time, and keep him away from his father. Mama Joyce doted on her handsome grandson, so she would surely have a huge piece of chocolate cake or peach cobbler made with fruit from her orchard along with a big scoop of homemade vanilla ice cream waiting for him.

"Queenie, you go with him," Albertina said, "so you can make sure she knows how to use it and how often. I'll get Sugar to help me clean up." Sugar opened her mouth in protest, then closed it abruptly when her mother looked over at her. She glowered resentfully as she watched Henry Lloyd and Jenna excuse themselves and hurry out the door, laughing as they clattered down the stairs, headed down the lane. Already plotting her revenge, Sugar slowly smiled at her stepfather, taking in his reaction with satisfaction before turning back and finishing her dinner.

Chapter Two

"I sure am glad Ma'dear sent us to Mama Joyce's" Jenna said happily, skipping along beside Henry Lloyd, her two steps barely matching his one long stride. "Mr. Pettigrew was spoiling for a fight tonight. I just hope he does not take it out on the little ones."

"Naw, I'm the one he was after," Henry Lloyd replied. "I'm usually the one he's rarin' to beat. I swear I'm going to kill that man someday."

"Henry Lloyd, don't say that," Jenna said anxiously. "I would not care if he were dead, but I don't want you to be the one to kill him. You would just wind up in jail for murdering that ornery, hateful old cuss."

"Well, he needs to leave me alone." Henry Lloyd bunched his hands into fists. "One day he's going to hit me, and there's no telling what I'll do." Following a brief, tense pause, "Let's talk about something else," he said, smoothing the scowl on his face, loosening his hands, turning a warm smile on his sister, reaching over to tousle her head of curly, shoulder-length inky-black hair. "We're away from that old fart, Mama Joyce is sure to have something good to eat, we can stay away for a long time, and since we're doing something for his mama and Ma'dear sent us, there ain't nothing he can say or do about it except choke on his own meanness."

Jenna smiled at Henry Lloyd. Of all her siblings, he was her favorite, the one she loved most, her confidant, champion, and best friend. Older by just under a year, one would not have known it by looking at the two of them. Henry Lloyd was tall for his age, with a well-shaped head covered by shiny dark brown curls that he kept cropped close, otherwise, "I look like a girl," he often complained disgustedly. His perfect features, high forehead, long lashes, intense brown eyes and square chin with a cleft in the middle made for a face that drove the girls crazy. Broad shoulders, strong arms rippling with muscles and powerful well-shaped legs developed from years of heavy farm labor made for a compelling, eye-catching combination that was the epitome of handsome, virile manhood, while his smile could light up a room.

Like his sister Sugar, he drew the opposite sex like bees to honey. He could have his pick of any girl in the county; even white girls tried to insinuate themselves into his good graces for him to notice them. Luckily, he had sense enough to ignore them, not willing to risk a visit from the local Ku Klux Klan. With black girls he was friendly but distant, unwilling to tie himself down or allow himself to be trapped by a girl looking to have a pretty baby. He was totally caught up in his music, his guitar playing accompanied by a powerful singing voice that he hoped would propel him out of Crawford Hollow into the big time, maybe Memphis or Kansas City. At thirteen he still had years before he could strike out on his own; he only hoped he could avoid a major showdown with his much-despised parent before then.

"Oh, Lord, here comes Glory Richardson," Jenna said disgustedly, looking up the road at the figure hurrying toward them. "Get ready for some major kiss ass."

"You better not let Ma'dear hear you talkin' like that," Henry Lloyd warned, smiling when Jenna grimaced.

"Well, it is true," she muttered, just managing not to roll her eyes as the older girl simpered up, with eyes only for Henry Lloyd, ignoring Jenna completely.

"Hey, Henry Lloyd," Glory said softly, moving close, lifting one hand to toy with one of the straps of his denim overalls, "Why didn't you come to my party? I was lookin' for ya."

"Because one – he was busy, two – Ma'Dear would not have allowed it, because three – he is not nearly old enough to be fraternizing with you and your friends," Jenna answered for him.

Unwilling to admit she had no idea what 'fraternizing' meant, Glory continued to ignore the irritating girl who used big words and had an air about her that made those inclined to be unfriendly hesitant about doing anything about it. She had a way of looking at you with those big, bottomless almost-black eyes that made it seem she could see right through you, that all your secrets were revealed, exposed to that dark gaze. Everyone knew she was destined to follow in her mother's footsteps; and it probably was not a good idea to get on the bad side of someone who could make potions, part the mists of knowledge, see beyond time and space, and ultimately wield magic.

"Well, cain't you just come for a friendly visit?" Glory asked. "Our watermelon patch has been giving us melons bigger than pumpkins and sweet as sugar. I'd jus' love to share one wit' chew."

"I ain't got much time for visiting," Henry Lloyd said with an easy smile that made Glory catch her breath. "Workin' the farm takes up most of my time."

"Speaking of time, I am sorry, but we do not have any more to spend on idle chit-chat," Jenna said firmly. "Ma'dear has us on an errand, and we still have considerable ground to cover."

"Yeah, we got to get this to one of her patients right away," Henry Lloyd said, holding up the burlap sack containing the wax-sealed jar with the poultice inside. "So, I'll see you later, hear?"

"I'll look forward to it," Glory said, moving even closer and lifting her face towards his. She halted and stepped back when

Jenna loudly cleared her throat, crossing her arms, dark eyes flashing in warning.

"That girl gets on my one good nerve," Jenna said angrily, watching as Glory continued on her way, throwing soulful glances over her shoulder. "I swear she was about to kiss you full on the mouth and would have if I had not reminded her I was standing there watching. I mean, really! She has to be at least seventeen, no-good cradle snatcher."

"Yeah, well, I'm lucky I have my big sister to protect me," Henry Lloyd said. They both laughed. Jenna was considerably shorter and built on a much smaller scale, so the term 'big' invariably made them chuckle. "Now, let's forget her. Race you to that big, ole oak tree!" Jenna took off running; Henry Lloyd giving her a sizable head start before he began to run, even so he caught and passed her, reaching out to touch the rough wood seconds before she touched it, panting from the effort. The two continued on their way, exchanging stories, confidences, their dreams, and future plans.

* * *

"Well, if it ain't my two favorite grandbabies! Y'all came all this way just to see me?"

"Hey, Mama Joyce! Ma'dear sent us to give you this for your ulcer. Jenna's going to show you how to use it."

"That was certainly nice of her. Before we get to that, come give me some sugar. I know y'all must be hungry. Come in, have a seat, and let me see what I can find."

They came through the back door into the large, spacious kitchen with its modern wood-burning stove, ice box and deep double sink with a pump that carried water directly into it. After kissing Mama Joyce on both cheeks, the two children seated themselves at the big, polished wooden table located near the center of the room. Looking around, Jenna immediately spotted the chocolate cake under a glass dome residing on one of the shelves of the stand-alone carved cabinet in a corner of the room. A large bowl of peaches stood next to it with what was surely a peach cobbler nearby. Jenna's mouth started to water, her dark eyes sparkling with anticipation. She loved coming to Mama Joyce's house; the order, peace and tranquility soothing to her soul, comforting to her spirit.

"I'm going to get y'all both some dessert. I made a cake and a peach cobbler; my trees are really growing some good peaches this year. I'm going to send some back with y'all, too. I got so many I don't hardly know what to do with them. I'm gonna give y'all some preserves and canned peaches, too. Now, let's see...I got some leftover fried chicken I made today, some macaroni and cheese and some green beans. Oh, there's some leftover cornbread, too. Y'all want some of that? I know you do, Henry Lloyd, a growing boy is always hungry. How 'bout you, Queenie? You want some of that, too?"

"Yes, please, ma'am," Jenna said. "That all sounds delicious."

Mama Joyce smiled. "You sure have a way of talkin'– sounds like a white girl sitting in my kitchen. Baby, you jes' keep talkin' that way. It'll help you more than you know in your dealings with them peckerwoods. I got the feeling you gonna be dealin' wit them a lot."

Jenna smiled. The support she received from her grandmother (who was really her step grandmother) provided emotional nourishment just as comforting as the physical nourishment received with the food offered in abundance each time she visited. She watched Mama Joyce reach into the oven and pull out a cloth-covered basket, unfolding the cloth to reveal a pile of crispy golden-brown chicken which she placed on the kitchen table within easy reach of the two seated there. Another trip to the oven produced a metal pan containing the macaroni and cheese, a dish Jenna loved above all others, but which was reserved for Thanksgiving or Christmas or other holidays at home. The final offering was a pot of green beans removed from a stove burner and placed on the table on top of a folded dishcloth.

"Now, y'all eat all you want," Mama Joyce said. "There's plenty. Papa Pete and I have already eaten. Henry Lloyd, you be sure to get one of them breasts. When you finish that, I'll get the cake and cobbler. Y'all want some homemade ice cream, too?" smiling when they both nodded eagerly. "Here're the plates, silverware and napkins. Dig in."

Needing no further encouragement, Jenna and Henry Lloyd piled chicken, macaroni and green beans on their plates and began eating. Jenna closed her eyes in bliss at her first mouthful of macaroni, savoring the combination of firm noodles, creamy sauce and chunks of flavorful cheese. Sinking her teeth into crispy chicken, breaking off a piece of lightly browned cornbread, she savored every bite. Across from her Henry Lloyd was making short work of his heaping plate of food. After leaving behind nothing but the bone on the chicken wings she had chosen, Jenna sat back with a satisfied sigh around the same time her brother popped the final bite of cornbread on his plate into his mouth.

"Y'all ready for some dessert now?" Mama Joyce asked, smiling at their enthusiastic nods and moving over to the sideboard, plates in hand. "Henry Lloyd, how's that music coming?" she asked as she placed a sizable piece of cake, peach cobbler, and a generous scoop of ice cream in front of each of them.

"It's going good, Mama Joyce," Henry Lloyd said eagerly. "I done taught myself a new song; it's called 'Stormy Weather'. I learned all the words so I can sing it, too."

"He sounds really good, Mama Joyce," Jenna agreed. "Henry Lloyd should be on the radio."

"Well, I sure would like to hear you," Mama Joyce said. "You should have brought your guitar so'sn I could."

"I didn't dare. Daddy…wasn't in such a good mood, and he'd already said something about my playin' it too much. I keep it hid and try to stay out of his way when I'm playin'. I don't want it to get broke."

"Your daddy," Mama Joyce sighed. "I swear I don't know where I went wrong with that boy. I tried to raise the mean out of him but couldn't. He's just like Papa Pete used to be before he got too old to raise Cain like he used to." She walked over to a chifforobe against a far wall. Leaning down into it, she pulled something out. "One of my tenants couldn't come up with his monthly rent, so we worked out a trade. I wouldn't charge him for the next few months if he let me have this," holding out a slightly battered guitar. "I don't know how well it works, but I thought you might could fix it and keep it here so you can play for me whenever you come see me."

Henry Lloyd, his face alight, caught his grandmother in an enormous hug, careful not to crush the precious instrument. Reverently taking it from her hands, he plucked the strings, holding it close to his ear to gauge its sound. "Sounds good," he said, with a huge smile. "I can get some sandpaper to smooth out these marks in the wood and some wax to polish it up. It'll be a lot better than the one I got at home. Thank you, Mama Joyce."

"Well, you need all the practice you can get," Mama Joyce said briskly. "Does it sound good enough for you to play somethin' for us now?"

"Oh, yeah," Henry Lloyd said happily. He spent some time tightening strings, listening to sounds as he stroked them. Satisfied, he lifted his voice and began singing. "Swing low…

sweet chariot..." beginning with one of his grandmother's favorite spirituals. His voice was a full, rich tenor, clear and strong and in perfect pitch.

Several songs later, Henry Lloyd's hands stilled, his voice quieted. "Wonderful," Jenna said with a sigh. "You sound better than anyone I have ever heard."

"I don't believe I'se ever heard better," Mama Joyce agreed. "You keep practicin' and your music will take you far."

"If it gets me away from this place, I'll be satisfied," Henry Lloyd said.

"We should get back," Jenna said regretfully. "We have been gone long enough. Mama Joyce, let me look at that ulcer on your leg, put some poultice on it, and show you how to dress it yourself." As her grandmother obediently sat down in her favorite rocker and Jenna knelt beside her, unwinding the bandage covering it, Henry Lloyd stood up abruptly.

"I'll wait for y'all outside," he said, cradling the precious guitar in his arms. "It'll give me a little bit more time to play."

"He doesn't want to admit the sight makes him queasy," Jenna said with a slight smile. "Ma'dear sends him to do something else when it comes time to butcher anything. The first time he saw her cut a hog's throat, he fainted and woke up throwing up. He cannot stand the sight of blood or the smell of anything sick."

"I see it don't bother you none," Mama Joyce said, wincing as Jenna pulled away the last of the bandage which was stuck to the seeping ulcer as gently as she could.

"No, I need to see it in order to make it better," Jenna said, examining the open wound closely. Reaching into the burlap sack, as she extracted the poultice, her fingers encountered another packet. Pulling it out recognizing its contents, she nodded, talking as she unwrapped it.

"That ulcer is not looking so good, Mama Joyce. Have you been to see Doc Edmonds?"

"Naw, I ain't. You know I hate going to his office, all them white folks gaping at you and them stuck-up nurses looking down they nose at you. I would jes' rather let you and Albertina take care of me."

"Mama Joyce, some things Ma'dear and I cannot do," Jenna said gently, "like testing you for diabetes…sugar," she added when her grandmother looked confused.

"I ain't got no sugar," Mama Joyce said emphatically.

"Have you been extra tired lately?" Jenna asked softly "Or extra hungry? Have you had to pee a lot more? Are your feet and legs numb? I know it takes a long time for sores and ulcers and such to heal. This ulcer is not getting any better."

"Everything you said is jes' a sign of getting old," Mama Joyce stated obstinately. "That don' mean I got sugar."

"Maybe not, but let Doc Edmonds tell you that," Jenna said. "Please, Mama Joyce, don't be stubborn. Go see Doc Edmonds. I do not know what I would do if something happened to you. Henry Lloyd and I need you here with us, healthy and your usual feisty self. I do believe Henry Lloyd would run away if you weren't here to give him support and a place to get away from his daddy."

"Awright, chile, I'll go." Mama Joyce said. "You gone be a great nurse, Queenie. You can make anybody do just about anythin', and your knowin' the old way of doing things and the book learning you gone get are going to make you a force to be reckoned with."

"Thank you, Mama Joyce," Jenna said, smiling, her heart warmed by her grandmother's comments. "Now, let me tell you how to use what I brought. This is toadflax," she said, holding up a packet of dried greenery interspersed with specks of yellow and orange. "I want you to measure two tablespoons and put that in a half-quart of warm, not hot, water. Then dip some of those big cotton balls in it, put them on a clean dry rag and wrap that around your leg. Do that twice a day and just before you go to bed. Now, when you wake up each morning, I want you to rub this poultice into it because it has a lot of yarrow. Let it breathe for about three hours or so before you put the compress on. It should start healing in about three or four days, but you be sure and let Doc Edmonds see it, hear?"

"Yes, ma'am, Miss Queenie, I sure will," her grandmother promised. "I'll send somebody to get me set up wit' an appointment tomorrow morning."

"Good," Jenna said, standing up and giving Mama Joyce a tight hug, "I love you, and you be sure to follow everything just like I said, all right?"

"I will," Mama Joyce promised.

"Good," Jenna said smiling, "We must go now. Ma'dear is going to think something happened to us."

"I sure enjoyed y'all," Mama Joyce said, starting to rise, but subsiding when Jenna gestured for her to remain seated.

"You want me to clean this kitchen before I go?" Jenna asked.

"No, chile, jes' leave it. I'll get to it in the morning," Mama Joyce said. "Take that bowl of peaches sitting on the cabinet and reach into it and grab two or three jars of canned peaches and a coupla jars of preserves. There's a sack hanging on a peg over there you can put them in. You be sure and thank your ma for this medicine."

"I will, Mama Joyce," Jenna said. "Henry Lloyd, it's time to go," calling out to her brother who was sitting on the porch still strumming his new guitar. He came through the door as she was putting the last peach into the sack, striding over to give his grandmother a big hug, walking to the cabinet and carefully placing his guitar on an empty shelf within. Waving goodbye, thanking Mama Joyce again for the wonderful dinner, the pair headed out of the door, clambered down the steps, and toward the road, Henry Lloyd taking the sack from Jenna and slinging it over one shoulder. Laughing and talking, full of excitement over Henry Lloyd's new acquisition, they began the long walk home.

"Queenie is that you?" a voice asked plaintively. A figure stepped out of the shadows cast by the massive tree that marked the beginning of the land owned by her stepfather.

"Yes, it's me," Jenna said, opening her arms and hugging the figure that ran into them. "It's all right, Sidney," she said soothingly. "I'm back, see?"

"You were gone a long time. I thought you'd left me."

"Now Sidney, you know I would never leave without telling you. Were you there when Ma'dear told us to go to Mama Joyce's, or did the spirits have hold of you?"

"They close tonight, real close. They bothering and worrying me so much I forgot. I'm glad you're back home and didn't leave me. You the only one who believes me and knows what I'm talking about and understands what they be telling me."

Sidney, the seventh child, had the 'gift'. Shy, retiring, and small for his age, his pale brown eyes were often vacant, focused inward, grappling with the spirits who rarely left him alone. Born with a veil over his face, everyone knew from the start he was destined to follow in his mother and older sister's footsteps. Male healers were especially powerful and highly respected for their knowledge and abilities. As a seventh child, Sidney would be even more so until it became obvious that he was too close to the spirit world, that he had pierced the veil separating them from the real world, and that the spirits would not leave him alone. He would often become detached, removed from the physical world, wandering through the pathways of his mind into another realm altogether. His vacant stare that could last for hours was unnerving, making anyone who did not know him, and even those who did distinctly uncomfortable. He had a way of discerning, of seeing the secrets hidden in other's minds and hearts that caused people to actively avoid him, afraid of having those secrets revealed. Jenna was the only one of his siblings who understood and supported him. He had no friends because he could not go to school. Even his brothers and sisters were somewhat afraid of him. He clung to Jenna as the only stability in a shifting, confusing world.

"Look what Mama Joyce sent," Jenna said, stepping back and taking the sack from Henry Lloyd, reaching into it, removing a peach and handing it to Sidney who immediately bit into it, savoring the sweetness, wiping his mouth on his sleeve as the juices ran down his chin.

"Wan' me to tell you what the spirits told me?" Sidney asked, walking beside Jenna as he consumed his peach.

"I'm gonna go on up ahead and take these things to Ma'dear," Henry Lloyd said hastily, retrieving the sack from Jenna and increasing his pace, "I'll see y'all at the house." Sidney gave him the willies, and he sure did not want to hear whatever it was the spirits had told him. Let Jenna deal with their strange brother.

Putting one arm around his shoulders, drawing him close, Jenna patiently listened to Sidney's difficult to unravel ramblings, asking questions, leading him home as he shared with her his latest journey into the spirit world.

Chapter Three

"Queenie, are you awake? You promised to collect some herbs and plants for me, the kind that grow wild. You know most of them are best picked with the morning dew still on them, so you need to get movin'."

"I am up and dressed, Ma'dear," Jenna said, running a comb through the tangles in her hair, wincing whenever she snagged it on a particularly stubborn snarl. She glanced over at her sleeping sister, who, mouth open, was snoring slightly. *You think I do not know you sneaked in here at some god-awful hour of the morning,* she thought, *and if Ma'dear ever finds out, she is going to have a fit…mark my words, you will get caught…and there are many ways and kinds and definitions of getting caught.* Putting the comb down on the battered dresser, Jenna hurried out of the room.

"I am getting ready to leave, Ma'dear," Jenna called pitching her voice to be heard through the closed door of the bedroom shared by her mother and stepfather. "You do not need to get up," she scolded, watching anxiously as her mother slowly came out of the bedroom and stopped, leaning heavily on a wicker chair catching her breath, holding one side of her swollen stomach, before landing on the seat of the chair with a thud. "I know what to look for and where to find it. You could have stayed in bed and rested before everybody else gets up."

"Bed don't give me no rest, chile," her mother said wearily. "This baby just keeps kicking and moving and squirming so much I lay awake most of the night."

"You should probably stay in bed until the baby is born," Jenna said worriedly. "You will need all of your strength when you go into labor, the last set of twins almost killed you. You still were not recovered from that and bang!" She snapped two fingers together, "Pregnant again." Jenna choked back the bitter words of recrimination, of anger, of acute dislike, knowing that all she would do was upset her mother. "Have you talked to Mother Rose?" she asked instead. "Told her about the difficulties you were having?" Mother Rose was the town midwife who had delivered babies, black and white alike, for more than a generation.

"She came by here day before yesterday," Albertina said. "She told me I was doing well and that I would likely sail through the labor with not much harm done," she lied.

"Well, I do not believe that, but I do not have time to find out what she really said," Jenna responded, walking to the door, picking up the burlap sack she carried the herbs in, peering in to make sure her small but sharp knife was in there along with newspapers and absorbent rags for wrapping, a small cup for dipping water and a pen to label what each packet contained. "I am off," she said, blowing her mother a kiss. "You get some rest now, you hear?"

"Did you eat breakfast?" Albertina asked.

"I did," Jenna replied. "There was some cornbread left over from last night's supper, so I crumbled it into a bowl, added some buttermilk, ate a peach, and I am thoroughly satisfied. Talk to you later." She headed toward the door.

"Hold on, I'm going with you," Henry Lloyd appeared in the doorway dressed in his usual overalls and checkered shirt.

"You are?" Jenna said in surprise, "You are welcome, of course, but I thought you said gathering and looking for herbs was so boring you would rather watch snails race."

"Well, it gives me the chance to spend some time with you. I can look for signs of game while we traipse along, and besides, doesn't a queen rate an escort? I am at your service, your majesty," Henry Lloyd said, bowing deeply. Straightening he exchanged a long look with his mother, her eyes widening in understanding. A young black girl walking alone in a heavily wooded area had recently been attacked, savagely beaten and assaulted. Though her attackers had not been formally identified, word was the ringleader was the sheriff's wild son. Jenna would be an irresistibly tempting target, but with him there to protect her, she would be safe.

As comfortable in the woods as he was on the farm, Henry Lloyd could shoot the wings off a fly at thirty paces, was an expert tracker and could effortlessly disappear into the brush, invisible and undetectable. Hoisting his rifle over one shoulder, a huge coil of rope on the other, slipping his prized Bowie knife into a hidden pocket on the inside of his overalls, he pronounced himself ready to proceed. Albertina watched them go after first admonishing them to be safe, vigilant, and careful.

*　　*　　*

"There she is," Beau Richards whispered excitedly, "Didn't I tell you she comes out here all by herself? I been watching her. She's a pretty, little thing. It'll be a pleasure breaking her in."

"That there is one juicy black morsel," his best friend, Tom Reynolds agreed. "We gonna flip a coin to see who goes first?"

"For shore," Beau said, his eyes kindling in anticipation. "No matter who goes first she'll still be tight for the rest of us. I bet you any money she's a virgin."

"But ain't she the witch's daughter?" Jed Harris asked. "I shore don't want no root put on me 'cuz I spoiled her daughter. Them voodoo darkies can put a hurtin' on you."

"Ain't nobody goin' to put a root on you, 'cuz ain't nobody goin' to know. We'll sneak up on the gal, grab her, have our way, and then tell her we'll kill her whole family if she tells. You can bet she won't say nothin'. Rumor has it her mama and my daddy been keeping company for years. Hell, who knows? She might be my sister. So even if they suspect neither one of them gone say nuttin' either. That will teach that black bitch about what happens when you sleep with a white man, and it'll tie my daddy up in knots 'cuz he won't be able to do nothin' about it."

"I don' know," Jed said doubtfully, still not totally convinced.

"Ah, Jed, you worry too much," Tom said. "That other gal ain't said nothin' has she? Well, neither will this one."

"Yeah, you actin' like an old woman," Beau said with disgust. "You weren't so nervous last time, and there's no reason to be scared this time. C'mon, man, buck up! We better get a move on; much later and someone's liable to happen by." Reluctantly allowing himself to be persuaded, Jed trailed behind his friends.

Crouching behind the tall grass growing all around, using it as concealment the trio slowly advanced on the girl sitting on a fallen log, absorbed with writing something on a newspaper-wrapped package. Intent on reaching their target, they were shocked when their forward advance was halted abruptly. As each stepped over a small mound of disturbed earth, that foot sank to the knee before being grasped tightly around the ankle, a snap and they were jerked off their feet and simultaneously hoisted into the air where they hung upside down, arms flailing, spinning. Before they could recover from the shock of that, there was a whistling sound and a sharpened stake pierced their clothing just above their crotches, dangerously close to the male appendages they wielded so proudly but had caused much pain and heartache. Three gunshots rang out and a hole appeared in their clothing even closer than the stake. The three trapped adolescents began screaming. The screams turned into desperate pleas for mercy when three additional gunshots so close they singed tender skin rang out. Convinced the next shots would render them incapacitated, Jed fainted, a spreading wet stain appeared in Tom's pants, while Beau closed his eyes awaiting the inevitable. After an agonizingly long wait that felt like forever, three final shots tore through the rope binding their leg and they tumbled to the ground into the heap of earth they had stepped over earlier with such disastrous consequences. There was no sign of their intended target.

Beau was the first to break the awkward silence. "Now, I know how a snared rabbit feels," he said with a disgusted laugh. "I'm going home to clean up, and then I'm going to go bang Cindy Lou Frasier. She really thinks we're getting married, stupid cow."

"Yeah well, I'm going home and get washed, and then I think I'm going to stay there the rest of the day. I don't feel so good," Jed said shakily, his face pasty white.

"I promised my ma I would go to town with her and help her carry packages," Tom said. "That's after I clean up too, of course." The three boys started to stand, their arms sinking into the mounds of earth they had landed in. They each felt a wooden shape buried in the dirt at almost the same time. Pulling it out, they gasped, Jed's face turning even whiter, looking as though he might faint again. Tom dropped his like it was on fire while after one look Beau threw his as far as he could.

"It's a voodoo doll," Jed said wretchedly, "Her mama done put a root on us…oh, Lawd, how did she know? I knew it wasn't a good idea to try and mess with the witch's daughter."

"Would you shut up?" Tom said angrily. "Ain't nothing goin' to happen! Don't nobody know nothin' for shore. If we just stay calm, we'll be all right."

"Tom's right," Beau said. "We admit to nothing, we keep quiet about all of this, and we won't have nothing to worry about… but to be on the safe side, I say we leave the little bitch alone, tempting though she may be." Unnerved but in agreement, the three boys bid one another farewell and went their separate ways.

*   *   *

"Queenie, baby, would you go over to the hen house and see if you can find and coax some more eggs out of those hens? I'm goin' to need them for some bakin', and you the only one I know able to get them onery things to lay right away, and you know where they hide them."

"All right, Ma'dear, I will be right back." Jenna put down the medical book she was reading and jumped up, hurrying out of the open door. She loved reading the books on medicine given to her by Doc Edmonds after he had replaced them with a new, updated set for himself. A long conversation with the town physician when he had come to check up on Albertina during one of her many pregnancies ultimately led to his presenting her with his old books. He also invited her to ask questions whenever he saw her and encouraged her desire to acquire formal training. Impressed with the sharpness of her mind he tried to talk Queenie into becoming a doctor, but she found the care taking side of nursing more attractive to her nurturing nature. Now he was working to get Queenie her nursing credentials on the college level with the ultimate goal, an advanced degree.

Entering the fenced area housing the chicken coop, Jenna began clucking at them, reaching down to stroke them, making cooing noises, following them underneath the coop, moving aside covered dirt to reveal hidden eggs. Soon she held six eggs in her hands. Poised to crawl back from underneath the noisy, rickety structure, she paused, cocking her ears to listen, trying to hear over the cackling sounds of the noisy chickens.

Strange grunting sounds were coming from a tangled stand of trees and bushes behind the chicken coop. *It sounds like some of the pigs got loose*, she thought staying safely behind the fence and under the coop as she crawled close enough to see. Pigs were known to attack people, and she did not want to get in the path of one, let alone two or more. She would tell the boys who were dressing for church. They could rope and return them to their pen after they got back. She needed to hurry, or she would be late, and she had to wash up again after crawling around in the dirt. Still cradling the eggs, she crept closer until she could see the small patch of earth located in the center of the trees and bushes surrounding it. She gasped, inhaling sharply. Her hands clenched tightly, crushing the fragile eggs, covering her hands with golden yellow yolks and slimy egg white. She felt ill, lightheaded, trying to absorb what her eyes told her disbelieving mind she was seeing. Backing hastily away, regaining her feet, she fled.

The pig sounds were coming from her groaning and grunting stepfather, his pants and white drawers down around his ankles, his fat, hairy butt clenching, releasing, steadily pumping, pounding hard into the woman, who eyes closed, was keening steadily, her skirts wrapped around her waist, panties hooked over one leg. Finishing, they disentangled, rearranged clothing and separated, he headed for the barn, and Sugar to get ready for church.

"Queenie? Queenie? Good Lawd, chile, what happened?" her mother's voice brought Jenna back to an awareness of her surroundings. She still held remnants of crushed eggshells in her yolk-stained hands.

"I-I fell," she stammered, looking down at herself. "Oh, Ma'dear, I am so sorry," her voice broke, the tears fell.

"That's all right, honey," her mother said, enfolding her in a warm embrace, "accidents happen. You weren't hurt, were you? Well, that's all that matters," she said, feeling the wordless shake of the head, returning the hug from the arms clutching her so tightly. "Now, you go get cleaned up, and I'll send Sidney up the road to borrow a few eggs from Miss Essie. Go on now, dry your eyes and don't you worry about it no more." She watched, a slight frown between her brows as Jenna stumbled away.

"Queenie, are you all right?" Henry Lloyd's voice broke into her turbulent, troubled thoughts.

"Wh-what?" she said, turning to look at her brother. "What did you say?"

"I asked if you're all right. You acting real strange." She had been behaving strangely since before they left for church that morning and continued to act strange even after they had arrived. She sat stone-still throughout the service, never saying a word, staring straight ahead. She hadn't even moved when Henry Lloyd sang, which was totally unlike her usual enthusiastic, sing along, hand-clapping self. Henry Lloyd's soulful, heartfelt singing had the power to move, to cause ladies to shout and to elicit the kind of feeling that had both men and women jumping up to do the holy ghost d-a-n-c-e. The only time she had reacted was when Sugar came and sat down beside her. She had jumped up as if her backside was on fire and moved to the opposite end of the pew, separated by numerous brothers and Rolanda. Walking home she continued to keep her distance staying as far away from her sister as she was able.

"Has Sugar done somethin' to you?" Henry Lloyd asked in a low voice.

"Why do you ask?" Jenna asked, her voice shaky.

"'Cuz every time she comes near you, you get stiff as a board and move away as fast as you can," Henry Lloyd said.

"No, she has not done anything to me," Jenna whispered following a long silence.

"Then why you actin' like that?" her brother demanded.

"Leave Queenie alone," Sidney said, coming up beside her and placing an arm around her. "What she knows or don't know don't need to be spread around."

"Where did you come from, and what do you know about it?" Henry Lloyd asked.

"I came 'cuz I know Queenie needs me," Sidney said. He turned his head, his eyes following Sugar who had walked on ahead. His eyes went vacant, empty, a hollow voice totally unlike his began to speak from his lips. "Her days of creating havoc among the many are ending...vengeance in a brown suit...as she has given, so shall she receive...pain and suffering...until the penance is paid in full...."

Henry Lloyd's scalp prickled. As always when Sidney began prophesizing, he beat a hasty retreat. "Well, if you're sure you all right, I'll meet y'all back at the house." Lengthening his stride, he hastened away.

"Don't you worry none, Queenie," Sidney said, "Sugar gone get jes' what she got comin' to her real soon."

"Thank you, Sidney, that is just what I needed to hear," feeling much of the oppressive feeling that had been weighing her down begin to dissipate. Sidney's predictions always came true, so if he said Sugar was about to get hers, she was. Comforted, arm in arm, they headed for the house and the special Sunday dinner Ma'dear had prepared.

*   *   *

"Queenie? I need to talk to you. It's important."

"What do you want, Sugar?" Jenna asked tersely.

"One thing I want to know is what I did, 'cuz you ain't said 'boo' to me in I don't know how long," Sugar said, "but we can talk about that later. I'm in big trouble and I need for you to do something for me, to help me."

"How far along are you?" Jenna asked dryly.

Sugar's eyes widened. "How did you know?" she whispered.

"You put on some weight, you are eating like there is no tomorrow, and I hear you getting up in the middle of the night throwing up," Jenna said.

"You right. I am in the family way," Sugar said, "and I need you to give me something to get rid of it. I sure don't want no brat, and one thing we don't need is another baby in the house, especially since Ma'dear is going to drop hers any day now."

"Whose is it?" Jenna asked.

Sugar gave a crack of laughter. "I can tell you whose it ain't," she said. "But as to naming who the daddy is, that I can't tell you."

"How far along did you say you were?" Jenna asked.

"I missed my last period, and that was about two or three weeks, ago," Sugar said. "I always been real regular."

"So, you are about six or seven weeks along," Jenna said, calculating rapidly. "Have you told anybody else you are in the family way? Because you know what you are asking me to do is illegal, and I sure do not want to go to jail."

"I ain't told nobody," Sugar said. "You think I want the whole world to know? Besides, Ma'dear would well-nigh kill me if she knew. You the only person I've told, or that I'm gonna tell. You will help me, won't you?"

"It goes against the grain, everything I believe in, but yes, I will help you this one time. But this is the only time I will do this. If it happens again, you are on your own."

"It won't happen again," Sugar said. "I ain't never gone be so careless again."

"You better start using a rubber," Jenna said, "because getting pregnant is not the worst thing that could happen. You sure do not want to be known as the girl with the clap."

Sugar's eyes widened. "I never thought about that," she said. "How come you know so much about stuff like that?"

"It is all there in my medical books," Jenna said, "If you take a look at the pictures of what happens down there when you get the disease, you would definitely use some protection."

"I'm gonna do better," Sugar promised. "When will you help me take care of this?"

"I will have what you need tomorrow morning," Jenna said. "Meet me by the well after breakfast, and do not make any plans for the next week or so. You are going to be bleeding heavily."

"I'll start ripping rags today," Sugar said, "and I'll meet you by the well in the morning. Thank you so much for doing this for me, Queenie. I'll do something for you some day. I'm blessed to have you for a sister."

"One more thing," Jenna said as Sugar turned to leave, and when she turned back inquiringly, "I want you to leave Mr. Pettigrew alone."

"Do you know everything?" Sugar asked in amazement tinged with awe. "Is it 'cuz you're a witch?"

"Never mind how I know, I just do. You must stop, otherwise Ma'dear is bound to find out. When she does, she will kill you both. Not that you deserve it, but I would hate to see her go to jail, and for the little ones to be without their mother. So, you better promise me and mean it, or you will be sorry."

"I promise," Sugar said. "I won't do it with him no more. It wasn't that good anyway, and I was always afraid of getting caught."

"Well, you did get caught. Next time it might not be me. If not killed, you would have such a bad reputation, nobody would have anything to do with you."

"I said I would, so you ain't got to say no more," Sugar said, a touch of irritation creeping into her voice. "I will see you by the well in the morning. Good night."

"Good night," Jenna said, watching until she was out of sight before going to check on her mother. *That baby better come soon...Ma'dear cannot take much more.* Swamped by a wave of worry mixed with fear, she picked up her pace.

Chapter Four

"Queenie! Queenie! Wake up…"

Jenna sat up, sleepy eyes focusing on Sidney's frightened face. "What is wrong?" she asked, swinging her legs over the side of her bed, "What has happened?"

"It's Ma'dear's time! Daddy sent Henry Lloyd for Mother Rose…oh, Queenie, I peeked in…there's blood….so much blood…"

Jenna jumped up, racing to her mother's room, pushing past her stepfather standing uncertainly in the doorway. Albertina lay in the center of the bed, clutching her midsection and moaning. The bed sheets below her waist were stained red, the stain spreading every time she thrashed around. Rushing over to the side of the bed, sitting down carefully, reaching over, she grasped her mother's hands. "All right, Ma'dear," she crooned. "We are going to be welcoming another baby into the world soon, and he or she is going to need you fit and healthy. All the rest of us need you, too…be strong Ma'dear…be strong…" Jenna stopped abruptly, swallowing hard. Looking into the doorway at the scared faces crowding it, she forced herself to calm. "Mr. Pettigrew, I need for you to lift Ma'dear very carefully while Sidney and Dexter strip the sheets and turn the mattress over… Rolanda, look in that drawer and get me a fresh nightgown, then you go put a big pot of clean water on the stove and set it to boil…Sugar, you get another pot to boiling and drop our sharpest knives into it....Lorenzo, you go look in that big basket in the closet and get those clean rags out. Alfonso, you go get some fresh sheets and some of those big rags to lay across the mattress...hurry, now." Everyone rushed to comply.

Mother Rose came through the door just as Mr. Pettigrew was laying Ma'Dear down into the freshly made bed. Tall, gaunt, her heavily wrinkled careworn face reflected her many years of delivering babies, the healthy and the stillborn, the wanted and unwanted, the loved and the reviled. She had aided her share of mothers as well from first timers to seasoned veterans, the frail, the hearty, and had closed the eyes of those not strong enough to survive the ordeal of childbirth, at times joined by their newborn, other times leaving behind a husband and other, suddenly motherless children. She prayed that this would not be one of those times. "You did just right, Queenie," she said, looking around, "Now, I think you should send the young uns away until this is over; it would just upset them. Is there somewhere they can stay?"

"Henry Lloyd can take them to Miss Essie's," Jenna said. "Sidney can stay here in case we need him to help with something. Henry Lloyd cannot stand the sight of blood; he was looking a little unsteady on his feet when he saw the bloody sheets."

"You do what you need to," Mother Rose said. "It's gonna be a while. We got lots of time." Reaching into the bag she brought with her, she extracted a small packet, took a pinch of the powder contained therein and sprinkled it over one of the pots of hot water. Dipping one of the clean rags into it, she squeezed out the excess water and placed it on Albertina's hot forehead; Jenna picked up a paper fan and waved it up and down her mother's damp, perspiring body. The moans were getting louder, the writhing harder, breathing turning into gasping pants, the red stain between legs reappearing, spreading. Mother Rose picked up another clean rag and packed it between Albertina's legs to try staunching the blood flow. Removing the rag to check her progress, she sighed. Still no sign of the baby.

Hours later, gasping cries turned into screams of pain, the blood flow was heavier, Albertina's strength was waning rapidly, and still no baby. "We need to send someone for Doc Edmonds," Mother Rose said, "I've done all I can do. This is a breech baby, and from what I can tell, the cord is probably wrapped around its neck. If he don't get here fast, we're going to lose them both."

Jenna jumped up, calling loudly for Sidney, sending him running when he appeared in the bedroom doorway. Running back to her mother's side, she turned to Mother Rose. "I read about how you can turn the baby if you insert your hands...up there... my hands are small...I can unwind the cord and turn the baby around...I have to try, or they are both going to die."

"All right, chile. I'll be here...if things go wrong."

Jenna dipped her arms up to the shoulder in the large bowl of hot water on the bedside table, Mother Rose pouring alcohol on them to disinfect. Taking a deep breath, murmuring encouragement, she slowly slid one hand in the slippery, dilated opening and did the same with the other. Her hands encountered tiny feet, further probing found the tangled cord. She carefully unwrapped it from the baby's throat and gently turned the baby positioning it head-first in the birth canal. She withdrew from her mother's body, moving over to the bowl she had used earlier, washing and rinsing her hands free of blood and body fluids from the placenta. Her mother began straining, pushing down, answering nature's call. A tiny head appeared and moments later the rest of the baby slid into the cupped hands waiting to receive it. After an agonizing moment of silence, wails from an unhappy infant filled the air.

Doc Edmonds came hurrying through the door a short time later. Tall, well-built, handsome with salt and pepper hair, he was one of only a few doctors in the area who accepted colored patients. Albertina lay unmoving on the bed; a closer examination showed that she was deeply asleep, the baby asleep next to her, both had been cleaned up and the bed sheets changed again. Jenna was sitting in a chair on the side of the bed, holding her mother's hand. She watched as Doc Edmonds performed his examination, listened to Mother Rose explaining the sequence of events. Nodding, Jenna moved away from the bed when the doctor asked to speak with her privately.

"Well, Queenie, I think we can safely say that your mother and your new sister owe their lives to you," Doc Edmonds said. "You should be proud. You knew what to do from reading one of the books I gave you?"

"Yes sir, I reread difficult pregnancies, just in case," Jenna said.

"It's a good thing you did," Doc Edmonds said. "Giving you those books was one of the best things I have ever done." Sobering, he said, "It looks like Albertina is going to pull through, thanks to you, but I'll be honest with you – she won't survive another pregnancy. She almost didn't survive this one. I could make it so that there won't be any more babies, or pregnancies, but I need your father to sign the papers allowing me to perform the procedure."

"He is not my father," Jenna said fiercely, "and he will never sign it, not if he knows what he is signing."

"What if he does not know?" Doc Edmonds said. "What if he were to think he was signing his permission for something else altogether?"

"I think he would sign it then," Jenna said looking up at him. "Do it, please? I will not say anything, so no one else will know.

37

Please, Doc Edmonds. We need Ma'dear a lot more than we need any more babies around."

"All right, I'll do it," Doc Edmonds said. "Give me a few minutes to draw up the papers, and I will do it right now. Where is your...stepfather?"

"Probably sitting in the rocker by the kitchen door waiting to hear something." Jenna said.

"Good, I will need to talk with him some place private," Doc Edmonds said.

"You can use the table in the kitchen to write on," Jenna said. "I am going back to sit with Ma'dear."

A short time later Doc Edmonds came into the bedroom, signed paper in hand. "Here it is. I want you to put it away someplace where only you can find it. I don't think we'll ever need it, but you never know."

"Yes sir, I know just the place," Jenna said. She was going to bury it in the metal box in the herb garden where she kept all her special papers and memorabilia; it would be safe there.

"I know you are probably exhausted. You have had quite an evening," Doc Edmonds said. "But do you think you can assist me? I want to get this done now, before the healing starts. We don't want to have to open her up again."

"Sure, I will. Just tell me what to do," Jenna said. She stood up and closed the door. Opening it sometime later, she thanked the doctor, thanked Mother Rose who was waiting in the kitchen, and sent Sidney to collect the rest of the children to tell them about their new sister so they could peek in and see for themselves that Ma'dear was all right, stumbled into her room, fell across the bed, and promptly fell into the deep sleep of the physically and emotionally exhausted.

* * *

"I'm going out for a while. I cain't stand sitting in this house another minute," dressed, perfumed and heavily made up, Sugar made her way toward the back door.

Jenna was holding her new baby sister, Rhonda, feeding her formula from a warmed bottle. Albertina was too weak to hold the infant and her milk was drying up rapidly. Looking up she said, "You feeling well enough to leave the house? I know you do not want to be embarrassed by leaking all over the place."

"It's slowed down to no more than the end of a regular cycle would be," Sugar said after first looking around to make sure no one could overhear the conversation. "I padded up real good, so I'll be fine. I'm just going over to the *Blue Note* for a little bit, have a dance, conversate a little, and then I'll be back ready to take my turn at nurse and nursemaid again." Picking up her purse from the side table where it lay, she opened it, checked the contents, nodded her head at sight of the folded money inside, smoothed the folds of the snug skirt she was wearing, made sure her stockings were run-free and that the seams were straight before sashaying out the door.

"Where that gal goin'?" Rodney growled walking over to the door, watching as Sugar moved down the pathway leading to the road, "and who said she could go anywhere?"

"Sugar is almost twenty years old, Mr. Pettigrew," Jenna said. "That makes her pretty much grown, so she does not have to ask anyone for permission to do anything." Her stepfather watched Sugar like a hawk, and his increasingly bad temper attested to the fact that he and Sugar were no longer intimate.

"She don't need to be going nowhere this time of night by herself," Rodney grumbled. "She liable to get into all kinds of trouble. Did she say where she was going?" he asked.

"No," Jenna lied calmly. "She will be back before too long. She said she was tired of being cooped up in this house."

"I'm gonna go sit outside and get me some air," Rodney said. "It's hot up 'n here, and what wit' that baby cryin' all the time, a man cain't get no peace." He stalked out the door, slamming it behind him.

The sound startled an almost-asleep baby, who immediately raised her voice in protest. Rocking and making cooing noises, Jenna soothed her little sister back to sleep.

*　　*　　*

"Lord, I either done died and gone to heaven, or an angel done escaped from Paradise." The voice making the statement lacked the Southern drawl normally heard when someone spoke, indicating the likelihood of an out-of-towner.

Sugar turned. A young man she had never seen before stood boldly looking her up and down, lingering on full breasts peeking over the top of the low-cut, tight-fitting wool sweater she wore, his eyes slowly traveling downward, and back up, meeting her eyes, a slow smile forming on well-shaped lips. "Girl, I'm gonna have to have you arrested for larceny, because you surely done stole my heart."

Sugar took her turn at a close perusal, looking the unknown man up and down as boldly as he had examined her. Nattily dressed in a brown suit with matching hat, patent leather shoes and a red and brown checkered vest, with smooth brown skin the color of ripe pecans, dark eyes, processed black hair, and a thin black moustache, he had an air of sophistication not present in any of the men she knew. Instantly intrigued, she wasn't going to let him know it, not yet. So, she snorted, turned away and said, "Do the girls where you come from fall for them pitiful little come-ons?" she asked scornfully. "I may be from the country, but I sure don't fall for lines like that."

"Oh, Baby, you wrong me," the man protested, "I ain't never seen nothing fine as you in my entire life. The words came straight from my heart," suiting action to words he placed one hand over his heart. "C'mon baby, don't be so cold," he said when Sugar continued to walk away. "Let me buy you a drink, we'll talk, get to know each other, dance a little bit. What do ya say?"

"A drink might be nice," Sugar purred. "A little talking probably wouldn't hurt none, either."

"Bet!" the man said, grasping Sugar by the elbow and leading her over to an empty table near the tiny dance floor. "What's your name, baby?" he asked.

"My name is Shavonya, but everybody calls me Sugar."

"That's because you so sweet, I bet," the man said. "My name is Lawrence Green, but everybody calls me Larry."

"So, what brings you to Crawfish Holler, Lawrence Green?" Sugar asked.

"I got kinfolk living in the bottoms. It's been years since I seen them, so I figured it was about time, and man, am I glad I did."

The waitress came by bearing a tray containing a bottle of bourbon, an ice bucket full of cubes, a bowl of canned cherries, a pitcher of water, and two glasses. Opening the bottle, Larry poured them each a generous splash of bourbon, dropped in a couple of ice cubes, filling the glass the rest of the way with water. Handing Sugar a glass, he took a large swallow of his before leaning forward and saying. "Now Sugar-pie, I want you to tell me all about yourself. Don't leave nothing out." Heads close together, the two talked and danced as the level of liquor in the bottle dropped lower and lower.

"What time did your sister get in?" Rodney demanded as he came into the kitchen from the back room where he was sleeping with the younger boys while Albertina recovered. "I went to bed at three o'clock, and she wasn't back yet."

At the stove flipping pancakes for Sunday breakfast, frying link sausages and scrambled eggs, heating up the molasses, Jenna hesitated. *How am I going to tell this man that Sugar did not come home at all*, she wondered. He was certain to react badly and would probably take it out on the boys. Setting full plates in front of her brothers she said, "You all eat up now and get on to Sunday school," Jenna said. "Hurry, you do not want to be late." Taking the hint, the boys picked up their forks and began quickly cleaning their plates.

"Gal, I asked you a question," Rodney said angrily. Hearing the tone in his voice, Henry Lloyd got to his feet and hurried to the back returning moments later with the sports jacket and bow tie he wore to church every Sunday. "I'm practicing a new song that I gonna sing today, so I'll see y'all at church." He disappeared through the open doorway.

"I heard you, Mr. Pettigrew. I am just getting the last of the food on the table, and I did not want to burn or spill anything," Jenna said. Footsteps on the stairs outside had them both turning towards the door.

Mincing her steps, walking the careful walk of the inebriated, Sugar came through the door. "Looks like I'm jes' in time for breakfast," she said with a giggle. "Too bad I ain't got time to eat. Larry's going to pick me up in a few minutes and take me to Orangesburg. We going to eat there...in a restaurant. I need to hurry and change clothes."

"Who is Larry?" Jenna asked.

"He's this man I met last night. He ain't from around here; he's jes' here visiting family. Drove down in his new car. He lives in Detroit and makes plenty money. I'll introduce him to y'all later. He's liable to see all these young'uns and get scared away. Now, I ain't got no more time to talk. He'll be here any minute. I'm gonna meet him on the road." She hurried out the room.

Rodney watched her go, eyes narrowed. He stood abruptly; his right hand clenched into a fist. With a wordless roar he swept all the dishes within reach off the table. He stood, looked around balefully, turned and stalked out of the kitchen, down the outside stairs and stomped away. Jenna looked around at the shattered plates and glasses, at the molasses pooling into a sticky puddle on the floor, at the buttermilk splattered everywhere, and sighed. She hurried into her mother's room when she heard her name called.

"What was that crash?" Albertina asked. "It sounded like somebody knocked the kitchen table over."

"Mr. Pettigrew knocked some dishes over when he was getting up from the table," Jenna said. "I was just getting ready to clean it up."

"Well, I don't want you to miss church," her mother said, "Do what you can and leave the rest. Miss Essie is going to come by and stay with me while y'all are in service, and she's going to cook dinner, too. I'll pay her to clean it up. After church I want you and Henry Lloyd to go over to Mama Joyce's for a while. You take a look at her leg and see how it's healing. I don't want Henry Lloyd around when his daddy is in a mood. Y'all take your time, and I'll see you after a while."

"Yes, ma'am," Jenna said walking over and kissing her on the cheek before turning and going to her room to dress for church.

*   *   *

"Hey babies, it's good to see y'all, come on in. You jes' in time, I'm about to put dinner on the table."

"Hey Mama Joyce, Ma'dear sent me to look at your leg," Jenna said, kissing her grandmother on both cheeks.

"I came 'cuz Daddy is in one of his moods," Henry Lloyd said with a smile, also kissing his grandmother.

"I'm glad y'all here; I got a surprise for y'all. I was going to come to the house, but you all the first to see. Go on in the parlor."

Stepping into the kitchen, moving through it into the parlor, Jenna checked in surprise. A slim, stylishly dressed woman, her hair in a fashionable French twist, a strand of pearls around her throat, and several gold bangle bracelets around her wrists stood up and approached them, hands extended.

"Don't tell me this is my niece and nephew! Why, you're just about grown up. The last time I saw you, none of y'all were any bigger than this," she said, holding her hand about knee high. "Mama, who are these beautiful young people?"

"That there is your niece, Queenie, and your nephew Henry Lloyd," Mama Joyce said proudly, "Ain't they good-looking? All of Albertina's children are."

"My name is really Jenna, but everybody calls me Queenie," Jenna inserted.

"Well, I'm your aunt Loretta, but everybody calls me Lori," the woman replied, smiling. "Y'all come over here and give me a big hug! I'm your family."

After exchanging hugs, Loretta looked over at Henry Lloyd. "How old are you, handsome?" she asked. When told, she said, "I guess that means you aren't old enough to drive yet, huh? That's too bad," she said when Henry Lloyd shook his head no. "I was going to let you drive the car I'm paying this white man to let me drive while I'm here, and if you did a good enough job would have hired you to drive me in my car in California."

"Girl, you stop trying to turn that boy's head," Mama Joyce said. "He ain't nearly old enough to leave home yet, so you just hush, and let's go in to dinner."

Looking at her brother's bedazzled face, Jenna was glad he was not old enough to go anywhere; otherwise, he probably would have abandoned them without a thought. Loretta laughed. "I'm just getting to know my kin, Mama," she said. "It gets lonely all by myself in my big old house in California." Placing a scented arm around Jenna's shoulder, hugging her lightly she asked," How old are you, Jenna? I guess you too young too," she said with a disappointed sigh when told. "I'm going to have to wait a few years before I can talk you all into coming to live with me, but I just know you two would love it."

Loretta continued to talk about her life in California as they all sat down to dinner. Papa Pete came into the room from the bedroom where he spent most of his time and sat down, smiling slightly when Jenna gave him a hug and a kiss and Henry Lloyd hugged him. Sitting down, Jenna looked at the dinner offerings eagerly. A large baked chicken, skin glistening a crispy golden brown was flanked by a big, clove-studded ham, several slices cut from the bone and arranged around it. A big bowl of mashed potatoes, a melting pat of butter at its center was surrounded by bowls and platters of green beans with small pearl onions, candied yams, fresh rolls, sliced tomatoes, fried okra, cornbread, and deviled eggs. A pitcher of iced tea was sitting on the cabinet, next to a cake that by its color made Jenna think it was probably caramel, a peach cobbler and a pecan pie. She bowed her head as Papa Pete blessed the food and watched with eager anticipation as Mama Joyce carved the chicken, placing a wing and a thigh on her plate, helping herself as the bowls and plates of food were passed around.

"Henry Lloyd, are you going to play for us before you leave?" Mama Joyce asked. She turned to her daughter. "That boy can sing and play the guitar like nobody's business," she said proudly. "You think you listening to the radio when he play."

"Really?" Loretta said eagerly. "Now, I know you need to come to California! I know a lot of people that could help you get your singing career started; and you are so handsome, we might even be able to get you in the movies."

"Do you live in Hollywood, Aunt Loretta," Jenna breathed, "and you know movie stars?"

"Do you know Lena Horne?" Henry Lloyd asked reverently.

"I live in San Francisco," Loretta answered, "but I do know some movie producers and directors. They come visit me whenever they come North. I don't actually know Lena Horne, but I could probably arrange an introduction."

"Loretta, I done told you to stop trying to turn these children's heads," Mama Joyce said, "Henry Lloyd ain't going nowhere for a long time, and Queenie is going to be a nurse, so stop trying to get them to come to California."

"Alright, Mama, I'll say no more," Loretta said, "but I just want you all to know my door is always open. I would love to get to know my family better."

When she had eaten all the dinner she could hold, Jenna rose and helped Mama Joyce clear the table, replacing the dinner plates with dessert plates and utensils, helping to cut the caramel cake, scooping cobbler into a separate bowl, placing a piece of pecan pie next to the cake. Reaching into the icebox Mama Joyce pulled out a bowl of whipped cream, placing a large dollop on the pecan pie. Jenna was so full of dinner, she could only manage a small piece of caramel cake which she loved. Then she watched in amazed wonder as Henry Lloyd ate two pieces of cake, an enormous helping of cobbler, and a big slice of pecan pie.

Loretta refused any dessert saying, "Mama, I can't eat all that sweet. I already ate more than I usually do, and I want to be able to still get in my clothes when I go home."

"How long are you staying?" Henry Lloyd asked. "I hope it's a long time."

"Well, aren't you sweet," Loretta cooed. "I wish I could stay awhile, but I really have to get home. I'm leaving day after tomorrow, but I'll definitely be back now that I know I have such interesting family members here."

Henry Lloyd beamed. But Jenna, looking at her glamorous, sophisticated step aunt, tried to suppress a growing feeling of disquiet. Something about Loretta did not ring true. Telling herself she was probably imagining things and admitting to some jealousy over Henry Lloyd's obvious infatuation, she brushed those feelings aside, making a point to engage Loretta in conversation and sitting beside her when Henry Lloyd performed for them.

Before they left, Jenna examined the ulcer on Mama Joyce's leg while Loretta took Henry Lloyd outside to look at the car she was driving while there. "It looks a lot better," Jenna said as she applied more poultice. "What did Doc Edmonds say?"

"He said it was healing nicely," Mama Joyce replied. "He did say I was showing early signs of sugar and gave me a list of things I shouldn't eat."

"You be sure to do what he says," Jenna said. "We must keep you healthy."

"Since I can't have it, Papa Pete don't need it, and Loretta won't eat it, why don't you take the rest of them desserts home wit' cha," Mama Joyce said. "There's some more peaches in a basket on the porch, y'all can take it, too."

"Thank you, Mama Joyce," Jenna said giving her a warm hug and a kiss. "Henry Lloyd, we must go now," Jenna called.

Henry Lloyd and Loretta came through the door as Jenna was wrapping up the last of the cake slices, taking the bag she handed him and going outside to collect the peaches. Coming back in, he gave his grandmother a warm hug, turning to his newly discovered aunt and hugging her as well.

"I sure enjoyed you all," Loretta said, hugging Jenna who hugged her back, not quite as warmly as her brother had, still fighting those uneasy feelings. Promising to see them again soon, Loretta waved until the pair disappeared around a curve in the road before going back into the house and closing the door behind her.

Chapter Five

"What's Daddy got his drawers in a knot about?" Henry Lloyd asked as he came through the kitchen door, "He's been meaner than a double-headed rattlesnake for days."

"Who knows?" Jenna said with a shrug. "He is always angry about something. Maybe he is upset because he still cannot sleep in his bed, or maybe someone at work made him mad, or maybe he is just furious because the sky is blue."

Henry Lloyd smiled. "Yeah, you right. Does Ma'dear know that Sugar ain't been home in two days?" he asked.

"I have not told her, and Mr. Pettigrew has not either," Jenna said. "She has gone crazy over that slick city-man who is in town visiting his family. Larry-something, I think."

"That dude in that car I saw her in?" Henry Lloyd asked.

"Uh-huh, a man in a brown suit," Jenna said with a slight shudder. Every time she thought about him a shiver ran down her back, thinking about Sidney's prediction.

"Where did she meet him?" Henry Lloyd asked.

"At the *Blue Note*, I think," Jenna said. "That is where she said she was going the last she was in this house."

"That dive?" Henry Lloyd said in disgust. "And she's spent the last two or three days with him? It don't take much, does it?"

"Never has," Jenna agreed.

As if their conversation had conjured her up, Sugar came through the door, pulling a man dressed in brown behind her.

She was wearing an obviously new dress with matching shoes and handbag. She smiled at those gathered around the radio; they had been listening to *The Lone Ranger* radio program. Jenna walked over and turned down the volume, frowning when numerous voices were raised in protest.

"Is Ma'dear up yet?" Sugar asked. "I want her to meet somebody."

"She has been sitting up a little bit, but she has not gotten out of bed yet," Jenna said. "Doc Edmonds says she has to stay there for at least another two weeks or so."

"You think I can just peek in for a minute?" Sugar asked.

"Is it that important?" Jenna asked.

"Well, I think her meeting my new husband is pretty important, don't you?" Sugar said with a coy smile, holding up her left hand, where a gold band and a sizable diamond encircled the ring finger.

"You, you got m-married?" Jenna stammered, looking from one to the other. "After knowing one another for only a few days?"

"Little girl, when it's real there ain't no reason to wait," the man said, wrapping his arms around his new wife, "besides, I want to take her with me when I head back to Detroit."

"And when might that be?" Henry Lloyd asked, eyeing his new brother-in-law.

"I got a few days yet," the man said easily, "then it's off to the Motor City."

"Where are you going to stay?" Jenna asked, putting an arm around Sidney who had crept up beside her and stood staring wide-eyed at the man dressed in brown from head to toe.

"I was going to ask Ma'dear if we could stay here," Sugar said, nestling more closely into the arms encircling her, "Larry's folks ain't got no room."

"And we do?" Henry Lloyd asked quizzically, looking around at his numerous siblings who had gathered around to gape at the newcomer in their midst.

"I thought we could stay in our room; Queenie, you could sleep in here on the trundle bed," Sugar said coaxingly. "It's only for a few days," she said when Jenna stiffened in protest. Before she could answer, a heavy tread on the outside stairs had everyone turning toward the door.

Rodney walked in, halting when he saw the strange man in the house with his arms around Sugar. "Who you?" he asked, his voice gruff, hostile, his right hand curling into a fist.

"Hello, sir, you must be Sugar's daddy. It's nice to meet you. My name is Lawrence Green, but everyone calls me Larry," the man said walking over and extending his hand. He lowered it after a moment when Rodney just stared at it, making no move to shake it.

"Daddy, this here's my new husband," Sugar said sweetly, looking up at her stepfather. "Even though we just met, we fell in love straight away and just knew we were supposed to be married. We went to a justice of the peace this afternoon, and he married us. Isn't it exciting?"

A long, awkward silence ensued. "I'm goin' to milk the cows," Rodney said turning away and walking out the door. "You boys go slop the hogs."

"Don't mind him, he always like that," Sugar said. "He jes' an evil ole man." Turning back to Jenna she said, "Go see if Ma'dear can talk to us."

Tossing her sister a look of disbelief, Sugar still wanted to stay with them after the way Mr. Pettigrew had reacted? Jenna walked over to the closed door, opened it softly, and slipped in through the narrow opening. Albertina was sitting up, alert, her eyes on the door.

"What's going on?" she asked.

"Sugar went out, was gone for three days, and came back with a husband from Detroit," Jenna replied. "Now she and he want to stay here until they leave for Detroit in a couple of days."

If the news surprised her mother, she did not show it. "What does Mr. Pettigrew say?" she asked.

"He did not say anything," Jenna said, "Nothing at all. He just stared at the man as if he had two heads and walked out."

Albertina closed her eyes, breathing deeply to expand her consciousness. "It's just as well," she said after a time, "Sugar was headed for big trouble, mayhap marriage will settle her down some. Tell them they can stay here. Queenie, you can sleep on the trundle bed in here with me since Mr. Pettigrew is still sleeping with the boys, and they can have you and Sugar's room until they leave. But first, I want to meet this man Sugar done gone and married. Send them in. What's his name?"

"Lawrence Green," Jenna supplied, as she walked to the door, "but everybody calls him Larry."

Dinner that evening was a silent affair. One look at Rodney's face and the boys took care not to meet his eyes, concentrating on the greens and cornbread on their plates, not even looking at the stewed chicken in front of their father's plate. The smell of moonshine hung in the air and grew stronger every time Rodney breathed out, the expression on his face growing blacker and blacker the more Sugar giggled, every time she whispered in Larry's ear, each time he kissed full lips. Gritting his teeth, he reached for the clay jug of liquor on the floor next to him, raising it to his lips and drinking freely. He reached into the pot and pulled out a chicken leg, biting into it and chewing loudly.

"Are you going to offer the rest of us some chicken, Mr. Pettigrew?" Jenna asked. All eyes turned to Rodney.

He shifted narrowed eyes to Jenna's face. "Who tole you to kill one of my hens?" he demanded. "A dead hen cain't lay no eggs."

"Ma'dear told me to catch one of the older ones," Jenna said calmly. "We got company, so she thought it would be nice to have a little extra something for supper tonight."

"I sure appreciate that," Larry said brightly. "I ain't ate like this in years, that good ole Southern cookin'."

"Well, help yourself, honey," Sugar purred. "Daddy, would you pass the pot, please?"

Rodney slowly stood on his feet, deliberately picked up the pot of stewed chicken and heaved it at the nearest wall. Chicken parts, gravy, and vegetables crashed against the whitewashed sheetrock, ran down the wall, dripped in heaps onto the faded wooden floor. "Help yourself, honey," he snarled into the stunned silence, picking up his jug and staggering out the door.

"Rolanda, you go tell Ma'dear everything is all right and do not say anything about Mr. Pettigrew, so she does not worry." Rolanda jumped up and ran to her mother's room. "Looks like we are going to have to make do with greens and cornbread," Jenna said, surveying the mess.

"Looks like," Henry Lloyd agreed with a smile. "At least the pigs will eat well tomorrow."

"I wish I was a pig," Dexter said wistfully, looking longingly at the tempting pieces of chicken scattered across the floor.

Jenna started laughing and after a startled moment was joined by everyone else sitting at the table. Looking over at her younger brother, Jenna said, "Well, sweetie, at least we can have the peach cobbler I made. It is really good and better than anything the hogs will eat!"

Dexter brightened. "I s'pose I'll stay a boy, then," he declared.

"Well, I am certainly glad of that," Jenna said to more laughter. She made certain he got an extra helping when serving

53

the still-warm sweet, rich with brown sugar, vanilla extract and cinnamon, an abundance of tender peaches and crispy, well-browned crust sprinkled with sugar.

"Well, Little Sister, you 'bout to see the last of me for a long, long time," Sugar said early the next morning, putting the last of her toiletries into the battered suitcase that had been sent full of used clothes by an unknown aunt in Chicago. "Why, I do believe you goin' to miss me," she said looking at Jenna's downcast face.

"I am," Jenna said, her eyes full of unexpected tears. Memories crowded her mind: she and Sugar picking blackberries and eating until their faces were stained purple; splashing in the shallows in the pond behind the house; climbing apple trees in the orchard, picking up the rotten ones and throwing them at unsuspecting men in hats, running away laughing; walking to the town general store to spend their pennies on candy; helping Ma'dear make biscuits; trying in vain to teach her about medicinal herbs; churning ice cream on hot summer days and licking the blades clean; laying in the lush grass looking up at the sky while identifying faces and figures in the clouds.

"I'm goin' miss you too, Queenie," Sugar said, her voice tender, thick with tears. She opened her arms and Jenna ran into them, hugging tightly, being hugged just as tightly in return. Stepping back, Sugar picked up an unpacked handkerchief lying on the bed, using it to dry both their eyes.

"Now you be good, take good care of Ma'dear, don't let the children run you ragged, and don't take no shit from Daddy Rodney, you hear? If you ever need some place to stay, you'll always be welcome in my house, all right?" One last hug, a quick look in the mirror to repair smudged makeup, reaching over to pick up her suitcase, a final look around the room she had lived in so long, and Sugar was ready to go.

"You ready, baby?" Larry reached over to take the suitcase, turned and headed out the door to the car parked at the end of the long tree-lined lane.

"Y'all come give me a hug," Sugar said to her siblings, hugging each one in turn, admonishing them to be good and to listen to Jenna and Ma'dear. They all promised solemnly. "Now, let me say goodbye to Ma'dear, and I'll be on my way." She disappeared into the bedroom where her mother was, returning a short time later carefully wiping her eyes. "Well, I'm gone," she said moving down the stairs to the pathway leading to the road. Halfway down she turned and waved goodbye to her family assembled on the back porch. They all waved and called out their goodbyes until Sugar was no longer in sight. They heard the car engine as it roared away, churning up pebbles on the rocky road, listening until all they could hear were the usual signs of life in the country. Returning to the house they crowded around the radio, just in time for another episode of *The Lone Ranger*.

*   *   *

"Ma'dear is getting better, you think?" Jenna asked Henry Lloyd as she skipped along beside him. They were on their way to the general store to collect groceries and pick up mail, if any, maybe even a letter from Sugar. She had written several times since her arrival to the Northern industrial city. Everyone gathered around to hear about her new life, fascinated with her descriptions of big buildings, tall structures, traffic, apartment buildings, and supermarkets.

"She is getting better, thank the Lord," Henry Lloyd agreed, "but Daddy is getting worse. He drinks just about every day. He's always on my back about something, and quick to pick up a belt or a switch. He even yells at you girls, and he never used to do that. I wonder what's wrong with him?"

He has never gotten over Sugar ending things with him, Jenna thought, *and he really lost it when not only did she move far away, but she has a husband now, and a baby coming.* "Maybe he is mad because Ma'dear is still recovering after all this time, he still has to sleep in the room with you all, and the baby starts hollering whenever she sees him."

"Smart baby," Henry Lloyd said. They both chuckled as they mounted the stairs and entered the general store.

"Hey, Miz Day," they both said respectfully. Carolina Day, wife of the store owner was standing behind the main counter, fanning herself with a fancy lace-edged silk fan.

"Good mornin'," she said with a heavy Southern accent. "How y'all doin'?" Taking in Henry Lloyd's tall, muscled handsomeness, her smile grew sultry, her eyes heated as she examined him through lowered lashes. "What is your name, handsome?" she asked throatily, propping her arms on the counter while fanning languidly.

"His name is Henry Lloyd," Jenna said tartly. "Our mama sent us to collect some groceries, and then we need to be on our way. She has not been well, so we cannot leave her by herself for long."

Big blue eyes cooled considerably when they turned in Jenna's direction. Her lip curled as she looked Jenna up and down. "Aren't you the healer's daughter?" she asked haughtily. "Your mama makes potions and does conjuring for people, don't she?"

"Yes ma'am, my mother is Albertina the healer; and this is her son whom she watches over very closely," Jenna said deliberately.

"I don't blame her," Carolina breathed, focusing on Henry Lloyd again, "Do you do conjuring as well, Henry Lloyd, honey? I would dearly love to get a love potion from you, made by you."

"No, ma'am," Henry Lloyd said, "Only my mama and my sister can, and my little brother, a little."

"That's too bad," Carolina cooed. "Well, tell me, darlin', do you do any handy work? Several things at my house need... taking care of and my husband is not at home a lot and so busy with his businesses that he can't do it. I would pay you very well, and I could offer you a cold ko'cola to cool you down when you become...heated."

"Henry Lloyd is much too busy on the farm, with his schoolwork and other endeavors to come by your house," Jenna said forcefully. "I am his older sister, so I ought to know...not to be rude, ma'am, but we need to collect these groceries and be on our way. Thank you very much."

Blue eyes darkened with annoyance, flashed with irritation. "Of course, don't let me keep you if you're in that much of a hurry...but should you find yourself with extra time, Henry Lloyd...please feel free...I usually can be found at home... alone..."

"Thank you, ma'am, but like my sister said, I don't think I have time for any more than I'm doing already..." Henry Lloyd said respectfully.

"My loss," Carolina sighed. "Let me see this list of yours, so y'all can be on your way." Taking the list from Jenna's outstretched hand she moved away, turning to pick up the items written there, making it a point to stretch, bend, and extend, drawing attention to legs, hips, and breasts. Walking unhurriedly over to a small area surrounded by iron bars she rummaged around for a moment, returning with two envelopes. "Y'all have a couple of letters: one from California and another from Michigan," she said. "Who do y'all know living in Yankee territory?"

"Kin," Jenna said shortly, reaching her hand out for the letters. She made certain to keep herself between Henry Lloyd and the flirtatious white woman as she loaded groceries into the cardboard box they had brought with them. Trouble and danger he sure did not need; thankfully, he did not seem the least bit interested or even aware of the woman's attempts to entice him. Shopping complete, they politely thanked the woman still eyeing Henry Lloyd hungrily, clattered down the stairs and moved up the road, Jenna making a mental note to bring Sidney with her next time.

"Letters from Sugar and Aunt Loretta," Jenna said. "Loretta probably begging you to come to California and Sugar pretending everything is good in her marriage."

"I guess if you know all that, you don't even have to read them," Henry Lloyd said with a smile.

"Soon we will not have to wait on letters," Jenna said with a skip and an excited smile. "The telephone is going to be installed next week. Then we can actually talk to Sugar and hear her voice, a lot more than just words on paper. I can hardly wait."

"And we can talk to Loretta," Henry Lloyd said. "She's got a telephone, too."

"Oh, yeah, her too," Jenna said with markedly less enthusiasm. She was still finding it hard to warm to her step aunt; something about her was just not right. Henry Lloyd on the other hand was crazy about his aunt and talked constantly about visiting her in California. He had even mapped the train route and had looked up schedules and times. Loretta was offering to pay his way; even so, Ma'dear was resistant to the idea, uncomfortable with the idea of Henry Lloyd traveling so far away.

*   *   *

"Are you the healer? The one with a pretty daughter and a handsome son?"

"Ma'am, I have a lot of pretty daughters and handsome sons. What might I help you with?"

"I'm just making sure I have the right one. Are they here? If I see them, then I'll know that you're the one I've heard about."

"No ma'am, they're in school. Classes started last week."

"Oh, they go to school? Every day? That's unusual for colored children, isn't it?"

"I can't speak for all colored children, ma'am, but mine go to school."

"What time do they get out? Maybe I can wait."

"They going to be a while, ma'am, and then they'll have chores, and they ain't around when I'm consultin'."

"Oh well, I wanted to ask you…would you send your son over to my house this Saturday? I have some handy work that really needs to be done…I would pay him…and y'all could always use a little extra money, couldn't you?"

"I'm sorry, ma'am but my sons work the farm on Saturdays and Sundays to make up for the times they in school. They ain't got time to work for nobody else."

Carolina's eyes flashed with irritation. "I wouldn't keep him long, just time enough to help me a little. I could use the assistance. I would drive him to my home and bring him back. I pay well."

"I might can help you," Albertina said, watching as the white woman's eyes sparked with anticipation. "If you would go down the road a piece, there's a cabin on the left. That's where the Edwards live, and they could really use some extra money. Jim Edwards is a really good carpenter and an all-around handyman. He'd do a good job for you."

Carolina's face tightened in frustration. "I must say I find your lack of cooperation very disappointing, and verging on insolent, missy. I came here to help you, to get some assistance in my home and all you have done is refuse me."

"I offered you someone who could do the work for you ma'am," Albertina responded calmly. "Someone who could really use the money and who I know would do good work for you. I'm sorry if that does not satisfy what it is you say you need."

"Well, I never met a niggra who couldn't use extra money," Carolina said. "Who owns your land?" she asked looking around. "Who is it you sharecrop for?"

"The land is owned by my husband's family and has been for generations," Albertina replied. "The taxes are all paid, and everything is owned free and clear."

"I see. Well, I'll be on my way, and I thank you for your suggestions. Mayhap I will take you up on it." Carolina climbed down the back stairs and began walking down the long path leading to the road where her shiny new car was parked. Albertina listened as it roared away, noting that it did not turn toward the Edwards' cabin, instead headed for the road leading into town. Lifting the pot of green beans she had been snapping before being interrupted and resuming her task, her mind busy, her thoughts troubled.

Chapter Six

"Queenie, honey, would you go get the clothes off the line for me please? They should be dry by now."

"Of course, Ma'dear, I will be back shortly." Picking up the large basket used to hold clothes, Jenna headed for the clothesline strung up between two trees a short distance away. On arrival she reached up and began releasing the sun-dried clothes, sheets and towels from the pins holding them on the thin rope, dropping them into the waiting basket. Working quickly, methodically, she slowed, stopping as she reached her panties hanging near the end of the line. She gingerly pulled a pair down and looked in. A thick, milky white substance covered the crotch area, soaking into the cloth, a strong musky odor emanating from it.

"There it is again," Jenna said in disgust. "What is that, and why is it only in my panties? Now, I must wash them again. I am getting sick of this." A sudden thought intruded; a passage from one of her medical books flashed through her mind. Horrified, she dropped the panties on the ground, using a stick to pick them up, walked over to a bare patch of ground, dug a hole deep enough to drop them in and did so, covered them with earth, and stomped the ground flat.

"I do not believe it," she said as she made her way back to the house, "Mr. Pettigrew has been ejaculating in my panties. That is why they are always stiff in the crotch or gooey wet. Lord, what should I do? I cannot tell Ma'dear. She would probably shoot him dead and even the sheriff could not get her off. I cannot tell Henry Lloyd either for the same reason. He is Mama Joyce's son, so I cannot tell her, and Sidney is too young to hear something like that." Unsure of what to do, Jenna debated with herself all the way to the house.

That night Jenna awakened with a start. On the verge of sitting up she froze. Eyes wide open she lay still, trying to control her breathing, sensing danger. The sound of heavy breathing filled her ears, interspersed with low grunts; the floorboards by her door creaked, and she could hear flesh rubbing against flesh. Her heart pounding wildly, Jenna edged closer to the side of the bed furthest from the door, planning to jump and run if she heard footsteps entering her room. Endless moments later she heard a strangled moan and a panting gasp. Silence fell and then the sounds of a heavy tread moving away from her door reached her straining ears. Sitting up, shaking uncontrollably, eyes trained on the door, she remained that way until the first rays of sunshine coming through her bedroom window signaled the start of a new day.

"Queenie, I'm going to send you to stay with Mama Joyce for a while," Albertina made the announcement during breakfast that morning, watching Jenna pick over her food, startled at every sound, dropping her fork more than once. "And I'ma send Sidney with you. He needs to get to know his grandmother better."

Jenna turned questioning eyes in her mother's direction. Did she know? Heartfelt relief warred with guilt. Had she done something to cause what was happening? Was she somehow responsible? "You-you are sending me away?" she stammered. "W-why? Are you mad at me?"

"Of course not, honey, but Mama Joyce is getting old and she could use some help in keeping her house up. Sidney can help when you at school, and like I said, he should get to know her as well as you and Henry Lloyd. I have plenty of help here. Rolanda is old enough to start learning how to keep house, and the younger boys can help too. I'll come see you, and you can come here. I'm not putting you out. You can apply yourself to your schoolwork better without constant interruptions, too. I been thinking on this for a while. Besides, now that Mama Joyce 'nem got a telephone, we can talk just about every day."

"Yes, ma'am," Jenna said quietly, "I will put my things together and help Sidney get his together, too. Since it is Sunday, we can go right after church." She moved toward her bedroom Sidney close behind.

"We gonna go live with Mama Joyce?" Sidney asked excitedly, using both hands to maneuver the string-wrapped box containing his belongings and which he had insisted on carrying himself.

"Uh-huh," Jenna responded, "for a while anyway. Mama Joyce is getting old, and I know she has sugar, so we are going to take real good care of her, you and me."

"I'm glad," Sidney said, lifting the box higher into his arms. "We get to be together. I get to know Mama Joyce, and you'll be safe."

Jenna looked sharply at her brother. His pale brown eyes were smiling up at her, free of the emptiness and shadows that indicated the presence of spirits. "That is a good thing," she said, deciding against asking him what he knew. Walking along, they speculated about the changes that living with Mama Joyce would bring.

*   *   *

"I'm back and insisting that you do two things for me," Carolina Day stood on the back porch, her eyes searching. It was early afternoon, and she had timed her arrival perfectly. Henry Lloyd and the rest of his brothers and sisters were coming up the road from school. Carolina's face grew brighter, her eyes heated, caressing, as they took in his tall, solidly built good looks. "I will not take no for an answer," she added as Henry Lloyd walked up.

"Boy, I need for you to go straight to the meadow and collect the cows," Albertina said. "They been out there all day and need to be brought in for milking. Hurry, now." She purposely did not use his name.

"Young man, it is considered polite to greet someone who comes to your door," Carolina said, her voice playfully admonishing, fanning coyly and batting her eyes, "at least it is for civilized people."

"How 'do, ma'am," Henry Lloyd said respectfully, nodding his head, "But s'cuse me, I got to be leaving. I've got chores. C'mon y'all," he called to his brothers. "Y'all can help me." Climbing rapidly down the stairs walking briskly, they were soon out of sight.

"What was it you wanted from me?" Albertina asked deliberately, her eyes watchful, fury flashing in their brown depths.

Carolina watched the boys until they were out of sight before turning back to Albertina. "I want your son to come to my house to help me get it in order," she said, "and I want you to use your healing know-how to prepare a concoction for me, something to help invigorate my blood. I've been a bit rundown lately."

Albertina studied her in silence. Carolina's eyes fell; she squirmed, feeling increasingly uncomfortable under that unreadable gaze. The silence stretched on a moment before Albertina said, "I'm sorry, but I think maybe you didn't understand me the first time you were here. I do not hire my son out and have no plans to do so. He has too much to do at home to send him to work elsewhere. As for your health complaint, I think Doc Edmonds is the person you need to see for that, not me."

Carolina's face grew red with temper. "I do not need you to tell me who to see," she said hotly. "I am sick and tired of your uncooperative attitude. Who do you think you are, sassing me this way? You should be glad I want to spend some of my husband's hard-earned money on you and yours. I have yet to meet the niggra who does not need money."

"You have now," Albertina said quietly, deliberately. "Get the hell off my porch, bitch, and don't come around here no mo'. I ain't got nothing you need, and I don't want nothing you got."

Carolina inhaled sharply. "What if I were to tell my husband to inform you that your business is no longer needed or welcome at our establishment? Where would you buy what you need then, missy? Or what if I told him your son has been making eyes at me? Saying improper things? Trying to put his hands on me, even trying to kiss me? You'd be getting another visit, all right, but it would not be from me, it would be from those out to teach y'all a lesson about proper respect."

Albertina approached her until they stood face to face. "I am going to tell you something, and I want you to listen real close," she said. "If you say or do anything – and I mean anything – to put my son in danger, there is nowhere on this earth you can hide. Do you hear me? Nowhere. I will find you, and I will kill you. A long, slow, painful death. By the time you get to hell where the devil will be waiting for you with open arms you will be begging for death, crying for it, praying for it. You have been warned. Do not come here anymore and forget you ever laid eyes on my son...threaten me and mine again, and you will be very, very sorry." There was no doubting the lethal sincerity in the quiet, menacing voice and cold, dark eyes looking into hers. "Now, get your sorry ass out of here, and don't ever come back!"

Carolina gasped, taking an involuntary step backwards, her face as pale as it had once been red. Turning, she fled, running down the stairs and the path leading to the road, jumping into her car, driving rapidly away. Albertina stood where she was for a time before going into the house walking over and picking up the telephone.

*   *   *

"Guess what, Queenie? You ain't the only one goin' somewhere new to live. I'm going to go stay with Aunt Loretta. Ma'dear called her, and she's sending me a train ticket. I'm gonna go live with her in California." Henry Lloyd's voice bubbled with excitement over the phone, his eagerness obvious. "Now, I can leave this hole-in-the-wall for good, and better yet about as far away from Daddy as I can get."

Jenna gripped the phone so tightly she was afraid it might crack. "You are leaving?" she said, her voice choked. "Moving all the way to California? When?"

"I'll be leaving in a couple of days, as soon as I get my stuff together and Ma'dear can arrange for someone to take me to the train station in Orangesburg."

"Does Mama Joyce know?" Jenna asked swallowing past the obstruction in her throat.

"Naw, I'm coming to tell her and to see you tomorrow evening. Let her know I'm coming, but don't tell her why. I want to tell her myself."

"I will stay quiet," Jenna promised.

"All right then. I'll see y'all tomorrow," Henry Lloyd said.

"Bye," Jenna whispered, holding the phone to her ear long after the click on the other end signaled Henry Lloyd had hung up. Running to her room, throwing herself across the bed, one arm over her face, the tears came.

*   *   *

"Where's your son at, Albertina?" The heavyset man with fleshy arms and large belly hanging over his tan trousers asked, dark sunglasses hiding his eyes.

"I have six sons," Albertina replied. "Which son are you talking about?"

"That tall one, your oldest. Henry Lloyd."

"What you want wit' him, sheriff? He ain't done nothin'."

Sheriff Calhoun Richards hitched up his trousers, arranging the holster hanging from his belt more comfortably. "I ain't said he done anything, I jes' need to talk with him a bit."

"What about?"

"About the danger in attracting too much attention to himself in the wrong places and to the wrong people."

"My son rarely leaves the confines of this property except to go to school and church, Calhoun. How can he attract attention minding his own business? If he did attract unwelcome attention, how is it his fault?"

"I'm not saying it is his fault, Albertina," Sheriff Richards said, "but the talk is out there, and it's starting to reach the wrong ears. There has been rumbling about teaching upstart nigger boys a lesson on what happens when white women start showing too much interest in them. Talk about reducing his height, taking away his manhood and making his face something no one would want to look at – before or after they string him up first."

"Calhoun, you wouldn't let them hurt my son, would you?" Albertina asked. "My son? Any one of my children?"

The sheriff slowly removed his sunglasses, faded blue eyes gazed into hers. "I'm trying to prevent that from happenin'," he said. "That's why I'm here, to warn you and your son to lay low for a time until the talk dies down. If he's seen anywhere any time in the next few weeks or so, I can't answer to what might happen. So, tell me, where is he?"

"He ain't here," Albertina said.

"Where is he?"

"On his way to California as we speak," Albertina said, her eyes bright with triumph. "He gonna live there with kinfolk."

After a short silence, "Well, I reckon that takes care of the problem," Sheriff Richards said replacing his sunglasses. "I'm glad you found a way to nip this thing in the bud, with no harm done so that no further action need be taken." He walked over and put his arms around Albertina, who stood stiffly before slowly relaxing into his embrace. "I would have done the best I could, but I might not have been able to stop them."

"I know you would have, Calhoun; and I'm glad, real glad he's out of reach," Albertina said quietly.

Lifting her chin with his thick, beefy fingers, lowering his head, Calhoun joined his lips to hers, deepening the kiss when she opened her mouth, inviting him in. Stepping back after a time, reaching up to remove his sunglasses to look into his eyes, she grasped him by one hand, leading him into Sugar and Jenna's old room and closing the door.

* * *

"Excuse me, Miss Queenie, but is this seat taken?" the male voice asked.

Looking up from the medical book she was reading as she ate her lunch, Jenna's eyes fell on Michael Edwards standing a short distance away, holding the paper bag carrying his lunch in one hand. She looked at the bench that except for her was empty.

"No, there is no one here but me," she said.

"May I sit with you?" Michael asked.

"Please, have a seat," Jenna invited. As Michael sat down and reached into his bag extracting a sandwich, Jenna studied the boy who she had known since kindergarten and who was in her English and chemistry classes.

Michael Edwards was tall, dark, and lean. A top student, he was the star of the school's basketball team. Everyone expected him to be offered a basketball scholarship at South Carolina A&M or one of the other colored colleges and universities interested in having him on their team. Outgoing, funny, popular – he could have any girl in school he wanted, so Jenna wondered why he was taking the time to talk to her.

"What are you reading?" Michael asked, looking at the girl with the strange, beautiful eyes and curly inky-black hair. He had loved Jenna since their first day of school, but she had never noticed his quiet devotion. Like with most of her classmates, with him she was friendly but distant. Her only close friendship outside of her family had been with Charlesetta Marshall, who had dropped out of school last year at sixteen to get married.

"It is a medical book," she replied in her clear, precise voice that he loved to hear, could listen to for hours. "I have been reading about diabetes."

"Are you going to be a doctor?" Michael asked with interest.

"No, a nurse," Jenna said, looking at the boy most girls would give their eyeteeth to talk with, to have notice them. Michael was not bad looking with strong, rough-hewn features, large nose, full well-defined lips, and brown eyes with thick, curly lashes any woman would kill to have. Not exactly handsome, but powerfully compelling, he could attract women like moths to a flame.

"Wow, that's great. We need more colored nurses. Have you picked out a school yet?" he asked. "Where did you get the medical book?"

The extraordinary eyes looking at him warmed. She told him about Doc Edmonds giving her his old medical books years earlier. They began talking about school, medicine, basketball, and other topics until the ringing of the bell announced the end of the lunch period. Jenna stood and smiled at Michael, as if looking at and really seeing him for the first time. "It has been nice talking to you," she said, "I really enjoyed it."

"So did I, maybe we can do it again, soon," Michael said, that smile hitting him like a punch, leaving him slightly giddy.

"I would like that," Jenna said, still smiling. "See you in chemistry."

They met for lunch regularly after that, their conversations interesting, stimulating, covering a wide variety of topics. He tried hard to make her laugh and was gratified when he succeeded, being able to chase the sadness out of her eyes, to lift the shadows behind them. She confided in him about how much she missed her brother, how much she had depended on him, how hard it was to be without him. "He was my best friend – he and Charlesetta – and with them both being gone…" her voice trailed off.

"I understand," Michael said gently, "but I want you to know that I'm your friend and you can tell me anything. I promise to never repeat it. I give you my word."

"Thank you, Michael, it is nice to know there is someone out there I can count on," Jenna said. "It helps me feel less alone."

Michael held out his hands; Jenna put hers into them. "You can count on me. Know it. Believe it." Giving him one of those smiles that never failed to enchant, captivate, dazzle, going to his head like fine wine, he pulled her to her feet. Retaining hold of one of her hands, he walked her to class, his heart light, at peace. As they walked, she mentioned that she would be spending the weekend visiting her mother. He asked if he could come to see her while she was there, and they made tentative plans to meet after church on Sunday. As he left her at the door to her class, he had no idea that it would the last time seeing her for years.

Chapter Seven

"There she is!"

"She's here!"

"It's her!"

"Queenie's home!"

"Queenie!"

Laughing, screaming excitedly, Jenna's brothers and sisters ran to greet her, running into the open arms waiting for them. Hugging as many as she could, she stepped back so that she could hug each one in turn; Dexter, the twins Lorenzo and Alfonso, Rolanda and her twin Renard all hugged their older sister as hard as they could, delighted to have her back home. Chattering nonstop as each tried to gain her attention, they headed for the back porch where Albertina stood waiting, holding two-year old Rhonda in her arms.

"Hey, Ma'dear, hey baby," she said kissing and hugging her mother, lifting the laughing toddler into her arms, kissing baby-soft cheeks, smiling as she received baby hugs and kisses from her little sister.

"Hey, Queenie, it's so good to see you," Albertina said with a smile. "It's good to see you too, Sidney. Come over here and give your mama a hug."

"Hey, Ma'dear," Sidney said. "It's good to see you, too. I'm gonna go play baseball with Ernie and Willie up the road." He jumped off the stairs and ran. Ernie and Willie were part of the Edwards' clan, younger brothers to her friend Michael.

"Be back in time for supper," Albertina called after him. "The rest of y'all go play, too. Give your sister some room. She can't move the way y'all crowding her."

Reluctantly, her siblings stepped back, watching as Jenna and Albertina entered the house, Jenna still holding Rhonda. After a moment they decided to play a game of hide-and-seek, running to hide as Rolanda began counting.

"C'mon, baby," Albertina said. "We can talk while we fixing dinner. I got a ham out of the smokehouse, and it's in the oven, and there's some beans cookin'. You can help me make whatever else we decide to go with it."

Putting the baby down who immediately toddled after her as fast as baby legs would allow, Jenna and Albertina moved around the kitchen, talking animatedly as they worked to get dinner on the table. "When's the last time you heard from Sugar?" Albertina asked.

"I have not talked to her since she had her last baby," Jenna said. "Three babies in two years! If she keeps this up, she will have more than you, Ma'dear." They both laughed.

"How's she sounding?" Albertina asked.

"I am not sure, Ma'dear. She sounded as if she was trying her best to sound cheerful, but there was something–something I could not quite put my finger on…" Jenna remembered Sidney's prophesy about Sugar's unhappy life and shivered.

"I know what you mean, whenever I talk to her, which is less and less, she's always alone. Larry is never home, and she never seems to go anywhere. Whatever's going on she won't talk about it, so I guess I jes' need to mind my own business unless she says otherwise."

"You are right," Jenna said, "We can do nothing until she asks for help."

"What about you, Queenie?" Albertina asked. "How are you? Have you got a fella? You 'bout the age you should be interested in boys," She watched with interest as a slow smile came to her daughter's face, her eyes brightened.

"Well, there is this one boy, you know Michael Edwards?"

"He one of the Edwards who live in the shack down the road?"

"Yes, he is a really good basketball player and is sure to get a college scholarship. He wants to major in Business and Finance. Anyway, he is really popular, and we have kinda been talking. He is supposed to come by for a visit after church."

"That will be nice. I look forward to it," Albertina said smiling.

Smiling with a mixture of embarrassment and anticipation, poised to ask about Henry Lloyd, a heavy tread on the stairs announced the arrival of Rodney Pettigrew. He came and stood in the doorway, leaning against the frame. He was dripping from the dousing he had given himself, washing off the blood and bits of meat from his job at the town's meat locker, using the tub filled with water Albertina kept at the foot of the outside stairs, a cake of soap beside it. But to Jenna no matter how much he washed, he always smelled of dead meat. He eyed Jenna standing at the stove stirring a pot of beans. Her fingers tightened on the spoon.

"Gal, you dun come home to stay?" he asked, his voice rumbling deep in his throat.

"No, Mr. Pettigrew, I am here to visit for a while; Sidney and I will be going back to Mama Joyce's. She needs us."

He regarded her in silence a moment longer before moving from the doorway, going to his room, and slamming the door behind him. Sidney appeared in the doorway and ran over to where Jenna stood frozen. "Can we go, Queenie?" he asked pleadingly, "back to Mama Joyce's? I want to leave now."

Jenna looked down into Sidney's wide, frightened eyes. "Everything is all right, sweetie," she said putting a comforting arm around him. "You know Mr. Pettigrew always acts like that. We will be going home right after church on Sunday. Now, you help Rolanda set the table so we can eat dinner." Sidney slowly walked over to the sideboard, picked up plates and began setting them down on the table.

Dinner that evening was a noisy, boisterous affair with everyone talking at once and all of them vying for Jenna's attention. Only Rodney was noticeably silent. As the noise level rose, the silence surrounding their father grew darker. He stood suddenly, slamming his fist on the table, silencing everyone instantly. The boys all shrank in their chairs, refusing to meet his eyes. Taking a deep breath, he visibly calmed himself, slowly sitting down, reaching for the jug beside his chair and taking a long pull. A rusty chuckle escaped his lips.

"Scared y'all didn't I? Sorry, I was jes' trying to get y'all to quiet down a little. I couldn't even hear myself think. I know y'all glad to see Queenie, we all are. I jes' think she need to be here all the time where she belong, but that's between her and her mama. To show I ain't mad, c'mon Albertina, join me in a drink." He reached over, picking up her water glass, leaning down and pouring from his jug into it, carefully adding the white powder he'd taken from her medical supplies when he'd gone into their room. He watched in satisfaction as she drank the water spiked with his moonshine, grimacing at the taste. It would take some time for the slow-acting sleeping powder to take effect, but when it did Albertina would slumber completely unaware of anything around her. Looking around with a smile, Rodney's gaze was caught by his son Sidney who was staring at him, his eyes unflinching on his father's face, intent, watchful, his face unreadable.

Later that night Jenna looked over at a visibly drooping Albertina, who eyes heavy, kept yawning over the game of Old Maid they were all playing. "Ma'dear, you should go to sleep. I will help everybody get ready for bed, then I will turn in too. See you in the morning."

"All right, thank you, honey," Albertina said. "I don't know why I'm so sleepy. I can hardly keep my eyes open. I think a good night's sleep is just what I need." Getting slowly to her feet, wishing them all a good night, Albertina entered her bedroom, closing the door behind her.

"Alright everybody, it is off to bed," Jenna said over noisy protests and pleas to be allowed to stay up just a little longer. It took a while for everyone to wash, brush their teeth, get undressed and redressed in sleep attire. Finally, they were all ready for bed. They gathered in the older boys' room to listen as Jenna read from the book she had brought, *The Three Musketeers*. They were all caught up in the swashbuckling tale.

Coming to the end of the chapter, Jenna closed the book and said, "Now, it is off to bed for anyone who does not sleep in here. I will be in to tuck you all in, and no getting up to practice your swordplay!" smiling at the giggles her admonishment elicited. She kissed them all goodnight before retiring to the room she and Sugar had once shared. Turning off the light she got undressed in the dark, pulling the long nightshirt on over her bra and panties. Climbing into her old bed she lay for a time tense, listening intently before she was finally able to relax and drift off to sleep.

She was shocked awake by a large, fleshy object that covered her mouth and part of her nose, making it difficult to breathe. She clawed desperately at the hand preventing her from screaming, terrified whimpers coming from her throat. Her hands were grasped in a punishing grip, pulled over her head and held so tightly it cut off her circulation, making it impossible for her to free herself, to fight back. A heavy weight fell on top of her, breathing excitedly; she could smell the moonshine he had consumed every time he breathed out, the smell of dead meat overpowering.

In the moonlight she could see Rodney's face looming over hers. She screamed in her throat, the sound unable to get past the hand covering her mouth. Rodney lowered his head, whispering harshly in her ear. "You better be quiet, gal. Your mama is sleeping so hard, I don't believe anything would wake her up; but if you wake those young un's, I'll break your arm before I knock you out. It won't be quite as good with you just laying there, but I'm gonna make you a woman whether you awake or not, understand?" Jenna moaned in terror. "You walkin' 'round here like you really think you a queen, looking down your nose at me, leaving home to get away from me...I got you now! I'm gonna use you real good before I'm through, and you bet' not tell nobody."

His hand over her mouth lowered to her throat and he squeezed, slowly choking the air out her body, unable to inhale, Jenna started to lose consciousness. Just before she passed out Rodney eased up, and Jenna was able to draw air into her tortured lungs. He swiftly brought her arms down and held them behind her back. He positioned his body over hers. Through her nightshirt she would feel his aroused hardness pressed against her abdomen. Slow tears leaked from the sides of her eyes. She inhaled sharply, panting wildly, whimpering despairingly when he began roughly fondling her breasts through her nightshirt. He frowned when his questing hand encountered the cloth of her bra. He frowned even more heavily when he felt her panties; reaching under her shirt he fumbled to pull them off, his hand returning to her mouth when unable to control them the screams rose again. "These ain't gonna stop me," he said, feeling for the elastic band holding her panties up. "You might as well lay back and enjoy it. I'm just doin' what I hear them white men do to their daughters, take them first before some other boy or man does. My daddy told me when I first married your ma it was my right to fuck y'all when y'all got old enough. It was one reason I married a woman who already had young uns. My sweet Sugar did like she was s'posed to – and so will you – one way or the other." Jenna heard a zipper lowering and then the rustle of cloth. Her whimpers coming nonstop, her frantic struggles growing weaker and weaker as her strength ran out.

Rodney lifted her gown higher reaching to pull down her panties. She felt the world spinning, growing dark. Then the sound of a muffled thud, another one, and Rodney slumped, a dead weight, unmoving on top of her. She felt something warm and wet flowing over her terrified body, soaking through her nightshirt. Scrambling out from underneath her stepfather who still had not moved, standing up beside the bed, she saw Sidney standing on the other side, holding a large, heavy cast iron skillet in both hands, a dark liquid slowly dripping down its sides. Looking down at herself she could see that the moisture she felt spattered on her face and arms, soaking her shirt, was Rodney's blood, pooling under his head as it lay on the bed, saturating the sheets and blankets. Overcome, raising her clenched hands to her face, Jenna began screaming, louder and louder, frenzied, out of control. Lost in a world of terror and darkness she screamed and screamed; a sharp blow against her cheek stopped her in mid-scream. Albertina was shaking her, her eyes streaming tears, begging Jenna to calm down – to not let what Rodney tried to do drive her mad. Trembling uncontrollably, she realized a small figure was pressed up against her, holding her tightly around the waist, helping her to stand, his face buried in her torso, his tears adding to the wetness already there.

Jenna gulped, forcibly swallowing the hysteria still trying to escape, to take over, the horror over what had happened and what might have happened overwhelming. Slowly lowering her hands from her face, enfolding Sidney in a shaking embrace, she tried to calm her brother who had just saved her from a brutal rape. "All right, sweetheart, don't cry. I am not hurt thanks to you. You did well, Sidney. You saved me. I am ever so proud of you, ever so grateful. Please, stop crying."

Sidney lifted his head, his face smeared with the blood covering Jenna, mixing with the tears streaming down his cheeks. "You proud of me, Queenie? Really? I really saved you?"

"You really did. You were so good, so smart to find a way to stop Mr. Pettigrew."

Sidney beamed. "Can we go home now? Back to Mama Joyce's?" he asked hopefully.

Jenna's eyes turned to her mother. Moving over to the light hanging from the ceiling, Albertina pulled the cord attached to the bare bulb, flooding the room with light. She knelt beside Rodney lying face down on the bed. Turning him over, she placed two fingers on his throat. "Is…is he…dead?" Jenna asked, forcing herself to look at the man sprawled across the bed. She started shaking again.

"No, he's alive for now," Albertina said, "but he is hurt real bad and could still die. We got to come up with a story about how he got like this. I don't want anybody in trouble behind this."

"We could place him at the bottom of the stairs and say he fell down because he was drunk," Jenna suggested.

"That's a good idea. That's what we'll do." She turned to the children crowded in the doorway, eyes wide, staring at their father, talking in hushed voices. "Mr. Pettigrew was hurt, and we going to move him so nobody will know where. He was up to no good and paid for it. Now we need to protect Jenna and Sidney, so we won't mention anything about this night ever again, all right?" They all nodded solemnly. "I need the boys to help me move him, take him outside, and put him at the bottom of the stairs. If anyone asks, we'll say he fell and hurt himself. I'll be back to clean all this up in a minute."

Nodding their heads in agreement, Dexter, Alfonso, Lorenzo, and Renard each grabbed an arm or a leg after Albertina wrapped his head in one of the bloodied sheets to prevent dripping on the floor. She retained hold of his head and he was lifted, maneuvered out of the door, through the kitchen, out the back door and down the stairs where he was deposited at the foot of them, his body arranged to look as though he had lost his footing.

"All closed eyes ain't sleep, all goodbyes ain't gone," Albertina said looking down at the inert body. "Ain't nothing able to keep me from my children when they need me. You jes' lucky Sidney got a hold of you before I did." She looked up.

"Dexter, you and Alfonso and Lorenzo run to fetch Doc Edmonds. Tell him we need help 'cuz your daddy fell down the stairs, and he's hurt real bad. Hurry, now." The boys ran down the road, still clad in their pajamas. Albertina hurriedly grabbed a bucket and scrubbing rags kept underneath the porch, climbed the stairs, and entered the house.

Doc Edmonds and the boys arrived shortly after Albertina finished cleaning up the mess in the bedroom. He bent over, raising an arm to check the pulse, turning Rodney's head to look at the wound. He looked up at Albertina, who looked back steadily. "Y'all get him into the house where we can lay him down, and I can examine him more closely," he said. The boys obediently lifted their father, who still had not regained consciousness, and on Albertina's instruction, carried him back into the room they had removed him from earlier. Doc Edmonds checked when he saw Jenna huddled in a chair in the kitchen, holding a steaming cup in her hands, staring blindly into the flames of the fire burning in the hearth. She looked up unsmiling, completely unlike her usual friendly, competent self.

"Hey, Jenna, I did not know you were here," Doc Edmonds said in surprise. Looking closer he said sharply, "Are you all right?"

Visibly rousing, Jenna sat up straighter, "Hey, Dr. Edmonds," she said, forcing a smile to her lips. "I am fine, just a little…upset over what has happened."

Doc Edmonds looked at her a moment longer before disappearing into the room holding Rodney Pettigrew, emerging a short time later.

"How is he, Doc Edmonds?" Albertina asked.

"He is in pretty bad shape," Doc Edmonds said. "He has a severe head wound and from what you told me has been unconscious for a long time. At this point it is touch and go to see if he will live. The next few days will tell. Lucky for him he is in good hands. I will leave some things for you to administer to him. Keep a close watch. Should his condition worsen, send someone for me. Otherwise, I will leave him to you." If he had any doubts about the story he had been given, it did not show on his face. "Jenna, you take care. If you need me for anything, anything at all, let me know."

"Thank you, Dr. Edmonds," Jenna said faintly. She watched Doc Edmonds exit through the kitchen door before returning to her contemplation of the dancing flames. She stayed there for the remainder of the night.

* * *

"Queenie? Honey, can you hear me? Queenie?"

Slumped in the chair where she had fallen asleep, Jenna awoke with a strangled cry, her eyes wild. "Is he dead?" she whispered.

"No, honey, he jes' like he was," Albertina said. "His breathing is better, but he ain't woke up yet. He may never wake up. I'm gonna send Sidney back to Mama Joyce's. I called her to tell her about Rodney and that Sidney was coming back early. I did something else; I told her to gather your things together 'cuz you were gonna be leaving on the noon train on your way to California to stay with Loretta. You need to get away from all of this, so your mind can heal, and you can find yourself again. Henry Lloyd is there. He'll be happy to see you and help you find your way."

"Sidney needs to stay close to what he knows and wouldn't do well anywhere else. I need for you to explain to him why you're going. He's gonna be really upset, and if you can help him see that it is not his fault you're leaving and that it's best for you, he'll accept it and be all right. I called around and found someone to swing by Mama Joyce's for your things and then drive you, me, and Sidney to the train station in Orangesburg. Miss Essie is going, too. She gonna be your chaperone, but she'll be turning around and coming right back."

Hours later Jenna stood on the platform at the train station in Orangesburg, her borrowed suitcase at her feet, her arm around Sidney who had not stopped crying since being informed that his beloved sister was leaving him behind. A distant whistle announced the imminent arrival of the train. Albertina walked up, placing a cloth bag in Jenna's hand, closing her hand around it.

"Here's some money," she said, "I saved up quite a bit over the years, and I want you to take it. Be sure to put it some place safe, and don't tell anyone you have it, hear me? You never know when you might need it."

"Thank you, Ma'dear," Jenna said, a catch in her throat, "I will keep it safe, and I promise not to tell anyone, not even Henry Lloyd, that I have it."

The whistle sounded again, closer, the train approaching in the distance. Jenna knelt beside Sidney, gathering him in her arms, gently rocking him back and forth. "Sweetheart, I have to leave you now. I must forget about what happened in a place that has no memories for me. When I am healed, I promise I will be back to see about you. I would never leave you forever. Didn't I always tell you that if I had to leave, I would tell you and let you know you why?" Stepping back, Sidney wiped streaming eyes and nodded, taking the rag his mother handed him to wipe his face and blow his nose.

Standing up, leaning over, Jenna kissed him on both cheeks. "You are my hero," she whispered in his ear. "I would not be standing here now if you had not saved me."

Sidney straightened proudly. "I love you, Jenna, and I'm really, really going to miss you. Will you write me? Call me on the telephone? Will you? Promise?"

"I promise," Jenna said hugging Sidney one last time as the train noisily pulled up to the platform. Walking to the colored section at the back, they all watched as the doors opened, the conductor stepped down, positioned two steps at the door's entrance and announced in a loud, clear voice, "All aboard for Atlanta, Memphis, St. Louis and Kansas City," the final stop where Jenna and Miss Essie would change trains for the first time on their long trip west.

Jenna turned to her mother. "Goodbye, Ma'dear," she said, her voice unsteady. "I will miss you. I am so sorry this happened."

Albertina hugged her tightly, her eyes bright with tears. "Don't you be sorry, honey, none of this was your fault. Now you be good, take care, and know that I love you more than ever. Live for the day we see each other again."

Jenna and an excited Miss Essie walked over to the open doors, climbed the two stairs, and entered the compartment where their berth was located. As those on the platform watched, a closed curtain opened. Jenna appeared, waving and blowing kisses, as the train pulled off. They waved back, Sidney running beside the train as it picked up speed, stopping at the edge of the platform, continuing to wave until the train was no longer in sight.

Chapter Eight

"Queenie!"

Stepping down from the train, Jenna turned at the sound of her name. Henry Lloyd was running toward her, followed at a more leisurely pace by a woman decked out entirely in pink – from wide-brimmed hat to pink gloved hands to high slingback heels. Jenna jumped the remaining stairs and ran into her brother's arms, laughing, holding on tightly as she was spun around in a dizzying circle, held securely in his warm embrace. Slowing down, stopping, helping her stand, stepping back, Henry Lloyd kissed Jenna on both cheeks before looping one arm through hers, leading her toward a smiling Loretta, her pink gloved hands extended.

"Here she is, Lori. Don't she look good? Hasn't grown any, but she do look a little older, even if she still ain't no bigger than a minute."

"She does look good, Silk," Loretta replied. "Queenie, you are pretty as a picture. I'll bet you have to fight men off with a stick."

Jenna abruptly stopped smiling as dreadful memories threatened to break free. Henry Lloyd, quick to notice the change in her demeanor said, "If I know Queenie, she been too busy watching over children and getting ready for nursing school to worry about men much. Which as far as I'm concerned is all to the good." He shot his aunt an unsmiling glance, a hidden warning in his voice. "Miss Essie how are you?" he asked, turning to the elderly woman who had accompanied Jenna, deliberately changing the subject. "How'd you like traveling cross-country?"

I loved it, I truly did," Essie said with a wide smile. "We stayed overnight in Memphis and Kansas City, which gave us a chance to do a little exploring. I think I could live in any one of those cities. Colored folks seem to live real well there."

"They live pretty well here too," Loretta interjected. "We have some really well-to-do colored areas in these here parts, and we are allowed to go most anywhere. We can't live everywhere, but most shop owners don't have a problem serving us. I think it's because a lot of foreign tourists visit, even Africans, and they don't want to run them away."

"Let's collect your stuff," Henry Lloyd said, "and then we going to take you to a nice restaurant that's right on the ocean. I think you really going to like it."

Jenna smiled good humor restored. "That sounds wonderful," she said. Linking her arm with her brother's again, they strolled away, talking animatedly. "Did I hear Loretta call you Silk?" Jenna asked curiously.

"Yeah, that's what they call me here," her brother responded. "Not many people know my real name. Those that don't call me Silk call me Slim."

"Why do they call you Silk?" Jenna asked curiously.

"Those that have heard me sing say I got a voice smooth as silk," Henry Lloyd said proudly, "so some folk started calling me Silk and the name stuck."

"I see why they call you Slim," Jenna said. "You are tall and got no fat on you." After a short silence, "So, do some people call you Silky Slim?" she asked with a giggle. "Am I to call you one or the other?"

"Only when we're around people other than family," Henry Lloyd said seriously. "When it's just the two of us or the three of us, you can call me by my name. You'll be Queenie. Don't tell nobody your real name, your first, but especially your last."

Jenna looked at Henry Lloyd inquiringly but decided not to ask any questions or point out the strangeness of it all. She was entirely too happy at their reunion to bring anything that might cause tension into the conversation. Not yet anyway. Her attention was diverted by Loretta who coming up on her other side, placed an arm around her shoulders, hugging her lightly.

"Have you ever had lobster?" she asked. "Crab legs? Well, you are in for a real treat," she said when Jenna shook her head no. "The seafood here is...unbelievable," Loretta said, bringing her bunched fingers to her lips and flinging them open with a kissing sound. "I just know you're going to love it." As they walked and talked, they approached a large, shiny automobile, maroon in color, trimmed in highly polished silver.

"Is that your car, Loretta?" Jenna breathed, and when her aunt nodded said, "Oh, my it is beautiful; and you are driving it, Henry Lloyd?"

"Yes, ma'am," Henry Lloyd said proudly. "This here's a Chrysler Imperial. It's got power brakes and power steering which makes it a dream to drive, and there's a lot of leg room in the back so y'all should be real comfortable back there." Walking up to the gleaming vehicle, reaching into his pocket and pulling out a set of shiny keys, he selected one, walked to the back twisting up a silver cover concealing the keyhole, inserting it and releasing the trunk. Lifting, he propped it open and swung the three suitcases into the space there, slamming it shut and locking it again. He walked over to one of the auto's rear doors, opening it with another key. Stepping back, holding it open, he bowed with a flourish. "My queen, your carriage awaits."

"Why, thank you, kind sir," Jenna said with a smile. Bending she slid across the soft leather seat over to the window on the other side. "Come on in, Miss Essie," she said, "there is plenty of room. Loretta, are you going to sit back here, too?"

"No, I'll sit up front with Slim," Loretta said, "and please, call me Lori – that's how everybody here knows me."

Essie climbed in, exclaiming all the while, running admiring hands over the butter-soft tan leather, using the handle attached to the door to roll the window down, admiring the push-button lighter that Loretta pulled out to light the cigarette at the end of the fancy holder in her mouth. "Even the white folks in Crawfish Holler don't have a car this nice," Essie said, "not even Mr. Moss, and he's the banker, the richest man in three counties. You must be sitting on a butter keg, Loretta...I mean Lori."

"I do all right," Loretta said modestly, delicately blowing smoke out of pursed, pink-lipstick covered lips.

"You doin' a lot better than all right!" Essie declared. "Are you married? Is he rich?"

"Everything I've done I've done on my own," Loretta said. "I don't have a husband. They're more trouble than they're worth most of the time. I found that out two husbands ago. I'm not getting married again, although I do have a gentleman friend or two."

"Cain't say that I blame you," Essie said. "I decided never to marry again when my husband died more than twenty years ago. He did leave me a sizable portion that lets me live comfortably, but it sure ain't like the way you must live, Lori. If you have a car like this, I cain't wait to see what your house looks like."

"Well, you'll see my house after we've eaten and driven around to see some of the sights," Loretta said with a smile. "It sure isn't going anywhere."

"Off we go," Henry Lloyd stated. "Welcome to San Francisco, Queenie! I think you gonna like it here." Pulling away from the curb, he merged with the traffic, picking up speed as they exited the area around the busy train station.

Rolling down her window, Jenna leaned out, relishing the cool wind blowing in her hair, eagerly looking around at the bustling, crowded city. San Francisco was unlike anything she had ever seen. As Henry Lloyd navigated through streets filled with cars, buses, and people she drank in the sights. Essie exclaimed continuously when first one thing and then another caught her wondering eye. "I have never seen so many people at one time in my life," Jenna said. "Some I have read about but never seen before."

"You talkin' about them Chinamen? Essie asked. "I heard about them. They wear pajamas and eat with sticks, and the men have ponytails so long they brush their rears. Have you seen any of them, Hen...I mean Slim?"

"The ones you talkin' about are the ones fresh off the boat," Henry Lloyd answered. "The ones that been here a while or that were born here dress like everybody else."

"Do the women have little bitty feet?" Essie asked.

"They used to wrap little girls' feet real tight and leave the wrappings on so their feet wouldn't grow," Loretta said. "But they don't do that anymore because the girls had a hard time walking, and they couldn't work. Their feet look like everybody else's now."

"There's a part of the city called Chinatown," Henry Lloyd added. "If you go there, you feel like you in China. Chinese people everywhere! More of them than anybody else. Everybody speaks Chinese, and they got the kind of food they eat in China, and clothes, and all the signs over the stores and in the windows are in Chinese, too. I'll take y'all there before you have to leave, Miss Essie."

"That would be wonderful. I sure am going to have a lot to talk about when I get back to Crawfish Holler."

"Have you ever tried any of the food?" Jenna asked.

"I've eaten some of they rice and some kind of noodle dish," Henry Lloyd said. "They got these fried rolls stuffed with shrimp and vegetables that are really good. If you look in the windows of some stores you see chicken feet hanging. There ain't no way I'ma eat that."

"Well, we eat pig's feet and chit'lins," Essie declared. "I bet that don't sound good to a lot of people."

"I guess it is all what you are used to," Jenna stated.

"If you look to your left, you'll see we've reached the ocean," Loretta said, pointing, "and we are not far from our restaurant. It is probably the most popular restaurant in San Francisco."

"They let colored folks eat there?" Essie asked in surprise. "Inside? With the white people, or do they have a separate section for us?"

"No, everybody eats together," Loretta said. "You put your name on a list and they call it as people finish eating and the workers clean it off. Whatever table is empty when it's your turn is where you sit."

"Well, ain't that somethin'," Essie said.

Fascinated by all that she was seeing, Jenna sat up straighter, tuning out the conversation in the car, riveted by her first sight of the Pacific Ocean. Water as far as the eye could see disappeared over the horizon. It shimmered in every shade of blue imaginable – pale greenish blue at the shoreline, darkening further out to a blue that was almost black in the far distance. The sun shining on the undulating water created pockets of glittering gold that illuminated the waters, so clear in spots that the ocean's sandy bottom was clearly visible. Some men had fishing lines in the water, large buckets full of water beside them to hold any fish caught. Rolling waves edged in white foam washed gently to shore, pulling back to be replaced by another wave edged in white. The movement was constant, unending, mesmerizing.

"Oh my gosh, it is so beautiful," Jenna breathed, "I have never seen anything more beautiful in my life."

"Well, if you like it so much, we are going to have to get you a bathing suit," Loretta said. "The best time to go swimming is in the afternoon, the warmest part of the day. The evenings and early mornings tend to be chilly."

"Oh, that sounds marvelous! I can hardly wait," Jenna said, smiling and bouncing in her seat.

"Yeah, but ain't they got sharks and octopuses and the like swimming around in there?" Essie asked fearfully.

"Among other things," Loretta said, "but they probably won't bother you, although you should definitely get out of the water if you see anything like that. Oh, we're here," she said, pointing to a building perched on the edge of a small cliff and extending out over the water.

"Cliffsview Fine Dining," Jenna said, reading the huge flashing sign attached to the building above green and white striped awning shielding several tables and chairs from the bright sunshine. All tables were full of people eating, drinking, and conversing while waiters moved among them carrying full trays of food and beverages. A steady flow of people entered and exited the bustling establishment.

"Oh, can we eat outside?" Jenna asked excitedly as Henry Lloyd eased into an empty parking slot and turned off the motor. Opening the doors, they all piled out.

"Not only are we going to eat outside," Loretta said, "we are going to wait until we can get a table on the ocean side. If we're lucky there might be some seals or walruses sunning on some big rocks in the water."

A short while later a smiling hostess, her Asian heritage obvious, seated them at a table next to the railing with a clear view of the ocean and the giant rocks jutting up from the rocky bottom. Sitting in a chair that faced that magnificent view, Jenna gasped in delight when she spotted three seals and two long-tusked walruses, their coats almost the same shade as the rocks on which they rested, sunning themselves, stretching occasionally and shifting their bodies into more comfortable positions. She watched as a fourth seal lumbered out of the water glistening, its coat a shiny dark brown, shaking off excess water as it found a likely spot on the rocks to catch the sun's rays. It took two tries before Henry Lloyd was able to capture her rapt attention.

"What did you want to drink?" he asked, smiling at her excitement.

"Oh, can I have a cola with lots of ice?" she asked. Ice was a rare commodity at home in South Carolina.

"A cola with lots of ice it is," Henry Lloyd said with a smile. Moments later a tall, shaped glass was placed in front of her filled to the brim with crushed ice and cola, a paper straw inserted in its bubbling depths.

Jenna sipped with pleasure, relishing the combination of icy cold, bubbling effervescence and slight burning sensation as it slid down her throat. "Here's the menu," Loretta said as the waiter handed each of them a stiff cardboard placard encased in shiny plastic. "Get anything you want. Everything is good here."

Jenna looked down at the menu with its many choices, most of the names of the entrees unfamiliar to her. Reading the descriptions did not help much, either. "What is a ca-la-ma-ri," she asked, "and lobster with melted butter and lemon? Is that all you put on it? Crab legs, what do you do with the rest of it?" Essie, equally mystified, nodded her head in agreement.

Loretta smiled. "Ordering for the first time can be a little confusing. Do you want me to order for you? If you don't like it, you can order something else." When they both nodded, she turned to the hovering waiter, issuing swift instructions as he nodded and scribbled furiously. Bowing slightly, he walked rapidly away as Jenna turned back to the ocean, to the waves splashing on the rocks and the sea animals still sunning on the rough terrain.

A short time later Jenna stared down in dismay at the plate in front of her where a giant, bright red bug with head, antennae and legs still attached, two of them with huge claws stared back, a cup with melted butter and a plate of lemon wedges beside it. She recognized the baked potato on a separate plate though the white cream and finely chopped green sprinkles next to it were unfamiliar. She looked over as Essie stifled a squeal when a plate of what looked like fried spiders was placed in front of her. Loretta's plate was covered with monster spider legs and Henry Lloyd had a mound of fried round things with tails sticking out of them on his.

"Wh-what is it?" Jenna asked faintly, her appetite rapidly diminishing as she gazed at the frighteningly ugly creature it seemed she was expected to eat.

"I ain't eatin' no spiders," Essie declared, pushing the plate away from her. "I don't care how good they s'posed to be."

"Girl, that's a lobster," Loretta said with a light laugh answering Jenna's question as she pulled her gloves off and placed them in her purse. "Essie, you have calamari, squid in English. I have crab legs and Henry Lloyd has fried shrimp. Come on, once you've tried it, I just know you'll love it." Picking up what looked like a nutcracker, she lifted a crab leg from her plate, inserting it into the cracker, crunching down, pulling out the pale piece of meat inside, squeezing lemon juice on it, dipping it into the melted butter and popping it into her mouth with relish. Wiping her fingers on the napkin on her lap, lifting it to dab at her lips, she said, "Now Queenie, here's what you do. Twist off the leg with the big claw, pick up that nutcracker and crush the outer shell," watching as Jenna gingerly picked up the leg and did as she was told. "Now squeeze some lemon juice over it, dip it in that butter in front of you, and eat it."

Jenna closed her eyes not to look at the creature looking back at her and placed what she had pulled from the claw into her mouth. Her eyes opened, widening in delight as she chewed. "Mmmm…delicious," she said, pulling off the other clawed leg and inserting it into the nutcracker.

"I knew you'd like it," Loretta said with satisfaction. "Essie, pick up one of the calamari on your plate. Dip it first into that red sauce, and then spread some of that white sauce on it and eat it."

Essie reluctantly compiled. A slow smile came to her face as she chewed. Swallowing, she said, "Well, I'll be switched! Them spiders are right good." Picking up another one, dipping it into the cocktail and tartar sauces, opening her mouth, chewing contentedly, she savored the flavors. She and Jenna both sampled one of the shrimps from Henry Lloyd's plate and shared a crab leg from Loretta's. Loretta showed Jenna how to access the succulent meat in the lobster tail and add the sour cream and sprinkle chives onto her baked potato. Key lime pie with a dollop of rich cream finished off the meal.

"That was so good," Jenna sighed as she scraped the last of the pie off her plate. "I am stuffed."

"It was good," Essie agreed, "once you get past the ugliness of everything, it was real tasty." She laughed along with everyone else at her candid observation.

"Well, if you all have had enough to eat, shall we do some more sightseeing?" Loretta suggested, placing several bills into a small, folded black leather case, placing a few additional bills on the table, pushing back her seat and standing, walking toward the entrance with its green glass doors, followed closely by Henry Lloyd, Essie and Jenna, stealing a final look at the sunning sea animals before hurrying to catch up. Back in the car, Henry Lloyd pulled carefully out of the parking lot and merged once again into the busy traffic. As they entered downtown, traffic slowed and at one point came to a complete stop.

"It looks like a train up ahead done stopped and that's what causing the holdup," Essie observed. "What's a train doing in a busy place like this?"

"That's not a train, Miss Essie," Henry Lloyd said. "That's a cable car, and people ride it just like you do a bus. Look, see those cables and the wires above them? That's what pulls them up and down the streets. Queenie, you'll definitely be riding them while you're here, and we'll take you on one if we have time before you leave, Miss Essie."

"I see why they need to be pulled along," Essie said, "I do believe these are the steepest hills and streets I've ever seen."

"People sure get their exercise around here," Jenna agreed.

Shortly thereafter they approached a wide expanse of road that continued over a huge span of water. The road was suspended between huge pillars in the water and held up by metal beams and thick wires high above the roadway, disappearing into the clouds and fog above it. "Is–is this a bridge?" Jenna asked wonderingly, holding her breath as Henry Lloyd joined the queue waiting to cross.

"It sure is," Henry Lloyd said. "That's the Golden Gate Bridge that hooks San Francisco with the rest of California. We gonna go across it so y'all can see more of the ocean. Then we'll turn around and head for home."

"You could almost believe you were floating on air," Jenna said dreamily as they sped along. "No ground, no buildings – nothing but clouds, cables, air, and sea."

"I'll be glad when we get back on firm footing," Essie said nervously. "I dun crossed bridges before, but you could always see where you been and where you goin' – not like this here."

"We got about two miles, then we'll turn and head back," Henry Lloyd said reassuringly. "We perfectly safe. They ain't nothin' to be worried about." He refrained from telling her how the bridge swayed in storms or high winds. Reaching the end, Henry Lloyd promptly turned the car around as they made their way back to San Francisco.

Jenna closed her eyes, delighting in the wind on her face, in her hair, ruffling her clothing. Leaning back into the seat relaxing, breathing deeply of the fresh sea air with its salty tang, slipping into a deep sleep from one breath to the next. She was awakened by a hand on her shoulder, gently shaking her awake.

"Queenie? Wake up, sweetie," The voice was Henry Lloyd's. "We here."

Sitting up, blinking rapidly, shaking her head to clear the mists of sleep away, Jenna sat up, looking confusedly around. At the top of a small hill rising majestically from the land around it, a huge, stately home surrounded by flowers, carefully tended bushes and tall trees, its dozens of windows shining, brick walls gleaming, was illuminated by the last rays of the setting sun. Catching her breath in disbelief, Jenna opened the car door nearest her and stood staring, transfixed by the most beautiful house she had ever seen.

Chapter Nine

"Th-this is your house, L-Lori?" Jenna whispered, gazing up at graceful lines and sparkling windows at the big bay window in the front of the towering residence.

"This is it," Loretta said with a satisfied smile at their reaction.

"Oh, my Lawd, it look like a movie star ought to live here," Essie said in awe. "You and Hen- I mean Silk live here all alone?"

"Not exactly," Loretta began. "You see..." they were interrupted by loud voices coming around from a paved walkway at the side of the house.

"Lori! There you are!" one of them exclaimed, staggering towards them. "We went 'round to the back and no one answered, and the door was shut. It was locked up tighter than a nun's..."

"Watch yo' mouth, man," the man accompanying the obviously inebriated one said, cutting in. "They's ladies present. S'cuse him, ladies," he said with a bow. His eye fell on Jenna who had stepped back behind Henry Lloyd when the men began talking.

"You been shoppin', Lori?" he asked, advancing on Jenna who shrank against her brother. Henry Lloyd pushed her behind him, straightening, his hands closing into fists. "MMmm, boy! She look like a sweet little thang...let me be the first to sample the new wares," he said, reaching into his pocket.

"Now, C.T., you stop that fooling around," Loretta said hastily, walking up and tightly clasping the arm with its hand in his pants pocket, halting its movement. "This is my niece who's come to live with me. She is my family and new to California. She doesn't know anything about the type of teasing you are doing, so stop it, understand?" Her eyes darted over to a tall, muscled figure who had appeared silently behind him. "We, all of us, are away tonight – and tomorrow, too. I'll send word when you can visit again." Looking back and up at the huge man watching them, the two men apologized profusely and stumbled away. After a moment the tall man melted back into the shadows without saying a word.

"Wh-what was that all about?" Jenna asked, peering around her brother at the rapidly disappearing men. "Who were those men, and what were they talking about?"

"Well, I was about to tell you. I get lonely in this big, 'ol house by myself," Loretta said, "so I decided to turn part of it into a boarding house for those young ladies new to the city with no place to stay. I give them somewhere to stay cheap while they look for a job, and they keep me company and help a little with expenses. I let them have gentlemen callers, but only those I approve of. Even then some uncouth ones sneak in – like those just now – who will never be welcome in my home again."

"Who was that big man that didn't say nothing?" Essie asked.

"That's Boots," Loretta said. "As you can see, we need a strong man in the house with so many women; he protects us. Now, let us go inside, shall we? It's getting chilly out here."

They followed Loretta up the main outside stairway into a marbled entryway with carved ivory posts and archways. Loretta continued through the central arch and a carpeted hallway leading to a sweeping two-sided staircase. "Oh, my," Essie breathed, looking up at the fifteen-foot ceiling, a many-tiered, glittering crystal chandelier at its center. "I ain't never seen nothin' like this, and I used to clean white folks' houses."

"Follow me. I'll show you to your rooms," Loretta said, beginning to climb the stairs.

"Do your boarders stay up here, too?" Jenna asked curiously.

"No, they stay in a different part of the house," Loretta said. "This section is for family only, where you'll spend most of your time, Queenie, especially at night. That's when my boarders' gentlemen callers tend to show up. We play a little piano, dance a little, maybe play a few cards, and if they're lucky, Silk might sing and play his guitar for them. Some of them get to drinking and a little loud and they might even get a little belligerent at times, so that's why it's best for you to stay in this part of the house. You'll learn the parts to avoid tomorrow."

"That suits me fine," Jenna said. Except for Henry Lloyd, she had no interest in contact with any men whatsoever.

The top of the stairs opened to a wide hallway with a landing on one side that was so huge it looked like a room with no walls, populated with a large sofa flanked by two big, cushioned chairs and a highly polished wooden coffee table at its center. A series of closed doors lined one side of the hall, wooden posts forming a balustrade encompassing the other side, wrapping around the entire floor.

"Queenie, this is your room," Loretta said, walking over to a set of glass doors with tall, floor to ceiling windows on either side, pushing them open, holding one as everyone stepped inside.

Jenna walked into a suite that easily could have held her family's entire cabin. Walls painted a cool blue held paintings of a wide variety of plants, complementing the real potted ones placed around the room. Dark green pillows were placed on the ends and spaced on the cushions of the richly blue sofa propped against one wall with deep blue pillows on the lighter green chairs placed on either side of it. Green urns streaked with blue and blue ones streaked with green were situated throughout, a small table in front of the sofa held wooden figures of long-legged birds; woven baskets held polished rocks and colorful dried seaweed. A large cubbyhole desk across from the sofa grouping held paper, pencils, a stapler, and a metal container full of pens of all colors. Walking over to an open doorway she peeked in. A tall four-poster canopied bed took up a large part of the room's available floor space. Sheer blue curtains hung from a central knot suspended from the ceiling, heavier silks hanging from rods fitted above and around the bed were a green and blue brocade held back with golden tassels. Blue, green, and gold pillows and shams covered the head of the bed; the quilted comforter of midnight blue was pulled back to reveal sheets and pillows of shimmering gold.

"Oh, my," Jenna breathed, trying to ignore the doubt nibbling at the edges of her consciousness. Despite her luxurious surroundings – and Loretta's graciousness – something still just did not ring true. Try as she might, she could not make herself like much less trust her fashionable aunt. *I wish Sidney were here,* she thought. *He would have her number right away.*

"Do you like it, Queenie?" Henry Lloyd asked anxiously. "If you don't, we can put you in another room on this floor."

"I worked hard to make it something you would really like," Loretta inserted. "This is the only suite. I thought you might like someplace private for your studying and such. But if you really don't like it…"

"I like it, Lor–i," Jenna said. "It is beautiful. I guess I was just a little…a little…overwhelmed. I have never had so much space to myself. It is just going to take some getting used to, and I am a little tired."

"Of course, you are, hon," Loretta said sympathetically. "You've been traveling for the better part of a week, then we kept you out most of the day. You must be worn out. We'll let you get ready for bed. I'll show Miss Essie where she's going to sleep, and I'll see you both in the morning."

After a flurry of good nights, Jenna hugged Henry Lloyd, waving goodnight as she closed the door. Looking down, her hand on the knob stilled, her gaze sharpened. "This door does not have a lock on it," she whispered, running her hand down the smooth wooden panel. Crossing rapidly over to the bedroom door she saw that it did not have a lock on it, either. Running over to the bench where Henry Lloyd had placed her suitcase, she quickly untied and unwrapped the rope holding it closed, dashed back to the double doors, and using the rope to bind them together, tied them securely in a complicated knot. Crossing over to the table she picked up a basket of smooth rocks and positioned it directly where the doors opened; anyone entering would knock over the basket, spilling the rocks onto the floor. Moving to the bedroom she closed the heavy door behind her, pushing the bench holding her suitcase in front of it and moving the chair in front of the vanity over to the door, tilting it under the knob to prevent opening.

"At least no one can sneak up on me," Jenna said. Moving toward her suitcase, she opened it to withdraw one of her nightgowns while ignoring the flimsy, lacey one draped invitingly over the bed. Walking into her private bathroom – the one luxury she truly relished – she stoppered the tub and began running warm water into it, then reached over to unstop a pastel-colored bottle, first sniffing then pouring a generous amount of its contents into the tumbling liquid, watching frothy suds form. Shedding her clothes, she stepped into the bubbling water and sat down, reaching up to turn off the faucets before leaning back, closing her eyes, and sighing luxuriously as she relaxed into the comforting warmth.

A short time later freshly scrubbed, teeth brushed, and hair combed and braided, Jenna stepped out the bathroom, walking over to the high bed, taking a small leap, jumping in. Stretching her arms over her head, yawning widely, she reached over to the lamp on the nightstand next to her bed and switched it off. Taking a deep breath, she relaxed, falling soundly asleep. Opening her eyes the next morning, she sat up blinking rapidly. Looking around at unfamiliar surroundings, it took a moment to remember where she was. When she did, she hopped out of bed, running over to the drape-covered windows, lifting one side to look out. A broad expanse of manicured lawn flanked by big beds of brilliantly colored flowers was being attended by two Asian men, a third man in the background pushing a motor-powered lawn mower. Beyond the lawn, a stretch of powdery white sand marked the beginning of the ocean, sparkling blue in the distance.

Jenna inhaled in delight. Pulling the drapes closed again, turning, she hurried into the bath. A short time later she emerged washed, refreshed, dressed and eager to explore her new surroundings. Pulling the chair from underneath the knob she slid it back to the vanity table and then pushed the bench back to its original position. Opening the door, she hurried over to the double doors, picking up the wicker basket full of rocks, replacing it on the table, unknotting the rope, wrapping it, and looked around for a likely place to put it where it would not be easily found. She settled on one of the many floor vases scattered around the room, deciding to change its hiding place every morning. Walking back to the glass-fronted doors, she turned the knob, opened them, and stepped into the hall. She started in surprise when a figure stepped from the shadows in front of her. It was an older woman dressed in a simple black skirt and white blouse and thick-soled laced up black shoes.

"Please forgive me for startling you, Miss Queenie," the unknown woman said. "I was waiting for you so that I could introduce myself and show you the way to the dining room. My name is Bertha. I keep house for Miss Lori. Later you will meet a cook, two maids, and three gardeners. If you have no questions, I'll take you down to breakfast."

She did not say anything about Boots, Jenna thought. *I wonder why.* Aloud she said, "I am ready, Miss Bertha, and I do not have any questions right now."

"Just Bertha, please ma'am," Bertha said briskly. "If you will follow me," turning and moving to the staircase and starting down it. Jenna hurried to catch up.

Several twists and turns after reaching the bottom of the staircase, they entered a wood paneled room with a polished wooden floor partially covered by a richly colored rug patterned with sharp angles and scalloped edges. Jenna smiled at the three people seated at the big table in the center of the room positioned underneath a glass domed chandelier. "Good morning, everyone," she said brightly, sliding into an empty chair.

"Hey, Queenie," Henry Lloyd said. "Did you get some good rest?"

"Can't you tell?" Jenna said. "I never sleep this late – not to mention the three-hour time difference – it is like, what? Noon in South Carolina?"

"Chile, don't feel bad," Essie said. "I just got down here a few minutes ago. I think all that travelin' and sightseeing caught up with the both of us."

"Well, I hope you are rested, Queenie," Loretta said, "because I have a big surprise for you. Dress shops from all over the city are coming here today to bring you some clothes. You can pick any and as much as you like, my treat and way of welcoming you to California."

"New clothes? For me?" Jenna said, torn between excitement and dismay, wondering what price she might be expected to pay for her aunt's generosity.

"For you, hon," Loretta said. "I want my niece to be as fashionable as anybody in this city. I can afford it and you deserve it, so where's the harm? Be sure and pick out two or three bathing suits for our trips to the beach. Can you swim? Good, you're going to love swimming in the ocean, the way the salt in the water holds you up. Now, have some breakfast," sweeping her hand to indicate the heavily laden table and sideboard. "After you've eaten, Bertha will take you around to show you the parts of the house that you can use as well as the sections you need to avoid. Then you and Miss Essie might enjoy sitting outside for a while until the people from the dress shops get here. In the meantime, I've got some work to do, so I'll see you when the dress shop folk arrive." Rising gracefully inclining her head to everyone still seated, she exited the room.

"Does the breakfast table always look like this?" Jenna asked, looking around at the large variety of foodstuffs on the table and sideboard.

"Pretty much." Henry Lloyd said with a shrug. "Lori likes to have a lot of choices at all her meals."

"We could feed the entire family for a week with what is here now," Jenna stated. "It looks like this every day?" she shook her head in disbelief. Finally deciding on a piece of buttered toast with grape jelly, a glass of milk and a cup of tea. She finished the last of her toast just as Bertha entered the room.

"Are you ready, Miss Queenie, Miss Essie?" Bertha asked. "If you'll just follow me," moving toward the dining room archway closely followed by Jenna and Essie.

"Do you believe this house, Miss Essie?" Jenna asked sipping on the cola with crushed ice one of the maids had brought her as she and Essie sat on the patio at the back of the family section of the house.

"I ain't never seen nothin' like it," Essie asserted, taking a large swallow of the iced tea she had requested, "and I sure ain't never seen one with two separate sections like this one."

"That is strange, is it not?" Jenna questioned.

"You'll get used to it," Essie said reassuringly.

Looking over at the woman who had traveled so many miles with her, one of her last links with home, she realized how much she would miss her, how alone her departure would leave her, and said on impulse, "Miss Essie, stay here, live here with me. Lori will not mind, why would she? She certainly has enough space and plenty of food if this morning was any indication. It would keep me from feeling so alone here. Please, Miss Essie? Say yes."

"You sure your aunt would be all right with me staying on?" Essie said doubtfully. "I'm s'posed to be leavin', headed back to South Carolina in the next couple of days. Although I wouldn't have a problem payin' my own way here, and there really ain't a lot waitin' for me back there."

"There, you see?" Jenna said excitedly. "I need you, Miss Essie. Say you will stay."

Looking into the bottomless, almost-black eyes looking pleadingly back, Essie nodded slowly. "All right, Miss Queenie. If your aunt says she don't mind, I'll stay." She laughed when Jenna jumped up, rounded the small table, and hugged her ecstatically. They both looked up when Bertha appeared at the patio door to announce the arrival of the dress shop merchants. Pushing back their patio chairs, they followed the unsmiling housekeeper.

"Well, Queenie, what do you think? Do you like it?" Loretta asked.

"I love it," Jenna said, spinning around so that the full skirt floated around her. "This is called a poodle skirt? I wonder why," she giggled, looking down at the felt poodle covered with hooked yarn sewn onto it.

"We will take all three," Loretta told the smiling clerk, "and the blue suit with the pencil skirt and Peter Pan collar, and the same suit in green and yellow, three white blouses, the blue pedal-pushers, the red checkered shirt to go with that, and the yellow flowered sleeveless dress with the full skirt and matching yellow cardigan sweater."

"Lori, are you sure?" Jenna breathed. "You already bought me three bathing suits, pants and skirts and blouses from that other shop—"

"Queenie, I'm enjoying this just as much as you," Loretta assured her. "It's like buying things for the daughter I always wanted, but never had."

"Chile, you gone be dressin' like a queen, that's for shore," Essie said in admiration. "You sure look pretty."

"She does, doesn't she?" Loretta observed. "Now, Queenie, why don't you take these into your room and put them away. Then change into one of your swimming suits. We'll go down to the beach. Essie, you're welcome to come, too."

"Well, I ain't got no swimsuit, but I will change into one of my older dresses," Essie said, standing and heading for her room. "Where do you want to meet?"

"Let's meet at the family patio doors in fifteen minutes," Loretta said.

"Fifteen minutes," Jenna agreed, grabbing an armful of clothes from the sofa and transferring them to the bed in her room, running back to grab a second armful, and a third. Hurriedly placing her new clothes into the spacious closet by the windows and folding others and putting them into the drawers of the large-mirrored dresser, she left out a two-piece red polka-dotted swimsuit, stepping into it, fastening the top, pulling the bottom up over her taut stomach. Surveying herself in the full-size mirror attached to the closet door, she smiled while twisting her hair into a ponytail before hurrying out the door, taking the time to move her rope from one vase to another, in an obscure corner underneath a stand of dried branches. Opening one of the double doors, looking around as she stepped into the hallway, she skipped down the stairs, headed for the family patio. Moments later Bertha opened the door, walked over to the vase where she had seen Jenna hide the rope that morning and reached in. Straightening, looking around at the dozens of places it could be hidden, she exited the room. She would report her lack of success and resume the search later.

"Oh, I just love swimming in the ocean. Loretta was right," Jenna said to herself, taking a deep breath and diving down into the crystal blue depths, swimming past a school of tiny fish, watching a desultory turtle swim by and the seaweed wave in the ocean currents. Coming up for air she looked to shore at the sound of her name.

"Queenie, time to come in now," Loretta called. "It's getting late. You'll have many more times to visit the beach."

"All right," Jenna called. "Here I come," ducking under the water and swimming to the shallows, standing up and walking the rest of the way, waves splashing over hips and thighs, lowering to her ankles and feet as she reached the sandy shore. Walking over to where Loretta and Essie awaited her, thanking Essie with a smile when she handed her a towel, she began vigorously drying herself off. "That was so much fun," she said toweling her hair dry. "Now, I need to take a bath to wash off this sand and salt." Chattering happily to Essie, the three made their way back to the house.

Chapter Ten

"Lori, Miss Essie, I will be down to eat after I wash off this salt and sand, put on some lotion, and change clothes," Jenna said, heading towards her room. "That salt really dries me out."

"It sure do," Essie said, looking down at her feet and ankles. "All I did was get my feet wet, and they so ashy they a completely different color than the rest of me! And that sand does get everywhere. I need to wash up some myself. I'll meet y'all downstairs."

"That sounds good," Loretta said. "Dinner will be ready by then so let's meet in the room next to the dining room. Then we'll all go in to have our supper." Her eyes met those of Bertha coming out of one of the unoccupied rooms, her lips tightening when the housekeeper shook her head slightly. "I'll see you all in a few minutes," she said while moving rapidly down the stairs, a silent Bertha close behind.

"That Bertha gives me the willies," Essie muttered to herself as she headed for her room. "Don't never say nothing and all the time popping out of strange places. This here's a mighty strange house, and I'm glad Queenie asked me to stay. That poor chile needs somebody normal around here."

Entering her room, Jenna closed the double doors, moving toward the vase where she had stashed her rope. Looking over at the earlier hiding place she saw that the slip of blue paper she had placed on the lip of the urn was now on the floor a short distance away. Bending down, she picked it up, crumpling it in her hand. Dashing over to the vase where she had hidden the rope she reached in, sighing in relief when her questing fingers encountered twisted roughness. Hurrying over to the doors she wrapped them securely, added the basket of rocks and went into her bedroom, closing the door behind her. As before she pushed the bench in front of the door and wedged the vanity chair underneath the knob.

"Somebody is trying really hard to keep me from being able to lock myself in," Jenna said to herself. "I wonder why? I need to find something more than just this rope and a place to hide it where whoever is looking for it cannot find it." Her mind busy, Jenna began running water in the bathtub, adding the bottled oil and foaming bubbles she liked so much.

"And you're sure there was a rope? The doors weren't just stuck?"

"I'm sure, ma'am. I saw her put it in one of those glazed clay vases. I couldn't go look for it right away and then when I did go, it was gone. She must have hidden it somewhere else. I looked and couldn't find it in her rooms, and I didn't see it in any of the other rooms on that floor, either."

"So, Miss Queenie thinks she's nickel-slick, does she?" Loretta said angrily. "First, she gets that country bumpkin to come live here, and then she finds a way to keep doors with no locks on them closed. I'm gonna think about this. We got to bring Queenie around to our way of thinking without getting Henry Lloyd involved or upset. We know how crazy he is about his sister, and we need him. His singing brings in a lot of people, and the girls love him – even if he does think he's sneaking to get with them 'innocent' boarding gals." Both women laughed. "All right, Bertha, let her keep her rope for now if it makes her feel safe. Find it, but don't move it just yet. If we know where it is, we can take it away when the time comes." Nodding in acknowledgment, Bertha left the room Loretta used as an office.

"Does your table always look like it's Sunday after church?" Essie asked, looking at the variety of offerings on its shining surface.

"Don't you like having a lot of things to choose from?" Loretta asked.

"I do, it's jes' that it seems so…wasteful," Essie said doubtfully, Jenna nodding in agreement.

"Well, you need not worry about that," Loretta assured them. "What we don't eat goes over to the boarding side for them to finish off. Believe me, by the time they get through, there isn't much to throw away."

"Oh, well, that's good," Essie said, obviously relieved. "In that case, pass me some of them mashed potatoes, Silk. They look delicious."

"I will have some chicken," Jenna said, placing a wing and a thigh on her plate next to the potato salad and greens already there. Reaching for the vinegar, she poured a small measure onto her greens, stirred them around to distribute it evenly, picked up her fork and dug in.

As they ate Jenna filled Henry Lloyd in on her first time in the ocean swimming experience that day; smiling, he promised to go with her in the next day or so. "But now y'all are going to have to excuse me, I got to get ready for my performance. I promised to sing and play my guitar for the ladies and their gentlemen callers tonight. They really like hearing me."

"Oh, can I come too?" Jenna asked eagerly. "I have not heard you sing and play in such a long time."

After an awkward silence, "Uh, no, I don't think so, Queenie," Henry Lloyd said slowly. "The other side of the house ain't the place for you, not at night, anyway. It can get a little loud, and if some of the men done had too much to drink, fights can break out."

"Don't worry. Slim is safe because one, he's a man," Loretta said reassuringly, taking in Jenna's shocked face, "and two, he isn't in the mix cause he's away from all that performing."

"I'll play just for you before we head down to spend our day at the beach," Henry Lloyd promised, rising and heading out the arched doorway. "I'll see you in a few minutes, Lori, and you, Queenie, and Miss Essie tomorrow." Moving quickly, he was rapidly out of sight, his footsteps fading.

"It's not nearly as bad as it might sound," Loretta said into the pool of silence that descended following Henry Lloyd's departure. "Most nights it's peaceful, and there isn't any trouble."

"It sound like you got a speakeasy in your house," Essie said, "drinkin' and fightin' and music and such."

Loretta laughed. "It does sound like that, doesn't it? I can assure you that I do not have a speakeasy in my house; the very idea is silly. No, I just allow my boarders to have company who can get a little out of hand at times, but we take care of it right away. I won't stand for disruption."

"Well, that's good to know," Essie said. "I would hate to think this beautiful house was involved in anything ungodly."

"Well, you don't have to worry about that," Loretta said. "Why, the Chief of Police has been known to visit. Now, if you all will excuse me, I need to check on Slim. Queenie, I'll have a radio brought up to your room – and yours too, Miss Essie. I ordered some books and magazines and puzzles and games you might like, and they should be in your room by now. So, I'll see you all tomorrow at breakfast, all right? Goodnight," and she moved briskly away, the sound of her high heels on the wooden floors slowly fading away.

"That old bitch! Her eyes are just a little too big, see a little too much," Loretta said furiously angry as she and Bertha headed for the indistinct sounds of tinkling music and the hum of many conversations occurring at once, punctuated by laughter and shouts of excitement by those with winning hands at the card tables. "She better watch what she say and mind her own business, or she won't be seeing anything. Ever. All I need is for her to make Queenie suspicious before I'm ready to explain to her exactly what it is I do, and what she's going to do to make us both a lot of money. Men will flock to that gal like moths to a flame. I think I'll keep her for our white customers, they pay more. That old biddy better not force my hand! She'll be really sorry if she does. So, she thinks my house might be ungodly? She ain't seen ungodly, and she better hope she don't cause the devil in me to get out. That would not be a good thing." Arriving at a large, heavy wooden door with a big keyhole under the knob, she stepped back as Bertha selected a key from among the many dangling from a metal ring attached to her belt, inserted it, turned it, and pulled the door open, following her mistress after pushing it closed and locking it again.

The noise level in the crowded drawing room rose dramatically when the woman in glittering pink was seen and recognized. "Lori!" from more than a dozen voices. "Pink Lady!" from even more. "Hey, Miss Lady!" "You prettier than ever!"

"Gentlemen, how are you? Good to see you. Are my girls taking good care of you? Ah, glad to hear it. Mr. Chief of Police, I was just telling someone how you honor us by visiting…you are most welcome…please, feel free to keep company with anyone that catches your eye – of course, you know your money is no good here." Smiling, laughing, exchanging light banter, Lori made her way around the packed room and to a darkened corner where her enforcer stood watching the people crowded into the limited space.

"Where's Nettie," she asked, "with a customer?"

"No, ma'am," was the response in a deep, raspy voice. "She say it was her time and she wasn't feeling well."

"It was her time two weeks ago," Loretta said testily, "and two weeks before that and two weeks before that. That girl wouldn't have a drop of blood in her body if it was her time as often as she say. Bring her to me in the room. Ask Bertha to join us." She watched the big man melt further into the shadows, headed for the staircase leading to the rooms where the women lived and serviced the men who paid handsomely for their time. She walked over to the tiny patch of space where couples danced, standing and smiling. As she was noticed, the noise level in the room quieted down.

"Good people," she said, "you all are definitely in for a treat tonight. My nephew, Silk has agreed to sing and play for us this evening." There was an excited rustling, murmurs of anticipation from many of the women. "For those of you that have heard him, you know he has a voice even smoother than the silk he was named for, and for those of you that haven't, well, let's just say that after tonight you'll be glad you have. So, without further ado, let's put our hands together for…Silk!"

Henry Lloyd walked up, guitar in one hand, the other raised in greeting. Pulling up a stool from the corner of the room, he sat, and after some final string adjusting, raised his head and began to sing. "Blue shadows falling…as my baby been gone away…" Women all over the room sighed as they took in the tall, extremely handsome young man with the caramel-colored skin, curly brown hair, and amazing voice.

Loretta moved away from the lights and the crowd captivated by Henry Lloyd's singing as he transitioned from heartbreak to complaining about the unwelcome change in his life since his woman gave birth, "Annie had a baby...can't work no more..."

Letting herself out of the back door, she moved over to the cellar door positioned flush with the lawn next to the back entrance. Reaching down, she pulled open the door, carefully climbing down the stairs illuminated by moonlight, finding and lighting a lantern on a shelf hollowed out from the dirt that formed crude walls. At the bottom of the stairs, she crossed a dirt-packed section of ground to a second door built into the side of the surrounding hillside. Unlocking it she entered a small, stifling room with bare floor and walls, a tiny, thin mattress, a metal chair, and a bucket beside it the only objects in the room. Pulling the chair over, she sat, fitted a cigarette onto the holder she pulled out from the slim, sparkling handbag she carried, lit it, inhaling deeply as she waited.

She was almost finished with her cigarette when she heard the outside door open and someone climbing down the stairs, crossing over, and pulling open the door to the tiny room where she sat. "I'm sorry I'm late, Miss Lori," Bertha said. "Someone fell into a table, knocked and broke glassware all over the floor that I had to supervise the cleanup."

"That's all right, Bertha," Loretta said easily. "Boots isn't back yet. Did you bring the leather gloves? The switch? The bottles? The belt?"

"Yes, ma'am," Bertha said holding up a large burlap sack. "It's all here."

"Good," Loretta said, "I think I hear Boots."

Moments later Boots entered the room, pulling a trembling, protesting young woman, little more than a girl behind him, depositing her in the center of the room and stepping back. "Thank you, Boots," Loretta said, "I think Bertha and I can handle this. I'll call you if I need you," watching the big man close the door, listening to the sound of him climbing the stairs and closing the outside door. Loretta took a final puff before removing the cigarette from her holder and dropping it on the dirt-packed floor. She eyed the obviously frightened girl standing, head down in the center of the tiny space. Bertha reached into the bag she held and pulled out a pair of stained, battered brown leather gloves, pulling them over her hands, flexing the fingers, closing her hands into fists, punching one into the palm of the other. Loretta let the silence continue, the tension inside the tiny enclosure increasing.

"I hear you are not feeling well," she said at last, fitting another cigarette into her holder. "What's wrong?"

"I-I jes' had cramps somethin' awful, Miss Lori," the girl said, her voice low, hesitant, "it being my time of the month and all."

"Well, now, that is a shame," Loretta said. "Cramps can hurt something awful." The fear in the girl's eyes eased, the tension in her body relaxing. Loretta lit her cigarette. "If I'm not mistaken it seems to me you were complaining of cramps and it being that time of month two weeks ago." She looked over at Bertha who had donned a plastic apron and was in the process of tying it around her waist. "Wasn't it about two weeks ago that Miss Nettie here had the same complaint?"

"It seems to me it was two weeks or so ago," Bertha said nodding. "Nettie said she couldn't take customers because she was riding the rag."

"That's what I thought," Loretta said, "and it's that time of month again? Already?"

The fear was back in Nettie's eyes. "I-I felt cramps, really bad ones, and thought the blood would come any time now…"

"But it hasn't started yet?" Loretta asked.

"No, ma'am," Nettie whispered wretchedly.

"When were you going to tell us you were able to work?"

"When-when I was sure it wasn't coming," Nettie said, her voice trembling.

"In the meantime, you was just planning to lay around and do nothing?"

"No, ma'am," Nettie said desperately. "I was perfectly willin' to help cook or clean or scrub..."

"I got Mexicans for that," Loretta snapped. "You know what I need you to do, and it got nothing to do with cooking or cleaning." She stood. "You know I don't like anybody to lie to me or try to deceive me, don't you?"

"Yes, ma'am," Nettie said, a catch in her voice, terrified tears running down her face, glancing fearfully over at Bertha.

"If you know that, then you know you must be punished, don't you?"

"Oh, Miss Lori, please," Nettie begged, falling to her knees. "I won't-won't do it no more...please..."

"Well, since you promise to be good...I'll have Bertha go easy on you, and you can go back to your room. But I expect you to take customers in two days. You should be feeling well enough by then." Nettie moaned. Loretta walked over to the closed door. "I'm going to leave you here with Bertha now, and I'll look forward to seeing you ready for work in two days." As she opened and closed the door behind her, she heard leather-covered fists methodically striking exposed flesh, followed by anguished gasps escalating into cries of pain.

"Where'd you go, Lori? You missed my whole set," Henry Lloyd walked up to his aunt as she entered the drawing room through the back door.

"I'm sorry, sweetie," Loretta said, running the back of her hand along his cheek. "I had some business that couldn't wait. I hate that I missed you. Tell you what, why don't you do an extra set tonight so I can hear you. It'll make the folks here happy too.

You know they can't get enough of your singing." She smiled at Henry Lloyd's enthusiastic agreement. Linking her arm through his, they headed back to the room where the noise had continued unabated.

"Miss Essie, how about you and I go explore our new town today?" Jenna asked the older woman who was pouring maple syrup over a generous stack of pancakes on her plate, an equally generous rasher of bacon next to it. "We need to learn our way around. I read that the cable car runs down the street in walking distance. We could catch it and see where it takes us."

"You know what? That's a good idea, Miss Queenie," Essie said with a smile. "I do feel like us getting out seeing for ourselves what San Francisco has to offer. It'll be my treat."

"Are you sure the two of you should be going alone?" Loretta asked. "What if you get lost? Or end up in a bad part of town?" What she could not say was that she did not want the two of them going anywhere by themselves, without supervision. "Maybe Boots should go with you all."

"I'm sure Boots got plenty to do right here," Essie said. "If we get lost, we know how to ask for help. After all, the two of us crossed the country by ourselves. I'm sure we can do the same in a city, even if it is San Francisco." Jenna nodded.

"Well, if you're sure..." Loretta said, "All right then, you all have fun, and I'll see you when you get back and look forward to hearing about your day," rising and exiting quickly before her anger and escalating temper got the better of her.

A short time later Jenna and Essie were walking down one of the steep hills that characterized the city, headed for the cable car stop they could see in the near distance. "I sure am glad you thought of this, Miss Queenie," Essie said with a wide smile. "I needed some fresh air" (and to get away from that house that was creating an increasing sense of disquiet in her).

"Me, too, Miss Essie," Jenna said. "While we are out, I need to pick up a couple of things that only you should know about." One of which was stout chains with locks for her doors. If whoever was searching her room found one chain and took it away, there would be others to take its place. Essie nodded in perfect understanding. "I want to go by this big Farmer's Market I have been hearing about," she continued, "to buy herbs, plants and seeds so that I can start a garden. Lori has a lot of land. She should be able to let me have a bit of earth." Her future garden was where she planned to hide money and another chain and lock.

"That's a real good idea, Queenie," Essie said. "I know how you love growing things and feeling the good, rich earth on your hands. That's the healer in you." Happy to be away from the almost menacing atmosphere of the beautiful but somehow oppressive house, the two transplants happily set out to learn more about their newly adopted city.

"We had so much fun," Jenna announced that dinner. "Miss Essie and I picked up a schedule and rode the cable cars all over the city."

"We shore did," Essie said. "We even went to that Chinatown you told us about, and it really is like being in China. We went to a lot of they shops. They real big on herbs and natural healing. Would you believe them China folks and Queenie could understand each other? It was a sight to see; everybody waving they arms and pointing to stuff and talking in English and Chinese! They healers and Jenna each understood what the other was talking about. I wouldn't have believed it if I hadn't seen it for myself."

"That's my big sis for you," Henry Lloyd said proudly. "Able to talk to 'bout near anyone about 'bout near anything."

"That is my little brother who still thinks his big sister can do anything," Jenna said. They both laughed, remembering previous exchanges about the meaning of big and little, and their years' long comparisons of tall, slim Henry Lloyd with his petite older sister.

"Well, it's certainly clear that you are happy to be back in each other's company," Loretta said with a smile. Henry Lloyd's devotion to his sister could create problems. It seemed as if she would need to delay her plans, at least until she could wean her nephew away from his sister, which was going to be a whole lot harder than she thought. Aloud she said, "So, tell me about these herbs that you and the Chinamen were talking about. What do you use them for?" pretending to be interested in the detailed description of the plants purchased that day, readily agreeing to allow her to dig a garden in a back corner, standing when she had all she could stand of talk of dirt and mulch and fertilizer and plants, excusing herself, and disappearing down the hall. She had no way of knowing that Jenna had purposely gone into such minute detail in hopes of running her aunt away.

Rising from the dinner table she was able to coax Henry Lloyd and Essie into playing a rousing game of Old Maid, followed by the board game *Sorry*, Jenna dancing in delight when she was first to get all her pieces on her side of the board. Pleasantly tired, wishing everyone good night, chaining the double doors closed with Essie standing watch on the other side, placing the basket of rocks on the floor, waving to let her staunch supporter know that everything was in place, Jenna entered her bedroom closing the door behind her. The sound of furniture being moved around was followed by silence. Essie moved away from the doors leading to Jenna's rooms, headed to her room, closing the door behind her. The sound of a lock turning marked the fact that unlike Jenna, the door to her room had a lock. The silence of sleep descended on one side of the house.

Chapter Eleven

"My first day in a new school! Do I look all right?" Jenna asked anxiously.

"You look beautiful," Essie assured her. "That poodle skirt and white blouse are real stylish, just like them white girls in those fashion books Lori has all over the place."

"Still, I'm glad you are going to help me register," Jenna said. "I would hate to have to go by myself." What she did not add was that she would have hated to have Loretta register her. As far as she was concerned, the fewer people that knew of her relationship to her aunt, the better.

"Well, I'm happy to do it," Essie assured her. "Ain't Henry Lloyd going to school today?"

"No, he says Loretta needs him to drive her somewhere up the coast," Jenna said disgustedly. "If Ma'dear knew he was skipping school, she would definitely give him a talking to. And her."

"Maybe someone ought to tell Sister Albertina," Essie said. "Keepin' that boy from school ain't a good thing."

"Well, it cannot be one of us," Jenna said. "They would know right away who told. It is already hard enough living here."

"You right 'bout that," Essie agreed with a sigh. "'Sides, that boy's getting old enough to make up his own mind. If he don't want to go to school, that's his business, I guess."

"I'll talk to him when I get the chance, when Loretta is not lurking around," Jenna said.

"Or that Bertha-woman," Essie said. "She worse than Lori."

"You got that right," Jenna agreed. "Well," she said taking a deep breath, "are we ready?"

"Yes, ma'am, Miss Queenie," Essie said. "Lead on."

"Class, please welcome Jenna Thompson, who is new to Bayside High. She has just moved here from South Carolina. Jenna, sit anywhere you see an empty desk."

"Yes, ma'am, thank you, ma'am," Jenna said softly, sliding into a chair with an attached desk in the second row. She looked at her class schedule to see which class she would be attending once homeroom ended and where her locker was in this huge school where there were more students than there were in people in her entire town. She listened attentively to the student reading the morning announcements, returning her attention to her schedule when that was over. She rose when the bell rang, mentally trying to figure out where her locker was in the massive facility.

"Need some help finding your locker?" The voice asking the question was bright and cheery with a slight accent.

Jenna looked up. A pretty girl with generous curves and long black hair braided into two thick ropes that fell past her hips was standing by her desk smiling at her. "It's Jenna, right?"

"Yes," Jenna said smiling shyly, "Jenna Thompson. I would love some help finding my locker, and if you could tell me where some of these classes are, I would be most grateful."

"Jenna Thompson, that is a pretty name," the girl said. "My name is Maria, Maria Fernandez, which in my neighborhood is liked being named Mary Smith."

"Still, I think it is a pretty name, too," Jenna said. "No one has that name where I come from."

"It is nice to know somewhere in the world my name is not as common as dirt," Maria said laughing. "Now, let me see your schedule. I will take you to your first class after I show you to your locker." Jenna handed Maria her schedule of classes.

"Oh, good! We have two classes together and the same lunch hour," Maria said happily, "and our lockers are not far apart, either. Follow me." Talking non-stop, pointing out classrooms as they walked to where her locker was, Maria guided her new friend through the noisy, crowded, teeming hallways. Depositing her in front of her first class and promising to meet her in front of the classroom which was her last before lunch, Maria hurried to get to her own class before the bell rang. She was waiting as promised outside of Jenna's English class when the lunch hour arrived, leading her to the cafeteria, pointing out the hot lunch line, walking with her as Jenna selected meat loaf and potatoes, corn, a roll, a piece of chocolate cake and a small carton of milk. After paying for her lunch, Maria led Jenna to a table with four girls already seated. They all looked up as Maria and Jenna approached.

"Hey, ladies," Maria said, "This is Jenna Thompson. She has come all the way from South Carolina, and today is her first day at Bayside, so be nice."

"Welcome to the League of Nations," a black girl with skin the color of burnt mahogany said smiling, "I'm Angela Waters. It's nice to meet you."

"I'm Julie Chin," the Asian girl sitting beside her said. "South Carolina, huh? It will be nice talking to someone who is not from around here – or the quote, unquote 'Motherland'."

"I'm Doris Golden, the Jewish one," a smiling girl with kinky hair said. "Welcome."

"Last but not least, I'm Susan Compton – the white girl," a blond, blue-eyed girl said with a light laugh. "Have a seat," gesturing at an empty spot on the bench next to her.

Once seated, the girls began plying her with questions, fascinated by her life in South Carolina, seeing glimpses of an America they were only dimly aware existed. Jenna in turn had questions of her own about the exotic environment where she suddenly found herself. The lunch hour flew by. As they stood on their way to afternoon classes, they made tentative plans for that weekend to go swimming at a local, popular beach. Jenna and Maria walked to the first of the two classes they had together, still talking animatedly.

"It sounds as if you're going to like your new school," Loretta observed as Jenna related her experiences that night at dinner. "I'm glad you're making friends," she lied.

"Why did they welcome you to – what was it? The League of Nations?" Essie asked.

"I think they were naming themselves after President Woodrow Wilson's League of Nations which was formed to create peace and understanding among nations – countries around the world – and to establish a solid friendship among them. The girls I met today are all good friends who seem to get along really well. One is colored, one is white, one is Mexican, one is Chinese, and one is Jewish."

"Oh my, all of them different, and all of them friends?" Essie said. "That's real nice. I ain't never had no white friends, never met a Chinese or a Jew, and Mexicans are pretty hard to come by in Crawfish Holler, too."

Loretta just managed to refrain from making derogatory remarks about Chinese, Mexicans, and Jews, knowing her observations would not be welcome. She stood, saying, "Well, I need to visit my boarders and make sure they haven't let any bad folk in my house. I'll see you all tomorrow morning." She briskly exited the room.

"You got anything you need to do to get ready for school tomorrow?" Essie asked. "Anything I can help you with?"

"Actually, there is," Jenna said. "I want to start taking my own lunch to school unless the cafeteria offers something I really want.

All I need is a sandwich and a piece of fruit and maybe a sweet of some sort. If you could make my lunch, that would really help."

"Why, I'd be happy to," Essie said, "beginning tonight. I'll just find my way to the kitchen and make up something for tomorrow. I think the cook goes home after dinner, so I should have the kitchen to myself with no one making me nervous by looking over my shoulder. I'll make sure I clean up real good after I'm done, so nobody can complain."

"Thank you, Miss Essie," Jenna said gratefully, walking over and giving her a big hug, "Now, if you will excuse me, I have some homework to do. See you in the morning." She noticed Henry Lloyd avoided looking at her each time she mentioned school or school preparation or homework. She would be willing to bet he had not been near a school since his arrival. She exited the dining room, determined to talk to him the first time they were alone together.

"I'm pretty sure the kitchen is this way," Essie said to herself. "I always see the maids carrying food from this direction." Reaching a pair of double-hinged doors, she pushed through, nodding in satisfaction as she looked around the large, modern, gleaming kitchen, night lights casting a soft glow. Looking around she spotted the light switch and flipped it on, flooding the room with light. A movement and scuffling noise drew her attention; watching as the curtains to what was probably the pantry twitched closed. Striding over to them, pulling them open, she jumped in surprise. A very young girl dropped the slice of bread she held, one of her eyes wide with fear, the other eye black and blue, swollen shut.

"Chile, you scared me to death," Essie gasped. "What you doin' in there?"

"Oh, please, ma'am, I'm sorry –" the girl pleaded desperately. "I know I'm not s'posed to be here, but I was jes' so hungry... But

I'll go now, and look," she said, reaching down and picking up what she had dropped, "all I took was this one piece of bread. I-I'll throw it away if you don't tell anyone I was here."

"Honey chile, come on out of there," Essie said gently, "If you hungry, you need to eat. Sit right here," leading the terrified girl over to the kitchen dining set, pulling out a chair and helping her sit. "Now, I'm going to fix my girl some lunch for school tomorrow. You want me to fix you a sandwich too?" She smiled when the unknown girl nodded hesitantly. Walking over to the pantry, pulling the curtain back, she inspected the well-stocked shelves, grabbing jars and placing them on the counter, opening the refrigerator to remove meat, lettuce, cheese, and fruit, moving over to the bread box and lifting out a loaf. Opening drawers, she removed a fork and a knife from one, and waxed paper from another, all the while keeping up a light conversation aimed at putting the girl, who jumped at the slightest sound, at ease. Ingredients collected, Essie began assembling sandwiches. "Here you go, hon. There's a ham, turkey and cheese sandwich for you, and I made this one to take with you," handing her a waxed paper wrapped package. "Eat up now while I make my girl's lunch." After a moment's hesitation, the girl bit eagerly into her sandwich, chewing rapidly, the extra sandwich disappearing somewhere on her person.

When the last bite was consumed, the girl stood. "Thank you, ma'am, for...for everything...but I-I got to go now before they start lookin' for me."

Poised to ask some pointed questions, there came the heavy tread of someone approaching. The girl looked around wildly, her fear increased tenfold. "Oh, Lawd, they must be lookin' for me. I'm goin' to be in such trouble...Lawd, Lawd! I cain't take no more," she said despairingly, her body shaking, her uninjured eye full of tears.

Thinking quickly, Essie grabbed the girl, pushing her under the tablecloth draped table, sitting in her place, pretending to be eating the last of a snack as Boots came into the room. "Hey... Boots, is it?" she asked, smiling at his slow nod, his eyes searching the room. "I came in here to fix Queenie's lunch, and everything looked so good I decided to make myself a little something. I do love to eat. Can I fix you something?" she asked brightly. "They's all kinds of good things in here."

"No, ma'am," Boots said after a moment's silence. "I jes' heard noises and movement in here and came to see who it was. S'cuse me for interrupting, now that I know it was you, I can move on. You have a good evening." Turning he melted into the shadows in the disturbing way he had, his heavy tread slowly fading.

"I believe he's gone," Essie said. The girl crawled out from her hiding spot underneath the table.

"Thank you so much, ma'am," she said, grabbing Essie's hand and kissing it. "I am ever so grateful…but I really have to go now."

"Don't you want to tell me what's goin' on?" Essie asked gently.

"No, ma'am, I don't dare," the girl said. "Thank you so much for the sandwiches…" She turned to leave.

"Won't you at least tell me your name?" Essie asked. Something very strange – even sinister – was going on in this house, and Essie was determined to find out what it was.

"My name is Nettie," the girl said after a short pause, "Nettie Jamison."

"Well, it's nice to meet you, Nettie Jamison," Essie said. "I'll be in here every weeknight, so please feel free to come back. I'll fix you some more sandwiches."

"Thank you, Miss Essie," Nettie said. "You've been most kind." Moving cautiously, looking around and listening closely, she moved down the hall leading to the other side of the house.

"What in the world is goin' on here?" Essie wondered aloud as she cleaned up. "Who was that child, why was she so scared, and whose been beating on her?" Cleanliness restored, Essie switched off the light, headed for her room, her mind troubled, busy.

"Good morning," Essie said brightly from one of the chairs in Jenna's sitting room where she was comfortably ensconced, a fashion magazine in her hands, a cup of coffee on the table in front of her.

Bertha froze for an instant, but swiftly recovered. "Good morning, Miss Essie, I was just coming to see if Miss Queenie's room needed sprucing up. Just making sure them Mexicans was doing like they're supposed to."

"They doin' fine. They been here already, but there wasn't much to do. Queenie makes up her own bed and keeps her bathroom spotless. Her mama taught her that."

"Well, that's good. Less for them to do," Bertha said smoothly. "I guess I'll go check some other things since there's nothing to be done here. You all right? Can I bring you anything?"

"No, I'm good," Essie said, relaxing back into her chair. "This room is right comfortable. I'm not in anybody's way, there's a radio here, plenty to read. I think this here will be my spot. I can help Queenie keep it straight, make it easier on her now that she's in school."

"I'm happy you've found somewhere you can relax comfortably," Bertha said smoothly. "Can I bring you some lunch later?"

"No, I know how busy you must be keeping this big ol' house running," Essie said easily. "I talked with the cook this morning, and so I'm jes' going to the kitchen where she'll have a plate waiting for me, or she'll fix me something and I'll bring it up and take the plate back myself when I'm done. I don't want my being here to put anybody out." *Ain't no way I'd eat anything you or that witch Loretta brought me*, she thought to herself.

"Sounds like you have things nicely arranged," Bertha said. "You have a good day."

"You, too," Essie said, watching the stout housekeeper walk out of the room, moving swiftly toward the staircase. "I guess you won't be meddling in her stuff today," Essie said with satisfaction, picking the magazine she had been perusing back up and resuming her reading.

"Do you think she knows anything?"

After a short pause, "I don't think so, ma'am," Bertha said slowly. "She didn't seem nervous or suspicious or anything. Boots said she was in the kitchen alone last night fixing Queenie's lunch and didn't seem scared or didn't appear as though she was meddling – sticking her nose where it didn't belong."

"Well, keep an eye on her. Don't do anything that might make her suspicious," Loretta said testily. "All we need is for that bitch to start asking questions we can't answer." Bertha nodded in agreement. "Enough about her. How is Nettie doing? Behaving herself? Learned her lesson? You are still locking her door when she's not working, aren't you?"

"Yes, ma'am, she hasn't had customers for a few days; her eye is not healed yet. I'ma give her another day or so. She'll be ready by then."

"That's good," Loretta said with a slow smile, "but I'm ready now." She watched Bertha walk to the door, close and lock it, walk back to where she was standing, reach up to wrap one hand around the back of her neck, pull her towards her, and kiss her hungrily. Eagerly divesting one another of their clothing, they fell on the overstuffed sofa naked, arms and legs intertwined.

"Henry Lloyd, are you not going to school?" Jenna asked quietly. She and her brother were seated on the patio at the rear of the house, Jenna sipping on her favorite cola with lots of crushed ice, Henry Lloyd drinking sweetened iced tea.

Henry Lloyd looked away and down. "Naw, I ain't been in a while," he admitted, shamefaced.

"How long has it been?" Jenna demanded.

"Really not since I been here," he confessed, head down.

"Why not?" Jenna demanded. "You know Ma'dear would not be happy if she knew. She wants all her children at least to be high school graduates."

"I know, but I ain't like you. I never liked school. I just went 'cause she made me," Henry Lloyd said.

"So, what do you plan to do when you start working? You can only go so far without a high school diploma."

"I really think I can go far as a singer," Henry Lloyd said earnestly. "Lori says she knows people, and folks really like me when I sing for the boarders and their friends on the other side of the house. She say that she can probably even introduce me to some movie people or record producers that will help me cut a record. What I want to do don't need no book learning." A short silence. "I guess you goin' to tell Ma'dear, huh?" Henry Lloyd asked, half-belligerently, taking in Jenna's troubled face and downcast eyes. "Then she'll try to make me go, or she might even want me to go back home."

"No, I am not going to tell her," Jenna said at last. "You should," she added when Henry Lloyd's shoulders slumped in relief. "If this is what you want to do and really think you will be a success at it, then stand tall. Tell her this is what you have chosen. You are old enough to make up your own mind. Just, be honest."

"You right," Henry Lloyd said straightening. "I been feelin' real bad, sneaking around and pretending. I'm gonna tell Ma'dear the next time she call." Reaching over, he hugged Jenna tightly. "I'm so glad you're my sister. You always tell me what I need to hear, whether I like it or not. Also, I'm real glad you here; I missed our talks."

"I missed our talks, too," Jenna said, returning the hug. "I will always tell you the truth, and let you know what I think. That is what big sisters are for."

Albertina called the following evening. "Hey, baby," she said when Jenna was called to the phone, "How you doin'? You been on my mind."

"Hey, Ma'dear," Jenna said happily, "I been thinking about you, too. I'm doing all right, settling in. I really like my school. It is huge! We have more students than all the people in Crawford Hollow. The classes are hard but interesting and challenging. I especially like my English and chemistry and biology classes, and I am making friends, too."

"Well, that's wonderful, Queenie," Albertina said. "You learn as much as you can, you hear? I got some news, too. It's about Mr. Pettigrew."

"Is-is he dead?" Jenna asked, her heart jumping.

"Naw, he ain't dead. The fact is, he finally woke up. He don't remember nothing. Would you believe, his brains must have gotten scrambled, and all the meanness in him knocked out, 'cuz he's turned into the nicest man you'd ever want to meet. He can't get around much and spend most of his time settin' on the porch, but he's sweet to the chillen' and jes' as gentle as he can be. Rhonda don't scream when she see him no mo', and the boys ain't scared of him no more, either. Not even Sidney."

"Really?" Jenna said, "Mr. Pettigrew?"

"It's the honest-to-God truth," Albertina said. "It's right peaceful around here now, so if you ever want to, you and Henry Lloyd can come home any time."

"That is so nice to know," Jenna said in honest, heartfelt relief. "You do not know how good hearing that makes me feel. Speaking of Henry Lloyd, I think he wants to talk to you. He has a lot to tell you."

"All right, then, put him on," Albertina said.

"Hey Ma'dear," Henry Lloyd said, "How you doin'?"

Jenna moved away to afford them some measure of privacy. The two spoke for some time, before he motioned her back over. "Okay, Ma'dear, I will…I love you, too. Here's Queenie," handing her the phone.

"Well, baby, I'm about to go, but before I do, Sidney wants to talk to you."

"Queenie? Queenie, is that you?"

"Sidney? How is my hero doing?" Jenna asked with delight.

"I'm all right. Every day I wish you were here," Sidney said. A pause. Then a voice vastly different from his normal one intoned, "Beware the nighttime drink from she who wears pink. Avoid the sneak attack from she who wears black."

Jenna's scalp prickled; she felt the hairs on the nape of her neck rise. "Thank you, spirits," she whispered, "I will."

Albertina's voice came on the line. "He done gone to the spirit world," she said, "so he can't talk no more. I'm going to hang up, too. Take care, baby. I love you."

"I love you all, too. Give Sidney an extra hug and kiss from me when he comes back," Jenna said. "Bye now," placing the receiver back in its cradle.

"Thank you for making me talk to Ma'dear," Henry Lloyd said. "It wasn't nearly as bad as I thought it would be."

"See, I told you," Jenna said, pushing Sidney's warning to the back of her mind for the time being. "Now, I must get myself ready to meet the League at the beach."

"Have fun," Henry Lloyd said. "Lori got some errands to run, so I'm gonna drive her. See you later." Giving his sister a hug, Henry Lloyd hurried away as Jenna made her way to her bedroom to collect what she needed for the afternoon of sun and fun ahead.

Chapter Twelve

"You have this carnival year-round?" Jenna asked in awe looking around at the teeming boardwalk: the Ferris Wheel, numerous rides including bumper cars and a carousel in the background, games of chance lining the causeway being hawked by rapidly talking men in straw hats with round brims and striped ribbons, the dozens of food stands many of them featuring edibles she had never heard of, stairs at regular intervals with wide wooden planks and handrails leading down to the crowded, sandy beach, and the rolling waves of ocean waters in the near distance.

"Yeah, the San Fran boardwalk is here all the time," Julie said with a smile. "Why, what do you have where you live?"

"Well, the State Fair comes to Orangesburg once a year," Jenna said, "and a carnival is always part of it, but it shuts down and leaves once the fair is over."

"What do you do the rest of the year?" Angela asked curiously, "for fun," she added when Jenna frowned in confusion.

"We do not have much time to worry about having fun," Jenna said quietly. "Most people I know are farmers or sharecroppers and work hard on the land... with all their children, too. Some go to school as well. That pretty much takes up everybody's time."

"What is the difference between a farmer and a sharecropper?" Maria asked curiously.

"Is your father a farmer or a sharecropper?" Angela asked.

"Mr. Pettigrew is my mother's husband, not my father," Jenna stated. "He is the daddy of my younger brothers and sisters. He owns the land our house is built on and quite a bit surrounding it, plus he works at the town meat locker."

"What is a meat locker?" Susan asked curiously.

"It is a place where raw meat is stored," Jenna said.

"Like a butcher's shop?" Angela asked.

"A lot like," Jenna said, nodding.

"I am ready to hit the water," Susan said, "then we can eat and catch some rides if we're feeling up to it."

"Jenna, do you know how to swim?" Doris asked. "Good," she said when Jenna nodded. "Have you ever been snorkeling?" insisting on stopping by a nearby beach shop to buy a snorkel when Jenna admitted that she never had. Once in the water, she was given detailed instructions on how to use it. Her first time in the water with it, she became a fan for life. Underneath the waves near the bottom, she examined seashells and small fish and the colorful coral reef. Sinking down with her friends, they swam out to the depths, floating and diving before swimming back to shore.

"That was so much fun," Jenna breathed, drying her hair and body with a large towel after rinsing off with a shower attachment spouting fresh water fastened to a tall pole near the stairs leading to the boardwalk, carefully rinsing out and wrapping her precious snorkel in an unused towel.

"That was fun, wasn't it?" Maria said. "Now, let's get something to eat. What can we introduce Jenna to today?" With a wide range of suggestions, they made their way to the stands offering foods of all kinds.

"This is called a…taco?" Jenna inquired, biting into the crunchy, meat, cheese and lettuce filled shell covered with a spicy, tomato-based sauce. "It is so good."

"And these are nachos," Maria said, picking up a spicy meat, black bean, salsa, melted cheese, pickled jalapeño and sour cream-laden tortilla chip, and popping it into her mouth, savoring the blend of flavors.

"Next time we go Chinese," Julie said, smiling with anticipation as she bit into a fried jalapeño stuffed with chiles and cream cheese. "I know just where to take you. You will love it: egg rolls, fried rice, kung pao chicken, egg drop soup..."

"Let us not forget Jamaican," Angela added, "jerk chicken, fried plantains...dirty rice...fresh fish..."

"What can we expect from South Carolina?" Doris asked. "And don't ask me about any Jewish good-to-eat foods, because there aren't any," she said to widespread laughter and good-natured ribbing.

"Let me see..." Jenna said thoughtfully, "fried chicken and macaroni and cheese and collard greens and peach cobbler and caramel cake..."

"I know! Next time we will have a picnic, and everyone can bring a dish," Maria suggested to enthusiastic agreement, "That will be fun, but for now, one last dip and then I need to head home."

"We all do," Susan said, jumping to her feet and running for the water with everyone else close behind.

"So, you really enjoy being with your menagerie, was it?" Loretta said with a light laugh.

"League, actually," Jenna said with a light laugh of her own, "but I can see where it would be confusing to people who do not have a very large vocabulary." Loretta abruptly stopped smiling. "I'm tired," Jenna said standing, "so I think I will call it an early night. Goodnight, all!" she headed up the stairs to her rooms.

"I believe I'm going' to do a little cookin'," Essie declared standing. "I do like to cook, and it's been a while since I stirred any pots, so I'm gettin' the urge. I'll jes' make somethin' wit' whatever I find in that big pantry of yours, Lori, some cookies for Queenie's lunch, maybe. Anyway, I'll be in there awhile so feel free to come get some nice hot cookies." She moved purposefully down the hallway. "I hope Nettie smells them and knows it's me," Essie said to herself, "I'll make up a coupla sandwiches just in case." Pushing through the hinged double doors, throwing open the curtains in front of the pantry, Essie began gathering ingredients for sandwiches and cookies.

A short time later the sound of light, hesitant steps coming from the boarder's side of the house, and the small figure of Nettie emerged from the shadows. Looking quickly around, she lifted one of the edges of the tablecloth and scurried under the table, accepting the plate of sandwiches from Essie with a murmured thank you as she dug in. "I was hoping you'd get to come," Essie said. "Nobody knows you're gone, do they?"

"No, ma'am," Nettie said. "When they lock the door, they think I can't get out, but I can. There's a big ol' tree next to my window. I jump over to it and climb down the trunk with none the wiser. Plus, I put a chair under the door's knob, so it won't open." Her face grew infinitely sad. "I have to go back to work tomorrow. My face done cleared up."

The sound of footsteps had Nettie dropping the tablecloth and crawling under the table. Bertha appeared, walking quickly into the middle of the room, looking around carefully. Essie walked over to the oven, opening the door and removing a sheet of fragrant cookies, placing them on a wire rack to cool. "Would you like a cookie, Bertha?" Essie asked, holding up a plate filled with cooled cookies. "I made some tea cakes, some sugar cookies, and something called chocolate chips. I saw that recipe in a magazine. They real good, and you welcome to as many of any kind as you'd like."

"They sure do smell good," Bertha said, sniffing appreciatively. "I'll take a couple with me while I'm doing my nightly walkthrough, so I'll just keep on moving." Thanking her kindly when handed two of each of the three kinds of cookies she had just made, Bertha took another look around, biting into a cookie before exiting the kitchen chewing.

"She gone," Essie announced. Nettie crawled from under the table again, munching on a tea cake Essie handed her along with two waxed paper packages to take with her.

"I got to go," Nettie said. "I got to be there to open the door next time somebody try it."

"Baby, what is going on?" Essie asked gently. "I cain't help you unless you ask for it. They's somethin' very wrong here, and I need for you to tell me what it is. That's the only way I can help."

After a long silence, "I-I'll tell you next time, I promise," the girl assured miserably. "I want to wait just a little while longer before you start to hate me."

"Chile, there ain't nothin' – and I mean nothin'– you could tell me that would make me hate you," Essie said without hesitation. "In fact, I believe I'ma take you home to live with me," smiling tenderly when Nettie's eyes filled with desperate hope and grateful tears. Grabbing one of Essie's hands, she brought it to her cheek before letting go and vanishing down the hallway leading to the boarder's quarters.

"Boarders, my eye," Essie said. A horrible suspicion was building in her mind. "Oh, my Lawd Jesus, could it be?" she whispered to herself. "Is it possible?" She ran some water in one side of the sink, adding a generous squirt of dish soap, placing the dishes, glasses, cooking utensils and cookie sheets down into it, deep in thought as she scrubbed.

"What took you so long? And how come I couldn't get the door open?" Bertha demanded as she pushed her way inside, looking around suspiciously.

"I–I'm so sorry, I didn't hear you. I must have been sleep," Nettie said, her head down, voice low.

"You know you goin't accept customers again beginning tomorrow, don't you?" Bertha said, watching with a satisfied smile as the young girl shrank in on herself with revulsion.

"Yes, ma'am," Nettie whispered wretchedly.

"You mighty stubborn! Thought I was going to have to starve you halfway to death before you decided to do as you were told or take you back to the room."

"No, ma'am, that ain't necessary," Nettie said softly, unable to suppress the shudder running through her.

"I'm off to finish my rounds," Bertha stated. "I'll send you up your first gentleman caller around this time tomorrow. Be sure and put your hair into pigtails. A lot of men like 'em young."

"Yes, ma'am," Nettie said, head still down, low voice filled with shame.

"Now, I could put it off a little longer," Bertha said, putting a hand on Nettie's shoulder, "another day or two," rubbing gently, "if you was to be nice to me," her hand wandering downward.

Nettie stepped back. "Well, maybe you'll change your mind after I send you some of our customers who aren't so careful with the merchandise," Bertha said with a bark of a laugh. "I'll be a lot nicer than they are…think about it." She turned and walked out the door, closing and locking it behind her, her brisk footsteps fading away.

Nettie fell to her knees. "Please, Lawd…please, Lawd…" she said brokenly, "Don't let Miss Essie forget about me, and please don't have her hate me once she find out what they make me do...Please, Lawd..." Rocking back and forth, Nettie prayed desperately.

"Hey, why you sittin' out here all by yourself?" Nettie shivered at the sound of the friendly male voice addressing her. She looked up; Miss Lori's handsome nephew was standing over her, smiling.

"It was hot inside, so I jes' came out to get some air," she said hesitantly. "Was there something I can get for you, sir? Something you needed?" Bracing herself for the indecent proposition.

"Naw, we can jes' talk. My name is...Silk, and some people call me Slim. What's your name?" Henry Lloyd asked, tempted for some reason to tell her his real name.

"They call me Baby Doll," Nettie said.

"Is that why you runnin' around in baby doll pajamas?" Henry Lloyd asked curiously, looking her up and down.

"Yea, it's s'posed to make men think about their younger days," Nettie said softly.

"Then what?" Henry Lloyd asked. Shooting him a look of disbelief, unsure of how to answer, they were interrupted by the sound of footsteps approaching.

"There you are," Bertha said. "Miss Lori's been looking for you. She wants you to meet some nice gentlemen."

"Why, so they can call her outside her name so they can feel young?" Henry Lloyd asked disdainfully. "Well, I saw her first. I'm gonna talk with her tonight. You tell Lori; she won't mind."

"Of course, she won't," Bertha readily agreed. "The two of y'all enjoy your talk, and I'll find someone else to introduce to those fine young gentlemen." She gave Nettie a long, hard look before walking briskly away.

"I-I better go," Nettie said, rising rapidly, "I don't want to make Miss Lori angry." She gasped, unconsciously trying to pull away, lifting one arm defensively when Henry Lloyd grasped her by the other.

"What's wrong?" Henry Lloyd asked. "You act like I'm gonna…hit you or somethin'…I would never hit a woman… don't go," he said coaxingly, "stay here and talk to me. I jes' want to talk wit' ya for a little while. I call you the little ghost. I hardly ever see you, if you ain't hidin', you ain't here at all, and sometimes you be gone for days. Where do you go?"

Nettie's eyes grew wide, frightened. "I don't dare say, mister," she said. "It's not for me to tell."

"You can't tell me where you go?" Henry Lloyd asked, frowning when Nettie shook her head in refusal.

"You can't say where you are durin' the day when most everyone else is up eatin', talkin', or listenin' to music? It's when the hairdressers and dressmakers come, too. How come you ain't never there?" Henry Lloyd demanded.

Nettie shook her head silently, eyes lowered.

Henry Lloyd was slowly realizing that something very wrong was happening on the boarder's side of the house – something involving the younger boarders. What he recognized now as fear on their faces, and those old men he had noticed hanging around helped fuel it. "Baby Doll, I want you to stay close to me for the rest of the night," Henry Lloyd said, patting the seat next to him. "We jes' gonna talk, and then I'll walk you to your room."

"All night?" Nettie whispered hopefully, "and that's all you want to do? Jes' talk?"

"That's all," Henry Lloyd assured her. "I jes' want to learn about you: where you from, what you do, what you did before you came here, your plans for when you leave here – everything."

"We ain't s'posed to say nothing about ourselves to…the gentlemen who call on us," Nettie said, "Jes' like we ain't to tell nobody our real names."

"I ain't no gentleman caller," Henry Lloyd stated. "I live here, so you can tell me anything."

"Miss Lori, she wouldn't like it," Nettie whispered. "I don't want to make her mad at me."

"How 'bout this? I won't tell her nothin' you tell me, no matter what," Henry Lloyd promised.

"Nothin'?" Nettie said, "What will you tell her we talked about? She sure to ask you."

"I'll jes' tell her we talked about my singin' and stuff like that," Henry Lloyd said. "She cain't get mad at you about that, can she?"

"No, sir, I guess not," Nettie said slowly, "but we better make sure we say we talked about the same things."

"Done!" Henry Lloyd said enthusiastically, "What do you want to talk about first, Baby...Dear?"

"It's Baby Doll, mister," Nettie said.

"It's Baby Dear to me," Henry Lloyd said, "and stop calling me mister and sir."

"Should I call you Slim or Silk?" Nettie asked.

Henry Lloyd hesitated, both names suddenly sounding tawdry and cheap to him. "My sister calls me Silky Slim," Henry Lloyd said. "Why don't you call me that, too."

"All right, Silky Slim," Nettie said, "but I still think you should call me Baby Doll when Bertha or Miss Lori can hear us."

"I can do that," Henry Lloyd said, "but just when they around. Maybe when you get to know me better, you'll tell me your real name."

Nettie lowered her head without answering. "Where did you want to go to talk...M – Silky Slim?" she asked after a time. "I'm s'posed to bring in a certain amount of drinkin' money, but I would be more than happy to pay for that myself," Nettie said.

"No, ma'am," Henry Lloyd said, reaching into his pocket and pulling a few bills off the sizable roll he carried. "Here, take these and get whatever you want. If you'd bring me some sweetened iced tea, I'd appreciate it. I'll wait for you out here. We'll talk out here, too."

"Now," Henry Lloyd said upon her return, "how'd you come to be one of Lori's boarders?" he asked. He watched Nettie's face go still, her eyes grow shadowed and sad.

She was silent so long Henry Lloyd was on the verge of changing the subject when she said, "I will tell you some day, but not tonight. Tonight, let's talk of nice things. How long have you been in San Francisco? Where did you come from?" Henry Lloyd obligingly began describing his life in South Carolina before coming to California and how drastically life had changed since his move to the West Coast. Nettie kept him talking by plying him with questions, at the same time somehow managing to reveal very little about herself. She got up twice to replenish their drinks, resuming the conversation where they left off.

"Well, I guess I need to walk you to the stairs," Henry Lloyd said regretfully hours later. "I sure enjoyed talkin' with you. We gotta do it again, soon. One day you gonna trust me enough to tell me your name and what's goin' on around here." Rising, he walked close to the very young woman in short-short pajamas, subtly protecting her with his presence.

"You certainly had the rest of the girls jealous of you tonight," Loretta said playfully, coming up next to Nettie and Henry Lloyd as they stood by the stairs leading to the boarder's rooms. "You had Slim all to yourself all night. What in the world did you find to talk about?"

"I jes' tol' her how different things are here than where I come from," Henry Lloyd said, "and we talked about music some. I'm gonna bring my guitar next time."

"Next time? You plan on taking up all his time again, Baby Doll?" Lori said, her voice and eyes hardening. "Surely, you don't plan on being that selfish."

"N-n-n-no, ma'am," Nettie gasped, stammering, "I-I-I would, would never…"

"I was the one being selfish," Henry Lloyd asserted, smiling down at a trembling Nettie, "and I was the one who claimed her time tonight. Nothing wrong with that, surely?"

"Of course not, dear boy," Loretta said. "You can spend as much time as you like with any of our boarders. I just know how much all of them love talking and…stuff with you." She was much more comfortable with the idea of Henry Lloyd being with the seasoned prostitutes – the ones who did it as a chosen profession, who knew how to keep secrets, ones who had not been forced into the business or had been coerced long ago, not ones who were still being broken in. Henry Lloyd did not appear upset or angry, so it was unlikely Nettie had told him anything shocking. Loretta would just have to make sure Nettie continued to hold her peace whenever she was with Slim, or until he knew and accepted what was going on in her boarding house. She had plans for him.

Looping her arm through that of her nephew, subtly questioning him about his time spent with Nettie, Loretta and Henry Lloyd headed for the family side of the mansion.

Chapter Thirteen

"Miss Thompson, you scored ninety-eight percent on your chemistry exam, one hundred percent on your biology final, ninety-nine in Advanced Algebra– Trigonometry, one hundred in English and another one hundred in Spanish. Your scores on the nursing entrance exams are equally high, so I will be writing your letter of recommendation. I have one from the physician who has known you since childhood and credits you with saving your mother's life; I'm putting the packet in the mail today, and we should hear something in a couple of weeks," running out of breath and information at the same time, pushing her glasses back up her nose, Gloria Fansler, Jenna's school counselor smiled at her recently-arrived star student. "Your grade point average is going to put you in the top ten of our graduates, but you come from a small school in South Carolina. Why do you think you are doing so well here?"

"I think it is because the classes I choose speak a universal language," Jenna said after a moment of reflection. "Like math, for example: equations are the same no matter where you are or where you learned them. Most sciences are built on the language of math. Our teachers in South Carolina do not play, either. Our schools are segregated with fewer resources, so our colored teachers work hard to teach their students what they need to know to compete academically with any white school in the state– and outside too, I guess. I like math-based classes and I love math, so I tend to do well, though I'm still trying to figure out where I messed up on my chemistry test and which algebra–trig problem I only got partial credit for."

Shooting her an incredulous look, just managing to refrain from asking how scoring a ninety-eight could be construed as messing up by any stretch of the imagination, Gloria said instead, "I truly believe you will be on your way to the Grayson School of Nursing in Birmingham, Alabama, this coming fall."

Jenna smiled, almost hugging herself in delight. She said, "Miss Fansler, "I surely do hope so."

"So, will you be spending the summer here," her counselor asked, "catching the sun's rays, lazing on the beach, learning to surf?"

"No," Jenna said with a sigh that was equal parts regret and anticipation. "I will be going back home to South Carolina. My mother is a healer, and I am still learning from her. I miss my brothers and sisters; therefore, I am going to spend the summer with them, gather what I need for nurse's school, and get ready to move to Alabama from there."

"You are a healer?" Gloria said, her eyes bright, interested, pushing her sliding glasses up her nose. "That is quite interesting! You are learning medicine using both natural remedies and scientific methods?"

"Exactly. I think each has something the other can use," Jenna said. "I want to meld the two and create something that is the best of both."

"I am happy to have met you, Jenna," Miss Fansler said. "I just wish our acquaintance could have been longer. You will be graduating this year; otherwise, I know you would have had a major impact on this school."

"Thank you, ma'am. I wish we could have known each other longer as well. I wish I could have known everyone I have met here longer." With two notable exceptions.

"Well, I will let you get back to class. I just wanted to share with you the fact that you made the honor roll and your great scores on the entrance exams." Handing her a hall pass, she watched smiling as Jenna skipped happily from her office.

* * *

"Where you been? I been lookin' for you. You disappeared for days again, and you weren't in your room 'cause I sent someone to look."

"I'm s-s-sorry, mister...I been a bit poorly," Nettie's head was down, her voice barely above a whisper.

"What's this 'mister', stuff?" Henry Lloyd demanded. "I thought we were past that." Lifting her chin with gentle fingers, he frowned when she winced and jerked away. He pulled her from the shadows despite her desperate attempts to get away, turning her face into the light cast by the full moon. "What happened?" he asked, his voice tight. "Who did this?" Nettie's face was bruised, one eye swollen almost shut, one side of her lips twice their normal size.

"I-I tripped coming down the stairs, sir," Nettie said. "I tend to be clumsy, and I banged my face when I fell."

"Baby, my daddy done whupped up on me and my brothers enough for me to know a beatdown when I see it," Henry Lloyd said, running a gentle hand down her cheek. "What I want to know is who hit you and why."

"I tol' you, I fell," she said, her eyes falling before his. "I can't, I don't dare," Nettie said when he continued to silently stare down at her. "I'll get in such trouble. I'm not even supposed to be talking with you now..."

"So, I'm the reason you got a beating?" Henry Lloyd asked, eyes flashing.

"Please, sir, I've said too much already," Nettie said, looking around for Lori, Bertha or Boots.

"Let's go over here, dear," Henry Lloyd said, taking her hand and moving them to a location on the outside patio where he could easily see anyone approaching. "Now," he said grimly, "you are goin' to tell me what's goin' on, and then we'll see what we can do about gettin' you away from here."

Nettie's eyes met his, hers wary, doubtful, desperately hopeful. "You ain't got to worry about me," he said earnestly. "I won't tell nobody what you tell me unless you say I can. I ain't out to trick you or hurt you in any way."

Nettie stared at him a moment longer before lowering her eyes. "I'll tell you my story, even if it means you won't be my friend anymore." She was silent for a moment as Henry Lloyd watched the play of emotions crossing her face. Taking a deep breath, she began. "I'm the oldest girl of thirteen children; three brothers are older than me. After me there were four more boys before the next girl came, so most of the housework fell on me and mama to do. It seemed all I did was wash and scrub and iron and cook and take care of babies that weren't even mine. I begged for them to let me go to school. They did, and I studied my books when I didn't have any chores, which wasn't very often."

"One day I was at the general store when I saw this paper pinned to the bulletin board. It was a notice offering maid work in California saying the job would pay for the train ticket and would provide room and board. Said once you got a job and your debt for the ticket and the room and board was paid off, you were free to stay if you liked or you could move somewhere else, with some money to get you started. I was so excited thinking this was my chance to get away from endless housework and cleaning and baby-rearing for free. At least this way I'd be paid for it. I sent a letter and got an answer about a month later. The letter contained a train ticket and an invitation to stay with a Miss Lori for a time to see how we'd suit. I knew my folks would never let me go, so...I ran away. I left the swamplands of Louisiana behind and arrived in San Francisco five days later."

"Ms. Lori and Boots met me at the train station. She was dressed all in pink. I thought she was the prettiest woman I had ever seen. I didn't know colored women could look like that. She took me to Fisherman's Wharf and bought me a sandwich at an outdoor eating booth. She asked me how I liked it and laughed when I told her it would have been better if the bread hadn't been spoiled. She told me it was called sourdough and was s'posed to taste like that. We walked around for a while and then Miss Lori had Boots drive us here. I had never seen anything like it. She showed me where I'd be staying: a room all to myself with a matching bed and chest of drawers and a bedspread that matched the curtains and the rugs on the floor. I thought I had died and gone to heaven. When she took me to meet the other girls, I thought I would finally have the sisters I had always wanted. The first days were wonderful, Miss Lori bought me clothes, I got my hair done, ate good food...and then came the day Miss Lori and Bertha told me what they expected me to do."

She fell silent for a time, Henry Lloyd brought her a glass of water. Several sips later she began again. "At first I laughed. I knew they couldn't be saying what I thought I was hearing. Then Miss Lori made it clear: 'I got all this on my back or on my knees with my legs or mouth or both wide open, and that's how you gonna help me keep it,' she said. I told them I wouldn't, couldn't do it. Then she reminded me of the money I owed. I swore I'd pay her back some other way. She asked me to reconsider, I said no, and then she said she was disappointed but accepted my decision and asked if we could drink to it. I agreed...and woke up with a white man I didn't know on top of me, inside of me. I screamed and he punched me, almost knocking me out, and then he jammed a scarf in my mouth. He got up when he finished... then came the next one...and the next one...and the next one..." silent tears were running down her face. "They tried to break me with the train, keeping me bloody and sticky with all them men's leavin's. When that didn't work, they tried to starve me. When they saw I didn't mind starving to death, that I wanted to die, they tried to beat me into giving in." She wrapped her arms around her shivering form, taking the jacket Henry Lloyd handed her with a murmured word of thanks. "They still trying to break me," Nettie said, her teeth chattering. "I've run away twice; the police brought me back both times 'cause the Chief is friends with Miss Lori. They still beat me and try to starve me, but they ain't broke me yet. One day I will get away from here, or they gonna have to kill me. One good thing that's happened lately is this lady I met in the kitchen. Her name is Miss Essie, and she real nice. She say she want to help, but I ain't told her my story yet...she may change her mind once she know."

"I've known Miss Essie all my life," Henry Lloyd stated. "If she say she'll help you, then she will help you. Her knowing everything will help us plan our getaway, and I think we should talk to my sister, Queenie, too. She'll be a big help."

"But Miss Lori! She'll come after us, and it won't be pretty."

"Let me worry about what Lori will or won't do," Henry Lloyd said quietly, angrily. "Right now we gonna get you to your room. Then I want you to come to me over on the family side of the house and tell Miss Essie and Queenie what you told me. Then we gonna find some place to hide you 'til we get out of here. Let's see, where can we meet?"

"I been meeting Miss Essie in the kitchen," Nettie said. "I could wait for y'all there."

"Good, that's what we'll do," Henry Lloyd said, helping her to her feet, "I'll come get you, and we'll find some place to talk so we can decide and do what needs to be done."

"Oh, mister! I-I am so grateful, so thankful. I can never repay..."

"My name is Henry Lloyd," he said gently, carefully cupping her face with his hands, "and I ain't asking you to repay me, hear? All right," he said when she nodded. "Wipe your eyes and laugh and smile like you havin' the best time ever." Tucking her arm into his, they headed for the noisy, crowded drawing room on the boarder's side of the house.

"Silk, are you lettin' this gal claim all your attention again?" Bertha asked with a sly smile as she strode up. "She just now feeling well enough to mingle, and here she go taking up all of your time again. We gonna have to teach her how to share." Now that he was aware of what was happening, the menace in the big woman's voice was unmistakable.

"No such thing," Henry Lloyd said easily. "I ain't seen Baby Doll in a few days, and when she told me she fell down the steps, I had her sit down, and we got to talkin' and time got away from us. Something wrong with that, Bertha?"

"No, of course not, Silk," Bertha said with a laugh, "I don't blame you. A lot of men like her company. She good at making them feel wanted." Nettie flushed miserably.

"She cain't help it if she got the sweetest face most men including myself have ever seen," Henry Lloyd stated, "I jes' count my blessings when I see her first, so's I can spend some time with her. Now, I'm jes' seein' her to her room, seeing as how she still getting' over that nasty fall."

"Well, that's certainly kind of you, Slim," Bertha said. "Good night, Baby Doll. Have a good rest. We'll look forward to seeing you tomorrow." They both watched her climb up the staircase and disappear around the corner at the top of the landing.

"Well, should we go say good night to everyone else?" Bertha said, "It's about time for our boarders to get some rest." They both turned, headed for the noisy drawing room, Bertha trailing behind a rapidly striding Henry Lloyd.

*   *   *

"You sure nobody saw you?" Henry Lloyd whispered when Nettie came out from behind the pantry curtains where she had been hiding.

"No, I was careful. I jammed the chair under the doorknob and pushed the chest of drawers in front of it. Then I came down the tree outside my window. I didn't have to hide once."

"Good. Follow me, we're goin' to Miss Essie's room. She and Queenie are waiting for us there."

"Maybe if you was to jes' let me get away," Nettie suggested tentatively.

"No, we need they help, and they will both be happy to do so," Henry Lloyd assured her. "They don't judge and don't forget Queenie is a healer. Now, we got to move before we get caught."

*   *   *

"...and I don't like it at all," the voice was angry, frustrated. "Every time I look up that gal is sitting under him. I don't want or need for her to start running her mouth."

Henry Lloyd sat up straighter from his position among the branches of the thick bushes where he had been hiding for hours after unlocking and opening the window of his aunt's office. Voices carried clearly through the small gap.

"I don't like it either, ma'am, but what could I do?" Bertha asked. "Forbid him from talking to her? You know I couldn't.

Forbid her? She can't make him leave if he's not inclined. Beating her and starving her ain't come close to breaking her."

"This is one aggravation I don't need, especially with Queenie talkin' about going back home when school lets out, right after graduation. I thought I would have at least the summer to keep working on Slim and getting bids ready on Queenie. White men will go crazy putting up big money to be her first. They'll pay top dollar for her even after that cherry gets busted. She won't remember much once we share our 'farewell' drink. By the time she comes to herself, it will be much too late. Then maybe she'll listen to reason; but if push comes to shove, we might have to encourage her into getting into the 'habit' of something."

"That's one way of getting her to do anything you tell her, but men we cater to tend to dislike screwing junkies. They give them the willies, plus they don't last long once they get hooked."

"You are right," Loretta said with a sigh. "We'll worry about all that later, but the first thing we must do is keep her here."

"I think that's where the farewell drink comes in," Bertha said with a laugh. "Followed by a long time spent in the room. But what about Slim? He sure to notice something's wrong, especially if Queenie comes up missing."

"I'm gonna put two or three of my best boarders on him," Loretta said. "They will turn him out so, the poor boy won't know if he's comin' or goin'! By the time they let him up for air, he'll be saying, 'Queenie who?'" They laughed. Then, sobering, Bertha asked, "What do you want me to do about Baby Doll?"

"We've given her enough chances to behave. I'm done. She's got to have a terrible accident of some sort real soon. We should have gotten rid of her when she damn near bit that man's dick off when he tried to make her give him a blow job. The only thing that saved her was he hadn't paid for one and he knew it, so what could he say? Even so, I don't know that his ding-a-ling ever worked right again. He sure never came back." Both women laughed.

"You sure that's what you want to do? Get rid of her? Them big, brown eyes of hers bring in a lot of money," Bertha said.

"How you know so much about her big, brown eyes?" Loretta demanded. "What you doin' even lookin' at them?"

"Oh, baby, you know it's just business. The only eyes I really see are yours," Bertha said throatily.

"See that it stays that way."

"You ain't never got to worry about that, sweetheart," Bertha said huskily.

Conversation was replaced by murmurs ending in gasping cries. A short time later, renewing their discussion on ways to bring the house back under an iron rule, they dressed and exited. When he was certain they would not be coming back, Henry Lloyd stood, slid the window open and climbed in, pausing to listen carefully. Moving silently, he crossed to where overstuffed chairs and a coffee table covered a thick plush rug, pushing the furniture out of the way and lifting the rug to expose a narrow door built into the floor. Grasping the iron ring in the center he pulled it open, peering down into the opening. Money was the first thing he saw, stack and stacks of it on several rows of shelves built into the earthen walls. A gun on a shelf by itself, deadly, black, and lethal gleamed in the dim light. Henry Lloyd picked it up, tucking it into the front of his trousers. He ignored the jewelry and bolts of pink silk, looking for and finally finding what he had come for: a set of four accounting ledgers. Flipping through one he nodded in satisfaction, grabbing several bundles of cash on his way out, taking great care to return everything covering the door back to the way it was. With any luck it would be days before it was opened again. Exiting through the window, he pushed it closed until he heard the lock catch. Gathering up the things he had collected, he hurried to where Essie, Queenie, and Baby Doll awaited. After he handed over what Queenie had sent him to find, he needed to have a serious discussion with someone.

*   *   *

"...I had just been let out of the room and sent to accept customers again...I was trying to stay out of the way, hoping no one would notice me when...your brother found me and talked me into telling my story and coming with him..." Nettie's voice trailed off.

"I'm glad you came," Queenie said, reaching over and grasping one of the trembling girl's hands, stroking it gently. "What is your name?" she asked. "You deserve to be called by your name."

"My folks named me Nettie," she said softly. "Nettie Jamison."

"Nettie Jamison, ain't that a nice name," Essie said with a smile. "Now we all know what to call you."

"I-I don't think my people would want me to keep using their name," Nettie said, her eyes bright with tears, "seeing as how I done shamed it so."

Sitting down beside her, Essie put a comforting arm around her shoulders. "Chile, you ain't got nothing to be ashamed of. Running away from home may not have been the best thing, but a lot of women leave home to find a better life. You thought you were going to do honest work. That you were tricked and hoodwinked and something precious taken away from you without your agreeing to it, well, that's just awful, but not your fault. For Loretta to live like this on the backs of poor, innocent scared girls make me want to beat *her* ass."

"Are there others here that are like you?" Jenna asked. "Girls forced to entertain men? Locked up and beaten?"

Nettie nodded, "At least two that I know of," she said. "There was another, but she left, and Bertha told us she had gone off to greener pastures...I don't know if I believe that."

"The ocean is a mighty big dumping ground," Jenna said.

"Lawd, Lawd," Essie said, shaking her head, "talk about meeting the devil in a pink dress! We surely done that, and we living in her house."

"With her mean old demon disciple in big, black, rubber soled shoes," Jenna added.

"So, how we going to get out of here without us ending up in the ocean?" Essie asked, hugging Nettie reassuringly when she gasped, shaking with fear.

"These are going to be our ticket out of here," Jenna said, holding up the ledgers Henry Lloyd had delivered before disappearing. "They spell out in detail how much money Loretta brings in, who she pays off, who the girls are, liquor sales, purchases, client list, everything. I would be willing to bet she has never paid taxes – not to mention everything she is doing is against the law. If the right people get a hold of this information, Loretta will be going to jail for a long time. Once she knows we have the ledgers, she will be ready to negotiate – anything to keep that information from leaking. So, we are going to hide them. And we are going to make at least three copies of everything and mail them to ourselves in South Carolina. We will keep them all in a different safe place, then let her know we have them, so she will be too scared to ever try anything."

"And she honestly thought she was going to make me a part of it? To make money for her?" Jenna said grimly. "Now, here is what we are going to do..." Heads together they listened closely as Jenna spoke, nodding in agreement as she finished.

Chapter Fourteen

"Miss Lori, please forgive me for interrupting your breakfast and family time, but I need to talk with you about something very important." Bertha, looking more flustered than Jenna and Essie had ever seen her, stood in the dining room doorway.

"What's wrong?" Loretta asked sharply. "Has something happened?"

Bertha nodded. Standing abruptly Loretta said, "If you will excuse me."

Still seated at the table, Jenna, Essie, and Henry Lloyd all heard Bertha's voice rumbling and Loretta's muffled exclamation. Moments later she came rapidly through the door.

"Baby, is something wrong?" Essie asked, "You actin' like the house 'bout to cave in or something." She had had her first experience with earth tremors and had absolutely no desire to experience any more.

"No, nothing like that," Loretta said. "It seems one of my boarders...left during the night, uh...owing me money. That's bad enough, but Boots is nowhere to be found, either."

"Boots is gone, too?" Essie said. "You think they run off together?"

Bertha and Loretta exchanged a startled glance; it was obvious the thought had never occurred to either one. "I-I don't know," Loretta said. "I don't think so, but anything is possible. I should go on the boarder's side to see if either one stole anything. I'll see you all later." She and Bertha hurried out of the room.

The three at the table continued eating in unbroken silence. Henry Lloyd rose silently and crept to the open doorway peering out cautiously. He straightened, stepping into the hallway, motioning for them to follow him through a maze of back entrances and sets of stairs; his many trysts with the boarders had provided him an intimate knowledge of its many intricacies. Reaching a closed door, he knocked before turning the knob and opening. Nettie stood as they entered, a black cartridge ink pen in one hand. Neatly stacked piles of paper took up most of the space on the small cot, a chair and nightstand the only other furniture in the room.

"Hey, Miss Essie, Miss Queenie," Nettie said respectfully, bobbing her head.

"You been using that salve on your bruises I made up for you," Jenna said, nodding in satisfaction, "I can tell. You just keep using it like I told you, hear?"

"I will," Nettie promised.

Call me Queenie or Jenna, all right? We are close to the same age, so no need to call me miss or ma'am or anything like that."

"All right," Nettie agreed shyly.

"You look like you been busy," Essie said, gesturing. "Look at all this."

"How many copies have you made?" Jenna asked, picking up and rifling through one pile of neatly handwritten sheets.

"I finished the three you asked me to, plus what I copied into the empty ledgers that you gave me," Nettie said. "I've always been able to write fast."

"Excellent!" Jenna said with a smile. "Now, Henry Lloyd, put these copies of the ledgers back where you got these. We will keep the originals. Hopefully you can get them back before the witches notice they are gone." Taking the ledgers she handed him, Henry Lloyd left, saying he would be right back to help Jenna and Essie find their way to their rooms and promising Nettie he would make certain she was safe.

"Graduation is this Friday," Jenna said. "I think we should plan on leaving graduation night. We will already have our tickets, and Henry Lloyd will have taken our suitcases to the train station. It is good Loretta lets him use the car whenever he wants, so we will not need to come back here after the ceremony. We will tell them about the ledgers just before we leave for Bayside, so they are going to be really angry. When they find out we have kept the originals and there are even more copies...I wonder what did happen to Boots?"

"He and I had a little talk. He decided to search for greener pastures," Henry Lloyd said, coming through the door. Essie, Jenna, and Nettie all turned in his direction. "You and Boots had a talk?" Jenna repeated. Henry Lloyd nodded.

Diligent searching had finally run Boots to ground as he was coming back from the beach, his form-fitting t-shirt dripping wet, using a towel to dry his hair. "Hey man, I been looking for you," Henry Lloyd said easily. "Thought we could talk for a bit."

"'Bout what?" the big man asked in his deep, raspy voice.

"'Bout choosin' the wrong side in what's comin' or deciding to jes' walk away," Henry Lloyd said. "How long you been working for Lori?"

"Ever since she bailed me out of jail three years ago," Boots said. "They was goin' to keep me there for a long time for fightin'. I messed somebody up pretty bad when I was drunk. She came to the jail, said she was looking for an enforcer, paid my bail, and brought me here."

"When did you know you were workin' in a cathouse?" Henry Lloyd asked.

"Miss Lori let me know from the very beginning. She never did pretend it was a boarding house to me. All them different men coming in and out, with some women entertaining four or five of them a night made it pretty plain what was going on."

"Did you help kidnap and break girls in, too?"

"Some, but I never did cotton to that. Them that choose to be hookers on they own, I figure that's they business, but tellin' lies to young girls to get them here and then forcin' them to turn tricks don't set well with me. I been wit' Miss Lori when she go to the train station to pick up gals fresh from the country. I help in keeping them from running away, and I carry them to the room down in the cellar after they drink Miss Lori's knockout farewell drink knowing that they gonna get a long train run on them; but I ain't never raped or forced no woman to do nothin' she didn' want to do."

"Seems to me you jes' sit back watchin' and doin' like you told," Henry Lloyd said. "But you ain't going to be able to sit back much longer. 'Cause if you keep on doin' like you told by the wrong people like you been doing, I'm gonna have to kill you." There was no doubting his matter-of-fact statement. Boots' bloodshot eyes flew to Henry Lloyd's; his body tensed, poised for battle.

"You know I'm a country boy," Henry Lloyd continued conversationally. "A lot of city boys like you might not know what that means. I learned to shoot just about around the same time I learned how to walk. We have big families in the country, so we eat 'bout near anything we can catch for free: coon, possum, squirrel, rabbit. One thing all them critters have in common is that they little and fast. So, to put food on the table, you gotta hit something small movin' real fast. Telling you I'm the best shot in at least three counties pretty much says it all. Us country boys tend to be handy with a knife, too…I've had this one here," retrieving his prized Bowie knife from somewhere on his person, "ever since I saved enough money to buy it seven years ago…" He easily flipped the huge blade by its hilt from one hand to the other; Boots' eyes widened. "I've gotten pretty good using it." They strode along in silence for a time, Henry Lloyd slipping his knife back into its hidden sheath.

"Now, I really don't want to kill you," Henry Lloyd said reasonably, "but I'm taking Queenie, Essie, and anyone else who wants to leave out of here, and I'm not goin' to let anybody stop me. I'm givin' you this one chance…leave here, start somewhere fresh where don't nobody know you – with some money to help get you started. Leave before the craziness starts…and I'm sorry to rush you, but you got to decide now."

After a brief, tense silence Boots gave in with a short bark of a laugh. "I've always wanted to see what the rest of California looks like. Hell, I might even go to Vegas," he said. "I sure ain't got no special feeling or loyalty for Miss Lori. To be honest wit' you, I'll be glad to get away from that evil place. Can I get my clothes?" he asked, looking down at himself. "Swimming trunks are liable to get kinda cold once the sun goes down."

"If you'll look behind that tree," Henry Lloyd said, pointing, "you'll find everything that belongs to you in them two suitcases. They's Loretta's, but she got so many she won't even know those are gone; and here's the money I promised," handing him one of the stacks he had taken from Loretta's safe. "Now, you best be on your way…good luck, man."

"Thanks man, you, too," Boots said, his appreciative eye taking in the impressive height of the stack of bills now in his possession. "Miss Lori gonna learn the hard way what a mistake it was to even think about forcing Miss Queenie into the life and thinkin' you'd go along with it, ain't she?"

"She really think throwing some hair pie at me is going to make me sell Queenie down the river? Give up my sister to that life? Ain't that much pussy in the world. Then forcing innocent girls lookin' for a better way into such an awful life... keeping them locked up servicing strange men while she makes more money than she can spend. When we do leave, Loretta's life won't ever be the same. That I promise you."

"I wish you luck, man," Boots said, heading for the tree to retrieve his belongings. "But I don't think you gonna need it." Henry Lloyd watched him pick up the suitcases and stride away.

"I guess he believed you really would kill him," Essie said.

"It's a good thing, too, because he would have," Jenna stated positively.

"Henry Lloyd, I thought the sight of blood made you sick," Essie said. "I seem to remember faintin' and such when hog butcherin' time come 'round."

"I'd have to wait until after he was dead and everyone was safe and away from here before I could even think about getting sick," Henry Lloyd stated. "Queenie knows, I wouldn't have wanted to, I wouldn't have liked it, but I'da done it. Boots knew that and knew he couldn't outdraw or outshoot me. His switchblade looked like a butter knife next to mine. He knew that he would be dead before he could reach for any type of weapon. Deciding Loretta wasn't worth it, he took the money and left for parts unknown."

"One less thing to worry about," Jenna said. "Henry Lloyd, you need to take us back to our rooms. I do have school tomorrow." She and her friends were planning a senior ditch day. Essie was going to fry a chicken and make a potato salad which was going to be her contribution to the picnic they had been planning since shortly after her arrival. They were going to spend the day at the beach culminating in a bonfire attended by most of the senior class.

"I still have to fry the chicken and make potato salad," Essie said, headed for the door, "Nettie, you get you some rest, hear?

Don't look like anybody comes up here; the dust all over the place proves that. Even though it ain't the most comfortable, you should be safe for the next few days. Be sure to lock the door."

"This is jes' fine, Miss Essie," Nettie said. "There ain't no where I'd rather be. A little dust never hurt nobody."

"I brought you some books and magazines to pass the time," Jenna said. "Henry Lloyd will bring you food and clothes and make sure you are all right. We probably will not see you for a couple of days and risk being found out, but we will be back to take you with us to graduation. After that it is to the train station and as far away from this house of ill repute as a train can carry us."

"I cain't never thank y'all enough. You all were God's answer to my prayers," Nettie said brokenly.

"You are so very welcome," Essie said, wrapping an arm around her. "After we leave here and you have some time to think, you can decide what you want to do: explore the world some more – older and considerably wiser – or you can come to South Carolina and live with me. I'd be proud to have you. Like I said, think about it and let me know what you decide."

Nettie nodded, her eyes glistening with grateful tears, her arms full of books, sitting in the chair and placing the books and magazines on the small nightstand, eagerly looking through her many choices for something to read to pass the time. The door closed softly behind Henry Lloyd, Jenna, and Essie as they quietly and carefully made their way back to the family section of the big residence.

Henry Lloyd continued to his room located closer to the boarding section as Essie and Jenna climbed the main staircase leading to their bedrooms. Once in her sitting room Jenna hurried over to where she had hidden the bicycle chain she used to secure the doors leading into her suite. Reaching into the urn, her hand encountered…nothing. Tilting it, peering down into the darkness, she could see the chain was gone. Moving over to the light switch, she flipped it off, looking as she did every night for light shining from suspicious holes cut in the wall. There were none. "I guess either they did not think about it, or they never had a chance to make any thanks to Essie coming in here and staying all day, every day."

Turning the light back on she walked over to the sofa, picking up and unzipping one of the cushions, pulling out a towel-wrapped plastic-coated bicycle chain. Zipping the cushion back up and returning it to the sofa, Jenna gathered the chain and moved over to the doors, wrapping it snugly and snapping it closed with the attached combination lock. She then grabbed the basket of rocks and slid it into its usual place under the door before going into the bedroom and closing that door, pushing the bench and the chair into their usual positions for the night. Shortly thereafter came the faint sound of water running into the tub. One of the handles on the double doors leading into the suite turned, there was a faint rattling sound, a thump, the other knob turned, more rattling, silence, and then the faint sound of footsteps moving away.

"What do you mean you can't get in? I thought you took away that chain she was using to lock the doors," Loretta pulled deeply on the cigarette jammed into her fancy holder, blowing a thick cloud of smoke out of her nostrils and mouth, pacing nervously.

"I did," Bertha said, holding up the blue plastic-wrapped bicycle chain, "and this is the rope that she was using first," holding it up as well. "She must have bought a lot of them chain locks and got them hid all over."

"That uppity little bitch is getting on my nerves," Loretta said angrily, taking another long pull on her cigarette. "She act

163

like butter wouldn't melt in her mouth, going around thinking she outsmarting us."

"She is so far," Bertha said. "She and that country bumpkin she brought with her. I can't search nearly like I want to with her sitting up in the room all day, every day."

"Things are getting out of control around here," Loretta said tightly. "First, that other gal disappears from a locked room, then Boots comes up missing, too. Do you really think they ran off together? That would explain how she got out."

"I don't know. He ain't never showed no interest in the broke-in girls, and as far as I know the two of them ain't never even talked," Bertha said.

"I called the Police Chief. He's got some of his men looking for them both – together and by themselves – but I haven't heard anything yet," Loretta said. "Queenie graduates Friday. We need everything in place by then. I want to get her alone to share the drink with her. I guess you gonna help me carry her down to the room since Boots isn't here to do it, and we know Henry Lloyd won't do it. I haven't been able to stir up the interest I wanted to, with her keeping her rooms shut up tight. There hasn't been a chance to drill the holes that would allow would-be customers to look at and bid on the merchandise. She's gone bring in top dollar, but they need to see what they're getting. I wanted their first look at her to be when she doesn't know she's being looked at."

"What if we take some Polaroids, so they get a look at her on her way to or from a swim?" Bertha suggested. "That way they'll be seeing her in as little as possible. She won't know it, and the bids will go way up."

"Now, that's a good idea," Loretta said. "We'll take them from the boarder's side of the patio where there's a clear view of the path leading to the beach."

"What we gone do about someone taking Boots' place?" Bertha asked. "Men get rambunctious without another man there to keep them in order...well, it could get ugly. I don't suppose Slim could do it, could he?"

"No, I don't want him doing strongarm stuff," Loretta said. "If he's got to discipline some rowdy man, I want him to just shoot him; but he's not ready for that yet. He's still too nice."

"Yeah," Bertha agreed, "the way he cooed over Baby Doll is proof of that. If I didn't know better I'da thought he had something to do with her disappearing, but he seemed as surprised as everybody else, and he ain't behaved no different than he normally does. He does ask about her, not as much since it look like she ran off with Boots."

"Maybe that'll toughen him up. Show him that women can't be trusted. I wish we could do something to make him turn against Queenie," Loretta said, "but I don't think there's anything that could make him do that."

"Naw, he crazy 'bout his sister," Bertha agreed. "Maybe we can make him think she ran off with a white man?" she suggested.

"That might work," Loretta said. "He'll think he's twice betrayed. That just might be an idea we can work with..."

* * *

"This fried chicken and potato salad is...a dream..." Doris said, biting into a golden-brown, crispy leg, scooping up a forkful of potato salad, pulling off a piece of bread.

"I love it," Julie agreed, "I've never had anything like it," placing a chicken thigh between two slices of bread savoring the crunch. "Jenna, you and your chaperone, or nanny, or cousin, or friend, or whatever she is," Jenna had described Essie as one or other at one time or another, "should stay here and open a food

165

stand on the boardwalk. You would do so swell! People would line up for your Southern food."

"You could serve caramel cake and peach cobbler and red velvet cake and greens…" Angela agreed. "All the good things my folks only fix at holiday time."

"Then you could stay in San Francisco and not have to move back East," Susan said eagerly.

"And you wouldn't break up the League," Maria said.

"What about nursing school?" Jenna asked. "Aren't you all going to college?"

"I'm not," Maria said. "*Mi familia* – my family – cannot afford it. After graduation, I'll be working in the family bodega as a waitress, clerk, and bookkeeper until I get married. Then I'll start having babies."

"I will be headed for Berkeley come fall," Susan said. "Since I plan on becoming a lawyer, I'll be majoring in Political Science with an emphasis on human rights."

"Human rights are the reason I'm headed to Central America to work in the Peace Corps," Angela said, "Nicaragua, to be exact, for at least one year, maybe two. Then I'm off to a colored college somewhere in the South to fight for human rights right here in this country."

"I'm headed for the American Jewish University in Los Angeles," Doris said, "to meet a nice Jewish boy, hopefully a doctor, and get married: my mother's words, not mine."

"I guess we are all headed in different directions," Julie said. "I am off to Harvard: my folks dearest wish, not mine. Well, if running a food stand is out, can you at least stay through part of the summer? Have some fun before fall?"

"I cannot" Jenna said regretfully. "I made plans that really can't be changed," thinking of graduation night, "but let us make a pact to keep in touch with a firm commitment to meet in person here in San Francisco no matter where we are or what we are doing in ten years' time."

"I am in," Maria said, extending her hand, "ten years."

"Ten years," Angela said, placing hers on top.

"Ten years," Susan said, "no matter what."

"In ten years," Doris said, adding her hand to the stack.

"Ten years it is," Julie said.

"Ten years from today, here in San Francisco," Jenna said solemnly, "The League will reunite."

"To the reunion," they all said individually, and then in unison, glasses of water or soft drink or iced tea raised, "To the reunion!"

*   *   *

"Queenie, I just can't believe that you've been here the better part of a year, yet we ended up spending so little time together," Loretta said, after knocking lightly and coming into Jenna's sitting room at her invitation. "Now you tell me you won't even be here for the summer. I had so many things planned; I am so disappointed."

I'll bet you are, Jenna thought. Aloud she said, "Time really did fly, did it not? I wish I could stay longer, but I need to get back to my healer training. I only have this summer if I go to nursing school this fall."

"Well, before you leave could we share a farewell drink, just the two of us?" Loretta asked coaxingly. "It'll be some time before we see each other again, so I think we should have some just-the-two-of-us time together." She pulled her fancy pink satin robe with a feather boa closer around her. "We could even wear our nighties, almost like a slumber party. Do you want to? It'll be fun."

Jenna regarded her treacherous false aunt in silence for a moment. *Beware the drink from she who wears pink*...her scalp prickled as Sidney's warning sounded in her mind. One sip of that drink and she would wake up days later in that horrific room Nettie had told them about. "Sure, that sounds like fun," she said. "We will be here until a week or so after graduation," she lied, "so maybe the night before we decide to leave would be nice."

"Let's plan on it," Loretta said, looking around, "You got everything you need for Friday?"

"I do," Jenna said, "I picked up my cap and gown today. Miss Essie has offered to press it for me. Bless her! I have already mailed my graduation pictures home and to Sugar in Detroit, so I'm good."

"Well, all right then. Be sure to let me know if there's anything you need. I'll look forward to that drink next week."

"Not as much as I," Jenna said sweetly, watching her aunt walk through the double doors and go rapidly down the staircase at the bottom turning toward the boarding side of the house. "She is gone," she called out, eyeing Essie as she came out of the bedroom. "You heard?" she asked.

"I did," Essie said, "I guess that's the drink Nettie was talking about, the one where you wake up days later being with a strange man."

"Who is just one of many," Jenna said.

"I think I need to start sleeping in here until we leave," Essie said, coming to a decision. "I would feel better, and they cain't do much with me laying right here."

"Good idea," Jenna said with relief. "I will feel a lot better with you here, too."

"I'll be right back." Essie returned a short time later, washed and dressed for bed, carrying a blanket and pillow with her that she arranged comfortably on the sofa. "Good night, Queenie," she said, rolling into a comfortable position. Tie up your doors, and I'll see you in the morning."

Jenna did as she was told, placing the basket of rocks against the closed doors, closing her door after a whispered goodnight, the sound of furniture being moved and the faint sound of running water. Shortly afterwards the light in the bedroom switched off, silence descended.

Friday could not come soon enough.

Chapter Fifteen

"Queenie – telephone – it's your mother," Loretta called up the stairs.

Jenna came clambering down the steps, eagerly reaching for the phone, "Hey, Ma'dear," she said happily, excitedly, "is it not a wonderful day?"

"It sure is, baby," Albertina said proudly. "My chile about to graduate from high school – the first one in our family. And with highest honors! I am so proud. I'm bettin' this letter sitting here for you from Grayson School of Nursing in Birmingham is telling you they'll see you in September."

"The letter is there?" Jenna said excitedly. "Oh, I can hardly wait to get home! I have so much to tell you."

"I'm looking forward to hearing everything in person, we all are," Albertina said. "Sidney can hardly contain himself. I love you, honey. Congratulations on your graduation day. We'll see you soon."

"Bye, Ma'dear," Jenna said brightly. "I will be seeing all of you really soon." She hung up smiling.

Skipping into the dining room she halted abruptly, then ran forward laughing with delight at the huge helium balloons, two of them spelling out the word "Congratulations," another the word "Graduate" tied to her chair at the table. Her smile grew even wider at seeing the gaily wrapped packages on her placemat. "For me?" she said delightedly, ripping the paper away.

She opened the present from Essie first, inhaling in delight, gently stroking the two petal-soft white woolen sweaters with tiny pearl buttons down the front. "Oh, Essie, they are beautiful!" she exclaimed.

"Look underneath them," Essie said. Obediently lifting a corner of the bottom sweater Jenna saw several pairs of white stockings. "Oh, my goodness, thank you so much," racing around the table to give her a huge hug.

"For you at nursing school," Essie said with a smile returning the hug.

"They are perfect," Jenna said eyes shining. She picked up the small package from Henry Lloyd. "Now, what could this be?" she asked, eagerly ripping off ribbons and tearing away gift wrapping paper, slowly opening the small, velvet-lined jewelry box. "Oh, Henry Lloyd, it is so beautiful," she breathed, lifting the sparkling diamond-cut golden cross carefully by its slender golden chain. "Here, put it on me now," she said, lifting her cloud of hair while her brother fastened the clasp, rushing over to a large mirror to admire it. "I will never take it off," she said fingering it gently.

"What a perfect start to the day," she said smiling, spreading butter and grape jelly on a slice of toast and biting into it, pouring herself a cup of coffee with lots of cream and several sugars. Henry Lloyd often laughingly asking her if she'd like a little coffee with her cream and sugar.

"So, what are you going to do on your last day as a high school student?" Loretta asked. "Spend it at the beach? Relaxing and getting ready for tonight?" Which would provide the perfect opportunity to take some Polaroids.

"No, my eyes get red from the salt water," Jenna said. "Essie is going to help me with my hair and help me get dressed. Other than that, I think I will read and just lounge around until it is time to get ready."

"Sounds like a good way to get ready for the excitement of tonight," Henry Lloyd said. "I'll be proud to see you walking across the stage, but in the meantime, I got a little running around I need to do, so I'll see y'all later." Suiting action to words Henry Lloyd rose and strode out of the room.

"And I," Essie said standing, "am headed for the kitchen. I'm going to make Queenie all her favorites for dinner: fried chicken, macaroni and cheese, candied yams, green beans, potato salad, carrot casserole, sliced tomatoes, rolls, caramel cake and peach cobbler, and anything else I think of and got time to make. So, I'll see y'all later too," strolling out of the room and heading for the kitchen. What she did not add was that she planned to cook enough to sustain them on the first leg of their journey home.

"Queenie," Loretta said, as Jenna stood on her way to her room, "I have something for your graduation day, but I wanted to wait until later to give it to you, maybe on the night of our little slumber party?"

"Oh, that is fine, Loretta," Jenna said. "That gives me something else to look forward to." She left the room immensely thankful that she would not be spending another night in her horrible aunt's horrible house.

"Miss Essie, that dinner was sublime. Thank you so much for making it for me – all my favorite foods." Jenna sat back with a satisfied sigh.

"It sure was good, Miss Essie," Henry Lloyd agreed. "I ate 'til I couldn't hold no more. So, I put me together a plate to take to my room to enjoy later." He stood. "I'm headed to my room to get ready for tonight. I'll meet y'all in the living room when you ready to go." He sauntered out of the room, the laden plate for Nettie in one hand.

"I am going to take a leisurely bath and then take my time getting dressed," Jenna announced.

"What are you wearing tonight?" Essie wanted to know.

"I am wearing that yellow flowered dress with the white collar and the yellow sweater Loretta bought me," Jenna said. "I have been saving it all of this time to wear tonight. I bought a yellow headband and a pair of yellow heels to match it."

"Girl, you gonna be sharp as a tack," Essie said admiringly. "I'll be in to help you as soon as you finish your bath."

* * *

"Jenna, you look beautiful," Essie said. "That yellow is perfect."

"Thank you, Miss Essie," Jenna said with a smile. Taking a deep breath, smoothing her skirt, she looked over at the woman who had stood staunchly by her side through all the past difficult months. "Ready?" she asked.

"Oh, yes, ma'am," Essie said, patting her purse.

"Let's do this," Jenna said, walking toward the living room where she had asked her aunt to meet her.

"You wanted to see me, Queenie?" Loretta asked. "I don't have much time. I'm short of help on the boarder's side, so I need to get back. That's why I can't go to your graduation."

"I will not keep you long," Jenna said pleasantly. Hearing footsteps approaching, she said, "Loretta, have you met my friend? Her name is Nettie. She is going to attend my graduation, and then she and I and Essie and anybody else who wants to will be leaving, headed for the train station. I know what you have been doing, what you were planning to do to me, what you are running here, and it stops now. Tonight."

Loretta opened her gold cigarette case, extracting a cigarette and fitting it into the holder. Pulling out a gold lighter she lit the tip, drawing the smoke deep into her lungs. Her eyes grew cold, narrowing as Nettie, accompanied by Henry Lloyd came into the room. Nettie was wearing a full skirt of pearl gray, white shirt, gray sweater, white socks, and black patent leather ballerina shoes. Her hair was caught up in a ponytail. "Gal, I don't know what you told these folks, but you owe me money and you trying to leave here without paying it."

Henry Lloyd reached into the inner pocket of his sport jacket, extracting a sizable wad of bills. "This should cover everything."

Loretta's eyes shifted to his. "I am hurt, Henry Lloyd, I truly am. That you could think that I am guilty of the things you are accusing me of just breaks my heart, it truly does. This gal," her tone shifting, pointing to Nettie, "is a known liar and troublemaker, and you can't believe anything she says."

"What about Honey Bun and Sweet Treat? Or Ginger Snap or Cookie?" Jenna asked. "The stories they tell are nearly the same."

"It's their word against mine. If you tell anybody any of this, I'll swear you ain't nothing but a lowdown, ungrateful liar," Loretta said viciously, "biting the hand that fed you, that gave you refuge when you needed it, that treated you like a daughter, and you Henry Lloyd like a son." Her eyes flickered to where Bertha was making a silent advance, wicked looking knife in one hand, hypodermic needle in the other. The distinct sound of a gun being cocked echoed through the room.

"I would stop right there if I was you," Essie said, coming through the wide doorway, competently holding the .45 in both hands. Bertha froze. "You know," Essie continued conversationally, "the only person that can outshoot a country boy… is a country girl. Drop what you have in your hands," Bertha hastened to comply. "Now, you go stand over there."

"Well, Mama," Jenna said ironically, "listen carefully. I said this ends now, tonight, and let me tell you why. Better yet, let me show you." Reaching down into a carryall she had with her,

Loretta gasped when she recognized what Jenna held in her hands. "I think these belong to you," Jenna said holding up the ledgers. "They contain all the proof needed to document what is going on around here. The police on your payroll, including the Police Chief, your client list which has some names on it that I am sure their owners would not want made public, bootleg liquor sales, the number of girls working for you, what you pay them – and that's just some of the interesting information in here."

"Who are you going to tell?" Loretta asked. "The police work for me. So do the judges and prosecutors around here."

"Oh, I was not thinking of sending it to them. Not at first, anyway," Jenna said. "I think the first people I would send it to would be the *Afro-American, The Black Herald, Colored Magnificence Magazine* and the *San Francisco Chronicle*. They would love to get hold of something like this, and we have plenty of copies. And I know the IRS – the Internal Revenue Service - would love to make certain you are paying your fair share of income taxes."

Loretta's eyes widened in horror. Her name in the colored community would be ruined, tarnished beyond repair, and she could well be looking at a jail sentence. Her jaw tightened, her eyes burning with hatred. "What's it going to take to keep you from doing that?" she asked bitterly, defeated.

"You let anyone who wants to go leave, you do not go after them or threaten them in any way, and you leave me and mine alone. Do not try to get even, do not even think about it, or you will regret it. We mailed copies to be kept by people we trust and that will go to the proper authorities if anything should happen to us. And one more thing: Do not plan on coming back to South Carolina. Ever."

Loretta stared into Jenna's eyes for one angry moment before nodding abruptly and looking away. "Now, I need the two of you to go sit on that sofa," Jenna said. "We are going to borrow your car to take us to graduation, and then the train station. You can arrange to pick it up there. Goodbye, Loretta, and with any luck I will never see or hear anything about you ever again."

"I cain't say as how I had a great time while I was here," Essie said doubtfully. "It has certainly been interesting, but I must say I'm glad to go home, and I'm just as glad as Queenie that I never have to have anything to do with you ever again." She stood holding the gun waiting until Jenna, Henry Lloyd and Nettie exited before backing away, turning and hurrying out the door. The sound of the car could be heard roaring down the driveway.

Upstairs in the boarding room section of the house, burning candles behind closed doors and locked rooms melted steadily, shimmering pools of liquor all around.

"Our Salutatorian tonight is a recent arrival to the Senior Class and Bayside High, but her talent cannot be denied. Let us give a hand to Miss Jenna Thompson, Salutatorian of the Class of 1958."

Applause rang through the auditorium punctuated by screams of excitement from the League, shrill whistles from Henry Lloyd and yells of encouragement from Essie as Jenna crossed the stage to collect her award, and later when she crossed again to collect her diploma. The ceremony ended when tassels were solemnly transferred from one side of the mortarboard to the other. The graduates erupted in screams, whistles, and boisterous noise, tossing their tasseled hats high into the air.

Afterwards Jenna was at the center of an excited, chattering group. "Will you sign my yearbook?" a fellow senior asked Jenna. "Sure, but only if you sign mine," she said with a smile. That was the first of many. "Are you coming to the after parties?" Maria wanted to know. "We are having friends and family over to celebrate my graduation. Say you will come."

"Oh, Maria, I cannot," Jenna said regretfully. "My train leaves in two hours, but do not forget our pledge to meet again in ten years."

"I won't," Maria said, hugging her tightly. "I love you, and we will keep in touch."

"Definitely," Jenna said, "I love you, too."

* * *

"All aboard! Last call to Las Vegas, Salt Lake City, Boulder and Topeka," the conductor called. Leaning over he picked up the portable steps passengers used to climb aboard and disembark. The sound of steam released into the air was followed by train wheels slowly turning, picking up speed, rapidly leaving the station behind.

"We did it," Jenna said excitedly. "Loretta's house of horrors is no more. Three girls being held against their will board trains for destinations unknown with enough of a nest egg to allow them to live comfortably until they decide what to do. The other ones are free to regroup in another cathouse if they want, but that will take time. And money."

There was knock on their berth door. The conductor entered. "Evening folks. Tickets, please? Thank you very much, y'all have a nice evening," closing the door behind him.

"I'm gonna wander around a bit, see if the porters playin' cards. I'll be back in a little while," Henry Lloyd said, rising and opening the berth door, closing it firmly behind him.

"Well, baby, how you feel?" Essie asked, looking over at Nettie seated across from her. "You free of that place and can do anything you want. Have you thought about what you want to do?"

"Yes, ma'am," Nettie said shyly, eagerly, "if your invitation is still open, I would love to come live with you in South Carolina."

"Well, that just tickles me to death," Essie said with a pleased smile. "I'm happy to have you."

"Oh, Nettie, that is wonderful," Jenna said with a smile, "I am so happy for both of you."

"Anybody hungry?" Essie asked, reaching into a wicker basket, extracting a plate of fried chicken and a bowl of potato salad, passing around forks, plates, and napkins.

*   *   *

"The fire is out, ma'am, but there is extensive water and fire damage on the eastern side of your residence, with a preliminary investigation pointing to arson," the firefighter's shouts could be heard over the noise of sirens, firemen issuing instructions, and policemen on the scene keeping the crowd back. A small group of boarders stood nearby, most holding what they were able to grab before being hustled out the building.

"Arson?" Loretta repeated stiffly. "You mean someone did this on purpose? Trying to burn my house to the ground?"

"Yes, ma'am," a policeman busily scribbling in a small spiral notebook walked up. "Several doors on your second floor in the eastern wing had to be broken into. Firefighters and investigating police officers found the remains of primitive incendiary devices in the locked rooms."

"What—what did you call them? Some kind of devices?"

"Incendiary devices, ma'am, fire making instruments," the policeman holding the notebook and pencil said. "In this case, someone used candles and liquor to start the fire. When the candle burned down and the flame touched that liquor, it immediately sparked a blaze. With liquor poured all over, the room was engulfed in flames in no time. At least three or four rooms were sabotaged that way. We will know more as the investigation continues."

"Investigation?" Loretta said in alarm. "What investigation?"

"Well, ma'am, whenever there is a suspicious fire like this one, it has to be looked into," the officer said.

"What's to look into?" Loretta demanded. "Two or three unhappy boarders decided they were going to leave without paying, so they set the house afire. That's all there is to it. They are long gone with no way of tracking them, so what's the point?"

"But, ma'am, a crime has been committed," the officer said.

"Like I said, you'll never catch who did it, and I don't want my business all out in the street," Loretta said. "I will get in touch with your Chief and tell him I don't want this to go any further." She turned to the fire official who had been hovering while she was talking to the police officer. "Is there something you want?" she asked.

"The fire's out, ma'am," the fire fighter said. "It was a clear case of arson, but everyone seems to have gotten out safely and that is the most important thing. I will be filing a report in the next day or so if you want to turn it in for insurance purposes."

"Uh-huh, thank you, I'll remember that," Loretta said. Her insurance had always been the payoffs she made to the right law enforcement authorities and public officials, not some monthly premium. She watched as Bertha walked up.

"You all right, Boss Lady?" the big woman asked, looking her over.

"I'm fine," Loretta said. "I hear everyone got out all right."

"Yeah, most everybody was long gone by the time the fire started," Bertha said. "Them gals over there were the only ones here. It's a good thing you decided not to open tonight."

"Thank heaven for small favors," Loretta said ironically. "Have the firemen let you inside yet? Have you been able to get into the office?"

"Most of the damage happened in the upstairs section where the bedrooms are," Bertha said. "The office had a lot of smoke and some water damage, but nothing actually burned."

"Do we know what, if anything, they left? We know some major things they got away with. I'm sure they had something to do with Boots disappearing like that."

"I was only able to get a quick look," Bertha said, "police and firemen were all over the place. They left cash, your silks, your car ownership papers, the deed to the house, that sort of thing. Of course, the original ledgers, a lot of money, and the .45 were gone."

"Now we know where Essie got that gun she was waving around," Loretta said.

"So, you ain't going to do nothin' about this?" Bertha asked, looking around. "I heard you talking to the policeman."

"What can I do? They have the ledgers and more than one of them gals willing to testify about that room and the type of life we forced them into. I, for one, don't want to go to jail," Loretta said.

"So, what we gone do?" Bertha asked looking around.

"We are going to start over, somewhere else," Loretta said decisively, "out of San Francisco. Las Vegas might be nice, and prostitution is legal in Nevada. Or Los Angeles, maybe? Near Hollywood? I've always wanted to live in Southern California. Maybe we can get more of them Hollywood types to come see us at our new house, and it'll be even nicer than this one here."

"We got money to start," Bertha agreed. "You get what you can for this and use the money as a down payment on a new house. I bet we can get them gals over there to go with us, and we can be making money while we're working on getting a new house fixed up."

"With no relatives this time," Loretta said. "They are too expensive and worrisome. Although I do wish we could have convinced Henry Lloyd to stay. Oh, well, let's talk to these ladies about going with us. Then we'll go to my soggy office, have a drink, and start deciding our next move."

"Sounds like a plan, Boss Lady," Bertha said, putting her arm around Loretta's waist. The two women began walking over to the small group of boarders standing around. Once there they talked about their plans while firefighters continued to soak the burned section, and police on the scene continued gathering evidence.

*   *   *

"Next stop Kansas City," the conductor's voice rang out.

"There's where we change trains to Memphis and then Orangesburg," Essie said. "Albertina will have someone pick us up to drive us to Crawfish Holler, and we'll be home."

"How long will that take?" Nettie asked.

"I suppose around two more days," Jenna said.

"I need to speak to Dearie before we get to Kansas City," Henry Lloyd said. He never called Nettie by her name; it was always some variation of the name she used the first time they met. "So, if you ladies don't mind taking a short walk, I'll say my piece and y'all can come back."

"I think a nice stroll to the observation car would be great," Jenna said. "I need to stretch my legs. Miss Essie, are you coming?"

"Right behind you, Queenie," Essie said, standing and stretching. "See y'all in a little bit," she said, closing the door behind her.

After a brief silence, Henry Lloyd looked down at the small figure that was having a hard time meeting his eyes. He sat across from the cushioned seat where she was and picked up one slender hand, noting how she flinched at his touch before visibly forcing herself to relax though she still would not meet his eyes. Gently stroking the top of her hand with his thumb he said, "So, you going to live with Miss Essie, huh? I think that is a good idea," he said when she nodded. When she looked up, he said, "You know I love you, don't you Baby Dee? I have from the first time I looked into those big, brown eyes. You the only one I want to make my wife and have babies by...but not for a while."

He could see the fear, the nervous apprehension ease in Nettie's expressive eyes, to be replaced by relief, still she asked, "Why not for a while?"

"Because you need to learn to like men again, not fear them. Time to heal, to look forward to a man's touch, not fear or dread it. I want our wedding night to be special. Plus, we both young with plenty of time. So, my very dear wife-to-be," he said tenderly, cupping her face with his hands, "I am going to leave you in the safe hands of Miss Essie, and I want you both to take good care of each other. I'll keep in touch, and you do the same."

"Won't you be there, Henry Lloyd?" Nettie asked anxiously. It was slowly beginning to dawn on her how much she had come to depend on the handsome young man who had rescued her.

"Naw, Baby," he said. "I cain't go back to Crawfish Holler. I guess I've outgrown it. I'll let you know how to reach me once I'm settled. When the day comes that you ready for us to be together, send me this here," he said, handing her the baby doll pajama set she was wearing when they first met. "That will let me know you ready for me, and I'll come, no matter where I am, or what I'm doing. You take your time. I don't mind waiting." Leaning over he placed a warm kiss on her forehead before standing going over to the berth door and quietly closing it behind him.

"All aboard! Last call for passengers for Omaha, Des Moines and Minneapolis," the conductor's voice rang out.

"Henry Lloyd, are you sure you are not going back home?" Jenna asked hopefully, standing on the busy platform.

"Naw, I don't think so," Henry Lloyd said. "I'm headed for Detroit. I already called Sugar, so she's expecting me. She said she lives in a big ol' house with plenty of room and takes in boarders from time to time."

"Oh, no, not more boarders," Jenna said in dismay. Looking at one another, they dissolved into uncontrollable, escalating laughter, holding onto one another for support. They laughed until tears streamed from their eyes, hugging one last time before Henry Lloyd sprinted for his train, managing to hop aboard just before the conductor closed the doors.

Standing side by side, Jenna and Nettie waved until the train carrying Henry Lloyd was no longer in sight before hurrying to catch their train to begin the final leg in a long journey home.

Chapter Sixteen

"Queenie! Queenie!" The rapidly running figure threw himself eagerly into the open arms which closed tightly around him.

"Sidney! I am so happy to see you. How is my hero doing? I missed you so much," Jenna said, hugging him even tighter.

"I missed you too, Queenie. I thought about you every day," Sidney responded returning the hug twofold.

"Thank you and thank the spirits for warning me about the woman in pink. You saved me again. It is because of you that I can come home," Jenna said, hugging him again. "I am so proud of you."

Sidney beamed. "Daddy is nice now, but you still going to stay with Mama Joyce like I do, right, Queenie?"

"That's right," Jenna said. "She needs looking after more than ever because she is getting older. Papa Pete needs help, too."

"He don't come out of his room much, anymore," Sidney said. "The spirits are going to carry him home soon."

"Well, then, we will just make sure his last days here are good ones, all right?" Jenna said gently.

"All right," Sidney agreed, grabbing hold of Jenna's hand, holding on tightly. "I know that you only goin' to be here for ninety-two days. I counted them."

"That is right, and do you know why I am only going to be here that long?"

"'Cuz you goin' off to school to become a nurse in Birmingham, Alabama. That's where the school is, right, Queenie?"

"That is correct. We will find it on the map, so you will know exactly where I am, all right?"

"All right," Sidney said, happily skipping along. "Look, there's Ma'dear."

"Ma'dear, Ma'dear," Jenna said, running and throwing herself into her mother's arms.

"Hey, baby," Albertina said, hugging her daughter tightly. "I am so happy to see you. You look good," she said, taking in the full skirt, white blouse with the Peter Pan collar and black ballerina shoes. "You look like a big city gal," she said with a smile. "You done outgrown Crawfish Holler, huh?"

"It will always be home," Jenna said. "My happiest memories and most of my family are here. What is that saying? 'Be it ever so humble, there is no place like home'. I cannot wait to see Dexter and Lorenzo and Alfonso and Rolanda and Renard and Rhonda. I missed them so much."

"They certainly missed you," Albertina said. "I don't think anybody slept much last night; they were so excited. Hey Essie, how you doin'?" she said, hugging the woman as she walked up. "I sure appreciate you traveling and staying with Queenie in California. I know it made her feel better."

"I was happy to do it, Albertina," Essie said. "San Francisco is definitely something else. I saw a lot and learned a lot, but I must say I ain't sorry to be home, especially since I brought someone to come live with me. This here is Nettie, she was staying in Loretta's boarding house, but decided she wanted a change, so she comin' to stay with me. Nettie, this here is Albertina, Queenie's mother, and the healer I was telling you about. She training Queenie to be a healer, too."

"It sure is nice to meet you, Nettie," Albertina said with a smile, "You were one of Loretta's boarders? I guess y'all heard what happened to her, didn't you?"

Jenna's eyes sharpened. "Something happened to Loretta? What?"

"Her house caught on fire, and there was a lot of damage. Nobody was hurt, but most of it ain't livable from what I hear."

Jenna and Essie exchanged satisfied glances. "Nice to know nobody got hurt," Essie said.

"What about Henry Lloyd?" Albertina asked. "You think he staying to help Loretta?"

"No, ma'am, Henry Lloyd is on his way to Detroit to stay for a while. He is going to live with Sugar and her family for a while," Jenna said. "We said goodbye to him in Kansas City."

"I think there's a lot I need to hear about your stay with Loretta," Albertina said, looking at the two of them. "I'll look forward to that. In the meantime, Mr. Brussels is going to drive us back to Crawfish Holler. We got a special dinner planned, and Essie and Nettie y'all coming, too. Y'all can tell me all about the city of San Francisco. The other part you got to tell me can wait until we alone."

"There she is!"

"Queenie!"

Clambering down the stairs, laughing and screaming in delight, Jenna's brothers and sisters ran to meet her. They crowded around hugging and kissing, welcoming her back after almost a year's absence. Everyone talking at once, they filled her in on everything that had happened since she had been gone. Looking up, she noticed Dexter still standing on the porch watching the wild reunion. Walking over to the bottom of the stairs, Jenna said, "So, you are too cute to hug your sister?"

Looking sheepish, Dexter climbed down the stairs and embraced Jenna warmly, kissing her on the cheek. "Hey, Queenie," he said. "I sure am glad to see you."

"You sure were not acting like it," Jenna said. "You were acting as if you did not know me."

"That's 'cuz Dexter is the man now," Lorenzo said with a laugh. "He got girls in two counties chasing him."

"He lettin' himself get caught, too!" his twin, Alfonso added, his smile wide.

"Dexter, you are only fifteen," Jenna said looking at her very handsome, very young brother. Of slightly below average height, Dexter looked like Rodney Pettigrew in his younger, good-looking days. Jenna was reminded of a photo she had once seen of Rodney, slim and trim in his army uniform, smiling at the camera, short, curly hair combed back, caramel-colored skin with hazel eyes and a dimpled smile. It was easy to see how he had turned girl's heads. Possessed of those same good looks, his skin a warm, creamy brown, Dexter was apparently following in his father's, and grandfather's, hell-raising footsteps.

"Dexter, are you messing with white girls?" Jenna asked worriedly. "You know they are nothing but trouble."

"Call me Dex," her brother said, "and no, I don't mess with no white girls. I don't need the trouble or the aggravation. I got all the colored girls I can handle. Besides, all cats are gray in the dark." He was shocked when Albertina walked up, reared back, and slapped him soundly across his face twice.

"I don't ever want to hear talk like that coming from you," Albertina said fiercely. "You show some respect for your sisters, your mother, grandmother, the women that helped raise you, and these our guests. You are young, obviously foolish. If you want to grow old, you will stop messing around like you are. Some gal's daddy gonna be showing up demanding you marry his pregnant daughter, and then where will you be? Now, apologize to these women for your ignorance and disrespect, and we'll go in to eat."

"Queenie...Ma'dear...Miss Essie...."

"Nettie," Essie supplied.

"Miss Nettie…Rolanda…little Rhonda…I beg all of y'all to forgive me," Dexter said contritely. "I didn't have no call to say what I did, and I'm really sorry for it."

"We'll let them think on whether you deserve forgivin' while we have our dinner," Albertina said. "Y'all come on in and eat," As they headed for the stairs, Jenna slipped her arm through that of her brother. "I forgive you, Dex," she said softly. "I know how boys talk. You just forgot who you were talking to."

"And where I was," Dexter said ruefully. "Ma'dear definitely packs a punch."

Jenna said. "I guess you will be careful about what you say and who you say it around. You love women in a lot of ways, now you need to respect them, too."

"Most definitely," Dexter said, rubbing his cheek. Laughing, arm in arm, they climbed the stairs and walked into the house.

Jenna halted abruptly, her hair rising on her neck, her hands clenching by her sides. Rodney Pettigrew sat in his usual place at the head of the table, looking much as he always had, heavier than when she had seen him last. Just as horrible memories of the actual time she had last seen him threatened, he raised kind, empty eyes to hers.

"Hey, baby, what's your name?" he asked.

"Queenie," she managed to choke out.

"Hey, Queenie, you doin' alright?" he asked.

"I am doing fine, Mr. Pettigrew," Jenna said carefully. "How are you?"

"I be doing well. My head hurts a little bit, but Albertina gives me somethin' to take care of that," he said, rubbing the spot on his head where the skillet landed. "Y'all come on in and sit down so we can eat," gesturing to the empty places at the table.

Reassured, Jenna chose her old place at the table, followed by Essie and Nettie, everyone else choosing a seat, bowing their heads as Essie led them in prayer, digging into the food Albertina had prepared to welcome the travelers home. Laughing and talking with Rodney smiling vacantly, they filled the fascinated listeners in on life in San Francisco, careful to leave out all mention of life with Loretta. During a lull in the conversation Albertina stood up, moving over to a small table near the kitchen door bending over to pick something up.

"Well, Queenie, here it is, the moment we all been waiting for," holding out the letter from the Grayson School of Nursing, placing it into her hand when she made no move to take it from her mother's hand.

Slowly, reluctantly, Jenna slid the envelope open, removing the several pages contained inside. Opening the folded letter, she began reading. A slow smile spread across her face, widened, turned into a crow of delight as she waved the papers in the air. "I am in! I have been accepted into the fall class, assigned a dorm room and a roommate. I have a list of things to bring, and they say they will see me in September!" Cheers of excitement and shouts of congratulations rang out as they celebrated Jenna's success, Rodney sitting in a rocker with a pleasant smile on his face at all the excitement in the room.

*   *   *

"Ain't you the healer's gal? I heard you were living a long ways from here. What, you back now? Wow, you quite the city gal now, ain't you? Prim and proper and all dressed up. I still say you a pretty, little colored thing. I kinda see why they call you Queenie."

Jenna looked up as she and Lorenzo and Alfonso climbed the wide stairs leading into the general store. Sheriff's son Beau Richards was leaning against one of the building's pillars, straightening as she drew closer.

"Hey, Beau," she said shortly, increasing her pace.

He stepped in front of her, blocking her path. "So, you back now? You going back to your voodoo ways? Where's that nigger brother of yours? What's his name? Henry Lloyd?"

Jenna stood silent, shaking her head at her brothers, halting their advance, fists clenched.

"I asked you a question," Beau said, "and I expect –,"

"Is there something wrong here? Some problem?" Sheriff Calhoun Richards stood at the bottom of the steps; his eyes hidden by the dark aviator glasses he always wore. "Beau? Anything going on I need to know about?"

There was brief, tense silence, "Naw, no problem," Beau drawled at last. "Jes' saying hello to a…friend I ain't seen in a while…be seeing you…friend…" He sauntered away.

"Thank you, Sheriff," Jenna said gratefully. "I sure did not want any trouble."

"Glad I could help," Sheriff Richards said. "How long you been home, Queenie?"

"I got home day before yesterday," Jenna said. "It is good to be back home."

"And it's good to have you home," Sheriff Richards said. "Where's that brother of yours, Henry Lloyd?"

"He has gone to live in Detroit," Jenna said.

"He gets around, don't he?" Sheriff Richards said with a slight smile.

"Tell you what," Sheriff Richards said, "I'll wait here until you finished your shopping. That way you can get in and out and be on your way quicker."

"Thank you, Sheriff, that would be nice," Jenna said with a smile, making her way into the store.

A short time later she and Alfonso and Lorenzo exited the store making their way down the dirt-packed road toward home.

Jenna waved her thanks as they passed by the sheriff's marked vehicle. Laughing and talking, sucking on a peppermint stick, they filled each other in on some things that happened to them during their year apart.

*　　*　　*

"Miss Queenie, I brought you these white shoelaces for your shoes at nursing school."

"Why thank you, Miz Issacs, I know they will come in mighty handy. Laces wear out so quickly. I sure appreciate your thoughtfulness."

"Well, we all real proud of you, chile," the elderly woman said. "I know you going to do great."

A steady procession of people like Mrs. Issacs, offered a dollar here, fifty cents there or contributed a nightgown or white stockings or toiletry items, all to aid her in getting through her first year of school. She had accumulated an impressive number of necessary articles that would help her immensely. Smiling, she added the pair of shoelaces to the pile of items waiting to be packed for school.

*　　*　　*

"Believe it or not, the dandelion, a plant most folks think is a pesky weed, has medical uses," Albertina said, plucking at a patch of the yellow flowers and putting them into her burlap sack. "The entire plant can be steeped into a tea that helps with digestion and mild constipation."

Jenna, scribbling furiously, made a note of the plant and its properties under the 'D' section of the notebook she was compiling about medicinal plants and their usage. "Does it work best fresh or dried?" she asked.

"Fresh is best, but the dried leaves and flowers make a good tea and a pretty good wine, too." She and Jenna walked along in companionable silence for a time. "Loretta turned out to be trouble, huh?" Jenna, Essie, and Nettie had shared the happenings in San Francisco with Albertina the night before.

"She did, but it was not all bad," Jenna said. "I met some girls who will be my friends for life; I spent some time with Henry Lloyd; I got to know Miss Essie a lot better; and Loretta bought me a lot of things. Once I figured how to keep everyone out, I had a beautiful set of rooms, plus a plot of ground where I grew herbs. I brought back seedlings from some of the Chinese herbs, and I have a couple of bicycle locks left which I think I might put to good use at nursing school."

"It's nice to know you got some good out of your experience," Albertina said.

"It was hard on Henry Lloyd." Jenna said.

"Why was it hard on Henry Lloyd?" Albertina asked, "Why was it harder on him than on you?"

"Well, Henry Lloyd really liked Loretta, but I never did," Jenna said. "He has been upset for a long while about being a Pettigrew. He knew Papa Pete was hell on wheels in his heyday; he could not stand his daddy; and look how his aunt turned out. He loves Mama Joyce, but he does not like anybody else in that family, and to think he has that blood running through his veins just gets him down."

Jenna noticed some rare Carolina bristle mallow, used as a poultice for inflamed areas. It could also be used as a tea and possibly to cure sores, swellings, broken bones, painful stomach problems, and other injuries. Cutting a patch of the sparse plant with the sharp little knife she carried, she reached into the sack for some dampened newspaper, wrapping it carefully and putting it into the sack. Prepared to go look for more, she stopped when her mother placed her hand on her arm.

"Chile, I'm going to tell you something, something I carried close to my heart, known only to me. Others suspected, but no one knew anything for sure, and sure couldn't prove anything. But now I'm going to share it with you and leave it up to you to decide whether to keep it to yourself or share it with somebody else. I want you to know – at least someone other than me to know."

Another silence ensued. "To know what, Ma'dear?" Jenna said at last when it seemed her mother was not going to say anything else.

"It has to do with you and Henry Lloyd," Albertina said slowly. When Jenna looked at her inquiringly said, "You and Sugar are sisters because I am your mother. But you and she don't share the same daddy. You and Henry Lloyd share the same daddy, and it ain't Mr. Pettigrew."

"So, Henry Lloyd and I are full brother and sister?" Jenna said with dawning excitement. "He is not related to the Pettigrews in any way, shape, form, or fashion?" When her mother nodded, Jenna exclaimed, "Hallelujah! Praise the Lord! No kin!" She looked over at Albertina. "Who is our daddy, Ma'dear? Does he know we are his children?"

Albertina hesitated a long second. "Your daddy ain't no colored man," she said at last, watching as Jenna's eyes widened in surprise, "and he is well known in these parts. Your daddy is...Calhoun Richards, the sheriff. He knows about y'all, and I think his white son suspects which is why he hates Henry Lloyd so much. Calhoun has kept up with y'all and protected you as best he could all your lives. He real proud of all that you have accomplished. He knows Henry Lloyd can sing and he real proud of that, too. He prouder of what you all have done than he is of that trifling white son of his who don't do nothing but drink and fight."

"Who would have thought it? Your colored children whom you have to pretend you do not know, make you proud while the white one whom everyone knows is yours is an embarrassment," Jenna said with a laugh. Sobering she looked over at her mother. "Are Henry Lloyd and I the only ones?" she asked softly.

"You know Dexter is a Pettigrew. He look just like his daddy did in his youth. Not only that, he starting to act like him." Jenna nodded in agreement. "Lorenzo and Alfonso I'm pretty sure are Pettigrews; Sidney, Rolanda and Renard I'm not sure about. I'm sure Rhonda is a Pettigrew."

"They are your babies which is all that matters," Jenna said staunchly, putting one arm around her mother and hugging tightly. "Oh, look, some yarrow, and we should get some bark from this willow tree." The herb gathering continued uninterrupted.

"Hey, Doc Edmonds," Jenna stood at the entrance to his inner office.

"Queenie, or should I say Jenna Thompson, how are you? Come on in here. I have been thinking about you. Congratulations on your graduation and your acceptance into the Grayson School of Nursing. I am so proud of you." Walking over to a glass cabinet he opened it, withdrawing a brightly wrapped package which he handed to a surprised Jenna. She tore it open after first admiring the beautiful paper. Pushing aside the tissue paper, she gasped in delight. Two beautifully bound medical books, *Grey's Anatomy* and *Taber's Medical Dictionary*, were revealed exactly what she needed for school. Very expensive, but important for success, her being given the books significantly increased her chances. "Thank you, Doc Edmonds," she breathed. "They are beautiful and exactly what I needed."

"Yes, ma'am! I live for the day you join my practice," Doc Edmonds said seriously.

"We will both live for that day," Jenna said. "I got a long way to go, but that will be the goal."

"I like that."

"I do, too."

Chapter Seventeen

"Queenie, try it on again," the piping voice pleaded followed by a chorus of agreement.

"You are going to make me wear this out or start believing it is real," Jenna laughingly protested, "Luckily, I will not receive my uniform until I get to school, or I would be modeling it for you all every day," lifting the nurse's cap they had made for her from a newspaper page and fitting it on her head, to her siblings' delight.

"You gonna be a pretty nurse, Queenie," Rolanda declared staunchly.

"The prettiest and the smartest," Renard agreed with a nod.

"Why thank you, just knowing I have your support makes all the difference in the world," Jenna said with a smile, removing her cap, folding it carefully and placing it in her brimming suitcase. Sitting on it to force it closed she said, "Read the list to me again, Sidney, one more time to make sure I have everything, not that I could find space for another thing if I have forgotten something."

Sidney looked down at the paper he held. "Wooden laundry rack, laundry bag, iron, clothespins, white sheets–two sets, white sweater, nurse's cap, street clothes, shoes, white stockings, nightgowns, slips, underwear, and shoelaces."

"Check to all of the above," Jenna said, pushing down hard to snap it closed. "How I managed to squeeze everything into two suitcases…but I did! I just cannot open them until I reach my destination. I would never get everything back in." She held up a large cloth bag patterned with roses. "I will have this one with me on the bus. It has toiletries, some unmentionables, and a change of clothes. I should be fine until I get to Birmingham. The bus stops at every single little-bitty town from here to there. Today is Wednesday, I will get there early Friday in time for dorm check-in, room assignments, roommate assignments, a tour of the campus and hospital where we will be working, picking up uniforms, ending in a picnic for the colored students in John White Park."

"Sounds like you better rest up on the bus while you got the chance," Albertina said with a smile, "Cuz you sure goin' to be busy once you get to school. Mr. Brussels will give you and Sidney a ride into town so you can catch the bus. I fixed you some food, so you'll have something to eat most of the way, and you got money to buy something if you need to."

"Yes, ma'am," Jenna said, patting her purse and the money belt located snugly inside the elastic garter around the stocking she was wearing.

"Y'all come say goodbye to your sister," Albertina said, "You won't be seeing her again until Christmas." Her siblings who had walked from their house to Mama Joyce's to say goodbye, crowded around. Even Dexter had made the trip, giving her a warm hug, and kissing her goodbye.

"You all be good. If I get good reports, I will tell Santa, and he will give me something to bring to all of you for Christmas from Birmingham. But only if you are good – all of you," noting the way Dexter rolled his eyes, his admiring twin brothers copied him. Walking over to him, giving him an extra hug, she said in a low voice, "I do not want you to do anything, and I mean anything to spoil Christmas or Santa Claus for your younger

brothers and sisters. If you do, you will have to answer to me…
and there are a lot of things I can do to make you very sorry…
you will just wish you were dead."

Dexter hastily straightened, stepping back. "I won't say or
do nothin', Queenie, and neither will anybody else. I'll see to
it."

"See that you do," Jenna said sweetly, embracing her siblings
one final time before making her way out the open back door
of Mama Joyce's house, the older boys all helping to carry her
luggage and arranging it in the back of the old car being driven
by the elderly man who was dropping her off at the bus station.
She hugged Mama Joyce, who had come outside. "Now you take
good care of yourself, Mama Joyce," she said. "Sidney is going to
help keep watch over you," looking down at her younger brother,
"like he always does, and Ma'dear can send some of the other
boys if you need help, okay?"

"I hear you, baby, don't worry about me. I got plenty of help
to call on if I need it," Mama Joyce assured her. "Now you take
this food I fixed for you and be sure to call us when you get to
Birmingham to let us know you all right."

"I will," Jenna promised. Looking around she took a deep
breath. "Well, I guess this is it," her dark eyes met those of her
mother, rising fear and uncertainty in their depths.

Albertina cupped her hands around Jenna's face. "You are
goin' to do great in Birmingham and make all of us – every
colored person in this town – proud. Me proudest of all. Now
you go do what you need to do – and can do so easily – and
before you know it, you'll be a nurse and a healer."

Reassured, Jenna hugged her mother tightly one last time
before moving toward the open door on the car's passenger
side, Sidney close behind, the only person riding with her to
the bus station. Waving to a chorus of goodbyes, blowing kisses,

she slammed the door shut, leaning out the window as it pulled away, still waving until the car rounded a bend in the road.

* * *

"Grayson...Grayson School of Nursing...students bound for Grayson School of Nursing...."The elderly man in the faded gray coat and hat held up an equally faded sign reading: GRAYSON.

"I am going to the Grayson School," Jenna said, hurrying toward the strolling figure, a young boy carrying her two bags following close behind.

"I am too," a second hurrying figure dragging her one bag stopped in front of the man holding the sign.

"So am I," said a third, gesturing to the three men each carrying at least two suitcases each, one pulling a wardrobe trunk in addition to the two suitcases.

"Well, it is always my pleasure to be the first to welcome y'all to Alabama, to Birmingham, and to the Grayson School of Nursing," the old man said. "My name is Sam, and I'm a Jack-of-all-trades for the school. I drive, I garden, I fix things, I clean up – you name it and I probably do it, have done it, or am about to do it. I been with the school for more than twenty-five years, so I seen a lot. This latest trouble with colored folks fighting white folks in the streets, well, this is trouble like I ain't never seen before, and Birmingham seem to be right at the center of it. You'll hear more about it during your orientation. Though the powers that be got to be real careful about what they say seeing as how the school is racially segregated with no plans to change anything as far as I can see. Y'all can c'mon, the bus is right over here." Sam led the three of them over to an old, battered bus that had seen better days, lifting a panel on the side to reveal a large empty space. "Y'all put your suitcases in there," he said, "Someone at the school will help unload when we get there." After the suitcases were deposited and the panel closed, he opened the bus doors, climbed aboard, and sat in the driver's seat.

"Y'all can sit anywhere you want to," Sam said. "It'll take us about twenty minutes or so to get to the school. It's right next to Birmingham Regional Medical Center. That's where y'all will do your practicums and residencies and such. The white girls have their dorm rooms and classrooms on the other side of the building from where you all have your lessons and such. The good thing is that all y'all, colored and white are using the same books, and the two sides look pretty much the same, can't really tell one from the other." He paused to concentrate on negotiating a sharp, narrow turn.

"Hi, my name is Gina–Gina Reynolds," a tall, brown-skinned woman build on generous lines with dark, chin-length hair, large eyes and full lips said into the lull in Sam's running narrative, "I'm from the southwest side of Atlanta, Georgia."

"My name is Petronella Wilson," an average height, plump, very dark woman with short, kinky hair and striking features said with a smile, "and I'm from Baton Rouge, Louisiana."

"My name is Jenna Thompson," Jenna said looking around and smiling, "I am from a small town in South Carolina called Crawford Hollow, but which everyone who lives there, colored and white, calls Crawfish Holler," smiling at the appreciative chuckles.

"Gina and Jenna, huh?" Petronella said, "That's liable to get confusing. Do you have any other names people call you?"

"They call me Queenie at home," Jenna said.

"I'm Gigi," Gina said.

"Gigi and Queenie – they fit you," Petronella said approvingly. "That's how we'll introduce you at the picnic tonight. I hear tell some fine-looking young men are going to be there."

"I can get with that," Gina said. "Some women have met their husbands, future doctors, at these functions."

"I've heard that," Petronella said, nodding. "Imagine finding your future husband your first day here. And a doctor? Icing on the cake!"

"I am not looking for a husband," Jenna said firmly. "Men almost always spoil things when you add them to the mix."

"Ain't that the truth," Petronella said, laughing lightly. "But I think some things taste surprisingly good...a little spoiled." Looking over at Gina she said, "Did you think you were coming to modeling school or something? What in the world do you have in all them bags you brought?"

"Just a few things: some clothes and things to decorate my room," Gina said, "You gotta be comfortable, right?" Reaching into her leather purse she pulled out a gold cigarette case, extracting a slim cigarette wrapped in dark paper, using a matching gold lighter to ignite the end. Taking a deep drag, she offered one to the women seated around her, shrugging her shoulders and putting them back in her purse when both refused.

"It looks like you going to be real comfortable," Petronella observed. "I was doing good to fill even one suitcase. Too bad we not the same size, or I'd be borrowing stuff from you all the time. I might still can use some of what you brought, though."

"Nice to know it's not a total waste," Gina said dryly. "I'd hate to disappoint."

Jenna giggled. "Don't think I didn't notice your two stuffed suitcases," Petronella said, turning to Jenna with a smile. "Even though you ain't but that big," she said, snapping her fingers, "I know I'm going to find something to borrow from you."

"We are here, ladies," Sam said, pulling slowly into the wide driveway. "This building has been around since 1890. They started accepting colored nurses about twenty years ago.

I remember the first class of ten. They all gone on to do really well. You all are the sixth class, I think, and it's a class of twenty-six. Y'all are the last ones to get here; they been coming since yesterday afternoon. They had kin here to stay with, I think. Here we are. We are just gonna stack your stuff inside the doors and transfer them to your rooms when you get your room assignments. Now, if you'll just proceed through those two sets of double doors and take the stairway to your right, you'll see the office straight ahead. That is where you finish your registration and get your room and locker assignments and such. They will tell you your roommate assignment then, too. I'll probably see you this evening when I drive y'all to the picnic at John White Park. I sure enjoyed talking to y'all, and I'm sure we'll see a lot of each other during the time that you are here." Reaching over he slowly pulled the lever that opened the sealed bus door, watching as Gina, Jenna and Petronella piled out. Climbing down the stairs he gestured for the two men standing around to come help collect the luggage.

"I hope we're roommates, or at least assigned rooms that are close to one another," Petronella said. "I think the three of us would get along really well. Especially if…is one of you smart?"

"Not me," Gina said, "I just got in by the skin of my teeth, and I think because my daddy gave a sizable donation to somebody. He would have done the same to get me into a colored college, but nursing school is only three years, and the hospital is where all the doctors are, so I chose nursing."

"Well, what about you, Queenie?" Petronella asked. "Are you the smart one?"

"I am not sure about that…" Jenna began.

"Where did you rank in your graduating class?" Gina asked. "I was so far in the rear I didn't even know we had that many students in the senior class."

"I was in the top ten percent, barely," Petronella said, "so I ain't dumb, but I ain't really smart or nothing. What about you Queenie? Where did you graduate? What did you rank?"

"I graduated from Bayside High in San Francisco," Jenna said. "I was the salutatorian."

"We got the smart one!" Gina crowed. "Wow, you were the second smartest kid in your whole class? That's impressive. I know who I'll be sitting next to whenever we have a test."

"And I'll be there on the other side," Petronella declared. "I bet ain't nobody else in this whole school scored any higher. Most of the valedictorians I know about are boys. Salutatorians too now that I think about it."

"Well, well, well, Sally Ann, it's only the first day of orientation and already we got niggra gals talking about cheating...not surprising, really...what is surprising is that we keep letting cheaters and ignoramuses apply, and even worse, accepting them. For what? To keep the peace, to give niggras their so-called civil rights? When all they seem to know is how to lie, cheat, steal and make babies?" The softly drawling, mocking voice dripped racial poison.

Jenna, Gina, and Petronella turned in unison. Two white girls, one blonde with short, bobbed hair, the other with curly brown hair caught up in a short ponytail were coming up the stairs behind them. Holding folded uniforms and carrying a stack of books, they were obviously part of the white nursing student population.

"Did y'all hear something?" Petronella demanded, strutting up to the two women, crossing her arms and staring them up and down. "I thought dogs weren't allowed, but I swear I just heard some bitches howling at the moon."

Mocking smiles faded as their faces became flushed with anger. "You better watch your mouth," the blonde woman said. "Or-."

"Or what?" Petronella demanded, walking up and thrusting her face into that of the other woman's, "What you going to do? Call your K-K-K brothers and daddies and uncles to rough me up? Call 'em! I ain't scared."

"You know what? Maybe you do need to be taught a lesson –," the woman hissed, her eyes narrowed.

"Is there something going on here? Something I should know about? That I need to address?" The stern voice came from somewhere behind them. A tall, spare woman dressed in hospital whites stood a short distance away.

"Ma'am, these, these, niggras–," the blonde began hotly.

"Stop right there," the woman, whose tag identified her as Emma Johnson, Head of Nurses in Training, lifted one hand, halting her mid-sentence. "You are all nurses-in-training and therefore worthy of respect. There is no room for prejudice here. If you cannot do that perhaps this is not the place for you. I expect you to show one another respect and consideration always, no matter the circumstances. Do you understand?"

"Yes'm." the blonde said, head lowered, but eyes flashing resentment.

"Now, I assume you all have things you need to do to prepare yourselves for Monday. If nothing else you still have your dorm rooms to put in order, beds to make up, clothing and other things to put away, giving everything a good scrub and dusting. My colored nurses will be catching the bus for the picnic in a short while. You don't want to miss that, so get busy ladies, there is much to do." She watched the two white nursing students exit the door leading to their portion of the building as Jenna, Gina and Petronella entered the office, beginning the process of collecting everything they needed before classes started on Monday.

"*Bedside Manner, the illustrated Nursing textbook, the First Aid textbook, Red Cross 4th edition, Human Anatomy, Aides to Hygiene for Nurses* – these are great books!" Jenna said excitedly, looking through the stack of books she had been given. "Plus, I have the latest edition of *Grey's Anatomy* from Doc Edmonds."

"Have you looked at some of these pictures in here?" Gina asked, thumbing through the anatomy book, "Lord, I hope I hold it together when I see some of this in real life." She carelessly tossed the book on her still unmade bed. "Come on, enough of that, we need to get ready for the picnic. Petronella will be here in a few minutes," lifting a suitcase onto the bare mattress and opening it, rummaging through its contents.

"I will make my bed before going to the picnic tonight," Jenna said, pulling out a set of the white sheets she had brought, unfolding one and snapping it across the narrow twin bed, smoothing the top and tucking in the corners with military precision, doing the same for the second sheet. She placed a pillowcase over the gray-striped pillow on her bed, arranging it dead-center at the top of her mattress. Picking up the waffled bedspread provided by the school, she smoothed it over the sheets, making certain it was even all around. "There," she said with satisfaction, "finished. Now when I get back all I need to do is get ready for bed and hop in."

"Girl, you are so efficient," Gina said. "I wish I was. I wonder if I could hire someone to come in and make my bed and straighten the room every day."

"I think those are part of our responsibilities," Jenna said. "It helps us learn to make a bed quickly and professionally since we are going to be making up a lot of beds during the course of our career."

"Don't remind me," Gina said disgustedly. "What am I? A nurse in training or a maid? I am not used to all this cleaning up. We hired folks to do it at home."

"You are not going to be able to hire anyone to make up your hospital beds," Jenna pointed out gently, "that is why you need to know how to do it yourself."

"Well, I'll worry about that later," Gina said, "Let's get ready for the picnic." Grabbing a towel and washcloth from the stack they had been given, they headed for the community bathroom down the hall.

"Wow, y'all look really nice," Petronella said as she came through the door. Gina and Jenna were roommates while their new friend had been assigned a roommate in the room next to theirs. "Queenie, I know you didn't get that outfit in no Crawfish Holler."

Jenna looked down at the blue pedal pushers, checked red and white blouse, blue sweater, and red and white sneakers she was wearing. "No, I got these in San Francisco the year I lived there with my aunt."

"You lived in California?" Gina said with envy. "You are going to have to tell me all about it. I want to go to California someday, maybe even to live. But for now, y'all ready to party?"

"Let's do this!" Petronella said enthusiastically as they made their way to where the bus was idling by the curb with Sam in the driver's seat. Climbing aboard, finding seats close together, they eagerly looked out of the bus windows at their new surroundings, making plans to go exploring on foot the next day.

"This is really nice," Petronella pitched her voice to be heard above the laughter and noisy chatter, "Look at all this food! I wish I could sneak some back to my room. Queenie, aren't you hungry? You haven't eaten a thing."

"I am just looking to see what is here," Jenna said. The truth was she was trying to find something that was not primarily composed of chicken or featured fried chicken. Every meal she had eaten since leaving home had contained some variation of chicken, most of it fried. She loved chicken but needed a break. Her eyes fell on an umbrella-covered stand offering hot dogs in a variety of forms. Walking over she settled on a hot dog with mustard and sweet relish on a warmed bun and her favorite drink: cola with lots of ice.

"That's all you want?" Petronella asked, biting into a large slice of caramel cake that had been preceded by a fried chicken sandwich, potato salad, and a large lemonade. "I'm going to get me a nice, big slice of watermelon after I let this cake digest some."

"That sounds good," Jenna said, "but I need to sit to eat watermelon; otherwise, I get it all over me."

"A watermelon ain't good unless it's really juicy," Gina agreed, "and sweet."

"Definitely sweet," Jenna said.

"What's that over there?" Petronella asked, pointing to where a crowd was gathering around a group of three or four men, one of them talking earnestly through a megaphone though they were too far away to hear what was being said. "Let's go see what this is about," she suggested.

"Separate but equal? Separate but equal? There is no such thing as separate but equal. Show me something you got that is equal to what the white man's got...schools, for example... what did your high school look like in comparison to the white high school? Did your books have shiny, new covers...or did your books even have covers? Do your schoolrooms have central heat? Or do you crowd around a fireplace or heater and hope no one's clothes catch fire?" The murmuring from the crowd grew louder with shouts of agreement.

"The only thing equal as far as the white man is concerned is the green of our money – and they try to give us as little of that as possible," chuckles of agreement. "I don't see them separating our money from theirs, do you?" More chuckles. "Yet they don't want us in the stores to spend our money...though they have nothing against sneaking y'all in the back way or coming to your house if you're one our privileged colored with money." Nods of agreement all around. Another young man took the megaphone. Jenna's attention sharpened.

"Separate but equal?" he said derisively. "Don't make me laugh…does your husband, father, son or brother make the same as the white man working in the same factory doing the same thing? How much does your wife, mother, sister make cleaning the white man's house, scrubbing out the white man's toilet? Less in a year than it costs the white woman paying her what she would spend shopping on a dress and a pair of shoes."

"Lord, these are some of those rabble-rousers," Petronella said. "When they start talking, the police are usually not far behind. We need to leave. Too bad, they all kind of cute."

"Yeah, we don't need trouble. Let's get back to the picnic," Gina said. "They are activists, not doctors anyway."

"You coming, Queenie?" Petronella asked turning back to Jenna who had not moved. "Queenie, are you coming?"

Jenna was listening closely to what the young men were saying, nodding her head in agreement, her attention particularly caught by the second speaker. Tall, handsome, articulate he was a dynamic speaker, meeting the eyes of many of those gathered, earnestly putting his point across. Moving across the crowd, his eyes collided with the most beautiful eyes he had ever seen. Sparkling, bottomless, almost black, they seemed to reach down into him, reading his intentions, gauging his sincerity. He checked in mid-presentation. Recovering quickly, he smiled, winking at the young woman with the inky-black hair and compelling eyes, smiling wider when she turned away quickly, joining two women who apparently asked her something that had her walking away rapidly, shaking her head violently. He was going to have to start asking around, determined that he and the young woman with the darkly beautiful eyes would meet again.

"Jenna, were you that interested in what they had to say?" Gina asked as she rejoined her friends, "or maybe it was that last speaker who caught your eye," she said teasingly.

"Who was it that said they weren't interested in men?" Petronella asked quizzically. "And look who's the first to fall."

"I-I did not fall," Jenna said indignantly, hoping her flushed cheeks were not obvious. "They were saying some interesting things; besides, I do not know any of them from Adam's housecat."

"Excuse me," Gina said, stopping an older woman walking away from the demonstration. "Could you tell me who is that young man speaking?"

"Oh, he is that young hothead Curtice Brooks," the woman said with a sigh. "He is always stirring things up. Already been arrested I don't know how many times, but he keep coming back for more. He and the ministers he run with are a big reason Birmingham is becoming known as Bombingham. I swear I don't know where this is all going to end." The woman walked away shaking her head.

"Curtice Brooks...Curtice Brooks...that's a nice name," Gina said.

"He ain't bad on the eyes, either," Petronella said. "Curtice and Queenie...Curtice and Jenna Brooks...Jenna Brooks...has a nice ring to it,"

"I told you," Jenna began hotly.

"I think she is protesting a little too much...a little too strongly," Gina said thoughtfully.

"I agree," Petronella said, her eyes twinkling.

Her new friends teased her about Curtice Brooks over her strenuous objections all the way back to the dormitory.

Chapter Eighteen

"Gigi? Gigi? Gigi, wake up now! You are going to miss breakfast, and you really should eat. Today is the first day of orientation, and you do not want to be late for that."

The lump underneath the ruffled bedspread moved slightly and made a gurgling sound before stilling again.

"You have ten minutes before the cafeteria opens," Jenna said, looking down at her brand-new Timex watch with the second hand, a stated requirement for their training. There was a knock on the door. "That must be Petronella. She said she would go with us to eat," Jenna said walking over to the door and opening it.

"Good morning," Petronella said breezily as she came sailing through the door. "Are we all ready for our first day on the path to becoming a nurse? Jenna, you look really nice – I love that pencil skirt – you have the cutest clothes. I just wish either you were bigger, or I was smaller so I could borrow some of them sometime. Now, I might be able to make some of Gigi's stuff work, she has so much of it." She halted abruptly. "Lawd, don't tell me the chile ain't even out of bed yet!" Walking over to the side of the bed, leaning down, and grabbing a corner of the bedspread and sheet underneath it, she snatched it off a slumbering Gina.

"Hey!" Gina protested, sitting up and staring blearily around. "What are you doing?" She sleepily eyed the two women standing in front of her. "Y'all dressed already? What the hell time is it, anyway?"

210

"Time for you to get up," Petronella said. "Now. If you hurry, you just might have time enough to grab something to eat. Queenie and I are leaving; we will save you a seat." They left Gina sitting on the side of the bed as they exited, talking excitedly as they speculated on what their first day would bring.

"Gina is missing a really good breakfast," Petronella said appreciatively as she added some extra butter to the generous pile of grits on her tray and the two pieces of toast with grape jelly on the side. She also had cold cereal and milk, sausage links, fruit, fried potatoes, scrambled eggs, coffee cake, and coffee. "Queenie is that all you are having?" she said, eying the apple, toast, jelly and two pieces of bacon on her plate.

"This is plenty and will definitely hold me until lunch," Jenna said, biting into her apple and stirring sugar into her milk-laden coffee.

"Ladies, you have five minutes before reporting to the auditorium for your orientation," the briskly efficient voice belonged to a black woman dressed in nursing white. "Be sure to put your trays on the table by that open window, and we will see you all in a few minutes."

"Looks as if Gigi will have to wait until lunch before she gets a chance to eat," Jenna said, "She will be mighty hungry by then."

"Maybe that will teach her to get up," Petronella said, "I just hope her stomach doesn't start growling, especially if we're sitting next to her. Folks might think it's you or me."

"That would be embarrassing," Jenna agreed, rising to take her tray to where they had been instructed to leave them.

"Definitely," Petronella said, scooping up the last of her grits before picking up her tray.

"Ladies, please be seated anywhere you like," the same black nurse who had addressed them in the cafeteria said to the chattering group of women milling around. "We will be closing the doors in two minutes. Anyone arriving after the doors are closed will be marked as late. If you are late three times within a semester, you will receive a demerit. Five demerits call for a meeting with the school disciplinary board, more than five could jeopardize your standing in the nursing program."

"Still no sign of Gigi," Petronella said disgustedly as she and Jenna chose a seat near the front. "Tardy on your first day? Really?"

Gina came rushing through the door just as the nurse who had spoken earlier stood to close it. Apologizing profusely, lamenting her uncooperative alarm clock, she looked around, spotting her two friends, and hurrying their way, still apologizing, promising it would not happen again because she was going out to buy a working alarm clock that very day. Clad in a full flowing skirt, peasant blouse and flat, buckled shoes, she stepped over and pushed her way past the people in the row containing her friends, sitting down with a flourish in the seat Jenna and Petronella had saved for her.

"Thanks for saving me a seat," she whispered. "Would you believe I fell asleep again? So, of course, I didn't have a chance to eat. Luckily, one of my suitcases…did not have clothes in it." Reaching into one of her skirt's deep pockets, she stealthily extracted a piece of taffy, propping open a textbook on her lap so that she could unwrap it, pretending to cough as she popped it into her mouth.

"Good morning, ladies," a tall, spare white woman whom Jenna recognized as the one who had witnessed the confrontation between Petronella and the white students as they were registering stood at the podium. "My name is Emma Johnson, and it is my great privilege to welcome you all into this year's class of nurses. The twenty-six of you are the sixth class to go through the program. We are delighted to have you here, look forward to getting to know you, and teaching you the craft of nursing. Now, if you will please open the booklet you were given at registration to page three, the calendar of events."

Jenna listened intently as Nurse Johnson talked about the calendar, emphasizing certain dates and times. The class schedule generated a great deal of interest, especially when informed where they would be taking many of their classes. "Your basic science and your social science courses – psychology and sociology, for example – as well as your English classes, will be taken at Milestone College. You will be attending classes with the students there. Most of you will have your lunch there; we will provide vouchers for you. The Grayson bus will transport you back and forth. At this point, we divide you all into sections and assign group leaders to each section who will make sure that her group catches the bus on time, takes roll, and reports any problems or concerns to the administrative staff. Are there any nominations for group leader?"

Petronella stood. "I would like to nominate Jenna Thompson as a group leader," she said, gesturing to a surprised Jenna. "She's smart, conscientious, organized. She cares about people, and I think she would make a great group leader."

"Do you accept the nomination, Miss Thompson?" Nurse Johnson asked, pen poised to write her name.

"Yes, ma'am, I suppose so," Jenna said hesitantly. "I would do my best."

"Her best is a lot," Gina interjected. "She was the salutatorian of her class in San Francisco."

"I would like to nominate Carey Armstrong," another girl said standing. Others stood in support of their candidates; Nurse Johnson called for a vote, and the four women who received the most votes were designated group leaders. Petronella and Gina hugged Jenna in excitement when her name was called first and were even more excited when they were both assigned to Jenna's group. Four more girls were assigned to Jenna's Group One; they all gathered in a corner of the room to meet and to discuss bus and class times and schedules.

"Classes start at Milestone today, and we report to the hospital on Wednesday," Jenna said looking at her notes. "English 101, which we are all enrolled, starts at 10:00. It is 8:45 now, so I think we should all plan on meeting at the bus stop by 9:00. The bus leaves at 9:10, for a ten-minute ride to the Milestone campus. We should get there in plenty of time to look around, find our class, the bookstore, and the cafeteria. Class ends at 10:50 and our next class before lunch starts at 11:05 ending just before noon, so we can walk to the cafeteria together. If everyone agrees, I will see you all at nine and will take roll once we board the bus."

"I really like your hair like that, Queenie," Petronella said admiringly, eyeing the smoothly twisted coil pinned to the back of her equally smooth head, a few errant curls framing her face. Your hair is so pretty. I am glad you didn't have to cut it." Regulations called for all hair to be short enough or styled in such a way that would prevent its touching the collar of the nursing uniform.

"It makes you look really chic and sophisticated," Gina said. "You sure don't look like you come from a small town in South Carolina, that's for sure. That year in San Francisco really shows."

"Thank you," Jenna said, "I really did not want to cut it. Being so unruly I would not be able to do anything with it. At least this way I can keep it out of the way. Oh, good, we are here and so are the other members of Group One. Walking over to where the four other young women were standing, extracting a piece of paper with grid lines drawn on it and the names of the Group One members, she marked everyone present, smiling as she gestured for them to climb aboard the bus being driven by the talkative Sam who had driven them from the train station on their arrival.

"Good day, ladies," he said as the women climbed aboard and found a seat. "It sure is nice to see all of y'all again. You sure look nice in your school clothes. You are a good-looking bunch, and I look forward to seeing y'all in your nursing uniforms which you will wear later this week – but without the hat. Y'all won't get the hat until the second year, and there is a whole big ceremony surrounding it. Now, if everyone is here, we'll get started. Group leaders, if there's anyone missing from your group, you need to let me know, and we will wait for them, though we can't wait long, or we'll all be late." None of the group leaders had anyone tardy, so with a belch of exhaust fumes, the bus pulled ponderously away from the curb, swinging into traffic, slowly picking up speed.

"Milestone College was founded in the 1890s by Quakers, who called themselves Friends, from up North who wanted to provide colored people down here with an institution of higher learning," Sam said, picking up where he left off. "The students here have been very active in these so-called civil rights events that are causing all of the unrest around here. Many of them, men and women have spent more than one night in jail and stood together when the po-lice was gonna raid their campus looking for some of the main instigators. The cops had to leave when they could not produce a warrant, but I say it was a good thing national newspaper and radio people were there watching otherwise it could have really gotten ugly. Y'all be careful. I know Nurse Johnson warned y'all against taking part in anything. Grayson is officially neutral in all that is going on, and they do a lot to stay that way, so be warned. We are here. Y'all have a nice day. I'll look forward to seeing you all later." Reaching over he pulled the lever that opened the door, watching as they all disembarked, closing the doors on the empty bus, and pulling away.

"It is too bad Sam is so shy with rarely anything to say," Gina said sardonically to a chorus of giggles. "Otherwise, I bet since he's been here so long, he could tell us a lot of things."

Smiling appreciatively, Jenna turned her attention to the bustling campus, looking around with interest at the Victorian architecture and the variety of students headed to class. She did not notice the man walking with a group of his friends and fellow activists, megaphone in hand. He halted abruptly, clutching the arm of one of the men walking beside him. He pointed at a smiling Jenna, walking with a group of women in the direction of the campus bookstore.

"Hey man, that's her," Curtice Brooks said excitedly, "that girl I was telling you about who was at the rally in the park last Saturday. She sure is fine. I think I'll go invite her to the Administration Building to hear what we have to say and what we stand for. Maybe she will join the movement."

"I don't know man," his friend said doubtfully. She looks like one of them saditty society babes who already have it so good, they don't even know what all the fuss is about. She probably wouldn't give you the time of day."

"Let's go find out," Curtice said, headed purposefully in her direction, his friend trailing reluctantly behind.

"Good day, ladies," Curtice said, moving in front of the group and stopping, causing them to stop too. Gina and Petronella's eyes brightened with interest when they recognized the handsome young man accosting them. His eyes sought out Jenna standing in the center of the group.

"My name is Curtice Brooks," he said smiling, his eyes warm, full of charm. "If I recall correctly, you ladies were at the rally in John White Park this past weekend. I hope you were able to take away something enlightening and meaningful from it."

"It was definitely that," Petronella said brightly when it became obvious that Jenna was not going to respond. "It was our first day in Birmingham, and after hearing some of the things you had to say, I understand better what it is you are doing and why."

"Me, too," Gina interjected, smiling flirtatiously, taking in dark hair and skin, brown eyes, beautifully shaped lips, and strong nose.

"We are going to be speaking about the issues in front of the Administration building in a few minutes. Why don't you all come listen to us?" Curtice said persuasively. "I think you'll find it quite illuminating."

"No, thank you," Jenna said coolly. "We have a class that we need to get to after taking a quick look at the bookstore."

"I guess moving ahead with your plans for wealth and privilege are more important than learning some things about the struggle your colored brothers and sisters are experiencing," Curtice said shortly, stung by the refusal, the iciness in the thickly lashed beautiful eyes looking back at him. "It must be nice not having to worry about being a colored person in this country."

Jenna slowly approached until she stood a hands-breadth away from the arrogant young man with the big mouth. "You do not know the first thing about me," she said deliberately, the ice in her eyes and voice heating rapidly as she looked him up and down, "so you have no right to make assumptions about me. For your information, I come from a small town in South Carolina where almost every single prominent white person and just about everybody else white is a card-carrying member of the local Ku Klux Klan. I have six brothers, one of whom was forced to leave home because a white woman would not leave him alone and the wrong people were beginning to notice. That same brother was instrumental in preventing me from becoming a victim of three white boys out to ravage me. My mother, who happens to be a healer, and I, also a healer, spend a great deal of time praying that my brothers and sisters remain safe. We all grew up in a small house that could not be considered rich by any stretch of the imagination; most of my nine brothers and sisters still live there. I know exactly what the struggle for our civil rights is about and support it fully, even if it does not call for me marching in the streets and attending rallies. I will fight to the fullest in my own way and offer my support in any way I can. If you are an example of what the movement is about here in Birmingham, then it is in trouble. No wonder you spend most of your time in jail if what folk say is true. Maybe that is a good thing; you cannot do much harm in jail, and you are obviously too thick-headed to attend class, presumably your reason for being here in the first place. Do not think you know everything – you don't – and do not jump to conclusions based on surface appearances. You will look and sound even more ridiculous than you do already. Now, if you will excuse me, you have already wasted enough of our valuable time, and we need to get to class. Ladies, shall we?" turning away, eyes flashing angry black fire, Jenna stalked away, followed by her awed group of fellow nursing students, leaving behind a chagrined, contrite, suitably chastened young man.

"Damn, man, I don't believe I've ever heard someone get read like that," Wilson Morgan, the friend who had accompanied him said, half-admiringly. "I do believe you have been thoroughly put in your place."

"And with good reason," Curtice admitted, shaking his head in bemused wonder. "I did jump to conclusions based on the way she looked. Just because she looks like a million dollars, I reached some hasty, unfair conclusions; and because she refused to come to the rally thought that meant she didn't care. I was wrong, obviously. I got a lot of fences to mend and lots of crow to eat to get into her good graces. Luckily, I am persistent."

"You still going to try and talk to her, man? She don't seem to like you at all." Wilson said doubtfully, "Girls all over this campus would jump at the chance to get next to you. Why not pick one of them?"

"Naw, man, it has to be her," Curtice said, gazing after Jenna's rapidly departing form, remembering beautiful eyes that seemed to see into the depths of him, assessing and finding him wanting, dark eyes that flashed with passion and conviction.

"Why, her, man?" Winston asked.

"'Cause she's the woman I'm going to marry," he said ruefully, smiling at his friend's shocked countenance. "Shut your mouth man, and let's go. We are going to be late for the rally we organized." Turning in the direction of the Administration building the two men hurried away.

"I guess you told him," Gina said with a snorting laugh. "Remind me never to make you mad. Still waters definitely run deep."

"I bet he ain't never had no woman tell him off like that," Petronella said, "cute as he is."

"Well, he deserved it," Stella Lewis, a member of the group said. "He had no business thinking he knew all about someone he had never really met." The other women in the group nodded in agreement.

"Can we talk about something else?" Jenna asked. "We have already spent entirely too much time on this trivial topic," trying to forget brown eyes looking into hers, anger and surprise followed by extreme remorse and contrition. Determinedly turning her mind to more important matters, she continued to the bookstore.

"Good morning, students, this is English 101 and I am Professor Ignatius Whitaker," the small, wizened man standing behind the podium said. Looking down at a sheet of paper, he called out the names written there. Once through that roll, he pulled out a separate sheet of paper and began calling additional names, one of which was Jenna's. "The second roll contains the names of the students who join us from the Grayson School of Nursing. Ladies, we are pleased to welcome you to Milestone. If each of you would, please stand and give your name."

Jenna looked around as she introduced herself, noticing how the women in the class glowered at her, their faces closed and unwelcoming. Sitting down, she wondered at the open hostility until the Professor began talking, passing out the class syllabus, discussing when papers were due and tests to be held. Odd looks aside Professor Whitaker proved to be witty, knowledgeable about his subject, and a dynamic public speaker. Jenna looked forward to the time she would spend in his class. They were dismissed early, book list and reading assignments in hand, allowing them time to buy the requisite materials for the class. Jenna and her group headed immediately for the bookstore. After standing in long lines and collecting and paying for the books they needed, they departed for the cafeteria, reaching into purses to find their lunch vouchers. Walking into the noisy, crowded room packed with tables that seated ten, they spotted one near a big window and claimed their seats, half of them holding the table while the others got into the hot lunch line, heading for their turn in line when the others returned and sat down. Even though the room was packed, the three empty seats at their table remained unoccupied.

"It's because the women here don't like us at all," Tonya Peters, one of the women in their group offered when Petronella wondered aloud why no one seemed to want to sit with them. "They think we steal their men."

"Can we help it if we're irresistible?" Gina asked, lowering her eyes and smiling at a young man seated at a nearby table. He smiled back, his eyes alight with interest. Gesturing to the empty seats, he lifted his brows inquiringly, standing with his tray and approaching when Gina nodded, waving her hand in invitation, entering an animated conversation with the man who had joined them.

"I guess if they're going to hate us, they should at least have a reason," Petronella said, watching as two other men came and occupied the remaining two seats, engaging two additional members of the group in conversation. "You all have been reeling them in all day, starting with Curtice Brooks this morning." She eyed Jenna sideways, smiling when Jenna opened her mouth and closed it abruptly, choosing with difficulty not to respond to the provocative statement. "Mmm, this lunch is as good as breakfast. They have good cooks in both these kitchens," biting into a crispy fried chicken breast.

"Eat up, ladies," Jenna said, directing her remarks at the women who seemed to be more interested in talking than eating. "We have one more class here before catching the bus back to Grayson, and we have a full schedule there tonight, so we need to get moving," watching as Gina and the man she was talking with exchanged numbers, as did the other two.

"Dwight is cute," Gina said looking seductively over her shoulder at the obviously smitten young man. "He told me about a party one of the fraternities on campus was sponsoring this weekend and invited all of us to come."

"Sounds like a plan," Petronella said enthusiastically. "Count me in. I'll be there with bells on."

"I won't," Jenna said. "I plan to use my weekend to clean my room, wash my clothes and study. I came here to work and learn, not to party."

"Oh, come on, Jenna, you know the saying about 'all work and no play'," Gina said coaxingly.

"We won't stay long," Petronella added. "There'll be plenty of time left for cleaning up and studying." They continued trying to convince their reluctant – and stubborn friend as they returned their trays and began the walk to their next class.

"Welcome back, ladies," Sam welcomed the women as they boarded the bus discussing their first day on the Milestone campus. "Hope y'all had a good day. Were the ladies on campus any friendlier than they have been in the past? I can see by your faces it was the same as it ever was – the men are friendly which makes the ladies mad, so they're not. That is a shame I say, with all the trouble in the world and here in Birmingham, all colored people should be trying hard to get along. Oh, well, one can always hope times will get better. Now if you ladies will look to your left, you'll see the 16th Avenue Baptist Church, The Reverend Frederick Huddleston is the pastor there. Lawd, is he a firebrand! He can sure light up a church, and he real active in the movement around here. He can cuss a blue streak, too. Some of the other pastors around here think he's too pushy and loud and is more of a detriment than a help, but a lot of people follow him anyway. It's a real good church for any of y'all looking for a church home while you here." The elderly man kept up his running commentary all the way back to the nursing school.

"Oh, man, I am bushed," Gina fell on her bed, kicking off her shoes, swinging her legs and bare feet onto the bedspread. "Who knew it would be so hard making up a hospital bed? The sheets must be so tight you could bounce a quarter off them, and the corners have to be tucked just so. I mean really! It won't make the patient no never mind what the corners of their bed look like. Not that you had a problem, Queenie. Your bed already looked like that, so for you it was about the same as making up the bed like you do every day, wasn't it?"

"It's not that hard, Gigi," Jenna said. "I can help you if you want."

"I do, but not now. I'm just too tired," Gina said with a sigh. "I'm just going to lie here until I muster the energy to get up and get ready for bed."

"Then, I will see you in a few minutes," Jenna said, gathering up her soap, toothbrush and paste and everything else needed to prepare for bed. She returned shortly, turning out her light and climbing in. "I will sleep tonight and not worry about studying until tomorrow night."

Closing her eyes taking a deep breath, she drifted off unaware when Gina stumbled up hours later, headed for the washroom, towel, and other toiletries in hand. Tomorrow was going to be another long day.

Chapter Nineteen

"C'mon, Queenie, come just for a little while? We won't stay long. Just a few dances, a little conversation, and we'll head back. Then you can study all you want."

"Girl, some fine men are going to be there," Gina said. "You know that fraternity has the best-looking men on campus."

"I know that's right," Petronella said. "It's going to be a blast, so why don't you put on one of them pretty party dresses you have and come on."

"We have mid-terms next week, so I intend to study," Jenna said firmly. "Maybe when they are over, but not until then. I do plan on going to church tomorrow, and you two are more than welcome to join me."

"After partying tonight, my plans are to stay in bed until supper time tomorrow," Gina said. "I've drawn the overnight shift and for once I'm glad. I get to sleep all day. I never thought I'd be looking so forward to something I used to do all the time."

The pace had been brisk, from their first orientation meeting to their present busy schedule. In addition to the classes taken at Milestone College, the nursing students were also required to take additional classes to hone their skills and knowledge base in areas specific to their craft. Emphasis on cleanliness was the first, last, and constant order of business. With their hands protected by industrial-strength rubber gloves (from the harsh jugs of Green soap and Phisohex hexachlorophene antibacterial cleansers), they scrubbed hospital beds and wiped down sinks and metal trays. They had also made up innumerable immaculate hospital beds.

"Are you sure we didn't stumble into a hotel, and they think we are maids?" Gina had asked irreverently more than once. "I swear I'll have a new respect for the people that clean my house," she added this time, lighting a cigarette and taking a deep pull. Her campaign for a doctor husband was moving along nicely. At least three or four doctors-to-be were showing signs of being greatly smitten, and an engagement would likely happen sooner rather than later.

"Well, that's awfully considerate of you," Petronella said dryly. "The good news is we'll be changing rotations next week. I think we'll be on one of the floors in the wards working closely with LPNs."

"Oh, Lawd, must we?" Gina half-wailed. "You know they hate me." She had inadvertently insulted them all by trying to hire some of them to clean up after her, the implication being that all they were good for was cleaning up behind their betters. Alerted to what she had done, since then Gina had done all but stand on her head attempting to appease them because as it soon became apparent, she was helpless without benefit of their experience, strength, and extensive knowledge. Forced to work together for the good of the patients, they were currently at a simmering standoff, cooperative but each wary of the other.

"Well, they don't like me much either," Petronella said.

"I thought they were nice," Jenna said.

"You would," Petronella said, "as soon as they found out you were a true healer, they have shown you nothing but respect. It was funny when they called themselves testing you, not only could you answer their questions, but you also added other plants to consider, broke down their chemical compositions and took it to another level in the nicest manner possible, leaving them with no doubt that they had been put in their place, that the healer was demanding her due and proper respect. And would you believe that, highly impressed, they broke into uproarious laughter, and she ain't been able to do no wrong since. Maybe we'll do more nursing type stuff this rotation."

"We are learning how to take temperatures," Jenna said. "Our nursing books and manuals and classes are just full of interesting information. Plus, as my final project in chemistry, I am comparing the chemical composition of a healing plant with that of a product in drug form currently on the market. My hypothesis is they will be so close in their chemical makeup, the difference will be virtually the same. My chemistry professor thinks I can get a paper out of it."

Petronella and Gina stared at her in silence for a moment. Turning almost in unison, they headed for the door. "We give up," Gina said, "enjoy your manuals and chemicals and hypotheses and what not. I'll dance one dance just for you."

"Thanks," Jenna said absently, immediately re-absorbed in the complicated chemical equation she was working on, jotting down notes and questions for her chemistry teacher.

Early the following morning, bathed, lotioned, perfumed and powdered, dressed in a bright blue sleeveless dress with a full skirt cinched at the waist with a slim cloth belt made of the same material, a light, three quarter length cardigan sweater the same shade of blue edged in white, and blue pumps on her feet, she put the finishing touches on her hair which she allowed to fall free – thick, wavy, lustrous. It brushed her shoulder blades. A few final swipes with her brush, and she was ready.

"I'm headed for breakfast and then Sunday School," Jenna announced to the slumbering, lightly snoring mound under the covers in the bed across from hers. "Anyone who cares to join me is welcome." No discernible movement came from the sleeping blanketed heap. "I'll probably stay for church, too," Jenna said brightly. "See you later."

"Would you just go?" Gina snapped, shifting into a more comfortable position. Smiling widely, Jenna exited the room closing the door firmly behind her.

"The doors of the church are open," the minister intoned fervently, spreading his arms wide as he walked up one aisle, crossed over in the back and down the second aisle, still imploring the hesitant or undecided to step forward. A spirited round of applause and shouted amens and hallelujahs erupted when a youth walked down the aisle and shook the minister's hand, followed by an older woman joining under Christian experience. Standing with the congregation, Jenna took the opportunity to look around. She had spent a good amount of time watching the Pastor's children misbehave, their young mother, an uncertain First Lady unable to control them.

"I see where my first contribution to the movement is going to be," Jenna said to herself. The Reverend Frederick Huddleston was one of the most dynamic civil rights activists in the city, known for his hot temper and equally fiery rhetoric. Looking away from the boisterous youngsters she was anxious to get a hold of, her eyes collided with a pair of dark brown ones trained on her face, watching her steadily. With a jolt she recognized Curtice Brooks. It must have been his gaze she felt, almost as palpable as a touch for much of the service. Her breath speeding up, catching in her throat, she looked away sharply, raising her hand for the benediction, singing the closing song. Scooting her way out of the aisle where she was seated, she walked swiftly down the sloping carpeted walkway, moving to where the First Lady stood surrounded by parishioners. Smiling, hand extended, Jenna politely plowed her way through the crowd.

"Sister Huddleston? My name is Jenna Thompson. It is so nice to meet you."

"It's nice to meet you, Sister Thompson," Rosalind Huddleston said, shaking Jenna's hand. "I'm Rosalind, and these are my children – Frederick Junior, Thomas, Edward and Rose. Children say hello to Sister Thompson."

Jenna was not surprised when their only response to their mother's instruction was to stare at her a moment before running off, yelling at the top of their lungs. "I'm so sorry for their rude behavior," the First Lady said. "They are a bit...rambunctious..." her voice trailed off.

"They are that," Jenna agreed. Moving closer she said confidingly, "I so admire the work you and the Pastor are doing with the movement. I would love to participate, but the rules of the Grayson School of Nursing prohibit any student or employee from taking part in any demonstrations. But I would like to help if I can and thought – maybe I could watch your children when you are busy with other things? I can come by on Fridays and Sunday afternoons. I could probably squeeze in a Saturday if I bring study materials. I have lots of experience with children – nine brothers and sisters, eight of them younger than me. Six of my siblings are boys, so if I can help just let me know."

"I–I would love to take you up on your offer," Rosalind said, her face lighting up, "as early as next Friday...and could you possibly spend the night? I'll have you back at the school bright and early Saturday morning."

"I think I can work something out," Jenna said, waving away Rosalind's effusive thanks, pretending not to notice the speculative way she was being examined by the children she would be watching on Friday. Reading the mischief in their eyes, she smiled. They were not going to know what hit them.

"Pastor, do me a favor. Introduce me to that young lady talking with your wife," Curtice said, tilting his head in Jenna's direction. "Her name is Jenna Thompson, and I need you to help me convince her I'm really a nice person worth knowing."

"Did something to get on her bad side, did you?" Reverend Huddleston asked with a knowing chuckle, his smile widening when Curtice ducked his head and sheepishly nodded. "Come with me boy, let's see what we can do about mending some fences with yon pretty lady."

"Honey, introduce me to this young lady that I have been noticing in the congregation these past few Sundays." When Rosalind did as asked, he said, "It sure is nice to meet you, but I noticed you have not officially joined us yet, Sister Thompson?"

"No, sir, not yet," Jenna said softly.

"Just know that we would love to have you as a member. Speaking of members, here's a member of our congregation who works hard in the church, works just as hard in the movement, and is a genuinely nice guy who I know would be happy to help you get acclimated in the church and the city seeing as how he's Birmingham born and raised. Curtice Brooks, meet Jenna Thompson."

"We've met, and not under the best of circumstances," Curtice said ruefully. "I let my big mouth get the better of me, as we both know, Pastor it has a way of doing –"

"That's why you end up in jail so often," the Reverend said with deep belly laugh.

"Yeah, well anyway, my mouth got the better of me. I said some things that weren't true, jumped to unfair conclusions, was thoroughly told off; I haven't been able to get the person I disparaged to give me the time of day since, so I can't apologize, to humbly beg pardon and ask that we start over...because I would really like for us to be friends."

"Now, there's as nice an apology as you'll ever hear," Reverend Fred said approvingly. "Do you accept his apology, Sister Thompson?"

"Jenna, please," Jenna said, "and of course I accept Brother Brooks' apology. It would be churlish not to."

Curtice smiled at the young woman with the fathomless dark eyes, who used words like 'churlish' with crystal-clear diction. "I'm happy that you are willing to give me a chance to redeem myself. May I call you Jenna?" Jenna nodded.

"Well, I'll leave the two of you to get better acquainted," the Reverend said. "And Sister Thompson, I expect to see you come walking down the aisle to join our church family in the very near future." Jenna smiled watching the minister walk away before turning back to Curtice.

"Jenna, may I walk you back to the nursing school?" Curtice asked. "We can get to know one another better, and have the chance to spend some together," presenting her with a wide smile when after a brief hesitation she nodded in agreement. They walked out side by side, their conversation growing increasingly animated after an initial awkwardness.

"Was that Curtice Brooks I saw you with? Who you were standing there talking with for such a long time?" Petronella inquired, a slight smile on her face, "Yes, that was him," Jenna said. "He goes to 16th Avenue, he had the minister introduce us, where he apologized for his previous boorish behavior, then asked to walk me home when I forgave him."

"Forgiveness for his previous boorish behavior, huh?" Petronella said. "I'll let you know whether that was a good thing – after I look up 'boorish'."

"While you do that, I'm getting undressed and studying a bit before dinner. Has Gigi gotten up yet?"

"I haven't seen her since the party, which was big fun, by the way," Petronella said. "I am determined to pry you away from your books to have a little fun, too."

"I don't know about fun, but I will be spending the night somewhere else this coming Friday," Jenna said with a slight smile.

"What?" Petronella gasped, "Where in the world are you going? With whom? Do you need to get permission?"

"I do not need permission. Just check out, let them know where I will be, and be back before Sunday night curfew. Anyway, I am just going to be minding Pastor and First Lady Huddleston's four children while they are attending organizational and planning meetings. Rosalind asked if I could spend the night, and I said I would."

"Oh, babysitting," Petronella said, deflated. "I thought it was something interesting."

"You had your mind in the gutter," Jenna said sternly, her eyes twinkling, "Shame on you!"

"I thought you had decided to let loose!" They laughed, laughing even harder when a bleary-eyed Gina opened the door demanding to know what was so funny.

*   *   *

"Jenna, welcome, welcome! Come on in! I can't tell you how much we appreciate your willingness to watch the children while we do the work that needs to be done." Pastor Huddleston stood back, gesturing for Jenna to enter. "We'll be leaving in a few minutes; the wife is still getting dressed. Let me show you where you'll be sleeping and give you a quick tour of the house, so you can begin to familiarize yourself with where things are."

"This is where you'll be sleeping, so just make yourself at home," Reverend Fred said. "My children have been anticipating your arrival all week."

I bet they have, Jenna thought, *and I bet they have all kinds of nasty little surprises for me. That is all right. I have a few surprises of my own.* Aloud she said, "I have certainly been looking forward to meeting them…so if you would be kind enough to perform the introductions before you leave, I would appreciate it."

"Of course," Reverend Fred said. "Put your things away and come to the living room when you're finished. I'll make the introductions."

"Thank you, Pastor," Jenna said. She reached into one of the bags she brought with her and placed two aluminum cylinders on the dresser. The words and pictures on one showed a variety of large, delectable mixed nuts heaped all around; the other displayed an array of tempting hard candies. Three other bags were placed underneath the bed, reaching into a fourth she extracted the gift she had made for Rose. Stepping out of the room, she headed down the hall, ducking into a nearby closet to await developments. She did not have to wait long. Giggling softly, each admonishing the other to hush, the three boys came stealthily down the hall, looking around before ducking into the room she was occupying. Coming out of the closet, Jenna stood on one side of the open door, listening carefully. She knew the exact moment the cylinders were opened. A rush of air, a loud springing noise, and the sound of several objects suddenly released from confinement. Startled exclamations and gasps of horror filled the air along with scrambling sounds and increasingly frantic whispers as they tried desperately to replace the coiled cloths that had escaped the first cylinder, and attempted to stop the insane, mechanical laughter coming from the second that started as soon as they opened it.

Jenna moved to the open doorframe where she stood silently watching, arms crossed. Their eyes widened when they saw her standing there. Caught red-handed, they sheepishly lowered their heads and handed her the opened cylinders. Reaching into one she silenced the maniacal laughter, motioning for the boys to pick up the wired cloth and place it on the dresser. Still without saying a word, she gestured for them to precede her out of the bedroom, down the hall and into the living room where the Reverend and Rosalind awaited. Jenna shook hands with each boy as they were introduced to their relief making no mention of their foray in her room. Rose was hanging onto her mother's skirts, her face buried in the billowing material. Jenna knelt beside her when introduced.

"Hey, Rose," Jenna said. "I am so pleased to meet you. I brought a friend of mine to meet you too. If the two of you get along, she just might decide to live here. But only if you both agree."

Rose lifted her head, peeking out to see the friend of Jenna's who might want to live with her. A rag doll with dark brown cloth skin, wooly black yarn hair, big stitched on black eyes, brown nose and red smiling yarn mouth, dressed in a blue dress with a white apron, black woolen shoes and white woolen socks was being held carefully in Jenna's two hands. Letting go of her mother's skirts, Rose, her eyes alight, reached for the doll, hugging tightly when Jenna placed her in welcoming, eager arms. "Her name is Emily Ann," Jenna said, "She is so excited to meet you. Do you think the two of you can be friends?"

`Rose nodded vigorously, hugging Emily Ann even more tightly. "I love her," she said, "I want her to live with me." She watched anxiously as Jenna whispered in Emily Ann's ear and appeared to be listening intently to what the doll was telling her. "Emily Ann says she loves you too, and would love to come live with you," smiling when Rose hugged them both fiercely. Tucking her hand in Jenna's she waved goodbye to her parents without bursting into tears and loud wails as she usually did whenever her parents left her with a sitter.

"Well, kids, shall we have some supper?" Jenna asked. "Your mom fixed spaghetti and wanted me to make a salad and heat up some bread. While I'm busy in the kitchen you can each bring one toy to the living room and stay in there until time to eat. No rough housing though."

Jenna turned on the burner under the spaghetti, stirring the mixture, moving to the refrigerator, and removing the ingredients for the salad. She had Rose tear the lettuce, add the chopped vegetables to a large bowl and with her assistance toss them all together. The little girl also helped butter the bread which Jenna placed under the broiler and collected napkins and silverware as the two of them set the table. The boys had never returned from their trip to collect toys. Putting a pitcher of water on the table, pouring it into the plastic cups on the table, adding dressing to the salad and a piece of toasted bread to the steaming plate of spaghetti, Jenna walked over to the hallway.

"Boys, supper is ready," she called, pretending not to notice their long absence. After blessing the food and making sure everyone was eating, Jenna strolled down the hall. Entering her room, she immediately noticed her bed was disturbed. Carefully pulling back the covers, she captured the scurrying water bugs in the large glass vase decorating the dresser. Shaking out the covers and looking under the bed to make certain she had captured them all she returned to the kitchen.

"I found these in my room," Jenna said walking over to the kitchen door and tipping them out of the vase. "I hope I got them all and none got away to lay eggs…they like dark, small spaces, like closets and shoes, the smaller the better. You boys need to be careful about putting on your shoes…you do not know what you might find." Calmly sitting down, Jenna continued to eat, ignoring the uneasy glances the boys were exchanging with one another.

"I brought some chocolates," Jenna said after everyone had eaten their fill. "Help yourself," holding a metal tin filled with tissue and waxed paper and a variety of chocolate covered treats. Reaching greedily into the tin they stuffed chocolate into their mouths. "You know," Jenna said thoughtfully watching them chew, mouths full, "If we had been in another part of the world, those water bugs would have become dinner. If fact, a lot of countries consider bugs good to eat, like candy…they cover them in chocolate, and crunch down…and they especially like their gooey insides," finishing her comment just as they bit into the caramel center of the chocolate covered pecan candy, smiling to herself when they abruptly stopped chewing. "Of course, we do not eat bugs…do we?"

With their mouths full of half-eaten chocolate and Jenna watching them, the boys had no option but to continue chewing and to swallow the sticky mass, trying desperately to not think about crunchy bugs with oozing insides and others lurking in their closet. Thomas was the first to lose the battle, racing for the bathroom, holding his mouth and gagging, followed closely by Edward. Frederick Junior managed to hold his down but was looking a little green around the edges, racing after his brothers when Jenna reopened the tin and offered him another chocolate-covered treat. Picking one up, she bit into it, offering one to Rose who chose a caramel chocolate candy, biting into it, and licking her lips.

"I guess that will teach them to pick on girls," Jenna said with a twinkle and a wink. Rose nodded, her eyes shining. She was often the victim of her brothers' pranks and was delighted when

Jenna whispered what the two of them were going to do while the boys were setting up an attempt to scare their babysitter.

"Are you all right?" Jenna asked with concern when the boys, still looking a little queasy, joined them in the living room, selected toys in hand. They all remained where they were until a short time later when Jenna announced it time for Rose to go to bed, taking the little girl's hand and walking to her room, decorated in a variety of shades of pink. Sitting in a wooden rocker, she held Rose close when the little girl climbed into her lap ready for bed.

"Have you ever heard the story of Beauty and the Beast?" Jenna asked when Rose shook her head, Jenna changed the heroine's skin and hair color so that she more resembled the story's listener. Enthralled, Rose listened closely, sighing in sleepy satisfaction at the tale's happy conclusion. Climbing into her bed, she hugged Jenna good night, arranging Emily Ann carefully beside her, quickly falling asleep.

The boys had not ventured from the living room as Jenna noted on her return. "Time for you to go to bed too," Jenna said. "If you want, I can read a chapter from the book I brought with me – *The Three Musketeers*, my brothers' favorite book. Lots of sword fighting and other adventures are in it."

"Is that all you got?" Fred Junior said disdainfully. "We don't want to hear about no sword fighting," ignoring his younger brothers' disappointed faces.

"Well...there is a story I could tell you..." Jenna began, "but it is not for the faint of heart – no, I cannot," she said shaking her head.

"Tell us! We ain't scared," Fred Junior insisted when Jenna still looked doubtful.

"Well, if you are sure..." Jenna said slowly, standing when they all nodded. Walking over to the kitchen, she reached into a drawer and took out a large flashlight, moving back to the living room and turning out the light, clicking on the flashlight, its beam the only light in the darkened house. "Gather around, and I will tell you the story of the Man with the Golden Arm," she stated solemnly. She proceeded to tell the story of a mining man who struck it rich, but not before losing an arm in a mining accident. Taking some of the gold he had mined, the man brought a gleaming golden arm to replace it, only to have it stolen and him killed by greedy claim jumpers. One dark night, a strange sound was coming from the nearby forest. The wind arose suddenly. The claim jumpers heard the moaning voice of the man they had killed in the wind asking the whereabouts of his missing golden arm. The rising wind suddenly blew out the campfire where they were gathered, and one by one the claim jumpers disappeared, after first letting out a muffled shriek following by a gurgling sound. The sole remaining claim jumper leaped running and screaming; the wind and the moaning voice following him. "Where is my golden arm? Where is my golden arm?" Jenna intoned in a low, moaning voice, "Where is my golden arm?" She went silent, suddenly switching off the flashlight, plunging the room in total darkness. She could hear the boys breathing heavily. Reaching over, she grabbed Fred Junior "YOU GOT IT!" she yelled to an accompaniment of screams from the closely listening boys.

Turning the lights on again, she turned to the wide-eyed boys. "Bedtime, fellas," she said briskly. "Do not forget to pick up your toys." Once in the room the three of them shared, she watched them prepare for bed, noting how they looked carefully in their closets, examining the house shoes they would be putting on in the morning, climbing into their respective beds, bidding her a quiet good night, their eyes looking around nervously as she turned off the light. She sat in the living room, opening one of the textbooks she brought with her. Then she heard Fred Junior calling her. "What is it, honey?" she asked standing in the doorway.

"Thomas is crying. He scared to go to sleep," Fred Junior said, refusing to admit that sleep was eluding him as well. Walking over to his bed, Jenna lifting a sobbing Thomas into her arms, rocking him gently and making soothing noises, putting an arm around Edward when he sat down beside her. After calming them down, she went into her bedroom, reaching under the bed, and taking something from one of the bags she had stashed. Returning to the boys' room, she plugged in the night lights she had brought bathing the room in soft light. "Here you go," she said tenderly. "The man with the golden arm is afraid of lights, so you will be completely safe. I will be right here and would never let anyone hurt you. They would have to go through me first." Hugging each boy tightly, even Fred Junior, she left them convinced that no one would dare take on their babysitter; she was much too formidable. Snuggling down, the softly gleaming nightlight provided them comfort and reassurance.

Jenna closed her chemistry book a short time later and prepared for bed after making sure everyone else was asleep. A peaceful silence descended the household, surprising the returning parents who had been bracing themselves for the usual upheaval that occurred whenever their children were left with a babysitter. Moving quietly so as not to awaken anyone, grateful parents were soon in bed and asleep as well.

Chapter Twenty

"You looking mighty nurse-y this evening, Miss Queenie," Petronella said admiringly, giving her friend the onceover, "Everything that should be white is very much so. Your crisply ironed blue blouse, white collar and cuffs are so starched they could stand up and walk around by themselves; the seams are perfectly straight on your white stockings; your white shoes polished within an inch of their lives with brand-new shoelaces; and your hair elegantly twisted. You look like one of them advertisements in *Colored Magnificence Magazine*."

"What a nice thing to say, Miss Petronella," Jenna said with a smile. "You are looking mighty nurse-y yourself."

"Gigi, you look nice, too," Petronella said carefully. The truth was both Jenna and Petronella were beginning to get seriously worried about their friend. Always frivolous but truly kind at heart, honest about her lack of true passion for the profession she had seemingly chosen at random, equally honest about her intention of finding a physician husband, always up for a good time and ready to party – her recent behavior had been so unlike her normal self that it was causing increasing alarm in her friends. She was brooding, snappish and angry often staring out into space, nibbling nervously on her thumb.

"Thanks," Gina said shortly. Looking at her friends' anxious faces, hers softened. Grabbing one of each of their hands, she said, "I'm sorry. I've been a real bitch, haven't I?" laughing when they both nodded. "It's just that – I can't go into it right now. The ceremony is about to start, but I promise to tell y'all what's been on my mind the first time we alone and can talk. Now, let's go get those nurse's caps. Lord knows we worked hard to get here, and at times I wasn't sure I would make it."

The Capping Ceremony was one of the most important events in nursing they would ever take part in, marking their official entry into the field of nursing. To get this far they had had to pass both their nursing and college courses; learn to scrub down a hospital room quickly, thoroughly and completely; wash and fold a mountain of sheets and pillow cases; serve countless lunches; take temperatures, pulses and measure blood pressure using their mandated Timex watches; assist physicians in a variety of capacities including the emergency and operating rooms; work closely with prickly LPNs – licensed practical nurses – the work horses of the nursing profession, the backbone keeping the whole together; the lack of a formal nursing education the only thing impeding an LPN's advancement. They had also formed friendships that would endure a lifetime.

Jenna had sailed through all of it. Her honest, innate love for what she was doing making it a pleasure and not a chore, learning all she could, absorbing everything like a sponge. Her paper on the chemical makeup comparison of natural remedies versus manufactured drugs had won a prize when presented in the student section at a medical conference and had been subsequently published. She was presently working on a second paper with her biology professor and a Birmingham Regional staff physician looking at the side effects resulting from natural remedies versus manufactured products. Petronella was also doing well, not nearly as well as Jenna, but easily within passing range. Gina was another story, always tittering on the brink of failing one or all her classes, of being expelled from the program, somehow managing to just get by, usually by the skin of her teeth. She had fainted the first time she assisted in surgery, her brief sojourn in the emergency room had not fared much better. Somehow, she had managed to persevere, and tonight was her reward, participation in the upcoming ceremony. They all turned as Prudence Brown, the black nurse who had guided them through their first difficult days of nursing school, came through the door where they were all gathered. She was dressed as always in snowy white with nurse's badge proclaiming Registered Nurse sewn to the arm of her uniform.

"How nice you all look," Nurse Brown said with a rare smile. "Let me be the first to congratulate you. You have come a long way, so enjoy this accomplishment this night. You deserve it. Now, if you all will get to your place in line, we will head to the auditorium."

The capping ceremony was simple but moving. The student nurses lined up according to academic standing, Jenna standing at the head of the line to no one's surprise. Each of them was handed a candle beginning with Jenna. The candles were lit by the person in front of them symbolizing their role as a comforting light shining in the darkness; the room they were in symbolically darkened. The featured speaker was a well-known member of the original class of colored nurses at Grayson. She spoke briefly but eloquently about the importance of nursing, its vital role in history, in the United States beginning with the pioneering work of Florence Nightingale during the American Civil War, and the often-unknown role that black nurses had played in the conflict known as the War Between the States. She ended by encouraging the new nurses to continue to fight for right, to stand up for what they believed in – the only oblique reference about the turmoil currently taking place throughout the South.

Head Nurse Emma Johnson stepped forward asking each second-year student to repeat after her the Florence Nightingale

Pledge. They all vowed to continue the tradition of caring for others, to do no harm, to always work for the good of the profession. Following the simple recitation, the newly recognized nurses were instructed to carefully blow out their candles, and the overhead lights turned on again. Crisp, brand-new perfectly folded, spotlessly white nurse's caps were pinned onto perfectly groomed heads as each student's name was called, and they were handed their first nurse's badge identifying her place in the official pecking order and which would be sewn onto her uniform. Following a brief prayer, the ceremony ended, and all attending guests invited to a small reception being held in the school's cafeteria.

"Pastor and First Lady Huddleston, you made it! Thank you so much for coming," Jenna said with a wide smile, hugging them both. "Hello, Monsters," she said to the four children gathered round waiting for their turn to greet the sitter they had quickly grown to love. In addition to being their staunch protector against all things wicked and scary, she was also warm, funny, caring and always coming up with fascinating things for them to do whenever she babysat.

"You look so pretty, Miss Queenie," Rose said admiringly. "I think I'm going to be a nurse when I grow up."

"Well, nursing is certainly a worthy profession," Jenna said. "That is wonderful if it is what you want to do. Boys, you were as good as gold," Jenna said smiling, "I am so proud of you. How about some punch, cake, and ice cream? I hear we have homemade peach and homemade vanilla." She watched them hurry toward the food line just managing not to run.

"The ceremony was beautiful. I would not have missed it for the world," Rosalind said. "First in your class! I had no idea. I am so proud of you."

"We are all very proud of you," Reverend Fred said in his booming voice. "Your church family is proud as well, although

I am still waiting for you to come down that aisle to formally join us."

"Thank you, Reverend," Jenna said, smiling softly.

"I can guarantee nobody in the world is any prouder than I am," a warm, caressing voice behind her said.

"Curtice, you made it," Jenna said turning, her face alight. "You are back from Greensboro? How did the lunch counter demonstrations go?"

"Same old, same old," Curtis said, "White folks acting ugly and us just sitting there taking it. Sometimes I wonder if we are having any impact at all, but I'm not here to talk about that. I am here to share in your good fortune, to tell you how proud of you I am, prouder still that I can call you mine, and to tell you how much I am looking forward to a future with you in it."

Silence. "Do you not agree with some part of what I just said?" Curtice asked carefully, his face tightening when Jenna looked down before looking up into his eyes, he as always falling headlong into bottomless depths. She turned away with a sweep of thick black lashes. "This is neither the time nor the place for serious discussions of any kind," she said. "I just got my nurse's cap. Let us celebrate!" She found herself at the laughing center of her Group One classmates, having that and other moments immortalized forever thanks to new Polaroid cameras that took and developed color pictures so easily. Someone started the record player and with a whoop everyone began dancing: Jenna holding hands with Fred Junior, Thomas, Edward, and Rose, clutching Emily Ann as they spun around the room, later holding Curtice and being held tightly in return as they gazed into one another's eyes, dancing to a slow love song.

"That was fun," Jenna said later that evening, as she lounged across her bed, her nightgown clad form wrapped in a matching robe, a similarly clad Petronella beside her.

"It was a lot of fun," Petronella agreed, stretching luxuriously. "You and Curtice make a nice, extremely good-looking couple. You can tell he thinks so. In fact, I thought he was going to propose tonight, but he didn't."

"That's 'cuz Jenna looked like she wasn't having it." Gina was seated on her bed, longingly eyeing her purse holding her cigarettes, but knowing she would face unpleasant consequences from her roommate if she even thought about lighting up in their room. She was nervous, uneasy because she had some major news to share with her friends.

"That's what I thought," Petronella said, "It would have been so romantic. You can tell he crazy about you. I thought you felt the same way. Don't you want him to propose? He's pre-law and wants to be a civil rights attorney. He'll make a good living and will probably make a name for himself on the national level. He might even become a Supreme Court Judge or get appointed to an appellate court or something."

"Smart, handsome, on his way to being famous – what more do you want?" Gina demanded.

"Maybe someone whose politics will not always land him in jail or place him squarely in the cross hairs of dangerously racist white people," Jenna said unexpectedly. "I love Curtice, I truly do. Part of me is thrilled with the idea of being his wife and the mother of his children. However, another part looks at what is liable to be a life under constant public scrutiny, upheaval, turmoil, and potential danger. I know that Curtice thrives on the rush, the adrenalin, that he lives to uplift his people whatever the cost and I would never ask him to change…but I do not know if I can or if I even want to live that way."

"It can't be easy for the person married to a firebrand," Petronella agreed. "Always worried about visits from the K-K-K or having rocks and bricks – even bombs –thrown through your windows, and crosses burning on the front yard, trying to protect your children while you support the partner who is working so hard to make things better for his colored brothers and sisters."

"Curtice is already well-known around here," Jenna said. "He has spent a lot of time in the local jail and accepts that he will be spending even more time in other jails across the South. We all know how vocal and outspoken he is. What if his mouth gets him into serious trouble – trouble he cannot talk his way out of? I do not want to be a short time wife and longtime widow. I do not want to be at home always waiting for him to return from his latest demonstration or protest or march praying that he makes it back safely."

"I never really thought about it, but it has to be scary for the other person in a relationship with someone like Curtice," Petronella said. "You have some serious thinking to do this coming year. Wow, even good relationships are complicated. Still, I wish I was in one," she said wistfully.

"You will be," Jenna said positively, "it will happen soon, you will be very happy, and it will last your entire lifetime."

Looking into the dark, uncanny eyes looking not just at her, but into her, Petronella felt the hairs on the back of her head rise. Although her friend would never admit it, Petronella was convinced Jenna could see into the future. "Well, I'll wait for that," Petronella said, "I'll just be patient."

Gina took a deep breath. "Speaking of relationships, it's time y'all heard about what's been making me act crazy these past weeks." She was silent a moment, gathering her courage. "Y'all know Harold Robbins and I are close," she said at last. Jenna and Petronella nodded. A future surgeon, they had always assumed the richly dark man with regular features and deep-set brown eyes behind black wire-framed glasses was the front runner in the competition for Gina's hand. "Well, he proposed to me last night." Still dressed in her nursing attire, she pulled a gold chain out from concealment under her blouse to reveal the large, sparkling square-cut diamond threaded through it.

Gasping, her two friends jumped to their feet. "Gigi, that's so wonderful. Look at the size of that diamond! I am so happy for you." Then looking at her more closely, Jenna said, "It is wonderful, right? Is it not what you wanted?"

"I didn't think it could happen to me, but I don't just like him, I really, truly love him," Gina confessed. "He is sweet and kind, and even though he's going to be among the rarest of the rare of colored doctors, a surgeon, he doesn't give himself airs. I thought they were interchangeable – the doctors-to-be, I mean. If one were to run, I would just go to the next one on the list… but then I started to fall in love with Harold…and I thought I could – that I wouldn't – that I would be able…" her voice trailed off miserably.

"Gigi," Jenna asked gently. "You have been acting funny for a while now. I thought you would be over the moon at getting the proposal from a doctor. To love the one who asked is just icing on the cake. So, what is the problem? Are you already married or something?"

"If only it were that simple," Gina said, standing and pacing up and down the narrow aisle separating the two beds, nibbling on her thumb. "I could divorce an inconvenient husband, but I cannot divorce my family."

"Why on earth would you want to divorce your family?" Jenna asked. Gina hesitated before inhaling deeply. "Have you all ever heard of Isaac Jennings?" she asked.

"Isaac 'Icepick' Jennings? The biggest gangster in the South?" Petronella said. "Everybody's heard of him. They say he killed dozens of people, most of them with an icepick which is how he got his name. Why do you ask?"

"Have I ever told you my full name?" Gina asked eyeing her two friends closely.

"Gina Reynolds," Petronella said, "I don't know what your middle name is."

"Reynolds is my middle name," Gina said unexpectedly, "my mama's maiden name. My full name is Gina Reynolds Jennings. Isaac Jennings…is my daddy."

Stunned, "Icepick, I mean, Isaac Jennings is your father?" Petronella said faintly.

Gina nodded. "Are you beginning to see the problem now? How am I going to tell the man I want to marry who his father-in-law would be? His future children's grandfather. What the hell do I tell his family? He will probably run like a rabbit, as fast in the other direction as he possibly can. Even if he doesn't, what about my daddy? He will want to meet him and his family – especially him - the man who wants to marry his only child. My mama will, too. He is my daddy and has spoiled me all my life and…I love him despite who he is or what he has done."

Petronella shook her head. "Y'all got some tangled webs to unravel on your roads to married bliss. I don't know which one is most tangled, though I think Gigi's might be a little bit more knotted than yours, Queenie. Telling a future high-powered doctor that his father-in-law is a straight up gangster ain't going to be easy. But then, marrying a hotheaded civil rights activist who often speaks before he thinks is kind of tricky, too."

"Maybe you can live somewhere other than the South," Jenna suggested. "You would only have to be around them when you visit and vice versa. Maybe that would be less obvious."

"Where is he from?" Petronella asked.

"Iowa," Gina said.

"Iowa?" Petronella repeated. "I didn't know they had colored folks in Iowa. Seems to me your problem is solved. Just keep your in-laws in Iowa most of the time, except for christenings and holidays and stuff like that."

"I still have to tell him," Gina said glumly, plopping down on her bed. "And that will probably be the end of that."

"Maybe not," Jenna said, sitting beside her and putting an arm around her. "Harold is a doctor, so he more than anyone should know that you have no choice about who your parents are. If he loves you, he will accept it."

"After he gets over the shock," Petronella added.

"I would appreciate it if you didn't spread this around," Gina said. "The fewer people that know the better."

"Mum's the word," Petronella promised as Jenna nodded her agreement.

"I'm for bed," Petronella announced, standing. "It has been quite a night in more ways than one."

"Good night, all," Jenna said. "I am babysitting all day tomorrow and well into the evening, so I will see you all Sunday after church."

"I'm going to lay here and think about what might have been," Gina said. "And decide when and how to tell Harold. I just hope I don't start wailing." She undressed swiftly, carelessly dropping her clothes on the floor, pulling her nightgown from under her pillow, putting it on, climbing into bed, and pulling the covers over her head.

*　　*　　*

"Miss Queenie's here!" Rose exclaimed happily, running to the front door throwing her arms around Jenna, Emily Ann in tow.

"Hey, Rosie," Jenna said, hugging the little girl. "Have you been good?"

Rose nodded vigorously. "I been real good, Miss Queenie, like I promised I would. Does that mean we going to make cookies?"

"It certainly does," Jenna said, holding up the grocery sack containing ingredients for cookies she had promised pending a good behavior report.

"Hey, Miss Queenie," Fred Junior hurried up, returning the hug Jenna gave him. "Are we going to work on our volcano tonight?" They had started a project that studied volcanoes and were in the middle of making their own papier mâché´ version that would flow simulated lava once finished.

"I think we will have time," Jenna said. "We have all day. Tomorrow is Sunday, so you can stay up a little longer. We just have to make sure you get enough sleep before Sunday School and church." She smiled and hugged the other two boys who came running to greet her.

"How you doing, Queenie? It's good to see you," Reverend Fred entered the room smiling. "I appreciate your willingness to watch over the children while we plot strategy today. I have a feeling it's going to be a long session. None of us hardly agree on what would be the most effective way to highlight the challenges and prejudices we face. Last night there was another bombing. Mr. Michael's grocery store was heavily damaged. A rumor that turned out to be wrong was that a bunch of us activists were meeting there. It's a good thing we weren't there, somebody would probably have gotten killed."

"I hate that Paul's store was so badly damaged," Rosalind came into the room shrugging into the lightweight tan woolen coat she was carrying. "That was the store where most of us shopped. Now we have to go somewhere out of our way if we want to patronize another colored man, someone we know won't cheat us or try to sell us spoiled food."

"Well, Hon, if you're ready we best be on our way," Reverend Fred said. "In case you need to reach us, we are going meet in one of the Sunday School rooms in the basement at 16th Avenue. Otherwise, we'll see you later tonight. Children, y'all will probably be asleep by the time we get back, so we'll see you tomorrow." Hugging each of them, they exited through the front door, closing it firmly behind them.

Hours later Jenna looked up from her sociology book when she heard the key turn in the front door lock as Reverend Fred came through followed by a harried-looking Rosalind and several others. "Got-dammit, how is it Montgomery, which is less than half the size of Birmingham, can organize an effective boycott," he was saying angrily, "but all we seem able to do is sit around flapping our fuckin' lips? Shit don't make no sense."

"Brother Fred, ain't no need to start using profane language," one of the men, also a minister, in the process of taking off his coat said chidingly.

"Hell, sometimes profane language is the only damned language to use," Reverend Fred said bitingly. "Maybe these mothers would sit up and take more notice if we did."

"You have heard the saying 'the squeaky wheel gets the grease', haven't you? I say the Reverend's right. We need to make some noise, some real noise in order to be heard – especially if we want to attract the attention of the national radio networks and newspapers, even television." Jenna looked up in surprise, recognizing the voice, her eyes meeting those of Curtice Brooks.

"And after we do, I say we call the U.S. Justice Department and demand that Bobby Kennedy get up off his ass and do something," Reverend Fred said. The room erupted in noise.

Easing her way out the room so she could not be accused of taking part should they get raided, Jenna headed for the kitchen where she had seen a harried-looking Rosalind disappear moments earlier. The 16th Avenue First Lady was standing in front of an open refrigerator door, anxiously examining its contents. She turned as Jenna entered the room.

"I – I was wanting to fix them something to eat, but I am not sure what…" her voice trailed off.

"Let us see what you have here," Jenna said briskly. "Why not get those big skillets out and a couple of large pots. I will bet we can rustle something up right quick." Reaching into the refrigerator she took out eggs, cheese, milk, a bowl full of watermelon chunks which had been cut earlier, and a big package of dark red sausage links. She grabbed potatoes and onions from the bin under the sink and a few large tomatoes ripening on the kitchen windowsill. Finally, she picked up the package of bread from the counter and began placing slices in the four-slot toaster on the counter.

"Sister Rosalind, you start cutting that sausage into smaller pieces about an inch or so," Jenna said, "fill that pot with water, and put it on the stove. We will make grits. After that, if you will start a pot of coffee and slice those tomatoes, I think we will have a nice meal to offer those hungry folk in there."

"Queenie, I honestly don't know what I'd do without you," Rosalind said gratefully.

A short time later, Rosalind invited everyone into the kitchen to eat the meal she and Jenna had prepared. Platters of fried potatoes and onions, grits, fluffy scrambled eggs with cheese, sausage pieces, sliced tomatoes, watermelon chunks and a stack of buttered toast with apple jelly in a cut-glass bowl on the side occupied one of the kitchen counters. A stack of plates, silverware, napkins, cups, and saucers were on the kitchen table. The smell of fresh coffee wafted from the pot bubbling on the stovetop. The final touch was the last of the frosted tea cakes Jenna and the children had made earlier that day on a plate next to the stove. "Y'all help yourselves," Rosalind invited softly.

"Everything sure looks tasty," Reverend Fred said. "Thanks for doing all this, darlin'," he said to his wife.

"You should thank Queenie," Rosalind said gratefully, "She's the one who pulled all this together."

"I was happy to do it," Jenna said, waving away the effusive thanks from the hungry group piling food on their plates, "Reverend Fred, if you could take me back to Grayson after you have eaten, I would appreciate it."

"I'll take you back," Curtice said immediately. "One of my buddies is letting me use his car, so I can drive you. It's the least I can do for someone who managed to feed us so well." Piling most of what was left on his plate between two pieces of toast, taking a huge bite, he stood.

Nodding her head in agreement, Jenna wished everyone good night as she collected her things and the money Rosalind handed her. The two exchanged a big hug at the door, Rosalind refusing Jenna's offer to help clean up, waving goodbye before closing the door. Polishing off the last of his sandwich Curtice took the stack of books, notebooks, and assorted papers from Jenna as they walked to the old, battered jalopy parked on the street. He, opening the door, helped her get seated. Placing the stack of assorted things he carried on the back seat, he slid into the driver's seat, leaning over to place a warm kiss on full lips before starting the car and pulling away from the curb. They rode for a time in companionable silence.

"You know, Miss Jenna, we rarely have any alone time. Someone is always around," Curtice complained. "There are some things that I want – that I need to say that are for your ears only. Christmas break starts next week – when are you going home to South Carolina?"

"The day after the break starts," Jenna answered. "My bus leaves at seven o'clock that evening."

"My buddy is leaving for Jackson, Mississippi early on the morning of the first day of the break. I'm taking him to the bus station, he's leaving his car here and I'll be here alone. Will you come spend the day with me? We can talk about the future, spend some rare time alone together, and then I'll take you to the bus station in enough time to catch your bus. I'll make sure we have some goodies, something to toast one another with, and we can just enjoy one another's company. What do you say?"

"That sounds like fun," Jenna said. "I'd like to see where you live."

"Great," Curtice said enthusiastically. "I'll come pick you up early so we can have as much time together as possible."

"I look forward to it," Jenna said softly as Curtice pulled over to the curb in front of the colored entrance to the school.

"Not nearly as much as I am," Curtice said, leaning over to place a final lingering kiss. "Good night, sweetheart."

"Good night," Jenna said, opening the passenger door and sliding out.

Curtice waited until Jenna was inside the building before driving off. He was greatly looking forward to next week.

Chapter Twenty-one

"City sidewalks, busy sidewalks, dressed in holiday style…" Gina sang lustily, slightly off-key.

"…in the air there's a feeling of Christmas…" Petronella joined in with a clear soaring soprano.

"…children laughing, people passing, meeting smile after smile…" Jenna joined in, her voice a husky contralto, "and on every street corner you hear…"

"Silver bells…" they all chimed in, "silver bells…it's Christmas time in the city…"

"I love that song," Gina said as she stuffed clothing into one of her suitcases. "I'm tempted to just leave everything and get anything I need after I get home," she said. "I hate packing."

"That's 'cuz you got so much to pack," Petronella observed, holding up her bag. "It takes me no time to pack. One suitcase with room to spare."

"Then you will have room for this," Jenna said, lifting a blanket on her bed and extracting two packages wrapped in brightly colored Christmas paper handing one to Petronella and the other to Gina.

"Oh, Queenie, you shouldn't have," they both protested. "We didn't say we were going to exchange gifts."

"You do not give gifts to receive gifts," Jenna said reasonably. "These are just a little something I wanted you to have, and you better not even think about rushing out to buy anything for me.

You just have a great holiday. I look forward to seeing you when we get back."

"Thank you, Queenie," Petronella said giving her friend a big hug, "You're the best. When are the two of y'all headed for home? I'm leaving this afternoon."

"I'm leaving this afternoon, too," Gina said. "and…Harold is going with me," she said, raising her left hand to show the diamond flashing on her ring finger. "I told him about my daddy, and he said he still wants to marry me. He's going to ask my father for my hand."

"He ain't scared?" Petronella asked.

"My daddy won't do nothing but give his consent," Gina said. "He's just anxious to meet the man who wants to marry his baby girl. It's not like he's going to attack him or anything."

"He still mighty brave," Petronella said. "Are his folks coming too?"

"Just his mother, and she'll be coming from Iowa the week of Christmas," Gina said. "In the meantime, I have a wedding to plan, and I want both of y'all to be my Maids of Honor."

"Gigi, I would be honored," Jenna said, giving her friend a big hug.

"I would love to be in your wedding," Petronella said, joining in the hug. "I'll be able to tell my future children about this wedding!"

"When is it?" Jenna asked.

"In April," Gina said. "Harold is doing his residency in Nashville, and we want to get married before he leaves. I guess I'll have to learn to like country music, huh?"

"You are going to the country music capital of the world," Petronella said. "You'll probably be hearing it blaring everywhere, so I guess you need to learn to love it."

"You will be so full of love, you will just love everybody and everything," Jenna predicted. "Even country music."

"I don't know," Gina said doubtfully. "It is going to take an awful lot of extra love for me to include country music in the mix – that guitar twanging, and folks caterwauling can really work my nerves."

"You will make it work," Jenna said with a smile.

"When are you heading home, Queenie?" Gina asked.

"My bus leaves at seven o'clock tomorrow night," Jenna said.

"I hate that you are going to be by yourself for a day," Gina said.

Jenna said, "Do not worry about me." She had not told anyone about her plans to spend time with Curtice. He would be picking her up later that morning; her heart fluttered with a combination of nervousness and anticipation whenever she thought about it.

"Well, I'm off," Petronella said. "Baton Rouge is still a long bus ride away. Gina, you coming?"

"Right behind you, girlfriend," Gina said with a smile, hefting the two suitcases she had decided to take with her. "Harold is going to meet me at the bus station, so you and I can share a taxi – my treat."

A last-minute flurry of hugs and holiday wishes and Gina and Petronella closed the door behind them leaving Jenna sitting on her bed.

A few hours later standing on the curb outside the school, Jenna watched the battered jalopy pull up beside her, Curtice climbing out from the driver's side, tossing her suitcases into the back. Opening the passenger side door, closing it behind her, rounding the car and sliding into the driver's seat, turning, he beamed as he leaned over to greet Jenna with a kiss.

"I sure am glad you decided to spend some time with me, Miss Jenna," Curtice said softly, "Your visit is like getting an early Christmas present."

Jenna smiled. "I am happy to spend some special time with you, Mister Brooks," she said. "It is a nice way to start the holiday season."

A short time later they pulled in front of what was once a stately home that had been converted to a boarding house. Like an elderly lady in a faded ball gown remembering better days, the house sagged in places, the paint was peeling and some of the flagstones leading to the stairs chipped and broken, yet arched windows and doors, a wide wrap-around porch and huge bay window in front retained echoes of former glory. Climbing out and opening the car door for her, Curtice kept hold of the hand he had grasped to help her out of the vehicle. Walking through the unlocked doorway and into the wide foyer, Jenna looked around with interest. Several faded sofas and worn coffee tables took up most of the floor space. Other doors opened to rooms where she could see tables and chairs. Twelve-foot ceilings added openness and a semblance of grace to what would otherwise be a crowded space; faded throw rugs covered what were once gleaming wooden floors. Leading her over to a sweeping staircase, the two of them climbed all the way to the top floor. Stopping in front of one of three doors on the floor, Curtice inserted a large, old-fashioned key and turned the lock, pushing the creaking door open, bowing with a flourish.

"Welcome to my humble abode," he said. "It isn't fancy, and this ole house has definitely seen better days, but I like it well enough."

"I can see why," Jenna said, looking around. "The wood paneling is beautiful and so are the windows. Which room is yours?" walking over to the door Curtice indicated and peeking in. A neatly made-up double bed occupied most of the floor space, a small nightstand and wooden dresser filling up the remainder. Books were stacked everywhere, on the nightstand, the dresser, the floor, the hallway, both desks in the main room and a tall bookcase in one corner. Pens, papers, and notebooks were scattered across one desk spilling onto the floor. Several megaphones occupied another corner piled next to a stack of wooden planks used to hold the protest signs created for the marches and demonstrations, blank poster paper and paint cans next to them. Walking over to a small screened porch perched in front of the apartment she sat down on a small wicker sofa, looking out at the park located across the street, at city office buildings rising in the distance, at the other former mansions on the street converted to boarding houses, its occupants coming in and out; and children playing outdooors, riding dilapidated bicycles, gliding by on old metal roller skates, jumping rope, drawing a hopscotch game on the sidewalk with chalk, a group of girls playing jacks. She turned, smiling when Curtice came to sit down beside her.

"This is a really nice neighborhood, Curtice," Jenna said. "You're not far from Milestone College."

"It is about a ten-or-fifteen-minute walk away," Curtice said. "That's why a lot of students live in these old mansions. They tend to be cheap, and they're close to campus."

"I like it," Jenna said. "It is really peaceful and quiet." They sat silently for a time absorbing the tranquility.

"You hungry?" Curtice asked, standing when Jenna nodded. "Stay here and get comfortable," he said. "I'll be right back with something to eat." He left. Jenna could hear him going down the creaky stairs, the sound of the car pulling away. He was back a short time later loaded with brown paper bags, delectable odors emanating from most of them.

"Come on over to the table," he invited, gathering up the books stacked there and transferring them to a nearby chair. "I went to Miss Lucy's – her food is good, I hope you like it," removing and unwrapping foil covered paper plates revealing crispy fried fish, shrimp and chicken, French fries, coleslaw, pickles, rolls, hot sauce and ketchup. "I got some fried peach and apple pies for later," he said, holding up a paper bag that he placed in the oven. Handing her a paper plate, napkin, plastic knife, and fork, pouring iced tea from the large pitcher in the small refrigerator, he urged her to eat as much as she could hold. Biting into the crispy fish, Jenna closed her eyes in bliss. "This is so good, Curtice, everything is," she said, popping a shrimp sprinkled with hot sauce and dipped in ketchup into her mouth.

"I am stuffed and cannot eat another bite," she declared a short time later, sitting back in her chair with a sigh. "Everything was delicious."

"I'm glad you enjoyed it, my queen," Curtice said. "Now, if you like, I can take you on a tour of Birmingham. I'm guessing you don't get the chance to explore much."

"You are right," Jenna said eagerly, "I am usually so busy with school and nursing, and I spend most of my free time watching the Huddleston children."

"Come with me," Curtice said, "I was born and raised here, so I know this city like the back of my hand," taking her hand he led her out of the room.

"What about your family, Curtice?" Jenna asked at one point as they drove around Birmingham. "You never mention them."

"My mama died about four years ago, just before I started at Milestone," Curtice said. "She literally worked herself to death providing for me and saving money to get me into college. I had an older brother who died when I was twelve. I never did know who my daddy was. I have an aunt and some cousins who live in Chicago, but I don't know them very well. My grandmother died before my mama did, and that's about it as far as family is concerned. I always envied people lucky enough to have big families."

"I have six brothers and three sisters," Jenna said, "whom I would be more than happy to share with you."

"I appreciate that, Miss Jenna," Curtice said, his eyes caressing, "and I'd be proud to take you up on that offer...and I'd love to have a big family of my own, lots of handsome sons and beautiful daughters like their mother." He parked in front of his boarding house as he made the statement, turning the car off walking around to open the door for Jenna, the two of them entering the building and climbing the stairs without encountering anyone.

"Just about everyone is gone for the holiday break," Curtice said. "It's usually a lot livelier than this."

Secretly relieved no witnesses were there as she entered a man's room alone, Jenna said, "Maybe next time there will be more people, and maybe I will have the chance to meet your roommate as well."

"I like that; it means you plan on coming back," Curtice said with a smile. Opening the door to his rooms, he stepped back allowing Jenna to precede him, following her, and sitting down beside her when she returned to the screened porch and sat back down on the wicker sofa. It was noticeably cooler, Jenna shivered, moving closer when Curtice put an arm around her, the warmth of his embrace comforting. "I'm glad, really glad you're here," Curtice said pulling her closer, "It has been a great day. I can't remember when I've enjoyed one more."

"A special day," Jenna agreed, looking up at him with the dark gaze that never failed to leave him breathless.

"Do you know, have you any idea how much I love you?" Curtice asked, his fervent voice catching, his eyes roaming her face, cupping it gently in his hands. "I have from the first time I saw you at the rally in John White Park and was hopelessly lost when you told me off so thoroughly, and then ignored me so completely after I let my big mouth get the better of me the first time I ever talked to you. Then after you forgave me, to have been blessed to be the one you chose to spend your time with fills me with pride. You are so smart, so beautiful, so accomplished, you could have any man you wanted. I know that you are going be successful at anything you do and that includes being a wife and a mother...and I would be the happiest man in the world if you were my wife and the children that you have are mine. I would always be proud of you and do all in my power to make you happy. I would never try to change you because there is nothing about you that needs changing. I'll work hard to give you a good life, Miss Queenie, my Jenna. Tell me that you feel the same way, that you'll marry me that we'll spend our lives together...say yes, Jenna...please, say yes."

Lost in the love she could see radiating from the eyes of the earnest young man who cared so much and wanted to make a life with her, smothering her doubts, letting her love for him surface, lighting her face from within, her beautiful eyes shining, Jenna said, "Yes, yes, I'll marry you, be your wife, have your children, and spend the rest of my life with you."

His face alight, Curtice lowered his head, bringing his lips to hers, sealing their pledge with a kiss that deepened, as their feelings blazed into life. Heated kisses led to sizzling tastes, little nibbles of tender throat and silken shoulders, hands lifting to stroke slim arms, pulling her slender curves close against his muscled strength. Pulling away, breathing heavily he said, "I would never disrespect you or do anything that you are not willing to do, Queenie, but I love you so much that if we don't stop now, I might not be able to."

Jenna lifted his hands to her breasts. Curtice, his face reverent, his hands gently stroking, caressing the precious gift he had just been offered, reveling in the promise of intimacies to come. They came together with a rush, pain and initial embarrassment giving way to overwhelming passion and crackling desire as two became one. Each turned to the other fiercely, ardently, tenderly more than once that first night of love before falling asleep, still entwined, physically drained and emotionally satiated.

Jenna awoke to kisses, hot biscuits with butter and honey, steaming hot chocolate and coffee the following morning. Sitting up, wrapping herself in the top sheet, she smiled with delight. "I have never been served breakfast in bed," she said, pouring one of the plastic containers of milk into her coffee cup.

"I'll serve you breakfast every Saturday morning," Curtice promised, placing another kiss on warm, slightly sticky, sweet lips before sitting on the bed beside her and biting into one of the biscuits. Thank you kisses quickly escalated into another heated lovemaking session after which they began to plan their future together, both agreeing that Revered Fred would be the one to marry them. The day flew by, full of love, laughter, and excitement about what was to come.

"Thank you for a wonderful two days," Curtice said as they waited in line for Jenna to board her bus that evening, "I can't think of when I've enjoyed myself more. You have a good time in South Carolina, be sure and give my mother-in-law-to-be my regards, and I'll see you when you get back."

"I had a wonderful time, too," Jenna said looking up at him. "Have a good Christmas and remember, this is a time of peace, so no demonstrations or rallies until after the New Year, all right?"

"All right, sweetheart," Curtice said, pulling her into his arms. "I'm so happy right now, I got no fight in me. I'll stay away from conflict and strife until after we've toasted in the New Year that's going to change our lives forever."

Kissing her deeply, holding her tightly, pulling away slightly, eyes caressing, he stroked one hand down her soft, smooth cheek. "I love you," he said, his voice tender.

"I love you, too," Jenna said, giving him one last kiss before boarding the bus and moving down the aisle to find a seat on the side where he was standing. She waved and blew kisses until the bus pulled out of its numbered stall moving down the street on the first leg of the long trip home.

"Queenie's home!" the excited lookout shouted: the announcement bringing the rest of the family pouring out onto the porch and down the stairs, running to greet the family member they were all happy to see returned to them, no matter how brief the visit. Laughter and group hugs were the first order of business as everyone welcomed Queenie home. Even Dexter and Alfonso and Lorenzo, the twins sauntered up and kissed Jenna on the cheek, hugging her tightly.

"My, you are the cool ones," Jenna said, eyeing the nattily dressed trio, large Afros topped with leather apple caps, bell-bottomed pants, and brightly patterned shirts. "Popular with the ladies, are you?"

Dexter smiled. "I do all right," he said. "Alfonso and Lorenzo ain't no slouches either."

"They Pettigrews through and through, that's for sure," Ma'dear said with a sigh. "They just like they daddy and granddaddy was when they were young and wild – girls acting crazy, fightin' over 'em, trying to get pregnant by 'em so they would have a pretty baby – all of that foolishness."

"Are you a daddy yet, Dex?" Jenna asked with concern. "And what about you Alfonso and Lorenzo? Gotten any girls in trouble yet?"

"There been some accusations made, but since they had been with other dudes they couldn't prove the baby was mine," Dex said, "so I ain't got no baby I claim." What he neglected to mention was that the other boys the girls had been with were usually Alfonso and Lorenzo.

"Blood will tell," Ma'dear said, shaking her head in disgust. "Come on in, sweetie, we done wasted enough time talking about them sorry boys. I fixed a good supper for you and invited some people I think you'll be happy to see. Here they come now," pointing to the two figures making their way up the long path from the road.

Gasping with delight, Jenna ran to embrace Essie and Nettie, the three of them laughing and embracing, happy at their reunion. Chattering happily, they made their way to the cabin and the big dinner Ma'dear had prepared, Sidney grasping the hand he had rarely let go of since his first sight of his sister at the bus station. "Miss Essie, Nettie, you both look so good, living together is obviously working out for the both of you."

"I didn't realize how much I would love having someone living with me," Essie said with a smile. "Nettie's the daughter I never had. I couldn't be happier."

"Neither could I," Nettie said with a shy smile, putting an affectionate arm around her benefactor. "Miss Essie is the easiest person in the world to live with. She don't hardly let me do anything – spoils me rotten."

"You deserve some spoiling," Essie said fondly. "Do you know she's spending her time writin' a book 'bout what she went through? She says it's her way of working through the pain and terrible memories of that time."

"What a wonderful idea," Jenna said enthusiastically. "May I read what you have written? I won't tell anyone what you wrote, but I would love to see it."

"You can read it, Queenie," Nettie agreed. "You already know most of it anyway. I'll bring it by tomorrow." The noisy group continued to make its way to the cabin where their dinner and a vacant-eyed Rodney Pettigrew awaited them.

"I have met the man I plan to marry, Ma'dear," Jenna made the announcement as she and her mother walked along the path they used in their search for medicinal herbs. It was not the right time of year for most of them, although a few grew year-round. It was these they were currently looking for, though admittedly not very diligently, being more interested in their conversation than gathering greenery.

"You have?" her mother said with an excited smile, stopping to grasp her daughter by the hands. "Tell me all about this man who has managed to turn my level-headed daughter's head," laughing softly when Jenna dropped her head, smiling in embarrassed self-consciousness, as she told her mother about Curtice.

"So, he's one of them civil rights people?" Ma'dear said. "One of them marchers and organizers and demonstrators, huh?"

"That is the only thing I worry about," Jenna admitted, "that we would be dodging rocks and bricks and dousing burning crosses most of our lives. That scares me."

"Maybe he'll take his fight to the courts when he graduates law school," Ma'dear suggested, "so he can fight his battles and yell all he wants to in the courtroom."

"I am hoping the same," Jenna said, "that he will continue the fight for our people but in a different way."

"I'm sure that's what he'll do," Ma'dear said, looping an arm through her daughter's. "He knows he's got a good thing going, and I think he'll do what he needs to keep it." Reassured by her mother's words, still linked arm in arm, the two continued their walk, discussing when and where the nuptials would take place.

Time spent at home flew by. Christmas came and went – a joyous, boisterous day filled with presents, food, friends and family, the little ones delighted with their gifts from Santa, the older ones excited about what Jenna had bought them in Birmingham. She was joyfully surprised when Curtice called on Christmas day to deliver holiday greetings, making it a point to meet and talk with an impressed Ma'dear over the telephone. Even though Rodney was no longer a threat, Jenna still elected to stay with Mama Joyce, Sidney, and Papa Pete during her stay. Mama Joyce still looked much as she always had, moving a little slower, but Papa Pete was visibly deteriorating, never leaving his room and rarely his bed, eating little and talking even less, his eyes distant, lost in memories of his tumultuous past, smiling occasionally when a particular memory surfaced. Jenna made it a point to see Doc Edmonds, older but still rigorous. he reminded her of their plans to practice together, delighted when Jenna told him of her plans to become a nurse practitioner.

"Jenna that is wonderful," he said, "Have you decided where you want to study?"

"Well, I have applied for programs in Birmingham, Atlanta and Detroit," Jenna said. "I have not heard anything yet, but I would be happy to attend any one of them."

"I read your paper in the *Journal of Medicine*," Doc Edmonds said, "It was excellent. The best thing I ever did was to give an earnest little girl my old medical books."

"I think so, too," Jenna said. "I am looking forward when the day comes that we have a chance to work together."

The days flew by and almost before she knew it, Jenna was hugging assorted family members goodbye as she and Sidney climbed into the car driven by the person who had agreed to pick them up and take them to the bus station. Waving from the window seat she had chosen, Jenna prepared herself for the long ride ahead. She thankfully climbed down from the bus that she had been riding two day later. Looking around, she smiled as she recognized a familiar figure.

"Hey, Sam," she said, greeting the elderly man who by his own admission did a little bit of everything at the school, "Come to collect the nursing students back in town from their holiday break?"

"Hey, Miss Jenna, it is good to see you. Your special friends arrived earlier today, and would you believe that Gina gal came loaded down with more suitcases?" He shook his head. "I'll be dashed if I know where she going to put them. Y'all's room is going to be awfully crowded. But come on, tell that boy to bring your stuff, we'll store it and be on our way."

Boarding the bus moments later, Jenna was happy to see some of the members of her group. Sitting on the seat they indicated, they exchanged greetings, filling in one another on their time spent at home. Gina and Petronella were waiting when she reached her room.

"Hey, Girl," Petronella said, hugging her friend. "Did you have a good holiday? Mine was pretty good, I guess. I was happy to see my mama. My daddy and his brothers got falling down drunk as usual and then started to fight as always, same old, same old. That's why I'm always glad to come back here where things are calm and normal. Thank you for the beautiful blouse. I had to hide it to keep my sisters from taking and wearing it, or my brothers from stealing it and trying to pawn it."

"And you think my family is bad?" Gina asked. "My daddy buys me stuff, not steals it from me. I know his reputation, but I have never heard him raise his voice, and I sure ain't seen him fight nobody, and we don't have a single icepick in the house. I don't have any brothers or sisters so I can't speak to that. My mama's always hovering over me, trying to get me to wear stuff she likes and stuff like that, but that's more annoying than anything else."

"Yes, well, like we said, you can't pick your family, so I just have to cope. But I don't want to talk about my trifling family. How did the meeting between the future in-laws go?" Petronella asked.

"The fact that we're getting married the first week in April should tell you something," Gina said with a smile. "My mama is going crazy with her planning – who to invite, where to have it, what to wear, decorations and all of that. I just tell her if I like something or not. She is doing everything else. Daddy just nods and says all right. He and Harold seemed to like each other, and his mother is nice, too. She talks real proper, like Jenna."

"How many are going to be in the wedding party?" Jenna asked. "Is it going to be a big wedding?"

"Well, the two of you, my Maids of Honor," Gina said counting on her fingers, "and two of my friends from high school, plus three cousins on my mama's side of the family, a flower girl and a ring bearer. How many is that?"

"If you count the men who will be escorting the bridesmaids and the Best Man and the groom it comes to seventeen," Jenna said doing some rapid calculations in her head. "That is a large wedding party."

"This will be the only wedding my mama will ever get to plan, so I know she is going over the top on everything. But we should have a really good time; I know the two of them will show everybody a good time."

"I'm going to be in 'Icepick' Jennings' daughter's wedding," Petronella marveled. "Who would have thought?"

"The daughter we met in nursing school," Jenna said. "The daughter who is going to fulfill her dream of marrying a doctor. You did it, girl, now enjoy it."

"I can tell already that it's going to be a wedding to remember," Petronella said.

"I hope so," Gina said, "Count on it," Petronella said. "With this cast of characters, it can't be anything else. On that note, I'm going to bed. Even though you don't do nothing but sit, riding on a bus wears you out. Good night, y'all."

"Good night."

"Good night."

Chapter Twenty-two

"Gigi, you look so beautiful! That dress is a dream; it is perfect for you." Jenna stood on one side of the full-length mirror admiring the double vision of her friend, the real and the reflected.

The translucent, square-necked, tightly fitted bodice was made entirely of delicate hand sown lace patterned with shimmering, luminescent pearls. Puffed sleeves, full at the shoulders buttoned snugly from the forearm to the wrist, a double row of pearl buttons softly gleaming. The narrow, elegantly draped ankle-length silk skirt was attached to a twenty-foot train; an enormous white straw hat, tilted to one side and tied under her chin with a big satin bow adorned Gina's head, a sheer white veil edged in pearls the same length as the train floated gently around and behind her. The flowers and greenery in her big bridal bouquet were the same colors as those selected for her wedding – buttercup yellow, green and yellow-gold. Actual buttercups glowed a bright yellow, green leaves and stems adding a vivid splash of color, the warm yellow gold of roses adding both color and fragrance. A white lace garter and lace-covered white heels with big satin bows completed the wedding ensemble.

"You look like you just stepped out the pages of the latest bridal magazine," Petronella said admiringly.

"She does look wonderful," Jenna said. "Gigi, I honestly do not see how you could look any prettier." Petronella nodded in agreement.

"Thank you," Gina said, her face beaming. "You all are looking mighty spiffy yourselves."

"I have ever owned a more beautiful dress," Jenna said reverently, looking at herself. "I am almost afraid to move. Thank you…"

"Please, not another word," Gina said, "I am having as much fun as you, so if you like it, I'm satisfied,"

"I love it," Jenna said softly replacing Gina in the mirror. Her buttercup yellow silk gown fell from a square-cut bodice in a straight fall to the floor in the front with a short train in the back. Short, puffed sleeves and long silk gloves the color of the gown covered her arms to her elbows. A bright green ribbon threaded through the bodice and tied into a big bow in back with long trailing ends adding a touch of vibrant color. Her hair was twisted into a curly mass on top, a rose surrounded by buttercups nestled in its depths adding rich color and texture. Her bouquet of bright yellow buttercups and yellow gold roses also included yellow and white daisies all tied together with wide yellow, white, and gold ribbon. She smiled when Petronella came to stand beside her, the design of their dresses the same, but yellow gold the dominant color of the other Maid of Honor's gown and roses the dominant flower.

"C'mon, y'all, we going to take a picture of the three of us before heading down the aisle," Gina said, gesturing to the photographer. "Hurry, I think I hear the wedding music starting. That's okay, they can wait. It can't start until we get there, right?"

Several minutes and pictures later, a last-minute exchange of hugs and well-wishes, a final straightening of the bridal train and veil, they exited the room moving into position slowly walking down the wide stairway as everyone seated in the glass enclosure stood, the grand piano and organ playing the wedding march. Bridesmaids dressed in green gowns with yellow daisy bouquets walked down the aisle on the arm of a tuxedoed groomsman. Jenna and Petronella walked side by side, smiling at friends and familiar faces. They were followed by the flower girl and a ringbearer who balked at his first glimpse of the large crowd and had to be coaxed down the aisle.

Gina was next on her father's arm. He lifted the veil to kiss her warmly on the cheek inches above his before taking her hand and placing it in that of the young man standing at the altar. All the women sighed when the groom raised the hand that he held to his lips before retaining hold of it and turning to face the minister. The kiss after the exchange of vows was warm, ardent, and full of passionate promise. Everyone laughed and applauded when the newlywed couple smiled and waved as they hurried down the aisle, followed by the remaining wedding party.

* * *

"Girl, can you believe all this? I ain't never seen nothing like it outside the pages of bride magazines, and I think this has got a lot of them beat," Petronella said, helping herself to another hot appetizer being offered by a hovering waitress.

"It is amazing," Jenna agreed. "The whole weekend has been incredible. Gina looks so beautiful; that gown is something else. To pull up to the hall in a limousine! I had to pinch myself a time or two to convince myself that I was not dreaming," she said, sipping on sparkling cider in a fluted glass.

"I know that's right," Petronella said with a short laugh. "I never expected to be at something this fancy, much less Maid of Honor, to a colored girl who lives like a princess...even if her daddy is a bigtime gangster," she said in a lower voice, looking around carefully.

"He is really nice, though," Jenna said, "her mother is, too."

"I guess you can be nice when everyone is scared of you," Petronella said, picking up another appetizer from a different waitress.

"Shhh! Somebody might hear you," Jenna admonished her. "Gigi would be hurt to the core to hear you talking about her daddy like that, and I know you would never willingly make her feel bad, especially on her special day, and you one of the Maids of Honor!"

Petronella ducked her head. "You right," she said sheepishly. "I need to think before I open my big mouth. Here I am staying in they house and eating they food and saying all kinds of mean-spirited things. I ain't never in life had a dress like this, and Mr. Jennings paid for it. Forgive me, Lawd – I hereby promise to have nothing but a good time and to say only good things from this moment on." Then she reached for another appetizer from the tray of a fourth solicitous waitress.

"What are the two of you talking about so seriously?" Jenna turned in delight at the sound of the warm male voice behind her.

"We were just marveling at everything," Jenna said, smiling up at the handsome man smiling down at her. Petronella strolled discretely away after first smiling at the two of them together. "It is all so beautiful," indicating the masses of flowers, trellises and statuary placed in strategic locations throughout the huge, glass-enclosed structure, late afternoon sun striking the glass at odd angles creating a glittering rainbow effect.

"It's nice," Curtice agreed, "I keep trying not to think about where the money that paid for all this comes from."

"I know, but Gigi cannot help who her daddy is," Jenna said softly, "plus lots of white dynasties today have family fortunes anchored in illegal activity."

Curtice cupped her face in his hands, "That's my Jenna," he said tenderly. "You see the glass half-full, don't you? Always seeing the best in everyone. It's just one of the many things I love about you."

Jenna looked searchingly up into the face so close to hers, placed her hands over his, still cupped around her cheeks, seemed about to speak when they were interrupted by the voice of the tuxedoed maitre'd inviting them all into the formal dinner. "You are seated with the bridal party, so I'll see you afterward once the fun starts," Curtice said, planting a soft kiss on her forehead.

"There you are, I've been looking for you," Gina said rushing up. "Well, what do you think, girlfriend? Did you like the ceremony? The location? Can you believe I'm married? To a doctor?" Jenna, Gina, and Petronella who had walked up as Gina was asking her questions, looked at one another, and squealed with excitement and delight, hugging each other tightly.

"Come on, let's eat," Gina said. "Then we gonna party hearty," walking up and planting a kiss on her new husband's lips that drew applause and whistles before sitting down in the large, overstuffed chair next to his.

Jenna kept up a friendly conversation with the two groomsmen on either side of her, both of whom she knew slightly. She watched as a parade of waiters brought the first course: a fruit salad resting in a fresh pineapple boat. Pasta sprinkled with fresh basil, thyme and Parmesan cheese comprised the second course, followed by rare beef sliced thin in a rich broth and roasted new potatoes. Leg of lamb with asparagus tips and soft fluffy yeast rolls followed a tiny bowl of strawberry or lemon sorbet intended to cleanse the palette, a small salad with a balsamic vinaigrette ended the meal. The enormous wedding cake along with a massive dessert table would provide the sweet.

"Girl, the banana part of this cake is delicious, the chocolate and lemon and coconut ain't bad either," Petronella said, placing another forkful into her mouth. "I didn't know you could have so many different kinds of layers with all them flavors."

"I have seen so many new things," Jenna agreed. "Lots of people will want to hear about this wedding."

"I bet it gets featured in *Onyx* and *Colored Magnificence Magazine*, both," Petronella said, "'Cuz it sure don't get more magnificent than this!"

"C'mon y'all, we got to get this party started," Gina said, walking up. "Ready? One, two, three!" gesturing to the band which broke into a sprightly number, Gina shouted, "Come on, ladies, let's Bunny Hop!" leaning forward, bending her knees, looking back at Petronella who placed her hands on either side of her friend's hips, and Jenna, her hands on either side of Petronella's, her hips held by Curtice who had joined in, his hips held by the person in back of him until a long line formed, snaking around the room, led by Gina and Harold whom she had collected on her first pass around the room. Tapping their feet and hopping forward and back, they danced around the room.

"Have I told you how beautiful you are tonight?" Curtice asked as he and Jenna danced to a soulful love song being sung by the band's female singer.

"I think you have mentioned it once or twice," Jenna said with a slow smile. "I am certainly glad you think so."

"Oh, I most certainly do," he said, "and I am looking forward to the day you are the one in a white dress walking down the aisle towards me."

"So am I," Jenna said after a brief hesitation. Poised to tell him something vitally important they were again interrupted by the song coming to an end and an excited Gina calling all women to gather round while she tossed the bouquet. Urged on by Curtice, a reluctant Jenna joined the group of excited women jockeying for position. Turning her back, Gina tossed the bouquet over her shoulder. A flurry of scurrying, good natured pushing and shoving, before a hand reached up and snagged the bouquet, its owner jumping up and down with excitement. Gina and Jenna both laughing as Petronella continued to dance around holding the caught bouquet high.

"Miss Jenna, would you take a walk with me? I would love the chance to spend some alone time with you," Curtice grabbed one of Jenna's hands, gently stroking its surface.

"I would like that very much," Jenna said, her heart speeding up.

Hand in hand they walked away from the boisterous crowd, moving to a quieter part of the glass enclosure. "This has really been something else, huh?" Curtice said, looking around. "I saw a photographer and someone else taking notes, so this wedding is probably going to be on the local society pages and some frou-frou magazines. I saw them taking your picture. You might become famous, but I hope you don't expect our wedding to be like this. I can't afford it, and I wouldn't want you to spend a lot of money just for show."

"I wasn't planning anything nearly this fancy," Jenna said, "just something small, nice and simple...even so, some people might question things...like should I even be wearing white when I walk down the aisle." She held her breath, waiting for him to understand what she was trying to tell him.

"Why would anyone question..." his voice trailed off as his mind began to race as he thought about the implications of what she had just said. He halted abruptly. Turning to Jenna his eyes searching he stammered. "J-Jenna? L-love...are you...are you saying...you're..."

"Pregnant," Jenna said looking up at him in some trepidation as she waited for his reaction.

His face alight, laughing with joy he lifted Jenna into his arms, spinning her around. "I'm going to be a daddy!" he said with excitement. "My wonderful woman is having my baby. We are going to be a family in what, about four or five months?" kissing her on the lips when she nodded. "We'll get married right after our graduations – yours and mine. Then we'll plan to relocate to whatever program you decide for the Nurse's Practitioner training and certification, and I'll go to law school there. We will settle there while we're in school, and then decide what we want to do and where we want to live after we both finish grad school."

"I like that," Jenna said, looping her arms around Curtice's neck, still held securely in his arms, greatly relieved that he was excited about the baby, at his unquestioning acceptance of impending fatherhood.

"Now that I am a man with responsibilities," he was saying, "I think I'm going to curtail my protesting and marching and learn to fight in a different way. After all, I got a wife and baby to take care of now. There is just one more meeting I promised to attend. Dr. Marvin Andrew Cates is coming to Birmingham to help us plot strategy and begin organizing a protest for the city's grossly underpaid sanitation workers. I will help with the planning, but I won't march, and then my protesting days will be over. I will just get ready for my baby's arrival and marriage to his or her beautiful mother. I'm so happy and excited I just want to shout it out to the world. I'm going to be a father! My sweetheart is having my baby!" Leaning down he kissed Jenna on the lips, pulling her close.

"We need to get back," Jenna said, "They will be wondering what happened to us."

"I just found out we are going to be a family," Curtice said with a wide grin, "That's what happened to us. Don't worry; I won't tell anybody until you say so," he promised. "Folks will just notice that I'm mighty pleased about something, they just won't know what. Come on, let's rejoin the party," he said, grasping one of her hands, lifting it to kiss slender fingers.

"There you are, girl! We have been looking for you. Gigi's getting ready to change clothes for the train station and the first part of their honeymoon. I think I heard New York – anyway, she wants us to help her get out of the wedding dress and into traveling clothes. She's upstairs waiting for us; I told her I would find you."

"Has she been waiting long?" Jenna asked as she hurried behind her friend.

"No, she just went up. This has been fun, hasn't it?" Petronella said, nibbling on a chocolate truffle from the massive dessert table.

"Wonderful," Jenna agreed. "I see you were talking to that groomsman over there. He is handsome." She watched with interest as her friend smiled slowly, ducking her head. "His name is Dayvon," Petronella said. "He goes to Williamsburg in South Carolina. He and Harold have been friends since they were little. He's from Iowa, too."

"He seems to really like you," Jenna said. "Are you all planning to see each other again?"

"We are going to write to one another and talk on the telephone on weekends, and then if things go well, he said he would like to come to my graduation," Petronella said shyly.

"Petronella, that is so exciting," Jenna said, as her friend pushed open the door where Gina awaited them.

"What is so exciting!" Gina demanded, equally delighted when Jenna filled her in. "I think it would be great if you met your future husband at my wedding," Gina said. "That would give us a forever bond."

"We have a forever bond anyway," Jenna said, slipping an affectionate arm around each of them. "It started our first day at

277

Grayson and will last forever and ever. God gave me two more sisters that day."

"And He gave me two sisters," Gina said, her voice choked as she wrapped her arms around her two best friends.

"He gifted me with two sisters who love me for me," Petronella said, hugging tightly. "We are sisters forever. That will never change no matter where we go or what we do."

"Sisters forever."

"And ever."

"And ever. Amen."

"Amen," they all stated solemnly before looking at one another and breaking into renewed laughter as they helped Gina out of her wedding gown and into her traveling clothes.

* * *

"What is it like being famous?" Stella Lewis, one of her group members asked walking up to Jenna waving one of the popular black newspapers. "All those goings on in Atlanta – messing around with gangsters and such – I didn't know Gigi's daddy was Isaac Jennings."

Looking at the paper Stella was waving around, Jenna saw a big picture of Gina and her bridesmaids, with Petronella and herself on either side of the smiling bride. "Gangster's Gilded Girl Gets Hitched" in large letters was spread across the page. The article went on to describe the wedding while naming some of those in attendance, including well-known gangsters; Jenna had had no idea any of those in attendance were not legitimate. "Pistol Pete' Peterson was there," Stella was saying, "and according to this article so was "Mickey 'Machine Gun' Martin" and "Sinister Sylvester' Simmons," she was saying excitedly. "Did you see any machine guns? Knives? Icepicks?"

"I doubt they were carrying them around a wedding," Jenna said dryly. "I had no idea anyone there was a criminal; they acted like normal, regular people."

"Here is another picture of you," Stella said. "You and Petronella looked so pretty."

"Mr. Jennings paid for everything," Jenna said, "otherwise we could not afford those dresses. He insisted that we keep them, though I do not know where else I could wear it. It is a nice keepsake."

"I cannot believe this is our last semester," Stella said. "Just a few more months and we'll be sure-enough nurses. Have you applied for any nursing positions yet?"

"I am hoping one of the Nurse Practitioner programs I applied for will accept me," Jenna said. "If one does, I will be headed for Atlanta, Detroit, or staying here in Birmingham. What about you?"

"I'm off to Charlotte, North Carolina to work at that big colored hospital they got there. Plus, I'm getting married, too, to an ambulance driver who's from Charlotte. We already got a house and everything. His folks are nice. They are working on the house for us, and it should be finished by graduation."

"Oh, Stella, how wonderful!" Jenna said warmly. "This is a happy-sad time for me. I am happy that we are all moving on with our lives, but sad because we will all be going our separate ways. Gina was first to leave us, but we all know she was not really into nursing, so it is really no surprise she decided to leave school early."

"Especially since she bagged that doctor she's been gunning for since she got here," Stella said with a light laugh. "Between her husband and her daddy, she ain't never going to have to work. What's good is, she already knows enough to perform minor first aid on her babies, so she's set."

"She is going to be a great wife and mother," Jenna said, "but some of us, like me, still have to work. I have emergency room duty tonight, so I must get moving or I will be late."

She was pinning her cap on elegantly twisted hair when she heard herself being paged. Opening her door, she stuck her head out. "I am right here," she said. "What is it?"

Someone is on the phone asking for you. He says he's your brother, and his name is Sidney."

Jenna's heart began pounding like a drum. She felt lightheaded. Her hands began shaking, the feeling of dread making her weak. Taking a deep breath, she hurried to where the receiver lay, picking it up and placing it to her ear. "Hello?" she said, her voice breathless, tense, gripping the phone so tightly she was afraid it would crack.

"Queenie? It's Sidney."

"You all have something to tell me?" her heart beating so hard and so loudly she was afraid she would not hear the message.

"…a whistle in the air…terrible pain and deep regret… followed by peace…do not forget life is for the living…heal and rejoice in the Miracle…" as usual the hollow voice speaking was not Sidney's.

"When Sidney?" Jenna asked, her voice calm, pulling him back from the spirit world.

"Oh, Queenie…" Sidney's voice was filled with sadness.

"When Sidney?"

"I'm so sorry, Queenie," There was a slight hesitation. "Now," he said softly. Even as he spoke, Jenna could hear the sirens in the distance, ambulances headed for the emergency room.

Dropping the phone, she ran down the hall, flew down the stairs and rushed out of the doors, ignoring the vehicles barreling rapidly up and down the street, not hearing the drivers honking at her, slamming on brakes to avoid hitting her as she ran across four lanes of fast-moving traffic, running up the sidewalk and pushing open the doors to the hospital emergency room. The increased level of activity was immediately apparent with emergency room doctors barking out orders, nurses scurrying to prepare temporary rooms by screening off beds with cloth-covered metal frames. Jenna immediately began searching. She found the face she was looking for in the third cubicle. Curtice was lying on his back, his chest covered with blood, the white shirt he was wearing, soaked. A nurse was pressing a bloody cloth against the gaping wound that was slowly, steadily pumping his life away. Moving over to his side, she picked up a clean cloth, indicating to the nurse her intention of taking over. Pressing hard, she leaned down, kissing him warmly on the lips. His eyes opened, love and recognition pushing aside the pain.

"Can it be?" he said with a smile. "Am I truly seeing my own personal angel standing before me? The one God gifted me with while here on earth? My baby's mother? My one and only true love? My miracle?"

"Except for the angel part, everything else is true," Jenna said softly. "This fall, we are going to be parents with our own little miracle to love."

"You'll love her enough for both of us," Curtice said tenderly. "I'm just sorry I won't be around to..." His voice trailed off. "Be sure she knows how much her daddy loved her. Never let there be any doubt about that."

"I will never let her forget her daddy," Jenna promised, trying to hide the fact that her heart was breaking, "because I never will. I will make sure she is proud to be a part of you." Reaching over she exchanged the bloody cloth for a clean one.

"Thank you, baby," Curtice said. "I'm glad I won't be forgotten. Nurse!" he called. A nurse pushed aside one of the sides of the makeshift room. "Could you find out if the Reverend Fred Huddleston is out there and have him come in here?"

He clasped Jenna's hands still pressed tightly against his chest. "I want you to promise me something," he said seriously, his voice noticeably weaker.

"What is it?" Jenna asked, swallowing hard against the constriction in her throat.

"I want you to promise me that you won't grieve too hard, that you will find someone to spend the rest of your life with. Promise me you will be happy, my queen, my love, my Jenna."

"I promise," Jenna said, trying unsuccessfully to keep the tears filling her eyes from falling. "I love you so much, Curtice Brooks. You are my best friend. I will never forget you; you will always hold a special place in my heart," her voice breaking.

"I like that," Curtice said, "You have held a special place in mine since the moment I saw you. My feelings grow stronger each time I look into your eyes." Reverend Huddleston walked into the room, his face somber. Before he could speak, Curtice said, "Reverend, I have a mighty big favor to ask before I go to glory," smiling tenderly and squeezing Jenna's bloodstained hands when a strangled sob escaped despite her best efforts to contain it.

"What is it, son?" Reverend Huddleston asked.

"I want you to marry us – Jenna and me," Curtice said. "I want Jenna to have everything I own, knowing our marriage will be blessed in the eyes of God. Will you do that for us, Reverend? Will you marry us?"

"Mr. Curtice Brooks, I would be happy to, proud to," Striding over to the narrow opening the Reverend called a doctor and two nurses over to serve as witnesses, along with another man Jenna did not know who she would later learn was civil rights leader Marvin Andrew Cates crowded into the small space. Pulling out his bible, Reverend Huddleston led the small group in a brief prayer before looking around and saying, "Dearly beloved…we are gathered here…" Looking deep into one another's eyes Jenna and Curtice exchanged vows. After the brief ceremony, the room emptied leaving them alone.

"I'm a lucky man," Curtice said, stroking a shaking hand down a smooth cheek.

"How is that?" Jenna asked, kissing him softly on the lips.

"Because I have been double, triple blessed," Curtice said. "I'm going to be the daddy of an angel, I married an angel today, I will leave here knowing I had the best this earth has to offer…I look forward to when we meet again…" his voice stilled, his eyes emptied of life. Reaching up, Jenna gently closed them, noting the time of death, walking out of the small enclosure, informing the doctor, turning to walk away, quietly dropping to the floor in a small, crumpled heap, doctors and nurses rushing to her side to offer assistance.

"Earth to earth, ashes to ashes, dust to dust, in sure and certain hope of the Resurrection into eternal life…" Reverend Huddleston intoned the familiar litany in a measured voice. "Lord unto thee we commend the spirit of Brother Curtice Brooks. Lord, another fallen warrior in the fight against injustice, Lord…"

Standing beside the open grave, Jenna tuned out what Reverend Huddleston was saying, willing herself not to throw up or pass out or both. Biting the inside of her cheek so hard she tasted the salty warmth of blood, she concentrated on staying upright. A short time later, immensely thankful that she had managed to hold it together she placed a yellow rose on the closed coffin, watching as it was slowly lowered into the ground. "Goodbye, my love," she whispered before turning walking away and climbing into the waiting limousine furnished by the funeral home.

Back at the church Jenna was seated and served first at Reverend Huddleston's insistence. Gina and Petronella and the Huddleston children seated around her. The table directly across from hers was occupied by the heretofore unknown aunt from Chicago and her six children, the woman frowning, all of them staring rudely. Gina stared back, looking them carefully up and down, spending considerable time staring at their shoes. Petronella joined in, her lip slightly curled, eyes sweeping over the seated figures, seeing but not seeing. Largely oblivious to what was going on around her, Jenna stared blindly at her plate. She looked up when Gina addressed her.

"Queenie, do you know what happened that day? Has anyone told you?" her friend asked, one arm on the back of the chair where Jenna was seated.

Jenna nodded slowly. "Both Reverend Fred and Doctor Marvin Andrew Cates have been by to see me and offer their condolences. They say they were meeting in one of the rooms at a local motel when someone threw a smoke bomb through the window. Everyone inside came out wiping their eyes and coughing, and that is when the sniper started shooting. He killed three men and wounded three others. He was gunning for Dr. Cates, but they got him back into the room, into the bathroom, taking cover in the bathtub. Curtice was hit just above the heart, everyone was amazed that he held on as long as he did, but he was determined to tell me goodbye." She stopped, drawing a shuddering breath, swallowing hard.

"And to marry you," Petronella said. "He was determined to do that."

"Yes," Jenna said softly, "he was determined to do that."

"I hope you don't think some fly-by-night marriage is gonna give you no rights about what happens to my nephew's things." Jenna looked up. A woman she had never seen before stood next to the table where she was seated.

"And who is you?" Petronella asked belligerently, standing up, crossing her arms and eyeing the woman carefully.

"I am Curtice's only living older relative. I'm his aunt, his mother was my sister," the woman stated. "My name is Eunice Buford, and these are my children, his first cousins."

"I never heard him so much as mention you," Gina stated, "and I know you ain' never been down here to visit him. And you claiming kinship? Really?"

"All I know is, he was my nephew in every sense of the word, but he was not your husband," Eunice asserted, stepping forward.

"Madam, I beg to differ," The voice was warm, resonant with rich undertones. The owner of that voice came and stood behind the chair where Jenna was seated.

Eunice's eyes widened. She had seen that face often in recent weeks on television and movie news reels. "Reverend Cates," she gasped, "I...was...I just...I..." she stammered to a confused halt.

"Now Madam, I was a witness to what transpired," Reverend Cates said in a carrying voice. "I heard the young man ask for his pastor, and then ask him to marry him to this young lady here," putting a hand on Jenna's shoulder, "which he proceeded to do with a number of witnesses including myself. I assure you that in the eyes of God, they were man and wife. And Sister you must remember that it was not that long ago that the only recognition colored folks got in terms of being married was among themselves when they jumped the broom." A chorus of amens resounded from listeners all around.

Looking around at the unsympathetic faces, Eunice sniffed and stalked away calling for her children to join her. "We might as well go home," she said. "They all going to make sure that all Curtice's stuff goes to that gal who they all claiming was married to him. Won't do us any good to fight it 'cause then the lawyers would get er'thang." Eunice, her children in tow stalked away vowing never to return, scowling when some listeners began applauding.

"Good riddance," Petronella said, sitting back down. "You need to try to eat something," she said coaxingly to her unnaturally quiet friend, Gina joining her in attempting to get Jenna to eat something as mourners came by to offer their condolences to the woman who was married or slated to marry depending on what one believed about the bedside marriage.

"Queenie, have you decided what you are going to do after graduation? It's only six weeks away." Petronella was sitting on the side of Jenna's bed much as she always did, with Gina seated on her old bed, the only difference being it had been stripped since her departure. Both of her friends were there to offer support, Gina coming from Nashville.

I am going home to South Carolina, have my baby," she said, smiling wryly at their shocked expressions, "and then I am going to the Nurse Practitioner program at the University of Detroit in Michigan. I want to get as far away from the South as I possibly can," the bitterness in her voice flavoring her words.

"Queenie, you're pregnant?" Gina said, hugging her friend and laughing with delight, "Did Curtice know? He must have been proud," she said at Jenna's nod.

"That explains it," Petronella said. "I thought you were putting on a little weight, but I sure ain't one to talk about nobody's size," looking down at her own plump, shapely figure.

"Are you taking the baby with you to Detroit?" Gina asked.

"Of course," Jenna said. "My sister Sugar lives in Detroit. She has already agreed to take care of the baby while I am in school and on call. My brother Henry Lloyd is there, too; so, I will have family there to help."

"We've come a long way since that first day we introduced ourselves, and Sam was driving us to school," Petronella said. "A lot has happened in the time we've been here."

"One thing that will never change is the friendship that began that day," Gina said firmly.

"Yes," Jenna said, "Friends forever, right?"

"Right."

"Right."

Chapter Twenty-three

"Ladies and Gentlemen, please join us in congratulating the nurse graduating first in her class. With two published papers to her credit, she has been accepted into the Nurse Practitioner's program at the University of Detroit in Detroit, Michigan. Jenna Thompson, please come forward and accept your award, knowing that we wish you every success in Detroit."

Whoops and cheers erupted among the graduates when Jenna stepped forward from her position at the front of the line to accept the plaque and framed certificate from Head Nurse Emma Johnson, shaking hands with the faculty and thanking them for their well wishes as she walked across the stage stopping to smile and wave at the loudly applauding audience. After the ceremony she was surrounded by well-wishers including the entire Huddleston clan, the four children spending what little time that remained with their dear friend and sitter, missing her already. Gina and Harold had driven in from Nashville, she excited for all her friends and former colleagues, not the least bit sorry that she was not a part of the proceedings. She whispered her exciting news into Jenna and Petronella's ears, all of them squealing in excitement about the baby – babies – to come. Petronella introduced them to Dayvon who as promised had come to her graduation.

"It is done. We worked and studied and washed and folded and fed and assisted and emptied bed pans and food trays and had to deal with snooty doctors and cantankerous LPNs, but we did it, girlfriend; and this patch right here proves it. I'm going to sew it on my brand-new uniform tonight." Petronella proudly held up her registered nurse badge.

"When do you leave for South Carolina, Queenie?" Gina asked.

"Early tomorrow morning," Jenna replied. "I have cleared my room and had most of it shipped to Detroit. I cannot believe how much I have collected since being here. My bus for home leaves at 5:45."

"What about you, Petronella?" Gina asked. "Are you headed back to Baton Rouge?"

"No ma'am," Petronella said. "If I never see my sorry family again, it will be too soon. I'm leaving on the same bus as Queenie tomorrow. She has invited me to stay with her for a few days and meet her family. Then I am going on to Charleston. That's where the University of Williamsburg is; I already got a job at one of the hospitals there. If things work out as planned, Dayvon and I gonna get married at the end of the summer. Then he'll start graduate school in the fall. He wants to get his doctorate in education."

"Petronella, that is wonderful. I am so happy for you," Jenna said hugging her tightly, joined by Gina.

Separating, the three friends looked at one another, happiness and excitement being replaced by sadness at the realization that they would not be returning this time around, and that the many hours spent together laughing, working, studying, gossiping, bonding, were coming to an end. Tears filled three pairs of eyes at the same time, clasping hands, moving closer, hugging, they pledged eternal friendship and promised to keep in touch.

"I sure enjoyed your friend," Albertina said with a chuckle. "That gal is something else! What comes up, comes out, don't it?"

"That describes Petronella perfectly," Jenna said smiling. "You never have to ask her to speak her mind, because she will always tell you, in no uncertain terms!"

"Even so everybody loves her, and she is welcome here anytime."

"I will make sure she knows," Jenna said standing, putting one hand to her back. "I am on my way to Doc Edmonds office. I will be back in a couple of hours."

"Is Dexter going to take you?" Albertina asked. "Don't let him drive like a madman," she said sternly when Jenna nodded. "That boy knows he drives entirely too fast."

"I will not let him speed, Ma'dear," Jenna promised. "See you when I get back."

"Is the baby all right?" Jenna asked anxiously a short time later, putting a protective hand on her midsection.

"The baby is fine," Doc Edmonds said, "with a nice, strong heartbeat and lots of movement, which is excellent. I don't see any problems with you giving birth at home."

"With you to watch over me and this little miracle," she said patting her stomach, "we are in good hands."

"That's it, Jenna – you're doing wonderfully, breathe, breathe deeply, now push...push hard...okay, relax, take a deep breath, breathe...I see the baby's head....breathe..."

"Push darlin'," Ma'dear said tenderly, "In a matter of minutes I'll be holding my sweet little grand baby in my arms."

An exhausted, perspiration-soaked Jenna, feeling like she was being torn in two, summoning the last of her strength, answering the call of nature, squeezed down as hard as she could, letting out a final scream, feeling the baby slip from the warmth of her body, into her mother's waiting arms. One agonizing moment of silence, then the wails of a newborn filled the air.

290

"Queenie, baby," her mother said tenderly, placing the precious burden into the eager arms reaching for it, "you got yourself a beautiful little girl."

Jenna looked down into the life she had helped create, her eyes shining with love and wonder. "Hello, my little one," she said softly, "I am your mama, and I am so happy to meet you. Your daddy is not here, but I know he's looking down at us from heaven smiling. And this is your grandmother," she said smiling, holding her up to Ma'dear who placed a kiss on the tiny forehead, looking into the unfocused eyes trying to look back, a soft smile on her face. As she watched the tiny face crumpled, the little mouth opening and closing.

"I think your baby girl is hungry," Albertina said, and proceeded to instruct the new mother, guiding her through her first ever breast feeding, laughing softly when Jenna jumped in surprised pain when the baby clamped down hard on her tender nipple.

Jenna watched in wonder as her baby took nourishment from her, the wave of love she felt unlike any other. Letting go of her mother's nipple, the family's newest member slid almost immediately into sleep. Yawning, Jenna, too, felt a wave of exhausted sleepiness take hold, first kissing, then handing her daughter to her mother, snuggling down into the changed sheets and blankets. Just before succumbing to the welcoming, beckoning darkness, she heard her mother ask, "Have you decided on a name for her yet, Queenie?"

Jenna nodded. "What is it?" Albertina asked.

"Miracle," Jenna whispered. "Her name is Miracle." She slipped into a deep sleep as her brothers and sisters gathered around Ma'dear to meet the new arrival, the first baby in the house since Rhonda's birth six years earlier.

"Queenie, do you and Miracle have to go?" the little voice was plaintive.

"I do, sweetie," Jenna said, putting a comforting arm around Rhonda, who was holding Miracle carefully in her arms. "I have to go to school in Detroit."

"You already been to school in Birmingham," Rhonda complained, "and now you're going to school in Detroit? Why?"

"I am going to learn more things that will help me be the best nurse possible. After that I will never have to go back to school again. Won't that be nice?" Rhonda nodded. They both looked around as Sidney came into the room carrying the brand-new suitcase that Jenna had bought him.

"Are you all packed, Sidney?" Jenna asked with a smile. When he nodded she asked, "Did Ma'dear look at what you packed?"

"Yeah," Sidney said eagerly. "She wouldn't let me pack my comic books. She said they take up too much room."

"We'll get you some new comic books when we get to Detroit," Jenna promised. Sidney was going with Jenna and Miracle; he would continue to be home schooled; he would watch over the baby while Jenna was in school or on call; and best of all as far as he was concerned, he would not be separated from Jenna this time – she was one of the few who knew what to do when he became overpowered by the spirits.

Rolanda and Renard would take Sidney's place at Mama Joyce's. They had moved in the night before and would stay to perform the chores Sidney had done helping their grandmother and Papa Pete who really did not require much in the way of assistance with one major exception since he rarely left his bed and never his room – emptying his chamber pot.

"Y'all ready?" Dexter asked as he came through the kitchen door from outside, calling for Alfonzo and Lorenzo to help him load the car when Sidney and Jenna indicated their readiness. The twin boys each grabbed suitcases and assorted baby paraphernalia heading for the car parked at the end of the long path leading to their house.

"Well," Jenna said, "I guess this is it. Sidney, you ready?" Reaching down she lifted Miracle into her arms.

"Bye, Miracle," Rhonda said sadly, "I'm really gonna miss you."

"And she is going to miss her littlest auntie who has taken such good care of her," Jenna said giving her youngest sister a warm one-armed hug, leaning down to allow her to kiss the baby one final time. She hugged all those who had gathered to say goodbye to her and Sidney, both of them waving as the car drove away, wheels spinning.

"Well, Sidney, what do you think of Detroit?" Jenna asked as she changed a cooing Miracle. They had arrived by train a week earlier and Jenna made it a point to spend that week taking him to local sights and the zoo and other entertainments including the movies and the nearest public library.

"I like it pretty well," Sidney said. "It's really big and loud and lots of people and buildings and cars and stuff." He took the dirty cloth diaper from Jenna and dropped it into the diaper pail which was used to collect and soak baby things before dumping them in the washing machine.

"It was really good to see Sugar again, and awfully nice of her to let us stay here without pay. Do you remember her, Sidney?"

"I do," Sidney said, "She used to like to kiss boys until she married the man in brown and moved here. Now he's the one who kisses a lot of girls."

Jenna looked sharply at her brother. "Who told you that?" she asked.

"The spirits told me," Sidney said. "They told me that Larry...does not tarry at home."

"Do not talk like that around Sugar, you hear me?" Jenna said urgently. "What does or does not happen in their marriage and their part of the house has nothing to do with us, understand?"

"I won't say nothing, Jenna, I promise," Sidney said.

"My hero," Jenna said giving her brother a warm hug.

"Queenie...Sidney...y'all come on, dinner's ready," Sugar's voice floated up the stairs.

Pulling her dress down over a freshly diapered bottom, dropping a kiss on a petal-soft cheek, Jenna lifted her baby into her arms. "Come on, Sidney," Jenna said, "and remember not to say anything about Sugar and Larry, okay?"

"I won't, Queenie, I promise," Sidney said, as they walked down the hall and stairs into the dining room. He seated himself at the end of the table with Jenna on his right and Sugar on his left. Three boarders occupied the seats on the other side and a fourth in the chair on Jenna's right. The chair at the head of the table was empty.

"You all dig in now," Sugar said to those seated. "I made some stewed chicken and boiled potatoes with butter and parsley. There's some cornbread and fried okra, too. And I made a nice apple pie for dessert. Y'all help yourselves."

Placing a chicken leg, stewed vegetables, and parsley potatoes on Sidney's plate, handing him a piece of cornbread and pouring him a glass of milk from the pitcher on the table, Jenna advised him to eat. She filled her plate as Sidney began cutting his potato into many much smaller chunks, spreading butter on his cornbread, pulling the chicken off the bone, and mixing it with his potatoes. Adding some okra, he spooned the mixture into his mouth.

"Sidney, I notice you mix all your food up together," Sugar said, and when Sidney, mouth full nodded, said, "I can't do that. I can't stand for none of my food on the plate to touch. I never could. You remember that Queenie?"

"I do," Jenna said looking over at her sister. The years had not been particularly kind to Sugar. Four children including a set of twins in rapid succession had taken their toll. Her breasts, though still large and full were starting to sag, her stomach was rounding as fat collected around her middle, her hips had widened, and rolls of fat hung from her upper arms. Her face was still pretty although faint frown lines were appearing on her forehead and the sides of her eyes, deep furrows had formed from nose to mouth on either side, and her mouth drooped downward in a perpetual frown. Though she seemed genuinely happy to have her family members living with her, she carried an air of discontent around her most of the time. The probable reason for that unhappiness came into the room just as everyone was finishing their meal.

"How's everybody doing this evening?" Larry Green said in a loud voice as he sat in the chair reserved for him at the head of the table. "Sorry I'm late," he said as everyone mumbled a greeting, "I had some pressing business to attend to," either not knowing or not caring that everyone could smell the alcohol on him.

"And just where was this business? At the bottom of a whiskey bottle?" Sugar said sarcastically. "You seem to get a lot of business that way."

"Don't you get smart with me, woman," Larry said frowning down the table at his wife. "As long as I keep food on the table and a roof over your heads, you need not worry about what I do and where I do it."

"Yeah, well there are some things more important than that," Sugar said, "like spending some time with your family. Your kids ain't seen you in days; you still sleep when they wake up and don't get up 'til they bout ready for bed. They need they daddy."

"What I done told you about airing our personal business around other people?" Larry demanded in a low, even voice, his eyes cold.

Sugar abruptly closed her mouth while most of those at the table beat a hasty retreat. Jenna managed to refrain from saying how much her baby's daddy would have loved the chance to spend time with his family; for one thing she did not want to throw gasoline on smoldering resentment and defensive anger, and the bottom line was that the situation between Sugar and Larry was really none of her business. The ringing of the doorbell had her rising in relief. Sidney had hastily excused himself soon after Larry came through the door.

"That is probably Henry Lloyd," Jenna said. "He was going to take me to the club where he sings tonight. You stay there. Sugar, I will answer it."

"I'm falling over Sugar's family every time I turn around," she heard Larry mutter as she walked by.

Jenna smiled happily as her tall, handsome brother came through the open door, hugging her tightly, planting a kiss on her cheek, shadow boxing with a grinning Sidney. "Hey, Queenie, hey Sidney, how y'all doing? Queenie, you ready? Where's that little niece of mine? Hey baby," he cooed when Jenna placed Miracle in his arms. "How's the prettiest baby in the world? You are definitely going to be a heartbreaker when you grow up with a smile like that," he said, kissing soft, baby cheeks.

"Henry Lloyd, we need to go now," Jenna finally said when her brother showed no sign of ending his time with the niece he had fallen in love with at first sight. Reminded of the time, he kissed Miracle one final time before handing her back to her mother, who began climbing the stairs to her room, Sidney close behind.

Sugar was standing in the living room talking to Henry Lloyd when Jenna came back down. "I put the baby down," she told her as she shrugged into her coral-red woolen coat, pulling on black leather gloves, arranging a red and black wool hat on her head, and looping a matching muffler around her neck. The weather was already cold in September, with much colder on the way. "Sidney is upstairs with her, but if you would check on them now and again, I would much appreciate it."

"I will do that," Sugar said. "Don't you worry none about that. You go have a good time, hear?"

Leaning down, Jenna kissed her sister on the cheek. "I will, thank you. You have to come with us one of these times."

"Yes, well, I'll definitely think about it," Sugar said. "Henry Lloyd, you take care."

"You do the same, Sugar," Henry Lloyd said, one arm around Jenna as they walked out the door, down the sidewalk leading to the street, stopping in front of a gleaming, highly polished bright red Chrysler 300G Coupe, reaching into his pocket for the keys, inserting one on the passenger's side, holding it open for Jenna to slide in, closing and climbing into the driver's side, starting it and pulling away with a powerful roar.

"This is a beautiful car," Jenna said admiringly, smoothing her hands over the leather seat. "Is it yours?"

"Yeah, I make good money singing at clubs around town," Henry Lloyd said. "The car is the only thing I splurge on. I live pretty simply."

"Do you have a girlfriend?" Jenna asked looking over at her handsome brother.

"Naw, I date occasionally, but no one I see regular," Henry Lloyd said easily. "My wife-to-be is healing in South Carolina. How is my Nettie?"

"She is so much better," Jenna said. "Miss Essie spoils her to death, and Nettie is writing a book about her experiences to help get all that ugliness out of her system."

"That's good," Henry Lloyd said. "Sounds like the day she sends for me is getting closer."

"So, where are we going?" Jenna asked excitedly. "What is the name of the club?"

"It's called the *Quarter Note*," Henry Lloyd said. "I sing there on Fridays, Saturdays and Wednesdays. A band there plays for me, a lot of people come to hear me sing, and I usually have a good time."

"Usually? Not always?" Jenna asked.

"Well, every once in a while, some woman decides I'm singing directly to her, calls herself falling in love with me, makes a nuisance of herself, is usually married, at some point her husband gets involved and wants to fight, and I have to try to convince him that I do not want his woman and that I don't want to fight him. Most times that's enough to calm him down, but ever so often I have to knock a man on his ass before I send him home."

Henry Lloyd pulled into a parking slot behind a brightly lit building flashing neon signs. "We're here," he said, turning off the engine, rounding the car to open the door for her. "We're gonna go in through the back door. I'll introduce you to the band, my backup singers and some of the other folks who work here. And then I'll take you into the club to one of our VIP tables just before the show starts."

"That sounds good," Jenna said ducking under Henry Lloyd's arm as he held the door open for her.

"Hey, Slim, who's that you got with you? That mysterious girl you supposed to be marrying back home but ain't nobody ever seen?" the female voice was smooth, sultry.

"Nah, this here is my favorite sister, Queenie," Henry Lloyd said proudly. "She here to get her Nurse Practitioner certification at the University of Detroit. Queenie, this is Rita, one of the club's singers."

Rita, dressed in a long, glittering silver gown and heavy makeup, her hair twisted into an elaborate design on her head, eyed Jenna up and down. "Hello," she said at last. "So, you're the sister – not the girlfriend."

"No, I am not the girlfriend," Jenna replied, "but I know her very well. She is great; we all love her."

Rita's mouth tightened. "Isn't that nice," she grated, "an in-law that everyone loves? Aren't you the lucky one, Slim, having someone your family likes. I couldn't stand my in-laws. The feeling was entirely mutual, and we all celebrated when my husband and I got divorced."

"Five minutes to show time, five minutes," a young man ran across the backstage area calling out the time "That's my cue," Rita said. "Slim, Queenie, was it? Well, Queenie, it was certainly nice meeting you, and I will look forward to talking more with you later. Hope you enjoy the show."

"Thank you," Jenna said softly.

"Come on, Queenie. Let's get you seated and get you something to drink before I have to get ready," Henry Lloyd said, lifting a corner of the curtain, gesturing for Jenna to precede him.

Stepping into the patron section of the boisterous club, Jenna looked around with interest. All the tables were full of laughing, talking, smoking, beautifully dressed people, waitresses in skimpy clothing circulating, serving drinks, bringing hot appetizers and catfish platters moved through the crowd emptying full ashtrays and collecting dirty dishes and glasses. Cigarette girls with trays holding a wide variety of cigarettes, gum, candies, and mints calling out what they had available, dressed in short, full skirts with sheer black stockings and high-heeled pumps conducted a brisk business. Leading Jenna over to a small table that seated two near the front of the stage, Henry Lloyd pulled out a chair for her and flagged down one of the waitresses who returned shortly, setting down a glass of cola filled with an abundance of ice.

"Here you go, Queenie," Henry Lloyd said with a smile. "I told Francine to keep it filled and no alcohol. I'm headed to my dressing room to prepare for my set. I'll come check on you after it's over, all right?" When she nodded, he added, "One more thing – see that dude over there sitting at a little table by the door? That's the man who takes care of things if anyone starts acting up. So, if anybody messes with you or you need help with anything, go see him, all right?" Giving her a quick kiss on the forehead, Henry Lloyd walked over to the curtain, lifted an edge, and disappeared behind it.

Jenna spent time before the start of the show taking in the club's décor and listening to the band playing a variety of old and new songs including several covers from artists from a new record company, based in Detroit that catered to and featured people of color, the artists on that label becoming increasingly popular and well-known nationwide. Several couples were gyrating on the dance floor, others sat at tables for two, gazing into one another's eyes, oblivious to anything going on around them. Jenna noticed a stately man in a tuxedo moving purposely toward the microphone and stand placed at the center of the stage as the lights dimmed and patrons hurried to find their seats.

"Ladies and gentlemen," the man stated in a deep, rich voice, "welcome to the *Quarter Note*. We sincerely hope that you are having a good time which will only get better when you see and hear our lineup of singers tonight. Ladies, I know you'll be happy to know that Slim is backstage preparing to serenade all of you. Ain't that good news?" A chorus of cheers, applause, and whoops of excitement followed. "And men, don't worry. We got something for y'all, too. Rita Fleming is waiting to make

you feel good with her dulcet tones…So, without further ado…
Here comes Rita! Let's give her a big welcome."The announcer
exited the stage as the curtains opened and Rita approached the
microphone, lifting it off its stand and beginning her opening
number. She was followed by a comedian whose ribald jokes
had listeners both shocked and rolling with laughter. Following
a brief intermission, the darkened stage was slowly illuminated,
revealing a tall, slim figure in a perfectly fitted suit, a tilted
forward fedora on his head. Lifting one hand to push it back,
lifting his head, Henry Lloyd began to sing. The room quieted
as the rich, soaring tenor with the incredible range sang a
variety of songs before quieting, his head lowering, his hand
pushing the fedora back to its forward position on his head,
the lights slowly dimming and then going dark, to thunderous
applause.

"Henry Lloyd, I swear you are one of the best singers I have
ever heard," Jenna said in the car on their way to Sugar's house.
"You are even better than you were in California, and that is
saying a lot."

"Speaks the person who has always been my biggest fan,"
Henry Lloyd said with a smile, "my big sister, even if she ain't no
bigger than a minute," both of them laughing at their old, well-
worn joke.

As they pulled up in front of the house, Jenna asked, "Why
did you leave Sugar's house, Henry Lloyd?"

"I couldn't take another minute of Larry," Henry Lloyd
admitted. "I had reached a point where I was either going to kill
the bastard or give him the beating of his life. It was obvious Sugar
didn't want that, that she tolerated the way he acted, so I left."

"I totally understand," Jenna said, "I cannot blame you." She
only hoped she would not be doing the same thing in the near
future. "Good night, Henry Lloyd, I had a really nice time."

"Good night, Queenie, I'm glad you liked it. We'll have to do it again soon."

"I look forward to it," Jenna said with a smile. "You stay there. I can open the car door by myself." Henry Lloyd watched until Sugar opened the front door of the house, returning their waves before driving off.

Chapter Twenty-four

"Excuse me, but aren't you Jenna Thompson?"

Jenna looked up from the microscope where she was examining a specimen. The man standing before her was unknown though his white lab coat and the stethoscope draped around his neck identified him as a doctor.

"Yes, I am Jenna Thompson," she said. "Is there something you need that I can help you with Doctor…"

"You don't remember me, do you?" the handsome doctor with pale brown skin, wavy hair and hazel eyes said, moving closer.

Jenna frowned slightly as she looked more closely. She shook her head slowly. "I am sorry; maybe if you were to tell me where I know you, I could place you."

"What if I were to tell you that I got my medical degree down South? Birmingham, Alabama for example."

"You interned at Birmingham Regional?" Jenna guessed, "Your residency too?" When he nodded, she said, "My time there was so full of new concepts and ideas that a lot of things got past me. We had no rotations at the same time, so I must have been busy when our paths did cross. It is funny that they cross again here in Detroit – all the way across the country."

"My name is Branson Radcliffe," the man said, bowing slightly. "I'm Detroit born and raised, but decided opportunities were better for aspiring colored doctors, or should I say black doctors in the South, so I moved down there to go to school. But

I must tell you, I could not wait to get away from them 'yassa boss' Negroes and red-neck peckerwoods. Where are you from, Nurse Jenna?"

"A small town in South Carolina chock full of 'yassa bosses' and red-necked peckerwoods," Jenna said with a slight smile. "It is nice to meet you Dr. Radcliffe," Jenna said, "Branson," he corrected, "Dr. Radcliffe," she said, "but I need to finish looking at this slide, so I can send the findings to someone who is waiting for them. So, if you will excuse me –"

"Only if you promise to meet me in the cafeteria for a cup or glass of something," Branson said.

"Friendships within the parameters of work is not such a good idea," Jenna said. "It can cause unnecessary complications. Thanks for asking, though." She resumed her examination of the specimen under the microscope.

Branson looked at the nurse he had first noticed years earlier hurrying down one of the corridors that housed colored patients, caught by the eyes that met his for a brief moment before their owner swept past him on whatever errand had her moving so fast. Possessing extremely good looks, family background, and coveted professional credentials, accustomed to being sought after and pursued, Jenna's seeming indifference rankled him. She had not been so indifferent to Curtice Brooks, he remembered, often seeing the two of them together, laughing, talking, hand in hand. He had read about the sniper incident that had killed him, and the prominent civil rights leaders who had attended his funeral. He had seen a picture of Jenna laying a rose on his coffin just before it was lowered into the ground. He had also read about the rumors of a bedside marriage before the mortally wounded man died, and he knew Jenna had given birth. With Curtice gone, it seemed fate was going to give him another chance with Jenna Thompson, and he was going to take advantage of it.

"Why in the world would you want to pursue some country bumpkin with a bastard child?" his mother asked that night at dinner when he told her about his meeting with Jenna.

"You are just saying that because you haven't met her," Branson said. "She does not look, talk, or dress country at all, and if you didn't know better, you would think she was from some big city – Detroit, even."

His mother sniffed. "All big cities have slums," she said dismissively. "Who is her family?" she asked. "Where exactly are they from?"

"All she said was that she was from a small town in South Carolina full of Uncle Tom's and racists," he said. "Growing up like that, she'll probably be happy to get with someone with a little sophistication."

"Oh, I am sure she will jump at the chance," his mother said. "She certainly could not aim any higher than you, especially with a baby in tow."

"She didn't seem much interested as I was trying to talk to her today," Branson said, "told me she couldn't talk because she had work to do."

"Probably playing hard-to-get so that you would stay interested," Dorothy Radcliffe said dismissively.

Thinking about the indifference in her eyes, he doubted it, but refrained from saying so. His mother would never believe that any woman he showed interest in would have the nerve or audacity not to want her son. "What color is she?" he heard her ask.

"Don't worry, she passes the 'paper bag' test, and she has a head full of black, curly hair and some of the most beautiful eyes you will ever see," he said.

"I would bet she has ten or twelve siblings and all of them from different daddies," Dorothy said disdainfully. "All country gals do."

"Now, Mother, you have to get rid of all these preconceived notions," Branson said with amusement. "At least wait until you meet her."

"So, you plan to pursue this girl?" Dorothy asked. At his nod she shook her head in disgust. "I don't know why, when so many more suitable girls are just waiting for you to show a little interest," she said. "I have been trying to get you interested in Althea Gordon for years, and I swear I don't know why you will not go on and get her. She is such a lovely girl – a debutante, Douglas College for Women, a member of my same sorority. This child probably knows nothing about sororities, much less belong to one."

Rising, Branson walked over and kissed his mother on the side of her forehead. "Mothers and daughters-in-law always seem to have their differences, so this won't be any exception. I am sure she will be open to learning the finer points of navigating society from you. Now, I'm off! I have some pregnant mothers to look in on." He walked away whistling, his mother looking after him, convinced she had heard incorrectly, that he had not said anything about...daughters-in-law...

"Woman, I done tole you about questioning me about where I been, what I been doing or who I been doing it with. Just be glad I come home at all with the way you looking these days." A muffled response followed. "What? I don't give a damn who might be listening. This is my house. I'll say whatever the hell I want to, however loud I want to say it, whenever I want to say it, and anyone who don't like it – don't let the door hit ya where the good Lord split ya."

Sidney, lying on the floor, looked up from the comic book he was reading, one of the two rooms he shared with Jenna. "Mr. Larry is not a nice man, and I don't like him at all."

"I don't like him either," Jenna confessed, "but unless Sugar asks for help, it is not our place to say anything."

"One day we will 'cuz we'll have to," Sidney stated before returning to his reading. Jenna continued to watch him for a time troubled by his last statement. At least the Spirits prompting that last remark had immediately retreated into their world without taking Sidney with them this time.

She turned back to one of the medical books that she had been studying when Larry began talking loudly. Arguments between Sugar and her husband seemed to occur at least once a week and sometimes more. Larry spent little time at home, rising late and leaving for whatever it was he did to make money (though he seemed to make a great deal of it) not returning until late in the evening. As Sugar had said earlier, his four children, three boys and a girl saw little of him and when he was at home showed little inclination to spend any time with them. Sidney promptly disappeared any time he laid eyes on him and had yet to exchange any words with him. Jenna was cordial but could not warm to the man with a proclivity for wearing brown. Mild distaste turned into active dislike the evening she answered the phone and a woman on the other end demanded to speak to Larry Green.

"He is not here," Jenna said mildly. "May I take a message?"

"Who is this?" the voice demanded.

"I might ask the same question," Jenna said reasonably. "After all, you are the one who called."

"Is this Larry Green's house, my precious man whose baby I'm 'bout to have? 'Cuz I'm pregnant," she cooed.

Jenna chuckled. "Girl, you cannot spell pregnant. If you are looking for his wife to tell such nonsense to, please be aware his wife's mother and his wife's sister are powerful healers who communicate with spirits; some folk call them witches. You do not want to make them angry because you would be so sorry you did. Don't even think just hanging up means they cannot find you. So, if you are pregnant, then good luck. You knew he was married when you fornicated. If he wants to leave his marriage, let him be a man and say so. My advice: Do not ever call here again. If you are messing with Larry Green, end it now and stop with the lies! Do you understand?"

"Yes, Ma'am, I won't call again," was the frightened response, "and…I'll do everything else too." Short pause. "Please don't put the witches on me," the pleading voice was agonized, quaking with fear.

"Behave and I will not have to," Jenna said sternly. "Now say good night and hang up."

"Good night." The line went dead.

Smiling, putting the receiver back into its cradle she turned around. Sugar stood a short distance away. Jenna straightened and crossed her arms. "How many times does that happen?" she asked her sister.

"Let's just say that's not the first time," Sugar said with a weary sigh. "Thank you for taking care of this latest one the way that you did. I know she won't ever call here no more."

Jenna looked at her vastly changed sister. "Sugar, even though you drove me crazy, you used to be so vibrant and full of life. What happened to make you this way, to be willing to live like this?" Jenna asked gently.

"Four children in six years had a lot to do with it," Sugar said with painful honesty. She stopped. "If we going to talk, let's get a little more comfortable. You want some coffee? I make a pretty good cup."

"I'd love some," Jenna said eagerly, draping an arm around her sister as they walked into her spacious kitchen. Jenna sat in one of the cushioned chairs surrounding a wooden table tucked into a large three-sided bay window as Sugar assembled cups, saucers, plates, forks, spoons, milk and sugar containers and snowy white cloth napkins. Using a padded cloth, she picked up the percolating pot from the stove pouring fragrant coffee into fragile china cups. She returned from the counter carrying a lemon Bundt cake glazed with a lemon-infused sugar icing. She cut a generous piece for herself and Jenna before sitting down.

"I got pregnant right away," Sugar said, using a fork to cut away a sizable bite. "We come from a very fertile family," smiling as Jenna, laughing ruefully in complete understanding and agreement, dug into her own slice.

"Anyway, I was already pregnant when we got here. I did get out early in the pregnancy to see Detroit, and I loved it. The more I saw, the more I loved it. Larry was proud to squire me around at first. I was cute, sassy. You know that better than anyone. He and his friends just couldn't get enough of me; and I couldn't get enough of him, of them, of the nightclubs he took me to, and of the house he bought me before this one. He taught me how to drive; it was just wonderful. Then Lawrence Junior came. After that, being pregnant and gaining more baby weight, I couldn't go out with him anymore. So, he went out by himself. I could see him losing interest in me little by little no matter what I did, however hard I tried to please him. I told myself another baby would bring us closer, and so I got pregnant with Morris and Maurice. I thought it had worked until I got a phone call like the one you answered. I was hurt clear through to the bone and said I was leaving him. For whatever reason he convinced me to stay, and nine months later Tina was born. Now it seems all I do is wash and clean and take care of the boarding house and babies and ever' so often answer the phone to hear a strange woman on the line, but what else am I gone do? The worst of it is, I still love him." Sugar took a sip of coffee.

"You do live well, so I see how it would be hard to leave," Jenna said. "What exactly does he do for a living?" Because no job she had ever heard of unless it was some type of shift work allowed someone to arrive at work late in the morning or early in the afternoon by one's choosing and still make enough money to afford a house like the one they lived in, the expensive car he drove, his extensive wardrobe of brown-themed clothes and hats, not to mention feeding and clothing a wife and four children. The boarders offset some of the costs of the big house, but Jenna suspected Sugar had them for companionship and human contact more than anything else. Unlike Loretta's house of ill repute, this was a true boarding house. The lodging members were especially close, knowing they could never find anything remotely like it anywhere else, most of them having been there since Sugar first advertised for boarders a few years earlier. To Sugar's children and now Jenna's little Miracle, three live-in "aunts" occupied the residence, delighted to help however they could. Jenna had been heard to say with mock regret that her baby would never learn to walk because she went from one willing set of arms to another, and under the careful eye of her uncle who the Spirits had thankfully not taken with them since her return from nursing school months earlier.

"I don't really know what he do," Sugar confessed. "He always got plenty of money and one thing I can say, he ain't never been stingy with it. He decide how much I get and when and what I can and can't spend it on. I don't especially like that, but where else could I go and what could I do that would let me live like this? With four kids? And no education and no job and no prospects?"

"You have a point," Jenna said, "but you can change your circumstances. Take some of that money he gives you and first, get your GED. Then take some college courses, a few at a time, to get your degree. Then you can write your own ticket. You could major in hotel management and finance, something you would be great at. The best thing is, you already have three built-in babysitters ready, willing, and able to watch your kids and can be trusted. All you have to do is want to do it."

Sugar was silent for a time. "But I love him," she said.

"I know he hits you, but it is up to you to decide when you have had enough," picking up her cup, Jenna took a swallow of its contents. She looked at her sister, "You need to learn to love yourself more," she said simply. Changing the subject, they began to talk of other things.

"Nurse Jenna Thompson, do you ever do anything besides work?" Jenna looked up from the patient chart she was examining and the lined pad she was using to make notes. "Dr. Radcliffe," she said pleasantly. "How are you?"

Looking into the unusual eyes that currently held nothing but friendly indifference, Branson's hunting instincts awakened. He was determined to turn that indifference into passion, to make her respond, to love him. And then he would make her pay for all the work she was making him do to win her. Aloud he said, "You must do something for fun sometime. Your whole life can't be work, work, nothing but work."

"I do not work all the time," Jenna said with a slight smile. "I spend time with my baby and my brothers and my sister and some cultural things this city has to offer. But when I am supposed to be working that is what I do – work." She started writing again.

"How about going out with me? I was born and raised here, so I could show you a lot of things around the Motor City." He saw the refusal on her face and added, "I know you said you don't like going out with people you work with, but technically we don't work together. Our jobs just happen to be in the same place."

"But I will be doing a midwife rotation, and you are an OB-GYN, so we just might be working together," Jenna said.

"And we might not," Branson said, "Even if we were, our contact would be extremely limited. Come on, Miss Jenna, let me show you what Detroit has to offer. What can it hurt?" Branson's voice was coaxing, soft and persuasive.

Jenna hesitated, looking up at the good-looking doctor so eager to take her out. Why not, she decided after a brief debate with herself. What harm could one date do? "All right," Jenna said. "When?"

"How about this weekend? We could go out to dinner and then maybe hit a few clubs. Let's make it Saturday. I will call you Saturday morning and we'll decide on times."

"I look forward to hearing from you Saturday. Here is my sister's number, I live with her. She has a boarding house so there is no telling who will answer the phone, but just ask for me. So, I'll wait to hear from you Saturday. Now I must get back to work."

"Saturday cannot come soon enough," Branson said, leaning against the counter where she was writing, tossing her his sexiest smile, his voice low, caressing. He straightened with annoyance when he saw that she was not paying attention, had not even looked up, more than ever determined to win her.

"You sure look pretty, Queenie."

"You sure do," Sugar, who had come to keep her company while she got ready, agreed. "That dress and those shoes are beautiful, and I love how you have your hair."

"It is nice to have admirers," Jenna said. "Hopefully my date will think so, too." Although in all honesty she really did not much care. Since Curtice had died she had little to no interest in any type of romantic entanglement, not even noticing the black doctors on staff, more than one of whom had certainly noticed her. The doorbell rang. "That must be Branson," she said. "Well, let us get this show on the road," The three of them headed down the main staircase.

Sugar opened the door. "Good evening, I'm Doctor Branson Radcliffe. I'm here to pick up Jenna Thompson."

"Come on in, Doctor Radcliffe. I'm her sister, Sugar. It's nice to meet you." Sugar stepped back to allow the handsome man room to enter.

"Call me Branson, please. It is nice to meet you Sugar. You have a lovely home." He turned, smiling as Jenna, Sidney close behind, came into the living room where her date stood waiting for her.

"Hi, Branson," she said. "I see you have already met my sister. This is my brother, Sidney. Sidney, this is Doctor Branson Radcliffe. We work together, and he was at Birmingham Regional when I was there, too."

"Hey, Little Man," Branson said, bending down until his face was on a level with Sidney's, "It's nice to meet you."

Sidney stared into the face so close to his for a long moment. "Hi," he said shortly. Backing up, he turned and stood next to Jenna, his face closed.

"Don't have much to say, does he?" Branson said. "Maybe he is just shy. You ready, Jenna? I made dinner reservations at *Matthew's* for eight, so we should get a move on. It was nice to meet you all," he said, helping Jenna into her coat, watching as she walked over and kissed Sidney goodnight, telling Sugar not to wait up for her since she had been given a key to the house, moving down the sidewalk as the door closed behind them.

"Nice car," Jenna said looking at the gleaming silver-blue Cadillac parked in front of the house, sliding into the seat on the passenger's side as he held the door open for her.

"Miss Jenna, can I tell you how beautiful you look this evening? You smell good, too. No one would ever think you came from a small town in the South," Branson said, leaning in to where Jenna was seated.

"Thank you, I think," Jenna said. "But you should know I am not ashamed of where I came from. Not everyone lives in the big city, and most of my family are still back home."

No insult intended, darlin'," Branson said softly. "The South breeds some gorgeous women. That is all I was trying to say."

They were seated across from one another at a small cloth-covered table at *Matthews*. The restaurant, comprised of a series of intersecting rooms on several levels, featured deeply piled carpets, heavy drapes, plush chairs, and cloth tablecloths covered by smaller ones edged in lace. Waiters in dark suits circulated pouring wine, taking orders, serving food. A five-piece band played jazz in a plant-filled alcove on the first level of the eating establishment which was filled to capacity. The two of them had one of the best tables in the restaurant, next to a big picture window, close enough to clearly hear the music, but not so close they could not hear one another. The window overlooked Lake Michigan, water as far as the eye could see.

"I'll bet there aren't views like that in your small town in South Carolina," Branson said, looking at the woman who chin in hand was looking out over the waters of the Great Lake.

"No, not like that," Jenna agreed. "It is beautiful. Lake Michigan is so vast; it reminds me of the Pacific Ocean."

"You've been to the west coast?" Branson said in surprise.

"Yes, I lived there for about a year," Jenna said, "and graduated from Bayside High in San Francisco."

"You are definitely full of surprises," Branson said, "a woman of mystery, Miss Jenna. I look forward to uncovering more." A waiter arrived, reaching to pour sparkling water into the stemmed glasses on the table, picking up the napkin and snapping it across both of their laps, handing them both a menu and a wine list to Branson. He left and returned almost immediately with a wooden slab that held a loaf of warm crusty bread and a small container of fresh butter. Promising to return shortly to take their orders, on his way to collect the wine Branson had ordered he walked away.

"What's good?" Jenna asked as she perused the dining options within the leatherbound menu she held.

"Well, I'm all man, so it's steak and potatoes for me, baby," Branson said with a smile. "I like to start with shrimp cocktail. Don't give me no rabbit food."

"Not a salad person, huh?" Jenna said, smiling back. "I happen to like salads with oil and vinegar or blue cheese dressing – yum."

"I'll let you tell it," Branson said, watching the waiter returned, pouring a measure of wine into a glass, handing it to Branson who tasted it before nodding his approval, the waiter then pouring wine into his glass before doing the same for Jenna.

"Just a small amount for me, please," Jenna said to the waiter, "I am not much of a drinker." She thanked him, smiling, when the waiter obliged with little more than a splash in her glass.

"Let us make a toast," Branson said lifting his glass. "To new beginnings," he said, clinking his glass against the one Jenna was holding.

"New beginnings," Jenna said softly taking a sip of the wine in her glass, managing not to grimace at the taste. She really did not like alcohol and would have much preferred a cola with a lot of ice; Curtice had always ordered a cola for her, asking that it be served in a wine glass. She hastily halted that line of thought. She would have a difficult time explaining why tears were running down her face. Clearing her throat, blinking rapidly, she made a concerted effort to pay attention to her date.

Branson could not remember when he had to work so hard to impress a woman. Learning she had spent considerable time in the environs of a sophisticated city like San Francisco had come as a surprise, finding out her brother was the well-known singer Slim another. Not to mention she was on friendly terms with some of the most renown civil rights leaders in the country: It was beginning to look like he was the one coming up short. She was studying to be a Nurse Practitioner which placed her almost on a par with doctors, and so even knowing that he was an MD was not particularly impressive to her. During their meal, he learned that she was also a healer with an extensive knowledge of herbal medicines and remedies, and she had two published papers in prestigious medical journals to her credit with three and four currently under review. Here was no country bumpkin or unenlightened person who would be grateful for his attention; it was dawning on him that she could have her pick of men and he needed to work fast if he wanted to hold her interest before someone with better credentials than his became interested and tried to beat his time.

"I am certainly enjoying my time with you, Miss Jenna," Branson said, pulling her closer on the dance floor after finishing their meal.

"It has been nice," Jenna said trying hard to sound enthusiastic. "My dinner was delicious – even my salad," she said with a smile that she hoped did not look forced.

"I would like to think tonight is the first of many," Branson said looking deeply into the beautiful almost-black eyes looking into his.

Jenna was spared having to answer when the song ended to applause from seated listeners and those on the dance floor. Seated back at their table, Jenna was shocked to see Branson reach into the inside pocket of his suit jacket and extract a pack of cigarettes. "You smoke?" she asked in disbelief. "You are a doctor who smokes?"

"I like having one after I eat or if I'm out drinking," Branson said. "What, you are one of those people convinced they're not good for you?"

"They are poison," Jenna stated unequivocally, "that will eventually kill you."

"Oh, wow, if you feel that strongly, I'll make sure never to smoke around you," Branson said putting them back into his pocket.

"You should not be smoking at all," Jenna stated. "It is a nasty habit, and those who do it rarely realize how they reek of stale, stinky smoke, how it stains their fingers and teeth, and how they scatter ash everywhere."

"Why don't you tell me how you really feel?" Branson said. "Tell you what: I am going to stop smoking effective tonight. See what a positive influence you have on me?"

"If you do quit, you will live that much longer," Jenna said unapologetically.

Removing the pack from his inner pocket, Branson pulled out his cigarettes, taking each one out of the pack and breaking it in half. "I have smoked my last cigarette. Now, if you are ready, we can stop by this club I know, and we can talk and dance a little more before I reluctantly take you home." What he did not tell her was that his original plan called for going to the *Quarter Note* to hear Slim, but that was before learning the headline singer was her brother.

What Jenna really wanted was to go home but agreed to visit the club to round out the date. She and Branson joined the other couples on the dance floor, asked for and received a cola with lots of ice, and pretended she was having a better time than she truly was. Branson was popular and well-known, everyone examining his latest lady with interest, wondering how long this one would last. Finally, back at home, Jenna thanked Branson for a lovely evening, accepted a kiss on the cheek, opening the front door as he walked back to his car and drove off.

"So much for that," Jenna said with relief, "Now back to business as usual." Climbing the stairs, she made her way to her room where Sugar was waiting for her, eager to hear about her evening with the handsome doctor.

Chapter Twenty-five

"Pardon me, ma'am, but are you Jenna Thompson? Miss Jenna Thompson?" The middle-aged man with the pleasant, well-worn face in the grey suit was not someone she knew.

"I'm Jenna Thompson," Jenna said. "Was there something I can help you with, Mr. –"

"Jeffries, Isaiah Jeffries ma'am. Am I addressing Miss Jenna Thompson of Crawford Hollow, South Carolina and a graduate of the Grayson School of Nursing?"

"Yes," Jenna said, nodding.

"Miss Thompson, I represent the Rely on Us Insurance Company," he said, pulling out a plastic encased card from his wallet with his picture and the company emblem, name, and address. "May I come in?"

"I do not need insurance," Jenna began.

"Oh, no, ma'am, I'm not here to sell you any insurance," Mr. Jeffries said, "I am here to pay out a policy listing you as the beneficiary."

"Me?" Jenna repeated in surprise, "Insurance policy? Please come in. Have a seat," she said, gesturing to the sofa in the living room, perching on the opposite end of the one he selected.

"Before I get started Miss Thompson, may I see some identification?" the agent asked, reaching into the briefcase he carried and pulling out a sheaf of papers.

He carefully examined her hospital identification tag that had her picture on it, and her nurse's certification and license. Nodding his head in satisfaction, he said, "Miss Thompson, I am officially turning over this cashier's check to you in the amount of fifty thousand dollars. The double indemnity clause applied entitling you to twice the policy amount." He reached out, check in hand, placing it between the fingers of one hand when she made no move to take it.

"Who took out this policy?" she asked in a low voice, already knowing the answer.

"Curtice Brooks took out the policy in December of last year," the insurance adjuster said, "and paid promptly every month. You were his only beneficiary. It took me a while to sort out the paperwork and then to find you, but here you are, the terms of the policy have been satisfied, and the payout delivered. I wish you the best, Miss Jenna, and if you'll see me to the door, I'll be on my way." He rose, following Jenna to the door, climbing behind the wheel of a gray sedan that had seen better days and slowly driving off.

Jenna made her way up the stairs to her rooms, crossing over and sitting down into a big, overstuffed chair. Staring down at the cashier's check in her hand, tears slowly filling her eyes, lifting her hands to her face, the first sob came. Lost in pain and sadness, overcome by grief, she felt loving arms steal around her; Sidney, held her tightly, tenderly as she mourned.

"I swear I do not know why you insist on pursuing this country bumpkin, but if she will not go out with you, maybe you should leave her alone. She has her nerve, trying to be standoffish – who does she think she is? A little nobody from the wilds of South Carolina who obviously has no taste. Forget her, darling, and move on. I hear Althea Gordon is in town and rumor has it she is moving back to Detroit. Why don't I have a small welcome home dinner for her and the two of you can become reacquainted."

"I don't want Althea Gordon," Branson said, frowning. Besides, he had already known Althea, in the biblical sense, so why buy the cow? It was Jenna Thompson he wanted, and so far, he was failing utterly. She had been pleasantly distant since their evening out and had politely refused all subsequent invitations. He had gone over the events of that night again and again, and except for the cigarette incident Jenna had seemed to be having a good time, he certainly had. Much to his surprise, it seemed Jenna Thompson and only Jenna Thompson would do. He needed to come up with an effective strategy immediately or Jenna Thompson was going to slip through his fingers.

"I swear we ain't going to have room for people if these flowers keep coming," Sugar said, looking around for a surface with enough space to place the latest floral arrangement. Jenna's rooms had run out some time ago leading to those that were still arriving being placed down the wide staircase and into the living room that was currently in danger of being overrun. The bouquets had begun arriving Friday evening and had been coming every few hours ever since. A casual mention during their conversation that gardenias and petunias, closely followed by roses, were her favorite flowers, had to be the reason why each arrangement contained an abundance of richly scented roses, sweet-smelling gardenias, and vividly colored petunias, one or the other or two or all three prominently displayed. Jenna's room was filled with the aromatic mixture of her favorite fresh flowers. The phone and the doorbell rang at the same time.

"Hello?" Jenna said, carrying the phone with its long cord with her as she answered the door and collected the latest arrangement.

"Hey, Nurse Jenna," the low masculine voice said.

"Branson?"

"At least you know my name and seem to recognize my voice. That is something, I guess."

"Are you the one behind this barrage of beautiful flowers?" Jenna asked, smiling despite herself.

"My way of apologizing for whatever I did because not only will you not go out with me again, but you also won't even talk to me and only acknowledge my existence when you have to," Branson said sadly. "Try as I might, I can't think of what I did to make you avoid me."

Feeling a twinge of guilt due to some element of truth in what he said, Jenna replied softly, "You have nothing to apologize for. I think I owe you the apology."

"Accepted," Branson said promptly. "And to prove there are no hard feelings, go out with me again. We will have a few laughs, and I will make sure you are back at a reasonable hour," his voice was coaxing, persuasive.

"All right," Jenna said looking around at the masses of vividly colored floral arrangements. "When? Oh, and please, no more flowers."

"So, she finally agreed to go out with you again? I knew she was playing hard to get." Dorothy frowned at her son. "And you fell for it. This bumpkin is more conniving than I thought, I will give her that. When are you going to bring her by to meet the rest of your family, your mother in particular?"

"On our wedding day," Branson said, laughing at his mother's shocked expression.

"Your w-w-wedding day?" Dorothy stammered. "B-b-but…" she stopped, taking a deep breath. "Your puny attempt at humor has fallen totally and completely flat. Talk of marriage is serious business and should not be taken lightly."

"I didn't mention it until you asked a question that was a part of one involving the upcoming marriage. I was going to tell you, when it got closer to happening, like the night before. I'm not sure I'm going to let you near her until after she has said I do."

"She has put a spell on you," Dorothy said tightly, angrily. "She certainly knows how – all those backwards Southern girls do. That explains your obsessive behavior. I have never seen you like this."

"Well, I have never met anyone like her," Branson said. "Everybody is going to know I got something special after I make her mine."

"That little heifer is going to regret the day she ensnared my son," Dorothy vowed as she watched Branson leave the room, determined to throw himself away on a backwards coon from some Podunk town in the South. There appeared to be nothing she could do to stop him, but she had to try. Walking to the small table where it resided next to the telephone, Dorothy picked up her address book, thumbing through it until she found the number she sought, reaching down to pick up the ornate gold embossed receiver, dialing a number, listening to it ring, waiting for someone on the other end to answer.

"Bitch! What I done tole you about questioning me about what I do or don't do. Long as I provide for you and that passel of young'uns, you need to just shut the fuck up." After a low murmur, "Did you not hear what I just said? What? You going to walk up on me? You think you can act like a man, walking up on me like that, then you'll get treated like a man." The sound of a loud thud slamming against a far wall caused Jenna and Sidney, who had climbed into bed with her when the arguing began, to both jump. They put their hands over their ears, eyes tightly closed when the thuds, accompanied by faint cries, continued, unabated.

"Is he a pimp?" Jenna asked her sister the following morning, examining her in the bright light of the rising sun. "He knows how to beat you up without it showing, and it is usually a pimp who knows how to do that."

"I don't know what you talking about," Sugar began, but stopped at the look on her sister's face.

"If you do not want to talk about it, just tell me and I will respect your privacy. But do not insult my intelligence by pretending what is happening is not happening. We all heard what went on last night and all the other nights even if no one says anything. Larry is a pig who, I think, needs to be tossed out into the pigsty where he wallows most of the time anyway. If you are worried about money, stop. Money will be there when you need it. Think about it, Sugar... just think about it." She rose and left the room without waiting for an answer.

"I expect you to be at the welcome home get-together I'm holding for Althea this Saturday," Dorothy said to her son as they sat at the breakfast table.

"Mother, you know I go out with Jenna on Saturdays," Branson said mildly, stirring sugar into his coffee.

"Well, she will just have to find something else to do this Saturday," Dorothy said, tapping a spoon against the soft-boiled egg in her eggcup. "She cannot expect to monopolize all your time. Tell her you have other plans. I'm sure she will get over it," reaching for a piece of toast.

Not only would she get over it, Branson also had a sneaking suspicion she would not much care. He had managed to secure dates with her on Saturdays when she was not on call, and she seemed to have a good time, yet he sensed there was a part of her that continued to elude him. One thing he did not want to do was forego her company to mingle with people he had known all his life or women for whom he had no desire. Coming to a sudden decision he said, "All right, Mother, I'll attend your little soiree on one condition,"

"What condition?" his mother asked.

"That I bring Jenna, and you promise to be cordial to her. Otherwise, count me out."

"You realize this is blackmail," his mother said tautly.

"Take it, or leave it," Branson said.

"All right," Dorothy said, her voice stiff. "Since I apparently have no choice, bring your country bumpkin, and I will be polite, but don't expect us to be bosom buddies."

"All I expect is cordiality," Branson said. "Everything else will fall in place." He took a sip of coffee before tackling the omelet on his plate.

"So, I hear you invited to one of them saditty black folks' parties," Larry addressed Jenna as they were all seated at the dinner table. "Dorothy Radcliffe is one of the snootiest bitches in the entire state, and women be falling all over themselves to get with her son. How is it you come to know them?"

"Branson Radcliffe and I both work at Detroit Regional," Jenna said easily. "We kind of met in passing and have since become friends."

"Friends, huh? That's what they callin' it these days? And somebody tell me what's wrong with that boy?" Larry asked testily changing the subject, watching Sidney sidle away. "Your freaky brother with the funny-colored eyes? Every time he sees me, he takes off like he thinks I'm going to attack him or something, and he ain't never said 'boo' to me. What y'all been tellin' 'em?"

"We ain't got to tell him nothing," Sugar said. "He sees beyond the ordinary in people, so he probably see the devil in you."

Larry stood. "Don't try me, woman," he said menacingly. "You don't want these folks to see you get an ass-beating." He stalked out the room.

An awkward silence. "I think I will get dressed," Jenna said, rising. "Branson will be here, and I want to be ready. If you will excuse me," moving out the door up the staircase and into her rooms.

"You look beautiful as usual, Miss Jenna," Branson said, his voice caressing. "I'm a proud man to have you on my arm."

"That is nice of you to say," Jenna said with a smile.

The sleek off the shoulder sheath hugged her slender curves, its deeply black color complementing her dark eyes, hair, and warm brown skin dusted with gold. Her sparkling heels were a metallic dark pewter, the same color as her purse and the rhinestone hair clip flashing in the ebony tresses. Holding out a deep, plush coat in black with a fur collar for Branson to help her into, pulling on black leather gloves trimmed in fur, wrapping a fringed black shawl around her for added warmth, walking over to kiss Sidney, holding Miracle, and her baby good night.

"What did you say was the occasion for your mother's party?" Jenna asked as they sped along.

"A friend of mine that I grew up with is in town," Branson said, glancing over at her. "My mother has always been close to their family, so she decided to have a welcome home party."

"That is certainly nice of her," Jenna said, "Are many of your childhood friends going to be there?"

"Several," Branson said. "A lot of them went away to school but returned after graduation. Even so, we don't see a lot of one another – different lives, different careers."

"How nice for all of you to reconnect," Jenna said.

"You'll get an opportunity to meet some of my oldest friends," Branson said, as they pulled into a small, paved courtyard with a stone sculpture at its center. The courtyard fronted a large, partially hidden two-story house, the tall, stately oaks and manicured bushes surrounding it providing privacy and seclusion.

They walked up a long, winding sidewalk to the wide portico leading to two immense wooden doors with leaded-glass insets, Branson pushing the doorbell next to one of the doors. A uniformed maid opened the door, bobbing her head respectfully as they entered, taking their coats, pointing them to the spacious family room near the back where the sound of dozens of conversations and voices lifted in laughter could be heard. A tall, fair-skinned woman with short blonde hair, built along generous lines approached, touching her cheek to Branson's in greeting.

"There you are, my dear, your timing is perfect. Althea just arrived a few moments ago. Now that the both of you are here, we can officially get started. She is here somewhere; come let me help you find her."

"First, let me introduce you to a special friend of mine. This is Jenna Thompson, who is studying to be a Nurse Practitioner at the University of Detroit. Her internship in one area and residency in another are both at Detroit Regional where our paths crossed, and would you believe not for the first time? It turns out we were both studying in Birmingham, Alabama at the same time. Almost seems like we were fated to be, doesn't it? Jenna, my mother, Dorothy Radcliffe."

"Very nice to meet you, Mrs. Radcliffe, "Jenna said clearly, meeting cool gray eyes that left hers to openly examine her from head to toe. Jenna looked deeply into the unfriendly gaze, instantly recognizing the bone-deep antipathy, hostility emanating from the icily polite woman standing before her, discerning, understanding what made her that way.

"How do you do," Dorothy said, her voice colorless. She was unexpectedly rocked, unnerved by the beautiful dark eyes that met hers, eyes somehow seeming to look beyond the polished Dorothy Radcliffe in her beautiful wool suit from a world renown designer, deeper than the perfectly matched diamond encircled pearls in the earrings adorning her ears and the three-strand choker tastefully circling her throat, her perfectly made-up face and elegantly coiffed hair, uncovering the person she did not want anyone to know still existed. Stiffening, her face hardened. Turning to Branson, she said, "You simply must greet the guest of honor my dear," clutching her son's arm and pulling him to where a large group of men and women were circled, talking animatedly, her face tightening when Branson grabbed Jenna's hand, pulling her along, looking down at her and slowly smiling – his grin widening when she smiled slowly back.

"Althea, darling, look who has come at last. My dear son who when he is not at work, which admittedly isn't often, is always fashionably late for every social engagement he is invited to. Including mine," laughing lightly.

"Mother, you wrong me," Branson said with a laugh, hugging the very fair, very slender woman with almost blonde silky hair that fell from a central part in a thick, luxurious tumble well past her shoulders and large, greenish-brown eyes that when she pulled away from the embrace examined Jenna almost as thoroughly as Dorothy had.

"Jenna, meet Althea. Althea, Jenna. Althea and I have known each other literally from the time we were babies. She moved away for a time, but she's back – no one who has lived here can stay away from the Motor City for long."

"Nice to meet you," Jenna said, bracing herself for more hostility.

Unexpectedly, Althea grinned. Reaching over she hugged Jenna warmly, whispering in her ear, "Thank God you are here! Now our respective mothers, Branson's and mine, will stop trying to throw the two of us, together. At least for tonight, anyway." Stepping back, she said, "Welcome, Jenna, it is nice to meet you. I love that dress. Come on, let me introduce you around. I know how hard it is being the new kid on the block, even worse if damn near everybody else grew up together. Branson, go away for a while, this is a girl thing. I'll let you know when you can collect her." Grabbing Jenna by the hand, the two of them talking animatedly, they walked toward the large group still laughing and talking.

Branson looked over at his mother, his smile saying it all. Dorothy sniffed and stalked away. There would be other opportunities.

"Did you have fun tonight, Jenna?"

"You know what, Sidney, I did. I had a very nice time, the best time I have ever had with Branson, even if his mother is a witch. I met a woman tonight who I really liked; we are planning on going shopping and to lunch this Saturday. Her name is Althea Gordon, and I think Branson's mother, and hers too, were hoping the two of them would see one another, the fires would ignite, and they would fall madly in love; but it did not work out that way."

"She will prove to be a true friend to you," Sidney said. "Trust in the strength of a friendship." Then in his own voice he said, "You had so much fun because there were a lot of people there, and the two of you weren't by yourselves."

"From the mouths of babes," Jenna murmured to herself. She liked Branson well enough and had a good time in his company, but she certainly did not love him and did not appear to be in any danger of that happening. Besides, his mother would be almost impossible to deal with. Still, something about him went beyond his movie star good looks and brash self-confidence an unexpected kindness – a rarely seen vulnerability that kept him from being a complete washout and had the ladies waiting months for an appointment just so he would be the one to see them. Nice enough to keep her conflicted, not nice enough to cause her to fall headlong. "Which is just as well," she said to herself as she prepared for bed. "It's not like I'm going to marry him or anything," climbing into bed, switching off the light and snuggling underneath the pile of blankets she had to keep her warm on a cold Michigan night, falling asleep quickly in the comforting warmth.

"So, are you looking to marry him or to have his baby?" Jenna looked across the table at the person asking the playful question.

"Oh, dear, please do not tell me those are my only two choices," Jenna protested. "What about 'none of the above'?"

Althea laughed, "If that's the case, then you're definitely in the minority. The female population has been chasing, fighting, and offering themselves to get with Branson since we were in junior high."

"Were you ever a member of his fan club?" Jenna asked.

"I did sample the wares, but that was years ago," Althea said candidly. "It just didn't feel right, almost like I was trying to get with my brother or a cousin or something. He felt pretty much the same way, so we never pursued it, even though our mothers are always trying to get us together, not willing to see that it's not going to happen." She looked speculatively at Jenna. "I saw the way he was with you at the party, and I honestly think you could land him if you wanted to. I think he's seriously smitten."

Jenna said. "Going on dates with him are okay, but he is a bit full of himself which would get on my nerves…plus, his mother hates me."

"Well, if you were equally smitten, I wouldn't say anything, but Branson…is a dog with women, an utter bow-wow, a straight up hound. He's broken hearts all over Detroit, he broke them in college, he's had a few flings with other nurses, there were some church sisters, and several girls who were a part of TicTacKnow." TicTacKnow was an organization formed by black women aimed at exposing their children to a higher degree of learning and culture and to make them aware of the contributions Blacks had made to the world at large. Membership was by invitation only and very exclusive.

"And you were not going to tell me?" Jenna protested.

"Well, I have found that when you try to caution someone about whoever they are involved with, it can get really messy. When confronted the guy will lie, which leaves you looking like a jealous, petty troublemaker. So, if you were head-over-heels in love with him, I would not say a word, but since you are not... forewarned is forearmed. You could still marry him, you know, take advantage of his social connections, spend his money, and have pretty babies. And you could limit the contact with Dreadful Dorothy. Best of all, that means you would stay in Detroit which I think would be absolutely wonderful."

Jenna smiled at her new-found friend. "I will keep that in mind but let us not forget: He has not asked me. Now, talk about something else."

"I know, let us have a toast to newfound friends," Althea said, raising her glass of wine."

"To newfound friends," Jenna repeated, raising her glass of cola with a lot of ice. Clinking their glasses together, they moved on to a different topic.

"Hey, Slim, you got a minute? Somebody here wants to talk to you." George Fillmore, owner of the *Quarter Note* stood in the door to Henry Lloyd's tiny dressing room.

"Sure," Henry Lloyd said. "Come on in, it'll be a tight squeeze, but I think the three of us will fit." He closed the door when the two men entered. "Now, gentlemen, what can I do for you?"

"Slim, this is Gary Britton, owner and CEO of Motor City Records. You may have heard some of his singers. They are getting lots of play on black radio stations all over the country."

"I have heard of you, and listened to your sound over the airwaves," Henry Lloyd said, rising to shake his hand. "It's a pleasure to meet you."

"It is a pleasure to meet you, Slim," Gary said, firmly gripping the extended hand. "I've been wanting to talk with you for some time. I'm thinking maybe we can do business together."

"I'll leave the two of you to talk," George said, "I got a club to run. Now, don't forget you got a set coming up in a couple of hours. As always, it's a full house come to hear you, so don't get so carried away you forget your fans." Opening the door and moving into the narrow hallway, he closed the door behind him.

"I hear you always perform to standing room only crowds," Gary said, "that your voice throws the ladies into a tizzy, and all the fellows wish they could sing like that."

"I don't know about all that," Henry Lloyd said easily. "I done real good during my time in Detroit. Lucky, I guess."

"You're too modest," Gary said, "I've heard you myself and I'm here to tell you, you've got a rare gift. One that should be heard in more places than Detroit, which is why I'm here. I'd like you to come into the studio and cut a demo record for me, with an eye to signing you onto the Motor City roster if all goes as planned. What do you say?"

"Well, I guess it can't hurt," Henry Lloyd said after a moment's reflection. "Tell you what, come by tomorrow late afternoon or early evening and we will work out times and such."

"Sounds like a plan," Gary agreed, opening the door. "I will see you tomorrow. Mr. Slim, I think we could make beautiful music together," closing the door behind him.

"I hear Althea and your country bumpkin are as thick as thieves these days," a disgruntled Dorothy told her son. "The two of them have been seen all over town and she has introduced her into her circle of friends and invited her to our Triple Pi luncheon. Althea is treating this woman like her new best friend or a long-lost relative or something." Her unhappiness with this latest situation was clear.

"Not what you expected, huh?" Branson said with a chuckle. "And her name is Jenna, mother, Jenna." He looked at Dorothy. "Why are you behaving this way, mother? You've been unreasonably hostile ever since I first told you about her, without having even met her."

Remembering the dark eyes that had pierced her façade, her veneer of sophistication so effectively, she said viciously, "Because I am convinced, she's just a conniving little gold-digging social climber who has set her sights on you, figured out the way to keep you interested, and whose butter wouldn't melt in her mouth demeanor is just an act, and nothing you can say will convince me otherwise."

"You are wrong, Mother," Branson said, "but no matter what you think, you just better get used to the fact that Jenna is likely to become a member of this family." He walked away with his mother looking after him in frustrated anger.

Chapter Twenty-six

"I had a nice time, as usual, Miss Jenna," Branson said, following her through the door to the living room, linking his arms around her.

"I had a nice time, too," Jenna began, "I liked the movie. I knew she would regret running away and denying her mother."

"Yeah, there is nothing quite like –" they were interrupted by the sound of rising voices coming from the Green side of the house.

"You been meddling in my stuff? Going through my things? Don't lie, bitch, I know when my things have been moved. What did you think you were going to find? You know better – you must be losing your mind…or maybe you just need reminding what happens when you stick your nose where it don't belong." A derisive laugh followed. "Where'd you get that, and what you trying to do with it, scare me? Since you ain't got the gumption to use it, all that thing going to do is get you a harder ass beating." The loud report of a large gun followed immediately by another had them racing to where the shots originated. The wails of frightened children filled the air.

Sugar stood in the middle of the family room still holding the large caliber weapon she had just shot her husband with. Larry lay at her feet unmoving. Her pajama-clad children stood in the doorway leading to the upstairs bedrooms, crying. Rushing over, kneeling beside him, Jenna placed two fingers at the spot on his throat where the jugular beat. "He is not dead," she said. "Help me turn him over," Branson knelt beside her, ripping away the bloody shirt to examine the wounds.

"I need somebody to go to my car and bring me my medical bag," Branson said, "He's got some pretty serious flesh wounds, but they aren't life-threatening," he said.

"I'll go," Sidney said, standing in the doorway that Jenna and Branson had used, reaching out to take the keys he was handed.

"One bullet grazed his head, which is what knocked him out, the other passed clean through his upper arm. We need to clean them up so there is no risk of infection and I'll give him a dose of antibiotics, too."

"I need a sheet, or something cut up into bandages, and some help getting him into the nearest bed. And then I need some water heated." Branson looked up from tending to his patient.

"I'll help you get him into bed," Jenna said, propping an unconscious Larry into a sitting position, standing and then leaning down, draping a limp arm around her shoulders, Branson doing the same, dragging him between them to the master bedroom, dropping him on the surface of the large bed, Branson stripping him of his clothes and dressing him in pajama bottoms before pulling the blankets over the still unconscious man, striding into the bathroom and returning with towels that he placed underneath the sluggishly bleeding arm, moving the bloody clothing bunched beneath it.

Jenna returned from a trip to the kitchen. "I put a pot of water on the stove to heat," she said, walking over and retrieving the medical bag and car keys from Sidney, handing them to Branson who stuffed the keys into his pants pocket before opening his black leather bag with filled with medical supplies, withdrawing cotton pads and two syringes.

"I got this," he told Jenna. "You see about your sister and calm down them youngsters."

Sugar was unnaturally calm as she had been since shooting her husband. She still held the weapon she had used, but offered no resistance when Jenna gently removed it from her slack fingers. Sidney had collected his niece and three nephews and taken them to the rooms he shared with Jenna, beginning a board game that succeeded in distracting them from what was going on in a different part of the house. The doors to all the boarder's rooms remained firmly closed. The less they knew, the less they could recount to anyone, particularly law enforcement, who might ask awkward questions. Returning to the bedroom Jenna stood by the side of the bed watching Branson bind up the wound and administer two shots, one for pain, the other to prevent infection. Larry moaned, and slowly opened his eyes.

"She...she shot me...the bitch shot me..." he grated.

"What? Someone shot you, you say?" Branson asked, "I heard you tripped, and the gun went off as you were falling. You are talking outside your head, man. I think you will remember what really happened after you wake up from this pain-killer medicine I pumped in you. I'm Doctor Radcliffe, and we'll talk more then." He motioned for Jenna to follow him out of the room, closing the door behind him.

Sugar had not moved from her position on the couch. Sitting down beside her, gently holding her hand, Jenna looked up when Branson came and stood beside them. "Your husband is resting fairly comfortably," he told Sugar. "I left some tablets for you to give him when he wakes up which won't be any time soon. I suggest you get some rest as well. Jenna, could I talk to you in private?" Jenna rose, following him from the family room into the big, immaculate kitchen.

"You know that by law we are supposed to report a gunshot wound to the police," Branson said.

"I know," Jenna said. "It was clearly a case of self-defense. You heard what went on before she shot him."

"Maybe so, but…you do know who he is, don't you?" Branson asked.

Jenna looked confused. "Who he is? No, I guess I don't. Who is he?"

"That's Luxury Larry. He is a bookie known for being a snappy dresser and wearing a lot of brown. He is also one of the biggest Numbers runners in the entire state of Michigan. He has got a lot of pull – even has some police officers on his payroll. It might not go so well for your sister no matter what we say."

"You mean she might be the one in trouble and not him?" Jenna asked incredulously. "Even with the two of us testifying to what happened?"

"Well, now, about that," Branson said slowly. "Cavorting with criminals might put a stain on both our careers. People do tend to think birds of a feather stick together."

"Are you saying you will not tell the police what happened?" Jenna asked, looking up at him in disbelief.

"I am saying we can probably get away with not having to say anything at all," Branson said.

"How?" Jenna asked.

"I could have a little talk with Ell-ell – that's what he goes by on the street, let him know I saved his life and that I don't plan to tell the cops. In return he can't tell anyone what happened. Not all the cops in the city are on his payroll and there are some who would be happy to arrest and get him off the street. Besides, he has been implicated in a couple of serious beatings and some deaths himself. And there is a sure way for him to know we are gonna keep all of this quiet." He moved closer looking down, his eyes kindling.

"What is that?" Jenna asked huskily, looking up.

"He would know I definitely wouldn't say anything…couldn't say anything…if I were a member of the family. We all know a man can't testify against his wife and vice versa. You were here in the thick of things…so if we were married, I could never reveal what happened here tonight, because it might implicate you. I'll continue to check up on him until he's all better. What do you say? Will you marry me, Jenna?"

"But I – I…" she stammered to a stop.

"What? Don't love me? I don't care, it will come in time. As a married couple, we will be spending a lot of time together, we'll get to know one another intimately, there won't be any others competing or in the way and the love will come, you'll see."

Thoughts, warnings, protests, objections, crowded Jenna's mind, chief among them the thought of what would happen if Sugar were arrested or if unwelcome attention became centered on Larry's financial dealings. She in turn could lose her scholarship for no other reason than her living there, giving the appearance of collusion. She could not risk it. Trapped, unable to think of a way out, "I will marry you, Branson," she said, managing not to stiffen when he embraced her.

"I swear you are the most solemn bride I have ever seen," Althea remarked, adjusting the small spray of flowers in her hair, her eyes meeting Jenna's in the mirror. "We talked about this not so long ago. You made it pretty clear you had no deep feelings, with no chance of any developing, and I don't see anything that has happened to cause your feelings to change so drastically that you feel compelled to get married now. Not to mention the groom is watching you in a way that seems more like a warden than a lover. Add to the mix a mother-in-law who looks as if she is being fed a steady diet of limes, peel and all, her face is so puckered and drawn up. And the fact that only two guests are on the bride's side: one of them your sister who looks as though she's going to burst into tears – not happy ones, mind you, at any moment, although you did get Slim to sing – I had no idea he was your brother. Anyway, add all of that up, and something mighty peculiar is going on."

Jenna looked into her friend's eyes a moment longer before turning away with a sweep of ebony lashes. "Why are you so suspicious?" she said. "I care about Branson, he cares about me, and I think we will have a good, solid marriage."

"I haven't heard a word about love," Althea noted.

"I love that you were willing to be my Maid of Honor," Jenna said with a slight smile. "I appreciate your concern, but I know what I am doing."

Althea still looked doubtful, but reaching over, hugging her friend fiercely, she said, "Just know that if you ever need my help, need me to do something, anything for you, just let me know."

"Thank you, Althea," Jenna whispered, returning the hug, "Everything is all right, you will see."

Henry Lloyd stood outside the judge's chambers where the marriage would take place in a few minutes, waiting for the wedding party to arrive. He frowned as he did every time he thought about this marriage – ever since Queenie had told him about it, days earlier. Something was not right. The bride looked infinitely sad when she thought no one was looking. Sugar looked miserable, and Sidney, who was not coming, was even more silent than usual if that were possible. Something else that seemed strange, the timing off – Larry Green's banishment from the boarding house. Had Sugar finally discovered how her husband made his money? The groom, meanwhile, seemed more smug than happy, and his sour-faced mother, the stuff of nightmares.

Yep, there were some mighty strange happenings in connection with this marriage and he was going to get to the bottom of it. He straightened as he saw the wedding party approach.

Dorothy Radcliffe walked beside her son so full of rage she trembled with it. She had been consumed by this impotent anger from the moment Branson announced his impending marriage. The little gold digger thought she had won the war, did she? "Well, we'll just see about that, won't we?" posing unsmiling as wedding pictures were snapped. She was not the only one – except for the groom – smiles were few and seemed forced from all other wedding participants, matching the strained atmosphere that surrounded the entire proceeding.

"I am pregnant," Jenna spoke into the stillness of the darkened bedroom.

The bedclothes rustled as Branson sat up. "What did you say?" he asked.

"I said I am pregnant…about three months along, which means your son or daughter will be born sometime in June."

Branson smiled. "That is good news, Jenna – our first of many. I was an only; I like the idea of a big family. Mother will be ecstatic. She has been after me about grandchildren for years. I can't wait to tell her. You aren't saying much. Are you happy about the baby?" he demanded.

"Of course, I am happy about the baby," Jenna said quietly. "Telling you just now made it…real somehow."

Reaching down Branson pulled Jenna into his arms, gratified when she relaxed into them, not stiffening like she usually did. "Are you going to continue working?" he asked. "You know you don't have to. You could be a woman of leisure with nothing to do but get ready for the baby, and even after if you want."

"I plan to work until the baby is born," Jenna said. It was the only way she could retain a tenuous grip on her patience, not mention her sanity in dealing with an awful mother-in-law who took every opportunity to correct, diminish, criticize, or admonish, her syrupy voice dripping poison. It had been worse until the day Sidney told her in no uncertain terms to back off, the look in his eye causing Dorothy to close her mouth mid-criticism, after which she avoided him like the plague, and vice versa. He was not much better around Branson, speaking little, eyeing him with unconcealed dislike.

"So, you are pregnant, huh? I guess we can be thankful that at least this one will be legitimate," Dorothy began.

"That is enough." Something in Jenna's quiet voice caused Dorothy to abruptly stop talking. "I am going to tell you this one time only," Jenna said in deadly earnest. "You can say whatever you want to about me, denigrate me, laugh at me, scoff, spit all the bitterness you want – I am grown and can take it…but you are never…do you hear me? *Never* to say anything negative about my daughter. She is innocent, the circumstances of her birth are not her fault, and none of your business. If I ever hear you saying anything that will hurt that baby or make her feel the least bit unhappy or inadequate, I promise you will regret it. I will hurt you, make you wish you had never been born, do you understand? I caution you to take heed because I will not have this conversation again." Jenna walked away leaving behind a shaken Dorothy. "Branson better find a house for us soon, or I cannot be responsible for what happens." They had moved into the Radcliffe guest house right after their marriage but took most of their meals in the big house with Dorothy, who felt free to drop in at any time.

"Your babies are beautiful," Althea looked in the twin cribs at the sleeping infants, one decked out in pink, the other in blue. "When did you know you were having twins?"

"When Bettina decided to make herself known just before birth," Jenna said. "My OB-GYN originally thought Brandon had a heart murmur or something, and then Bettina announced her presence. I am not surprised. Twins tend to run in my family."

"Was Dorothy the Witch happy?" Althea asked.

"Oh, she billed and cooed and fussed and went on-and-on about her fair-skinned, 'good'-haired grandbabies," Jenna said dryly. "She has been on a spending spree to furnish their room and buy their clothes and choose their toys. She even bought formula for them when I could not produce enough milk."

"Does it bother you? Her taking over like that?" Althea demanded.

"No, it does not, not really," Jenna said after a brief pause. Looking up at her friend she said, "Althea, can I tell you something?" she asked.

Althea grasped her by the hand. "You can tell me anything," she said. "Anything. And I promise you it will go no further. I won't, whatever it is, hold it against you."

Jenna fell silent a moment before she said quietly, "I do not care because...Althea, I do not like my children...and they do not like me. I know that is terrible for a mother to say, but I can feel it. We do not share any type of bond, no parent-child closeness whatsoever, and I tried, I have really tried to feel something, but nothing is there. I am convinced my milk drying up was a sign. Brandon, I think, likes me a little, but I can tell his sister – who is going to be the one with the strongest will – she, she does not like me at all; and as they grow up, he will do whatever she tells him."

"Are you sure you don't have the post-baby blues?" Althea asked anxiously. "It happens to a lot of mothers. You might feel differently given a little time."

"No, they do not like me because they were not conceived in love. I do not love their daddy (who is crazy about them) never did, and I truly cannot stand their grandmother who adores them. And…" she admitted wearily, "I do not care much. I wish I did."

They were interrupted by the sound of Branson and Dorothy coming up the stairs, talking excitedly, laden with packages for the babies and nursery. She watched detached as Dorothy lifted one and Branson the other baby from their cribs, using the baby monitor to tell the maid to bring up their formula, moving to the glassed-in porch off from the nursery, sitting down to await the maid's arrival. After a moment she turned and quietly descended the stairs, Althea close behind.

"May I speak to Branson, please?" the female voice was smooth, sultry. "Tell him it's his Cupcake calling."

Jenna put the phone down without comment and went in search of her husband, running him down in the den going over patient files. "Your Cupcake is on the phone," she said. "She wants to talk to you."

Branson hurriedly put down the paper he was perusing, stood and strode into the hallway where the phone was located. "Hello?" he said angrily, picking it up and heading into the half-bath located in the hall, closing the door, his voice raised in anger.

He emerged a short time later and went looking for Jenna, finding her in her office at her typewriter, working on her latest paper. "I can explain about the phone call," he began.

"No need," Jenna said. "I have a pretty good idea of who Cupcake is. She is the one who sent me this letter," holding up a sheet of scented paper with elaborate handwriting on it. Branson walked over, snatched up the paper, reading its contents. His face darkened in anger. He crumpled the paper in one hand.

"Do not be angry with her," Jenna said calmly. "She just thought I should know you were having an affair with her. I guess I could have told her to get in line." She resumed typing.

Branson looked down at Jenna consumed with rage, at the woman he was seeing who dared to contact his wife, and at his wife who obviously did not give a damn. All attempts at generating some type of emotion, any type, from Jenna as usual, woefully unsuccessful. His hands clenched into fists he gritted his teeth. "Maybe I should invite her over to dinner," he said. "My mother would probably be happy to meet her."

"Maybe you should," Jenna said indifferently, not looking up. "But to prevent any awkwardness, maybe you should wait until I leave for San Francisco." She was leaving in three days to take part in the ten-year reunion of the League. Everyone was coming. They had been exchanging excited phone calls and letters for weeks. They were all staying at the same hotel, and Maria (the only one who still lived there) had planned a carefully orchestrated reunion, complete with a stroll down memory lane. Sidney and Miracle would stay with Sugar at the boarding house while she was gone.

She would pick them up on her way back home from the airport. She did look up when Branson stomped his way out of her home office, slamming the door behind him.

"Jenna? Jenna is that you?" Hurrying through the San Francisco airport, Jenna turned at the sound of her name. A tall, sophisticated, beautifully dressed Black woman was running in her direction, arms outstretched. Jenna dropped her things and ran to embrace her, the two hugging tightly, both talking at once.

"Jenna, you look so good! All-grown up and with such an air! I am so happy to see you!"

"Angela, I can say the same thing about you. You are so sophisticated. I love that pantsuit. Where did you get it, Paris?"

"I think this one came from Milan," Angela said, "but you're no slouch yourself. That scarf is beautiful and perfect with that dress, which is stunning by the way. Wait – is that Julie?" both running to embrace the elegant Asian woman running their way. Arm in arm, chattering away, they reclaimed their scattered belongings, headed for baggage claim.

Dinner that evening was at the bodega owned by Maria's family which catered only to them that night. Maria Fernandez had married Juan Hernandez, which she said was like Mary Smith marrying John Jones, and had five children. She looked much the same as she always had, several pounds heavier, which in her culture, she explained, just meant she was *buen cuidada* which roughly translated into well taken care of. Her husband, one of the cooks and servers, obviously adored her. Doris, who had attended the Jewish American University in Los Angeles made her mother exceedingly happy when she married a Jewish doctor of Internal Medicine. As a reward, although they did not call it that, she had been gifted one of her family's jewelry stores located in downtown Los Angeles. She, her husband, who had a thriving practice, and her two children had a huge, ultra-modern home in Beverly Hills. Susan, the white girl of the group, was a junior partner on the fast track at a prestigious law firm in Chicago. She had just been presented with an engagement ring big enough to choke a horse by her affluent fiancé, an up-and-coming politician. Angela was unmarried, but currently involved with a fabulously wealthy Greek shipbuilding magnate who was trying, so far unsuccessfully, to coax the world traveler into marriage. Julie was also working at a law firm, this one in New York, resisting attempts by her parents to get her married to an Asian man of their choice – one of the reasons she chose to live on the other side of the country. Plus, she was still trying to find a way to tell them she was living with someone – a white man no less.

Though they had read about it and sent telegrams, they all felt keenly and cried anew when Jenna told them about losing

Curtice – the two lawyers staunchly declaring her married to him and offering to prove it in a court of law if only for Miracle's sake. Jenna agreed and the two immediately began plotting strategy, telling her not to worry about cost; of course, they would do it pro bono. The six reunited friends talked through the night, laughing, exchanging anecdotes, passing around pictures of children and significant others, eating the delectable dishes prepared by Maria's husband and family, picking up where they left off, their bond of friendship stronger than ever.

They met on the boardwalk the next day, strolling around the teeming decks, remembering Jenna's awed introduction to the busy year-round entertainment venue, and her first taste of Mexican cuisine. "It was so good – I had never tasted anything like it," Jenna said as she consumed a chocolate-dipped vanilla ice cream cone. "I still love Mexican food, and eat it whenever I get a chance, but I must say, nothing I have ever eaten can hold a candle to the food your family prepared for us last night." There was a chorus of agreement.

"Let's hope you all feel the same way when you sample my folks Asian cooking tonight," Julie said, sipping on a tall frozen drink. "They have been prepping for days."

"All this wonderful eating is going to make it difficult for me to get into my clothes," pencil-thin Angela laughingly protested as she polished off the last of a soft-shelled crab sandwich. "So, let's go swimming and burn up some calories. I have swum in many bodies of water, but there is nothing quite like the Pacific. Last one in is a mama walrus!" Laughing, they all ran for the water.

Back on the beach they lay on the towels they brought from the hotel, looking back on the many times they had lain much as they were doing now, reflecting on the many things that had happened in the decade since the last time they had seen one another. "Jenna, I remember you left immediately, and I mean immediately. The same night as graduation, right?" Maria said. Jenna nodded.

"You always knew what you were going to do," Angela said, "Your mind was focused on becoming a nurse for as long as I've known you. You were going to be a nurse, your mind set on it, so that's what you did, and in spectacular fashion, I must say."

"I'll say! Graduating first in your class – no surprise there – and then deciding to become a Nurse Practitioner and a Healer. You never did things by half-measure, did you?"

"I read about your papers published in the top two academic medical journals," Julie said. "Way to go."

"Did I read about your paper in the Harvard law review, and Susan arguing a case before the Illinois Supreme Court and winning?" Jenna asked. "And Angela, your time in the Peace Corps exposed you to some of the highest echelon of world society, did it not?"

"It did," Angela agreed. "I met a lot of the movers and shakers of various countries, and just managed to get away without become the first wife of the son of the king of a wealthy African kingdom. His Majesty had a dozen wives, so I knew I would eventually be only one of many, so I skipped. Been leery of marriage ever since."

"Even marriage to Nikolai, who is incredibly rich and has bombarded you with flowers, phone calls, and gifts the entire time you have been here?" Doris demanded. They all watched with a great deal of interest when Angela ducked her head, refusing to meet their eyes, determinedly changing the subject, allowing the topic to drop, though their sparkling eyes spoke volumes.

The last night of the reunion, Jenna stood in the mirror adjusting her attire. "I suppose I should be happy I can still wear it," she said to herself, eyeing her reflection in the full-length piece of reflective glass. Since the stroll down memory lane was tonight, Maria had instructed everyone to bring and wear – if they could – the outfit they had worn to their high school graduation. Clad in the yellow-flowered dress, lightweight yellow cardigan and yellow pumps, wearing a yellow headband like the one that had held her hair back, she took one last look before picking up her yellow leather purse and closing the door.

"This has all been so wonderful. I hate that it has to end so soon," Julie lamented as they made their way back into the hotel lobby where they were staying.

"I so agree," Jenna said blissfully. "I cannot remember a time in recent memory when I have enjoyed myself more. You all have given me a whole new set of marvelous memories to add to the ones I already have." A chorus of heartfelt agreement.

"Wasn't it great that the nightwatchman let us into Bayside for a while? But did it seem like it...shrank or something?" Angela asked. "I had memories of this ginormous building, but tonight it seemed...not so."

"I thought I was the only one," Susan said with a laugh. "I looked at the football stadium, at the soccer field, and it seemed diminished somehow."

"Still, there will never be another Bayside High," Maria said.

"And I wouldn't trade it for anything," Doris said. "After all, that is where I met my best friends in the whole wide world."

"Shall we drink to our next reunion, ten years from now?" Jenna said, raising the glass of champagne they had poured from the bottle waiting for them in the hotel lobby.

"To our next reunion," Angela said raising hers.

"In ten years," Maria said, holding hers high.

"Ten years," said Julie and Susan in unison.

Five glasses clinked together.

"Ladies and gentlemen, this is the captain speaking. We are making our final approach to Detroit International Airport. The Fasten Seat Belt signs have been turned on, please fasten your seat belts, and we'll be touching down momentarily."

"Ladies and gentlemen, the captain has turned on the fasten seat belt sign. At this time, please return your seat to the upright position, return your trays to their position in the seat in front of you, and the stewardess will be coming through to collect any last-minute trash you might have. We will be arriving at the terminal in a few minutes. We'd like to thank you…"

Jenna stopped listening to the stewardess's speech. She was thinking about her recent trip to San Francisco and her impending return home – a home that did not and never had felt like one, where she and Sidney and Miracle felt trapped and unhappy, to a husband she did not love and a mother-in-law she abhorred. Disembarking the plane, she made two calls, one to Sugar, the other to Henry Lloyd. She walked out the airport smiling.

Chapter Twenty-seven

Branson pulled into the winding driveway in front of his residence. The house was dark, no sign of any activity, and Jenna's car was not in its usual spot in front of one of the garage doors. His jaw tightened. It did not look as if she were home yet, but he knew that tonight was the night for her scheduled return and that her plane had landed on time hours ago. He had called to check. She must still be at her sister Sugar's house, obviously in no hurry to come home.

He had purposely timed his arrival for well after the time he expected her to be back, so that she could see that he had not spent his time at home waiting for her. That she was not even there to witness his late arrival only served to fuel his anger and frustration. His marriage was not at all what he had anticipated on the night he had coerced Jenna into it. He had expected to have the upper hand, was convinced that a grateful Jenna would soon fall into his arms, allow him to lead her, control her, would love him desperately. Once he had secured that love, he could return to his cavalier ways, his superficial emotions and carelessly cruel treatment of women, as in days past leaving a trail of broken hearts in his wake; ensuring that hers would be foremost among them – and in the process maybe then he could get his back.

He had nothing he could really complain about. She was always cordial, even-tempered, and never once had she denied him his marital rights, which he exercised on a regular basis, but after which left him equally torn between pain, hurt and rage. His affairs since marrying Jenna were empty gestures, futile attempts to trigger some sort of reaction in his all-but emotionless wife. He opened his car door, slamming it shut, his footsteps on the stone-flagged sidewalk loud in the quiet of the night.

At the door, inserting his key in the lock, turning the knob and entering the spacious foyer, turning to close and lock the heavy wooden slab, he turned as the lamp on a table next to the telephone switched on. Henry Lloyd sat legs outstretched, by the table in a chair he had confiscated from another room. He sat up as Branson slowly approached. "Hey, man," he said with a lazy smile. "How you doin'?"

"I'm good," Branson said. "What brings you here?"

"Got a few things I want to talk with you about," Henry Lloyd said. "You want to do it here, or do you want to go somewhere else?"

"We can go to my den," Branson said, walking in that direction. "Can I offer you a drink?"

"I'll take a Scotch and water," Henry Lloyd said, following Branson into his den, sitting down into a large black leather chair, thanking him with a murmur when he handed him his drink, taking an appreciative sip of the expensive liquor. Setting it down on the end table next to the chair, he leaned forward. "I'm here to talk to you about Queenie. You see she's not here... and you should know, she's not coming back."

He watched the startled surprise followed immediately by anger building in the hazel eyes looking into his and said, "I knew from the jump there was something funny about this marriage— something not quite right, but Queenie was determined to go through with it, so I let it go. Tonight, she told me what happened that led to you marrying her: about Sugar shooting her husband, and how you helped patch him up and kept the police from getting involved – which was an upstanding thing for you to do...if you hadn't ruined it by using what you knew to pressure Queenie into marrying you to protect Sugar. Queenie will do most anything for her family – even marry someone she don't love. But she wants to be free now, and I'm here to see that you let her go without a lot of fuss and unpleasantness."

"And how do you propose to do that?" Branson asked, sipping from his own drink.

"I thought we could talk things over man to man," Henry Lloyd said reasonably. "That we could come to terms, you and I, without things getting...ugly."

"And what exactly do we have to talk about?" Branson asked, stretching his legs out, taking another sip of his drink.

"I saw you the other night," Henry Lloyd said, at *Cleo's Place*. You were there with a...friend. And from what I could see, a very close friend."

Branson gave a snorting chuckle. "You saw that did you? My friend got a little too affectionate for a public place, and I don't want all my business out in the street, so I had to let her go... besides she was too young. I should have known better."

"That's not the first time I've seen you around the club scene with friends," Henry Lloyd said. "You got kind of a rep for loving 'em and leaving 'em."

"Yeah, well, what do they expect? They know I'm married with kids, but if they don't care about that, why should I if they fall too hard? We're both going in with our eyes open. I have no interest in a serious relationship."

"And they're not Queenie," Henry Lloyd said, his eyes unexpectedly sympathetic.

Branson broke the silence following Henry Lloyd's observation. "No, they ain't," he said with a heavy sigh. "I really fucked up, didn't I?"

"I think you took the wrong approach," Henry Lloyd agreed.

"Nothing else I tried was working," Branson said with another sigh. "I was never able to get her to warm to me; that had never happened to me before. All I had to do was wink at a girl, flirt a little, show her a little attention and she fell into my arms like a ripe plum. Hell, my first time was with one of my mother's friends, and she wasn't the only older woman who wanted – and got - a piece of me. I got to thinking no one could say no to me...and then I saw your sister at Birmingham Regional one day and was surprised and irritated that she did not notice me, even more so when I saw that she had no trouble noticing that rabble-rouser Curtice Brooks. I told myself to forget her – she was just one chick among many, so what if she obviously had no interest in me? I had more women than I could possibly keep up with. I told myself that I had succeeded until the day I was surprised and delighted to see her hurry by me in one of the corridors of Detroit Regional. Man, I searched that hospital top to bottom until I found her. I managed to convince her to go out with me after which she blew me off – pissing me off royally... and making me more determined to make her care...It took a while for me to realize that I was the one caught this time, falling for someone who was friendly enough, but if I never called on her again, wouldn't bother her in the least. And even though I told myself to walk away...I couldn't. Which only made me angrier and more determined to get her, to have her feel like I did so that I could teach her a lesson, could turn the tables...only it didn't work out that way. My feelings for her grew and hers for me didn't."

"Never been turned down before made you a little crazy, huh?" Henry Lloyd said.

Branson reached over and poured his brother-in-law another drink. "Yeah, I guess so, man. The closest I came to winning her over was the weekend I sent her flowers every few hours the entire weekend…she was really sweet to me behind that…I should have stuck with stuff like that. But when your other sister shot Ell-ell, I mistakenly thought that was what I needed to get Jenna and have something to hold over her to keep her in line… big mistake. She was never the same toward me and I lost the only woman I have ever loved – aside from my mama, of course."

"Queenie does not take well to being threatened or pushed around," Henry Lloyd said. "I think she felt like she owed you for not involving the authorities and taking care of Sugar's rotten husband without calling the police after she shot him but feels the debt has been paid in full."

"What about my children?" Branson asked, "Bettina and Brandon?"

After a short pause, "It took 'a great deal of agonizing, prayers, tears and thinking,' – her words, not mine – " Henry Lloyd said, "but the bottom line is, she is willing to grant you full custody to both of them."

Branson sat, barely holding searing pain at bay, torn between relief and bitter speculation. Was she so eager to be so totally rid of anything that even remotely belonged to him, that reminded her of him that she would essentially abandon her children? Did she hate him that much? Maybe it was her way of limiting contact knowing he would have fought for custody or insisted on joint at the very least. Or was it an act of kindness, knowing how much he loved them? A moot point now. Standing slowly, he walked over to the polished wooden cabinet built into the side of one wall sliding the door open, extracting an unopened bottle of the brand of Scotch they had been drinking. Reaching up to loosen his tie, unfastening the top button of his shirt, he looked over at Henry Lloyd and said, "Tell…Queenie that I'm not going to fight her, that I'll sign anything she wants. Most especially thank her for giving me the kids, I'll make sure they have the best life possible. But right now, this is the only company I need," holding up the bottle of Scotch, "So, forgive me if I sound rude, but... get out of my house." He walked over to the black leather sofa, kicking off his shoes, flinging himself down twisting off the top of the bottle of Scotch and bringing it to his lips, not bothering with a glass, taking a long pull. Henry Lloyd closed the door behind him.

"What's this I hear about you badmouthing Jenna to Brandon and Bettina?" Branson demanded as he came into the kitchen where his mother stood chopping vegetables on the large granite-topped island centered in the middle of the shining tiled floor.

"I have said nothing less than the truth," Dorothy said primly as she sliced potatoes, arranging them in an oblong glass dish, sprinkling them with salt and pepper and other herbs, covering them with a milky cheese mixture, sprinkling more cheese over the top and popping the casserole into a hot oven.

"That sorry excuse for a wife and mother abandoned the three of you without any thought or consideration, which is no less than I expected of someone of her ilk," she continued viciously. "Those darling children need to know what type of mother she was, and what type of wife you had. I think –"

"That's enough." His voice caused Dorothy to look at her son in surprise. "I have had it up to here listening to you talk badly about Jenna," he said, "to anyone who would listen...and me for allowing it. Maybe if I had stopped you and your venomous observations earlier, sooner, had truly defended her, she might not have left me. Just so you know, I would do most anything to get her back, up to and including cutting you out of our lives entirely if need be. Lucky for you I know that's not going to happen. But know this: if I ever hear you saying anything else negative to those children about their mother, I will not allow you to see them. You are not to poison their minds against Jenna, it is only because of her that they are here at all. I never want to have this conversation again, are we clear?"

"We are clear," Dorothy said softly, knowing she had finally gone too far, watching her son stride away, sensing his unhappiness, for the first time wondering about, and regretting the role she had played in the destruction, the dissolution of his marriage.

"And I just want the two of you to know that your mother loves you both very much, that she would love to see you, and that it is all right to want to see her. She has not deserted you. You will always have an important place in her heart, and if you should ever want to go to visit her, let me or her know, and we can make that happen."

He watched Brandon's eyes brighten, and some of the suspicious anger lift from Bettina's. "She's not happy to be rid of us?" Bettina asked almost belligerently.

"Of course not," Branson stated positively. "I know she misses you and thinks about you every single day."

"Then why did she leave us?" Brandon demanded the question foremost in their minds.

"She did not want to break my heart," Branson said. "And that's what would have happened if all of you had left me here all alone."

There was a thoughtful pause. "You would have been sad, Daddy?" Bettina asked, sitting on one of her father's legs, snaking an arm around his neck.

"Real sad," Branson said solemnly.

"Would you have cried?" Brandon asked, sitting on the other leg, draping his arm around Branson's neck.

"Every day," Branson said, nodding, pulling them close.

"Auntie Althea said that Mommy really loved us and not to believe what Glamma was saying," Brandon said unexpectedly.

"She did?" Branson said in surprise when the twins both nodded.

Jenna had called Althea to secure a promise from her friend. "Do not let Dorothy make my children hate me," she said. "Her voice should not be the only voice they hear about me."

"I won't," Althea promised. "I'll let them know what a wonderful woman their mama is. I'm sure going to miss you, girl. I guess I'll be traveling South sometime in the very near future."

"See that you do," Jenna said. "I love you, girl," she said softly before hanging up.

"Auntie Althea said the door was always open for us to see Mommy," Bettina said, "Glamma said it wasn't true, that she didn't want to be bothered."

"Your mother will always have time for you," Branson assured them. "So, think about it, and we'll talk about it again." They walked hand-in-hand toward the gleaming automobile parked in front of the curb.

"Are you sure, Sugar? This is what you want to do? Truly?" Jenna asked her sister, her worry apparent.

"I'm sure," Sugar said. "Detroit is home to me. My children were born here, I've joined a church, added some more boarders including a gay couple that compete in world weight-lifting competitions and have me on a fitness program, started school where I'm doing real well, so it looks like where I am is where I'll be. Larry don't come near here anymore, so if that's what you're worried about, don't."

"Well, I am sorry that you are not going back to South Carolina with us, but I understand you are already at home," Jenna said, giving her sister an enormous hug. "And when I start missing you too much, well, that is what planes are for."

"Exactly," Sugar said, returning the hug, holding on tightly. "Now I know what Sidney meant the night you got back from San Francisco. He had been acting funny like he do all day, and I expected him to fade away at any minute, praying them ghosts or spirits or whatever they are would wait until you got home. He had been smiling and packing boxes the entire week and all he would say was, 'Queenie's back and we're going home.' And I would say to him, I know that, when Queenie picks you up on her way home from the airport, y'all will be going home, meaning your house here. And then he would get one of them mysterious smiles like he do and pack something else."

Jenna, Sidney, and Miracle were moving to Crawford Hollow where she would begin her Nurse Practitioner practice with Doc Edmonds as her partner. She would offer Healer services at her home as well. Mama Joyce had deeded her granddaughter a big plot of land adjacent to hers; a big, rambling house with a wraparound porch was currently under construction and should be almost completed by the time they returned from their tour of Europe.

"Why are you goin' to Europe?" Sugar had demanded when Jenna informed her of her intention. "And ain't that going to be expensive?"

"We have that break between the kids being let out of school, school restarting in the fall, our move to South Carolina and the house being built," Jenna had replied. "I always wanted to go overseas and visit some of those European countries I've always heard and read about and decided that this would be the perfect time to do that. I'm going to use some of the money Curtice left me to pay for it – even then there will be plenty left over." She did not add that she still had ample funds from the money Henry Lloyd had lifted from Loretta, as well as the money Ma'dear had gifted her with when she left for California years earlier.

"And what made you decide to include them two evil children of yours? They so hateful they might spoil your whole trip."

"I have to, I want to establish a relationship with them," Jenna said softly. "It's not their fault their daddy and I were the way that we were, and it's time I stop avoiding them because of their father and their awful grandmother. I know now that despite what I've said in the past I do love them and want them to love me. I think that this trip will allow for that to happen in a neutral environment that is new and different and exciting to all of us. I asked Althea to come with us to help, and so that they won't be traumatized at the thought of so much uninterrupted time with just me. I think this trip will allow positive feelings between us to grow. And of course, I want Miracle to get to know her brother and sister. Family is family, and all family is important."

*　*　*

"And what did you say was the name of this we on is?" Sidney asked, looking down at the people, no bigger than ants, scurrying below him.

"It's the Eiffel Tower," Jenna said, "and it's one of the most famous structures in the world. What do you think, Sidney? Do you like Paris?"

"It's nice," Sidney said, "But I liked Rome and Italy a lot better. Especially the Coliseum." An admiring Brandon, who followed his uncle everywhere nodded in agreement.

That is probably because of the many spirits that walk its crumbing corridors, Jenna thought, remembering the weight, the heaviness of the millennia-old structure's atmosphere, and could, out of the corner of her eye, almost see the figures of the hundreds, thousands, perhaps hundreds of thousands who had lost their lives there. Sidney had to have been profoundly affected. Happily, he had managed to stay anchored in this world, even the powerful spirits of centuries past unable to lure him away. He had liked Spain, but said it was a very sad country, and had flatly refused to visit Germany or Poland. They had all voted that Italy had the best food, hands down, that Spain with its crusty *pan* and meaty *chorizo* and seafood-laden rice dish called *paella* came in second but agreed that the huge breakfasts in the Netherlands could not be beat.

"I like Paris, Mama," Miracle said clearly, one arm around her mother, her eyes sweeping the famed city landscape spread out before them. "It's so pretty and I really like the clothes." The five-year-old had her own definite sense of style and had taken to the city's fashion scene like a duck to water.

"I like it too," Rhonda said breathlessly, looking around eagerly, holding Miracle tightly by one hand, the other grasping Bettina's small fingers.

"We all do," Althea said enthusiastically. "Paris is – magic. And the shopping is unbelievable."

"I wholeheartedly agree," Jenna said with a smile, "we'll have to see about getting all of us a few more things before we go." They immediately began planning their latest shopping spree.

Back home in America they visited Canada, with Toronto favored over Montreal; had seen Niagara Falls up close and personal, attended a play in New York City and visited Coney Island, seen the Grand Canyon and stood on the corner of Hollywood and Vine in Los Angeles, floated in the waters of the Great Salt Lake, admired the giant stone portraits of four great American men at Mount Rushmore, gone to the museums and galleries of the many Smithsonian properties in Washington, DC, with their final stop in their home state of South Carolina with its history of the Underground Railroad, and a visit to a former slave auction block where humans were bought and sold. On the train to Orangesburg where Ma'dear would meet them at the station, they discussed their whirlwind summer of world travel.

The entire clan was at the train station to pick them up with plenty of room because Dexter, Lorenzo and Alfonso all had cars. This time there was even more cause for celebration because Queenie was home to stay. Laughing and chattering, they collected the luggage, divided themselves among the three cars, and headed home.

"So, Queenie, world traveler, how does it feel to be back where you started?"

"Miss Essie, it feels just wonderful, like I am exactly where I need to be," Jenna said, sitting on the porch of Essie's newly renovated and enlarged cabin, sipping on a mug of hot coffee. "My house is almost finished, and I start my practice with Doc Edmonds on Monday."

"It's been quite a journey, hasn't it?" Nettie said, looking over at Jenna. "You've come a mighty long way."

"That I have," Jenna said, "but so have you, Nettie. Congratulations on your book, I read it and was moved to tears more than once. You are a wonderful writer – a bestseller, no less."

"Thank you," Nettie said softly. "I have finally been able to put that time behind me, to purge the pain and actually look forward to the future. How, how is Henry Lloyd?"

"He is doing well in Detroit. Everyone knows him; he is the headliner for one of the biggest clubs in the city, and he is this close," holding her thumb and forefinger up almost touching, "to signing a record contract with Motor City Records, which is moving its operations lock, stock and barrel to Los Angeles. If he signs, he will be moving there, too."

"So, he could become a big record star?" Nettie said. "He would be really famous, wouldn't he?"

"He could, if nothing better comes along," Jenna said. "He has been waiting patiently."

Nettie's heart jumped. "You think, he still wants me?" she asked breathlessly.

"I know for a fact that he told all the women chasing after him in Detroit that he had a girlfriend," Jenna stated. "All you have to do is ask him. You will not be disappointed."

Nettie prayed desperately that she was right…that something on its way to him would be well-received…

"So, are you going to be leaving us, Slim?" Rita asked, slinking up to Henry Lloyd and wrapping a bare arm around his neck. "Headed to Southern California and fame and fortune as a crooner? All set to drive the girls crazy? To headline shows around the world?"

"Where'd you hear that?" Henry Lloyd asked, smiling as he stepped away. He did not mention the unsigned contract that had been sitting on his desk for days.

"Everybody know Motor City Records is hot to sign you," Rita said. "The only question is how much you willing to hold out for. I guess soon I'll be saying, I knew you when…"

Henry Lloyd walked away from the open speculation, from the expectant glances following him wherever he went, the whispered questions, the anticipation. Entering the cramped confines of his dressing room, his eye fell on a package sitting on his dressing table. Ripping away the brown wrapping paper, inching down the twine holding the box closed, he tossed it aside, using both hands to lift the top of the box away. He stared down at the contents revealed, his eyes brightening, a slow smile lighting his face. Replacing the lid, he picked the package up, striding over to the door and closing it behind him. Later they would find the words 'NO THANKS' on the contract signature line and a separate note that said: IT'S BEEN REAL BUT I QUIT, and with those words Slim forever became Henry Lloyd.

"Who is that making that racket at this time of morning?" Miss Essie said, lifting a corner of her curtained doorway to peer out. "It's somebody in one of them big, expensive cars," she said, looking for her glasses. Her eyes widened when she saw the driver climb out. "Nettie," she said, turning to see her standing behind her, "Oh, good, you're awake – I think you need –" the remainder of her words were interrupted by the sound of banging on the front door. Hurrying over to it, Essie opened the door, stepping back as Henry Lloyd came striding through.

Nettie gasped and ran, leaping into the open arms that closed around her, eager lips coming together, savoring, tasting, delighting in a love finally free to express itself without reservation. Essie looked on indulgently, happy that the two had found their way back to one another. Looked like it was time for her to start planning the wedding. Smiling, she started pulling out pots and pans, putting things together for a good old-fashioned country breakfast. She would call Queenie, Albertina, and their crew to come and join the three of them once it was almost ready. They were sure to be surprised and happy to see the guest of honor. Grabbing a sharp knife, she began slicing thick slabs of bacon.

"Henry Lloyd, Nettie, Essie, I do believe this is about the nicest surprise I've had in many a day," Albertina said with a big smile to a chorus of agreement from around the table. "First, Queenie comes home to stay, and now Henry Lloyd is coming back too? It just don't get much better than this."

"Are you going to have a church wedding?" Jenna asked, admiring the sizable diamond gracing the ring finger of Nettie's left hand. "Have you decided on a date?"

"Yeah, we don't want to wait long," Henry Lloyd said, placing an arm around Nettie's shoulders, hugging her tightly. "This marriage as you all know has been years in the making. I am ready to claim my bride," placing a warm kiss on full lips that responded instantly, flaring with passion.

"And she is more than ready to claim her husband," she whispered against the lips brushing hers, smiling when she heard the discreet clearing of a throat, a subtle reminder that there were others in the room, pulling back, sliding her hand down his arm, sliding her slender fingers through his, retaining hold of his hand. Turning to Jenna she said, "We want to get married two weeks from this coming Saturday, which will give us time enough to find outfits. I was hoping that you would be my Matron of Honor and that Rhonda would be a junior bridesmaid and Miracle my flower girl. Henry Lloyd is going to ask his brothers to stand up with him. And I'd like for Rolanda and Renard to sing." Their voices – hers, a soaring soprano and his, a rich tenor – harmonized perfectly, blended seamlessly, beautifully. They were much sought after for church services and weddings.

"I am honored to be your Matron of Honor," Jenna said. "And I know Miracle and Rhonda will both be thrilled to be in your wedding. If we can find a dress pattern and material we like, we can make the dresses ourselves. "Ma'dear and Mama Joyce both have sewing machines and so does Miss Essie, so I think we should make them." Smiling when everyone agreed, they began planning the first sewing and fitting session.

A steady pounding at the door to her home clinic had Jenna sitting up in bed. Swinging her legs over the side, slipping on a robe, and tying it as she stood, her feet pushing into the furry warmth of house shoes, moving to the top of the sweeping stairs, starting down, noting Alfonso and Lorenzo who had chosen to live with her standing at the bottom with baseball bats. Gesturing for them to remain where they were, she entered her office. "Hello?" she said. "Who's there?"

"It's me...Beau, Beau Richards," you know, the Sheriff's son?"

"What can I do for you, Beau?" Jenna asked, instantly wary.

"I need your help," Beau said, "your skills as a midwife. It's my wife, Carol Ann. She's in a bad way, and I'm afraid she might not make it –" his voice broke.

"Wait right there. I need to gather some things and put on some clothes. I'll join you shortly," Jenna said, packing a large tote bag with carefully sealed and labeled packages, adding medicines and pain relievers and bandages to the rapidly filling bag. She climbed into the running truck that peeled away as soon as she closed the door.

Jenna hurried through the open door, entering the front room of the ranch style home, absently noting the presence of several tow-headed boys as she followed a rapidly striding Beau Richards. The smell of blood, perspiration and other odors struck her as she entered the hot master bedroom. Moving to the windows, she opened them, breathing deeply of the brisk breeze blowing through, instructing one of the boys standing in the doorway to bring her some fresh sheets and blankets, instructing another to fetch a warm nightgown, and a third to get her a mug of hot water for steeping the willow bark tea she would prepare to bring down the fever. The fourth came in carrying a plastic container and a large pot of extremely hot water which she poured into the container, dipped her arms in grabbing a bar of antiseptic soap and scrubbing down, drying off with a towel she brought with her. She placed a gentle hand on the woman's distended stomach, nodding when she felt the faint kicks.

"You all need to leave the two of us, or rather the three of us alone for a time," Jenna said to Beau and those gathered at the door. "I will come fetch you if I need your help for anything. Go on now, you're just making all of us nervous."

She waited until Beau closed the door behind him. "Now," Jenna said briskly, "Let us get this baby born. Little One," she said to the baby struggling in utero, "I think you were so excited you got yourself all tangled up in the cord and got yourself all turned around. So, I am going to get you turned around the right way and untangle that cord and then you can come on into this world."

The strained silence was broken by the faint sounds of an infant's wails coming through the closed wooden door. Jumping to their feet, they all stood tensely as the door to the bedroom opened, and Jenna came through holding a squirming bundle in her arms. "Beau, you have a new baby," she began.

"How is little Josiah?" Beau broke in, "Doing well? Is Carol Ann okay?" he asked anxiously.

"Josiah?" Jenna repeated. "That's a strange name for a girl, but to each his own, I guess."

"Girl? It's a girl? I got a baby girl?" Beau repeated delightedly. "Boys, y'all got a baby sister. Nine sons later and I got my baby girl. She's beautiful," he breathed when Jenna placed his daughter in his arms, the boys crowding around for their first look at their little sister.

"Does Carol Ann know?" Beau asked, looking over at Jenna, "that she finally got the little girl she's been pining for?"

"She found out just before she fell into an exhausted sleep," Jenna said, "and let that be her last one. Her body is worn out, and I honestly do not know if she could survive another pregnancy."

"Then let little Jenna-Josephine be our last one," Beau said softly, looking up at Jenna before returning his enraptured attention to the sleeping baby in his arms.

"Jenna-Josephine?" Jenna repeated.

"Seems a fitting name for a little princess – to be named after a 'Queenie'," Beau said with a slight smile. "I think we're destined to be as close as...family," he stated with another knowing smile.

Jenna smiled slowly back. "Well, I am honored, I truly am that you would name your long-awaited daughter after me. I would be proud to be her godmother."

"Why, that would be just great, Nurse Jenna," Beau said. "Is there anything else I can do for you?"

"Put the word out that my family – all of them – is to be left in peace from this day forth," Jenna asserted. "That they are off-limits to any type of retribution or revenge or trouble."

"Done!" Beau said immediately. "Anything else?"

"Let Carol Ann sleep until she wakes up on her own," Jenna said, "and when she does, have her stay in bed for the next week or so, with feeding the baby the most strenuous thing she does. Also, make sure she knows there will be no more babies. That will make her get better faster than anything else possibly could. She should be fine, but if anything seems wrong, just let me know and I will come back. Other than that…I rode with you, so if someone could take me home, that would be great."

Climbing out of the truck in front of her office door, she waved as it pulled off and she opened the door disappearing inside.

Chapter Twenty-eight

"By the power vested in me by the State of South Carolina, I now pronounce thee husband and wife. Henry Lloyd, you may kiss your bride."

Looking deeply into the dark brown eyes gazing mistily into his, Henry Lloyd smiled. Reaching to gently stroke his fingers down her soft cheek, he leaned down, eagerly, fervently, lovingly joining his lips to those of the woman who had been through so much, who had overcome so much, and who was his at last. Their tender embrace drew sighs of contentment all around. Holding hands, smiling, waving to the friends and family gathered, the newly married couple walked down the heavily flower-strewn aisle courtesy of flower girl Miracle who had taken her responsibility very seriously.

"Nettie, that wedding was just beautiful," Essie said, wiping her eyes, "and that you would ask me to give you away – I can't tell you how much that means to me."

"There is no one in the world I would rather have had," Nettie said giving the woman who had been like a mother to her a big hug, her eyes bright. "You are one of the biggest reasons why I'm standing before you now safe and sound – something that I will love you forever for – and I'm so looking forward to the day my children call you Grandma." The two women laughed, hugging again in delighted anticipation.

"So, you decided against a singing career" Albertina asked Henry Lloyd, "and to leave Detroit behind?"

"Yeah," Henry Lloyd said, "I decided I want a different kind of life, with a wife and babies. I was real close to signing a record contract, so I was really happy to receive the package from Nettie telling me to come home. Mama Joyce deeded me quite a bit of land, so I think I'm going to do a little farming, maybe some ranching, and just enjoy my land with my family. I'll probably join the church choir again." He did not mention that he had saved quite a bit from his singing gig, as well as the considerable sum remaining from the money he had taken from Loretta's huge reserve of cash, ample even after paying off Boots so many years ago and who had used it as seed money for several enterprises that had proven wildly successful. Fabulously wealthy, he owned several casinos in Nevada, which were legal in the Western state. There was plenty left over even after sharing it with Nettie, Jenna, Essie, and the abused women given new lives on the day they all left San Francisco.

"Maybe Rolanda and Renard will be the ones who become famous singers," Jenna said. "Their voices are amazing. When they sing in harmony, well, I think even the angels stop to listen."

"Are Auntie Rolanda and Uncle Renard going to be famous, Mommy?" Miracle piped up looking admiringly at her stunningly pretty aunt and handsome uncle.

"Maybe, baby, if they really want it and work hard enough. They both have voices that could make them famous," Jenna said, looking fondly down at her daughter, seeing her own eyes, including the secret knowing looking back at her.

"Not if they stay in Crawfish Holler," Dexter said in disgust. "Ain't nothing here for nobody looking to be famous. Ain't really much for anybody in these here parts."

"It's Craw-ford Hol-low, Uncle Dex," Miracle corrected him, enunciating clearly. She studied him silently a moment. "Maybe you should move to Detroit," she suggested. "You might get famous doing something there. I don't know what, 'cuz you can't sing, but there is probably something you could do," she said earnestly, smiling when a laughing Dexter reached over and gave her a hug.

"Food's ready," one of the church volunteer servers announced, gesturing to the tables filled with food set up a short distance away from the stairs leading into the kitchen, an apron tied over the good clothes she wore to the wedding, "Y'all come on and eat."

Miracle had demanded and received an apron to put over her first long fancy dress. She had picked out the pattern herself, meticulously examining before selecting the silky materials for the dress in the royal blue, aquamarine, and pale blue colors Nettie had chosen. The puffed sleeves and full skirt edged in dark blue with a cloth belt in the same color drawing a host of compliments and admiring looks. She walked among the tables placed outside Essie's cabin and filling with hungry guests, carefully balancing a tray of Mama Joyce's prized and highly sought after deviled eggs, offering them to those seated. She did the same with the wicker baskets of warm homemade yeast rolls nestled in large cloth napkins, alternating offerings, returning to the kitchen to replenish trays and baskets.

The women had planned the menu and cooked the food, with most of the community's female population assisting. The entire church and most of the Black community had attended the nuptials and turned out for the dinner. Even several white neighbors were in attendance. Nettie was well-known in town, and everyone remembered handsome Henry Lloyd from the time he was a little boy growing up there. And of course, everyone knew and most had consulted the healers, Albertina and a newly returned Queenie.

Sheriff Calhoun Richards was seated at the same table where Ma'dear waited to be served as the mother of the groom, the reason, over her strenuous objection, that she was not helping to serve the food. Rodney Pettigrew had died peacefully in his sleep months earlier, his death unremarkable and unremarked for the most part. Sidney was seated next to his mother, smiling as he chatted with the person sitting on his other side. The happy noise level quieted abruptly when Beau Richards, a deputy sheriff in his father's department pulled up in his squad car and climbed out. Jenna hurried forward, and after exchanging a few words, escorted him to the same table where his father was seated. He nodded politely to those seated on either side of him, congratulating the married couple, shaking hands with Henry Lloyd when the newlyweds walked by greeting guests on their way to the head table.

"Well, if that don't beat all," Essie said to the person seated next to her. "I never thought I'd see the day that Beau Richards would break bread with a Thompson or a Pettigrew. Or any colored person for that matter."

"Nurse Queenie saved his wife and baby girl about two weeks or so ago," Alfonso told someone else questioning his participation in the festivities. "He came banging on the door saying his wife was in trouble and needed Jenna's midwife skills. Of course, she went without even thinking about it. She saved the baby and the mother and in doing so brought peace to the community. I hear Beau's hung up his white sheet and is disbanding the Klan in this part of the state."

"I declare wonders will never cease," one of the elderly men listening said. "This is definitely a case of the lion laying down with the lamb – without saying who is who, of course." Smiling, he snagged a chicken breast off the pile of freshly fried, golden brown crispy pieces being passed around.

Food was in abundance. In addition to fried chicken there was baked chicken, stewed chicken, chicken and dumplings, chicken with rice, and chicken seasoned with lemon and garlic. Several carved turkeys resided on large platters, tender white and dark meat prominently displayed. On the pork side there was ham, pork chops, bacon stuffed pork loin, chitterlings, pig feet and ears and hogshead cheese. Perfectly seasoned, glistening pork ribs turned slowly on a spit over a pit dug into the ground filled with smoldering wood chips and charcoal briquets, the roasting meat periodically doused with Ma'dear's prized secret sauce, watched over by Lorenzo who was showing quite a flair in the kitchen. White potatoes, yams and wrapped ears of corn were buried in the coals on the other side of the charcoal pit, roasting slowly. Hamburgers, hot dogs, and fresh sausage links sizzled on a large grill next to the ribs. Hot catfish was lifted out of bubbling oil frying over a wood fire, placed on large platters and offered to eager eaters.

Huge bowls of potato salad were passed around. There was also coleslaw and tossed salad with vegetables fresh from the garden. Large containers of cornbread dressing with bowls of cranberry sauce on the side were scooped up by the heaping spoonful, joining the macaroni and cheese piled high. Candied yams, sweet potato, and carrot casserole occupied pride of place on many plates, next to fried and stewed okra, collard greens and mashed potatoes. Huge pitchers of sweetened iced tea and lemonade circulated freely, as did the personal liquor bottles and containers of moonshine being secretly shared.

In addition to the four-tiered wedding cake, other pastries included chocolate, devil's food, caramel, lemon and three kinds of pound cake; also bread pudding and banana pudding, as well as sweet potato and apple pie. Blackberry and peach cobblers rounded out the dessert offerings. Volunteers sat under a tree patiently cranking the old-fashioned ice cream maker filled with Essie's prized homemade vanilla recipe, finished batches scooped out and carried to the freezer to chill until time to serve.

Guitar and fiddle players pulled out their instruments and began playing, others added a saxophone, a flute, a clarinet, and a bongo drum to the mix; dancing couples, young and old alike showing off their moves on the freshly mowed lawn. Henry Lloyd and Nettie danced together for hours with eyes only for one another to music that only they could hear.

"Okay, single ladies gather round! I'm getting ready to throw the bridal bouquet," a laughing Nettie said, watching as they maneuvered for optimum position.

"Mommy, you're not married," Miracle said. "Why aren't you over there?"

"Because one, I don't believe in it," Jenna said, "and two, I have absolutely no interest in acquiring a husband."

"Well, if you don't believe in it, you have nothing to worry about, right?" Dexter said. "Go on over there, just to show you're a good sport. Go on, I dare you."

"Oh, please," Jenna said impatiently, "I am not going over there, and that's that."

"Scared?" Lorenzo taunted softly as Alfonso smiled knowingly.

"Of course, I'm not scared. Oh, all right," Jenna said walking over to where the crowd of hopeful single ladies stood waiting expectantly, positioning herself in the middle of the last row, half-heartedly raising her arms halfway.

"Ready ladies? Here we go...one...two...three!" Nettie tossed the bouquet over her head where it sailed as if it had wings, almost striking Jenna in the chest, she instinctively closing her

373

hands around it, catching it securely as she stepped back. She stared down at it stunned, as disappointed hopefuls moved away.

"Mommy, you caught it!" Miracle said delightedly. "Does this mean you're getting married?"

"Sweetheart, we've talked about superstitions and the trouble believing in them can cause," Jenna said, "Remember? This is just another superstition," she said, ignoring her brother's laughter.

"Miracle and Rhonda are asleep on their feet," Jenna said a short time later, "so, I'm going to put them to bed. Rhonda can spend the night with us." Collecting both little girls, holding them by the hand they walked to their car parked a short distance away.

"That was some wedding," Albertina said as she and Essie walked to the Pettigrew cabin. "I was so moved when I saw Henry Lloyd's face as Nettie came walking towards him."

"I know what you mean. I cried what little makeup I had on off long before they started taking pictures, no telling what I'm going to look like."

"You'll look good like you always do," Albertina said with assurance, "You always take a good picture."

"We'll see," Essie said. "I feel like we in-laws, like our children are married. I have to keep reminding myself that I'm not her real mother."

"Our children are married," Albertina said firmly. "You are that child's mother as much as if you'd given birth to her. In a way you did, when you brought her out of that hellhole she was living in and gave her a new, wonderful life making it possible for her to put all that behind her and accept what Henry Lloyd offered. Ain't no way for anybody to be more of a mother than you are – up to and including giving over your cabin and staying here with me until they leave for their honeymoon in the Caribbean tomorrow." Putting an arm around her longtime friend, the two women continued walking in companionable silence.

Henry Lloyd stood staring out of the window of Essie's newly built guest bedroom, waiting, turning when he heard the soft rustle of material. His breath caught. Nettie stood before him, smiling tremulously, wearing the baby doll pajamas she had been wearing the first time he had ever seen her, and the contents of the package he opened in Detroit telling him to come home, the wait was over. Slowly smiling, his eyes kindling, Henry Lloyd opened his arms, closing them tightly around Nettie when she ran unhesitatingly into them, throwing her own around his neck, holding on tightly. The magic of that night, their first coming together something they would remember all their lives, laying all ghosts to rest, culminating nine months later with the birth of their first child.

"I do not know why I let you talk me into this," Jenna stood observing herself in the mirror, at the flowing deceptively simple red dress that highlighted slender curves, flaring gradually out from a narrow waist to the full skirt swirling around her ankles, the sparkling red high-heeled sandals adorning her feet glittering when their movement brushed aside the floating, filmy material of the dress. A black silk shawl patterned with large red roses was draped over her shoulders, her hair twisted into an elegant knot on top of her head. She had after a great deal of badgering agreed to attend the school reunion being held at the high school she had attended for three years.

"As I live and breathe if it isn't Jenna Thompson, although the last name may have changed," the deep voice warm with friendly excitement was decidedly male.

Jenna turned. A tall, dark man in a perfectly tailored suit was smiling at her with happy recognition. "As I live and breathe, I do believe it's Michael Edwards," Jenna said with a wide smile, holding out her right hand which he immediately grasped with his, retaining hold of it. "It is so good to see you."

"And you," Michael said, drinking in the face he had not seen in person for so many empty years. "So, did you become the nurse you aspired to be?"

"I did," Jenna said, smiling up at him, surprised he remembered. "I'm a Nurse Practitioner. I moved here from Detroit and am practicing right here in Crawford Hollow in a practice with Doc Edmonds, although he is semi-retired now. What about you, Michael? Did you play basketball at one of the black universities?"

"I did," Michael said, "did pretty well, too. Majored in business and finance and a few weeks before I graduated was offered a job playing basketball with Italy's team. The money was good and the chance for travel irresistible, so I went and stayed in Italy until about a year or so ago, decided to come back home, did so, and am trying to decide where I'm going to live. I started a small electronics company that's doing well, so I can locate anywhere I want – just taking my time before deciding."

"Are you married, Michael?" Jenna asked, looking at him with those incredible eyes he remembered so well.

"Nope, never got around to it, somehow." He had had relationships, even some good ones, but marriage had never been a part of the equation. "What about you, Jenna? Are you married?" Unaware that he was holding his breath. That his entire future and the decision about where he would spend it rested on the answer to that question.

"No," Jenna said shaking her head. "I was, but…it ended, and I decided to come back home. Doc Edmonds and I always said we would have a practice together, so here I am."

His heart light, happier than he had been since the day they had parted after having lunch so many years earlier, Michael said, "It's good that you're not married, because you owe me a date, you know."

"I do?" Jenna said smiling, thinking back, pushing aside the memory of why the date had never materialized. "Are you saying I stood you up, but you still want another date?"

"Absolutely and let me tell you why," still holding her hand, Michael led her over to a semi-secluded pair of chairs a short distance away. The years melted away as the two laughed and talked as they had years before, seemingly picking up where they left off.

"Miss Jenna, I don't believe I've seen you smile this much... ever," her mother said with a smile of her own. "You seem downright giddy these days. Is there a reason for this sudden burst of happiness?" she asked.

"Happiness, your name is Michael!" Miracle said giggling.

Jenna hoped her burning cheeks were not obvious. "Don't be silly," she said. "Michael and I are good friends reconnecting, that's all." Thankful no one could see how her heart was racing.

"Uh-huh," Albertina said as Miracle snickered. "Where are you and your reconnection going today?"

"We're going on a picnic. I put together the food and Michael offered to bring everything else."

"I think I hear his car," Miracle said running over to the large picture window. "Yep, it's him. Hi, Michael," she said running to open the door, giving the man ducking his head to clear the door jamb a big hug.

"How you doing, Jenna Junior, half-a-quart Queenie?" Michael said returning it, lifting the giggling, jeans-clad little girl onto his shoulders. "Where's your mama?"

"Right here," Jenna said with a smile hugging him warmly when he set Miracle gently on her feet.

"Ready, baby?" he asked, his eyes warm.

"Ready," Jenna said hers equally warm. Helping her into the passenger seat of his fancy two-seater sports car, sliding into the driver's side, they sped off.

"This is nice," Jenna said, lifting her face to the bright rays of the sun as they strolled along, having opted for a walk after thoroughly enjoying the contents of the big picnic basket she had prepared. Closing her eyes she slowed, breathing deeply of the fresh air, removing her scarf to allow her hair to blow in the brisk breeze that whisked through the trees, causing the grasses to lift and rustle, opening her arms as if to embrace it. Her eyes shining, she looked over at the man watching her, a smile on his face. The smiles on their faces slowly fading as their eyes met and held.

"You are so beautiful," Michael said fervently. "And you just get more beautiful every day, every time I see you."

"Let's hope you still feel that way twenty years from now – if you should be around, or see me, or be anywhere near uh, here then." Jenna's cheeks were hot with embarrassment.

Stepping closer, Michael enfolded her in his arms. "I would like nothing better than to be here near you – with you – twenty, thirty, even fifty years from now. I would feel infinitely blessed to be a part of your life, an intimate part of your life." His eyes looked into the dark ones that he had loved all of his life, seeing an answering response, a reciprocal heat burning in their swirling depths. "You know I love you, don't you?" he said tenderly, "I always have, and I always will. I would be the happiest man in the world if you would agree to spend the rest of your life with me. I'll do everything in my power to make it a happy one. Will you live with me and be my wife? Will you marry me, Jenna?" Reaching into his jacket pocket he extracted a small red velvet covered box, stepping back, opening it, and bending down on one knee.

A huge square cut sapphire in glittering dark blue flashed on an ivory velvet cushion, its platinum band supporting a trio of diamonds on either side of the darkly shimmering stone. "I thought a sapphire suited you better, but if you don't like it –"

"I think it's the most beautiful thing I have ever seen," Jenna breathed, close to tears, "and I would be proud to be by your side for the next thirty, forty or fifty years."

"Is that a 'yes'?" Michael asked.

"Yes, yes, yes!" Jenna cried, laughing happily, throwing her arms around Michael when he lifted her into his, holding on tightly, happier than he could remember, lowering her, eager lips joining, feelings burning hot, bright, the love delayed for so long finally free to express itself without reservation. They walked, talked, kissed, and hugged as they discussed their future.

*　*　*

"Jenna, you look gorgeous."

"Really? You don't think this is all a bit...much?" Jenna asked anxiously. "I have been married before –"

"Well, the first one only lasted a hot minute, if you'll forgive my saying so," Petronella said, "and the second one – or first, depending on how you look at it, seemed awfully strange to me. You didn't invite anybody, never talked about it much, and still don't. But this one, well, anyone can tell this one is right. He crazy about you, and you just as crazy about him. And he and Miracle love one another, too. Even Sidney likes him; and if that don't say it all, I don't know what does."

"And this is your first wedding dress," Gina pointed out. "Plus, I expect you'll be smiling for these pictures."

"Thank goodness," Althea said, "I was at the last one, and let me tell you, the mood was more like what you see at a funeral than a wedding. This one is how you expect a wedding to feel, and a bride to look, happy, a little nervous, and excited. The only good thing about this one and the last is that Slim, I mean Henry Lloyd is going to sing again."

"All my friends and family being here is more special than I could ever say," Jenna said, her eyes bright.

"And where else would we be when we heard there was going to be a wedding?" Julie said smiling as she walked up in her bridesmaid dress, a drop-waist, high necked floral tunic patterned in pale orange, pink, yellow and golden lace flowers over a flowing pale pink tulle skirt, one of the colors present in the tunic. Susan joined the group in her dress featuring a pale orange skirt, smiling as she handed Jenna a sealed manila envelope.

"What's this?" Jenna asked, turning the envelope over, hefting its weight in her hands.

"Open it and see," Julie said.

Tearing open the envelope, Jenna pulled out the official looking document, looking it over carefully. A slow smile lit her face as she looked up and said, "It's an official acknowledgment from the state of Alabama stating that Curtice and I were legally married, that extenuating circumstances prevented the marriage from following procedure, but the presence of the minister licensed to marry people in Alabama along with the witnesses made it all legal. So, Miracle is declared the legal offspring of Curtice Brooks and Jenna Thompson." The room erupted with cheers, laughter, and joyful celebration on top of that already present in the happily charged atmosphere.

Michael Edwards stood in front of the altar, looking out over the rustling congregation. The church was packed with every pew filled to overflowing, with extra chairs placed next to the aisles except for the center one, and many still having to stand in order to watch the proceedings. Smiling wide, his eyes bright, he awaited his bride, the one woman in the world he had loved since his first sight of her on the playground just before the start of kindergarten so many years ago. His devotion had never faltered had been steadfast and true and was finally being rewarded. Looking out over the congregation filled with friends and family, he nodded, greeting familiar faces and the friends, many of whom had traveled considerable distances to be there.

The excitement level in the church grew as the music changed and the first bridesmaid and groomsman came smiling down the aisle. The bridesmaids, except for the junior bridesmaid Rhonda, were all Jenna's high school classmates, a group of friends that called themselves the League; the groomsmen were made up of Michael's brothers and two of his teammates from Italy – single women were positively giddy as they eyed the handsome foreigners with the intriguing accents. Next came the Maid of Honor, Jenna's very good friend Althea from her Detroit days, followed by two Matrons of Honor, Gina and Petronella, their unbreakable bond formed their first day of nursing school. The ringbearer was next, under the careful eye of his mother, Gina.

The music changed to the familiar one announcing the arrival of the bride. All guests stood as a proud Miracle, meticulously sprinkling the colorful flowers in her basket, walked in front of her veiled mother, smiling happily as she walked down the aisle in her second fancy long dress. A smiling Henry Lloyd, his sister's arm tucked through his, escorted her, one of two people he loved most in the world, down the aisle. Lifting the veil, kissing her softly on one smooth cheek, he placed her hand in that of Michael's who since her arrival, had eyes only for the bride. Looking deeply into one another's eyes, they smiled, turning to face the minister, the Reverend Fred Huddleston who along with his entire family had made the drive to South Carolina earlier acquiring his credentials in the state in order to marry Jenna to her childhood sweetheart.

"I now pronounce you husband and wife. Michael, you may kiss your bride," Reverend Fred announced in ringing tones.

Oohs and ahs echoed all around as the newly married couple shared a fervent embrace, followed by laughter and applause as they came rapidly down the aisle, waving and laughing, reaching out to hug many of the excited well-wishers. The wedding dinner was held on the lawn at Mama Joyce's at her insistence. The entire town was in attendance, black and white – everyone who could come had come, eager to share in the happy occasion with the Healer and Nurse who took care of all of them, joining the well-wishers who had come from all over. Beau Richards, this time accompanied by his wife was in attendance, he tenderly carrying their newborn daughter in her infant carrier. The sound of music filled the air, with the celebration lasting well into the wee hours of the following day.

THE END

Review Requested:

We'd like to know if you enjoyed the book.
Please consider leaving a review on the platform from which
you purchased the book.

CPSIA information can be obtained
at www.ICGtesting.com
Printed in the USA
BVHW070021040122
625366BV00006B/69